MW00479685

KILL SWITCH

KILL SWITCH

WILLIAM HERTLING

LIQUIDIDEA PRESS

Copyright © 2018 by William Hertling

All rights reserved.

No part of this book may be reproduced in any form or by any electronic or mechanical means, including information storage and retrieval systems, without written permission from the author, except for the use of brief quotations in a book review.

People, places, and events are fictitious or used fictitiously. The Bureau of Research and Intelligence in the novel has no connection whatsoever to the real-life organization bearing a similar name.

If you enjoy Kill Switch, please sign up for my mailing list at www.williamhertling.com to find out about future book releases!

For Tasia

"In the future, all clubs are S&M clubs."
—Shane Brody

Note: This book contains depictions of consensual BDSM
relationships and activities.

A SUMMARY OF KILL PROCESS

Angie Benenati was once the teenage hacker known as Angel of Mercy. After college, she worked in cyber security under Repard, one of the great former criminal hackers turned white-hat computer security expert. When Repard was later arrested for one of the most profitable and secretive hacks of all time, Angie made a break with the hacker community, just in time to join a new social media startup, Tomo. Tomo eventually grew to become the largest social networking company in the world.

This period should have been the most glorious time of her life, but Angie fell under the sway of the man who would first marry then viciously abuse her. After years of increasing mistreatment and isolation, Angie, desperate for escape, killed her husband. Eventually exonerated of her crime, Angie returned to work at Tomo with a new, covert agenda. No longer would she sit idly by. She would use her access to Tomo's data, now the largest repository of information on nearly everyone in the world, to profile domestic abusers, hunt them down, and kill them.

Years went by, and one-by-one, Angie eliminated abusers, but there were a million more for every one she killed. She grew to realize Tomo itself was an abuser: by holding people's data and relationships hostage, and manipulating what people read and hence thought, the social platform was exploiting its own users, while making itself inescapable.

Angie could serve a greater purpose by eliminating Tomo.

Working with cofounders Amber and Igloo, Angie launched a new company, Tapestry, founded on principles of privacy, security, and personal ownership of data. Tackling the normal challenges of a startup would be challenging enough, let alone taking on the world's largest social networking company as a direct competitor.

At the worst possible time, a shadowy operative working for the super-black government agency, BRI, took a personal interest in Angie. Soon the resources of this agency were focused on Angie and her activities as a computer hacker.

With the aid of Igloo, Angie defeated the government agent and uncovered a link between the operative and the CEO of Tomo. When the revelations became public, Tomo fell into disrepute, and Tapestry surged ahead.

Now, two years later, Tapestry is winning the social networking war. Angie has gradually become buried under the crushing load of executive management.

Igloo, Angie's protege in the hacking realm, feels increasingly adrift. What is the purpose of it all? Why is Angie ignoring her? Her only solace is her relationship with her new girlfriend, Essie.

Little does Igloo know that the largest, most pivotal battle to be fought for control of the Internet is just a few months away, and she'll be front and center. Will she be pawn or queen? Will she, or anyone she cares about, survive?

Learn more about Igloo and Angie's history in _Kill Process_, the exciting prequel to _Kill Switch_.

CHAPTER 1

Igloo stopped short when she heard the bagpipes. The unicyclist came into view, dressed in a kilt, Darth Vader mask, and playing a flame-throwing bagpipe. She waited until he'd passed, then crossed the street to her office. Everything was weirder in Portland. That was why she was never going to leave this town.

Igloo rode up to the fourth floor, trademark white hoodie pulled up over her head, ignoring her coworkers on the elevator, none of whom she recognized beyond a basic vague familiarity to their face. Tapestry, the world's second largest social media company by number of active users, was now over three hundred employees. She'd lost track of individuals somewhere around ninety. So much for Dunbar's Number. Maybe that was just her social awkwardness. Other people didn't seem to have such problems.

She swiped her phone. An article at the top of her notifications had a headline about Judge Lenz being arrested. Igloo's heart thumped. She clicked on the headline knowing the article contents were cached and there'd be no click trail showing her interest in the Judge. She smiled as she read, a small knot in her stomach releasing. Evidence pointing to Lenz sexually abusing staffers had come out, and suddenly a chorus of women had come forward to share their stories.

Igloo held her phone close to her heart. She had followed razor-thin trails of suspicion over months of effort before finally discovering Lenz's photos on a heavily encrypted hard drive, then anonymously turned over those photos to officials. Lenz wouldn't be bothering anyone else. Finally, those who had been affected would at least receive the closure of a monster getting what he deserved.

The elevator door opened, and she tucked the phone in her pocket. No extracurricular activities here at work. She tried to mentally put it aside. She had to keep her ethical hacking compartmentalized. Like everything else in her life.

She headed down a corridor lined with glass-walled conference rooms. Many people nodded or said good morning to her, although she didn't recognize most. She mumbled a good morning back, and they'd look away quickly. They seemed as eager to get past the awkward encounters as Igloo. What was the point? If everyone said the same thing, it was meaningless. They might as well grunt, or better yet, ignore each other.

She wished people came with labels: their online handle, a tag cloud describing them, and a list of their prioritized personal needs. Hers would have a big red warning: Do Not Interrupt.

She slowed to a stop in the middle of the hallway as people flowed around her and wondered if she could build the labels she'd imagined. She visualized Tapestry's data scheme as a structure in her mind, a directed, cyclic graph. Here, the user name. There, unique word analysis providing a tag cloud. That only left user needs. Trending interests was the closest they had, with upward trends indicating increasing interests.

"Hey, Igloo."

The fragile mental image disappeared, replaced by the face of Amber, who bent to peer directly into Igloo's hoodie. Igloo sighed. Her mind could visualize code of incredible complexity, but all it took was one interruption to make her lose the picture.

"We need to get to the all-hands meeting."

Igloo brushed Amber's hand away. "I'm coming."

Igloo trudged along after Amber, now the VP of Engineering. She dressed like it, in some sort of pant suit thing. How'd she get so corporate?

Igloo looked at her own black jeans, picked up from a thrift store in high school. Twelve years later, they were still going strong. Well, maybe the threads around that hole could be trimmed.

Amber rambled on about an agreement with NPR to distribute their shows on Tapestry. Unlike competitors, Tapestry supported WebTorrent and IPFS, so content didn't have to be loaded from centralized servers. The files would be served up by topographically-near peers. Other users. The more people that used Tapestry, the faster the network ran.

Amber's words faded into the background, and Igloo visualized the data graph again. Her mind grasped both the logical structure, which was clean and neat, as well as the actual implementation, which was considerably messier. That complexity wrapped her like a familiar warm, fuzzy blanket. At least it did until they reached the main conference hall, where there was far too much chaos to think any more. Igloo headed toward the back, where the stadium seating would give her a bird's eye view of the entire room.

Angie was here! As Tapestry's CEO, Angie had become busy and remote as the company grew. They got together only rarely for their ethical-but-still-criminal hacking, and when Angie did show, she'd be hopelessly distracted by Tapestry business. There was little of the comradely mentorship Igloo loved.

Igloo tried to catch Angie's eye, but Angie was deep in conversation with the VP of Marketing. Her blood boiled, because they were probably discussing the acquisition of new content providers. Igloo had signed on to change the world, to make a difference in people's lives. She didn't give a damn about making more money. But that was all that seemed to get the executives' consideration these days.

Tapestry was founded on the principles of end user data ownership and privacy. The company was supposed to be different from the rest of the corporate web. But somehow all the leaders of the company had gotten their heads up their asses. They were focused on the wrong thing.

Igloo was head of the company's chat AI, the only thing that still seemed socially relevant. The seemingly sentient automated bots befriended users on Tapestry and talked to them about almost anything. They'd completed a year-long study of over ten million teenagers, finding the suicide rate was thirty percent lower for those who friended a Tapestry personality. For people who had no one to confide in, Igloo's AI became their friends, close confidants, even life coaches. That was worthwhile work. Not acquiring more content to feed the masses.

While Igloo spent her days coding stuff that mattered, Amber and Angie squandered their time in meetings or traveling. There was no way she was going to follow in their footsteps, but she hated the distance that had grown between them. When was the last time they'd had an all-night coding marathon? Or even eaten dinner together, the three of them? Or discussed anything of substance? She had a pit of unease in her stomach. She was losing the only friends she had, aside from her partner, Essie.

Essie was the one bright spot in her life lately. A shining star, really. She knew that was part of the reason she resented being at work.

Igloo sighed and gazed up front to find Angie still chatting with the other execs.

Despite all her frustration with the distance between them, Igloo yearned to hear Angie say something exciting and relevant this morning.

As important as the AI chat was, Igloo's contributions had plateaued. Now they had teams of psychologists working on the personalities to make them more effective—better able to console someone in grief, better able to engage a teenager in distress. Somewhere along the line, Igloo had realized the personalities were no longer hers. They were Tapestry's.

Part of her frustration with Tapestry stemmed from the whole CTO debacle. When Amber had become the VP of engineering, it had left the Chief Technology Officer position open. Igloo wanted that position. She walked into Angie's office with the intent of asking for the job, and that was when Angie said she was going to be both CEO and CTO.

The decision still pissed Igloo off. She deserved that role. But the desire to be CTO also warred with the part of her that resisted hierarchy in all forms. She wanted the company to be like it was when she started: a true democracy where everyone was equal, more or less, and they could all get together in a room and make decisions as a group. Life was complicated.

Angie stepped up to the microphone.

"Thanks for coming, everyone," Angie said. "If you look around, you probably see some new faces. Let me say welcome and thank you to all the new employees. We're here to change the world, and we need your help.

"Hiring, of course, also brings challenges. We brought on thirty new people last quarter, and we have plans to hire fifty this quarter."

Good grief. Igloo fidgeted. Please let it not be a discussion of hiring plans.

"Less than ten percent of our employees were with us at launch. Nearly half joined after we hit a hundred million users. We're in danger of losing the culture that got us here. We're so focused on the end goal that we sometimes forget why we're doing what we're doing, or that how we go about our work affects the outcome nearly as much as our explicit objectives. I'm going to let Maria take over here."

Maria Alvarez, the Chief Operating Officer, walked up to join Angie.

"Thanks, Angie." Maria smiled.

Igloo shrank into her hood. Something bugged her about Maria.

Maybe it was that she wasn't here at the beginning. Or maybe it was that Igloo had overheard one of Angie's conversations, and knew they'd spent a million bucks to hire her. Such a ridiculous way to spend money. Maria represented everything that was wrong with Tapestry today.

"It's often said that 'you can't motivate people, you can only create a context in which people are motivated,'" Maria started. "Culture is one of the largest components of setting that context."

Ugh. It was worse than a discussion about hiring. A talk about culture, and by Maria, who wasn't even here in the beginning to understand what that culture was! Did she even grok why employees had SHA keys instead of sequential employee IDs? The essentially random unique numbers generated by the Secure Hash Algorithm were the perfect antidote to the hierarchy associated with an employee number that ranked one employee above another by their time on the job.

Angie smiled and nodded as Maria talked, as though she was the best thing to happen to the company.

Fuck. Engineering culture comes from engineers working together, not executives. Why did they need bosses to tell them how to talk to each other?

Igloo fumed. She was wasting her time here. She stood, pushed past two people blocking her path, and left the room in a rush.

The air in the hall was cooler, but stale. She made her way back to her office. Her suite really. By far and away the best perk of being employee number three.

The outer room was full of abandoned music gear, punctuated by empty spaces left behind when the rest of the band had taken their stuff. Guitar, drum kit, keyboard, all of it seemed purposeless now. She hadn't played since the band's last practice session, just before the breakup. Not really a breakup, was it? No, her expulsion. They still performed, just without her.

A few months ago, she'd swapped out her white hoodie for a black one and checked out their show for the first time since she'd been kicked out. She'd been replaced by a preprogrammed synth track.

The thought was depressing. She pulled out her phone and sent a message to her partner.

Igloo > I miss you.
Essie > I miss you too. Love you.
Igloo > Work is killing me. Watcha doing?
Essie > Editing blog posts. At least we have Deviance to look forward to tonight.
Igloo > I can't wait.
Essie > Me too. I'll wear something sexy.

Essie's idea of sexy was slutty, but that was okay by Igloo.

Essie was a constant joy in her life, although the relationship was an immense distraction. Igloo missed a few too many band practices, showed up late, tried bringing Essie to practice. Essie was intoxicating. Was that such a bad thing?

She was sitting in the lounge chair holding her dusty guitar and fantasizing about Essie when Angie knocked and entered without waiting for an answer.

"What's up?" Angie asked, settling onto the drum kit's stool.

Igloo didn't know what to say. Too many thoughts raced through her head at once, a kaleidoscope of emotion and thoughts. Angie was finally here, and now she was speechless.

Angie picked up a drum stick and tapped at a snare. "Think I should take up drums?"

Igloo shook her head. "Too cliché. Def Leppard has that locked up."

"How can a lone one-armed drummer single-handedly exclude all other amputees from a career in drumming?"

Igloo glanced over to see Angie carefully staring at her. Angie's humor seemed like a genuine attempt to connect. But jokes were no longer enough to bridge the separation between them.

"I never get to see you anymore." Igloo didn't want it to come out petulant, but it was hard to keep the whine out of her voice. She hated *needing* someone like this.

Angie experimentally tapped at a few drums. "Things have been crazy lately...I have—"

"Are hiring plans and company culture what you should be spending your time on? Is that what's going to change the world?"

Angie sighed, and tossed the drum stick onto the floor. "I used to mock people who made slides. But you remember how many presentations I did to get our VC funding? Sometimes this is the stuff that needs doing."

Igloo wanted to talk about hacking, but they couldn't, not here at work where they couldn't absolutely control the environment. All it took was one compromised phone or laptop, and their conversations could be recorded, transmitted to someone in the government, and they'd jeopardize not only themselves but the entire company as well. This wasn't just paranoia. The government *was* monitoring them.

"Everything's good with chat?" Angie asked.

Igloo nodded. "Incremental improvements. The psychologists have a few ideas. I made tweaks around detecting non-consensual language patterns. If we intercede early enough..." She trailed off to see if Angie would understand.

"If we get preteens and teens to use consensual language patterns, then it will change how they think, and changing how they think will affect how they behave."

"Exactly." She set the guitar down.

They stared at each other. There was an ease in the quiet, and for a moment Igloo felt a hint of connection between the two of them. It went unspoken that what they were doing would be objectionable to most, that their out-and-out goal was changing how people behaved, manipulating them to be kinder, and more aware. Most would focus on the method, not the outcome. But they understood each other. They would do what it took, regardless of how socially unacceptable it would be to the masses, but *they* would still accept each other. It was such a relief to feel that connection with Angie that she almost cried.

"It's good work, but you've been working on chatbots for a long time."

"They're not chatbots—"

Angie held a hand up. "Sorry. What I want to know is if you'd like to work on something different."

Angie had a knack for being mysterious. Igloo pulled her hoodie back and shook her hair free. "Go on."

"The world hasn't had a really private communication network since the NSA cracked TOR. There have been a few islands, small oases in the desert of surveillance, but nothing totally secure."

"We're encrypting all our traffic. Tapestry is secure."

"Probably," Angie said. "We've gotten to a moderate level of privacy. But think about our users. Most of their traffic to anything other than Tapestry is still in the open. But it doesn't have to be. What does an onion routing network do?"

"*As you know, Bob,*" Igloo said, rolling her eyes, "an onion network routes traffic through multiple nodes, with each node unraveling a layer of the onion. None of the interior nodes know how far away the packet originated, nor how far it still has to go. So even if the government manages to insert themselves into one or two places in the network, they can't see the payload, the source, or the destination."

"Unless *they...*" Angie pointed a finger out the window, which meant nothing, but Igloo knew she meant the NSA. "...insert themselves into a whole lot of nodes. One of the problems with TOR was that there weren't enough nodes. If the NSA decided to run a few thousand nodes, well within their ability, they'd get to spy on most of the TOR traffic. If they ran a hundred thousand TOR nodes they'd have a total panopticon...statistically able to see virtually all TOR traffic."

Igloo stared down at the digital pickup she'd installed on her guitar. "The only way to avoid that kind of attack is if the network has vastly more legitimate nodes, enough so that the government could never hope to control a significant percentage. If the government could do a million nodes, then we'd have to make an onion network with at least a hundred million nodes."

Angie smiled and nodded.

"Tapestry has more than a hundred million clients running." Igloo raised an eyebrow at Angie. "You want to turn all Tapestry clients into a giant onion network?"

"With encryption we can really trust," Angie said. "AES isn't enough because we can't be sure it isn't compromised. Run Twofish and Serpent. Randomized numbers of hops."

The Advanced Encryption Standard, or AES, might be suspect, but what Angie was proposing just wouldn't work. "It'll be too slow," Igloo said, shaking her head. "TOR always was."

"Because in a traditional onion network, bandwidth is limited. With a hundred million clients, it's not. There's a surplus of clients sitting idle all the time. So you piggyback a torrent-style algorithm, using multiple downloads to make up for the slowness."

"Parallel downloads won't fix the latency problem," Igloo said. "Bulk downloads like file transfers will be fast, but not interactive stuff."

"Then you layer in other techniques: predictive downloads, prefetching, distribution of content through the network. You give publishers a way to run their code on intermediate nodes, not just the endpoints."

Damn. Marrying all these cutting-edge techniques together the way Angie wanted would be tremendously complex.

Angie caught the look in Igloo's eyes.

"Don't worry about all that. Just focus on the onion routing. We'll get into the optimizations later."

"Fine." Igloo set down the guitar and stood. "I get it, I do. But what do our users care about onion routing and encryption standards? Would they even appreciate what we're talking about building?"

"Most won't care about the details," Angie said. "They may not be thinking about privacy. But that doesn't mean they won't appreciate it when they get it. That's what leaders do—figure out how to satisfy needs people aren't even aware of, and that no one else has figured out how to do yet. Our users want data ownership, control over their communications, and deep privacy. Even if they don't know it. A secure network is the backbone on which all that is provided. Tomo's gradually changing their tune, emphasizing privacy, user opt-out. We need to stay ahead of them."

"This needs a whole team, not just one anti-social programmer."

"Then build up a new team. Hand over the chat stuff to Amber. Tell her you're working on a g-job for me, and I'm giving you dibs to poach anyone you want in the company. But keep it as quiet as possible. And only recruit people who can keep a secret. No leaks."

"It's too ambitious," Igloo said.

"That's why I'm giving it to you. You need a challenge. You're bored of chatbots, and you're getting bored of Tapestry. I have to fix that before I lose you."

Igloo was too startled to say anything before Angie got up and left. How did Angie know? Was her behavior that obvious? Was her distraction with Essie also evident? Was she as transparent to other people as she was to Angie?

CHAPTER 2

Igloo biked home quickly, eager to see Essie. She arrived slightly out of breath, her back damp with sweat underneath her messenger bag.

Essie greeted her inside the door, a glass of water held in the flat of one palm, the other hand steadying the glass, her head slightly bowed, eyes down.

Igloo let her bag slide to the floor.

Essie was a vision, as she always was. A blonde, elfin woman with a pixie cut and a septum piercing, she stood just an inch taller than Igloo. Igloo appreciated a range of aesthetics, but she had a type, and Essie was as close to her ideal as she'd ever dated.

Thirsty, Igloo took the glass from Essie's hand, and drank. The water was precisely the temperature she wanted it, just a hair warmer than the coldness of the refrigerator, the type of water you could take a long swallow of and feel perfectly refreshed.

"Thank you."

Essie raised her eyes to Igloo's with a smile. "Welcome home."

She leaned forward, and Igloo went in for a quick kiss, cognizant of her sweaty clothes.

"Salty," Essie said, wiping her lips. "Go shower."

"Don't go getting bossy," Igloo said.

Essie smirked. "Or you'll punish me?"

"Maybe." As she walked to the bedroom, she called back, "If you're lucky."

She entered the room and stepped over some loose rope, a vibrator, and a ball gag. Igloo had been mildly kinky before she'd met Essie, but together they'd gone deeper than she'd gone before. BDSM wasn't something they reserved for the bedroom. It was part of the fabric of their relationship. In less than a year, Igloo had gone from owning a pair of handcuffs and some clothesline to an entire closet full of specialized gear.

Essie had been way more experienced right from the start. She helped Igloo get more involved in the scene, the local BDSM community. Convinced her to take rope lessons. And brought the rituals of Dominance and submission, or D/s, into their day-to-day relationship, like when she'd been waiting with the water when Igloo had arrived home. Some part of it ran counter to everything feminist Igloo had ever learned and embodied, and yet it was more than undeniably hot, it was a source of happiness for them both.

Ten months they'd been together. Essie had moved in a month ago and Igloo was thrilled about her first romantic cohabitation. Waking next to Essie every morning was blissful, and she loved seeing Essie's stuff all around.

Igloo stripped off her clothes and showered. She hoped to feel refreshed afterwards, but mostly she felt tired, the caffeine from her last round of coffee wearing off.

Essie found her sitting on the edge of the bed. "You're tired. Take a nap before tonight."

"Do I have time?" Igloo asked. It was good to have someone to take care of her. Someone else to make the little decisions like whether there was time for a nap.

"Yes. I'll wake you and have your coffee ready."

Igloo pulled the covers back and crawled into bed naked. Her head hit the pillow, and she lay there, her mind racing back and forth between Essie and work. Angie was right, there was something wrong at work, but she couldn't put her finger on it. It wasn't that she was bored exactly. It was more like the fit wasn't right anymore. Shit, she was never going to fall asleep. Then she wouldn't nap, then she'd be tired for tonight.

She closed her eyes for a second, and the next thing she heard was the creak of the bedroom door. The bed shifted as Essie climbed in next to her. Essie cleared her throat, and Igloo opened her eyes to find Essie kneeling on the bed, presentation pose, coffee in the palm of her hand.

She blinked a few times, trying to focus. "Did I already sleep?"

Essie nodded without looking up. "An hour and a half."

Wow. No wonder she was so groggy. She sat up, took the mug from Essie. "Thank you."

Essie smiled and raised her eyes to meet Igloo's gaze. "Drink up, come have dinner, and then get ready. You have an hour before we need to leave."

Igloo took a bunch of small sips of coffee, trying to get as much in her system as possible without burning her mouth. She joined Essie in the kitchen and sat at their little table. Essie brought plates of jackfruit tacos.

Igloo glanced down and forced a smile to her face. She'd been vegan once and wasn't particularly excited to go back. Living together was mostly awesome, but it did leave her hankering for more meat.

"You gotta try steak tacos someday." Igloo said. "You'd love them."

Essie shook her head. "Gross. There's no way I'm eating meat."

"Just try it with me. You'll have more energy. We're made to eat animals."

"No, no, no. That's gross. You can eat dead flesh when you're on your own."

Igloo sighed. She'd grab a burger tomorrow at lunch.

They talked about each other's days while they ate. Then Igloo glanced at the clock. She had time to epilate, if she hurried.

"Gotta go," she said, giving Essie a kiss.

After she finished prepping in the bathroom, she went back to her walk-in closet.

The left half was all band t-shirts, jeans, and white hoodies. The same everyday clothes she'd been wearing since middle school, clothing that she used to hide away from the way men stared at her body. She could bury herself in an oversized hoodie, and in some part of her mind, she was concealed, just a blob with a mind, divorced from any physicality, any sense of being embodied in a very human body. Because to be human, to have a body, exposed vulnerabilities. A body elicited dangerous attention from men. Her body was something that could be used against her, to hurt her, not merely physically, but to control her mind. And that was so unacceptable that she'd spent the vast majority of her life building layers of protection against that possibility.

But the right half of the closet was for play parties and the scene. Aside from being all black, the clothes there consisted mostly of form-fitting latex, pleather, and mesh. Pretty much the opposite end of the spectrum from everything she'd allowed herself to be for the past fifteen years.

Entering the BDSM scene had allowed her to tackle her fears, even embrace them somehow. She'd taken back ownership of her deepest vulnerabilities. She controlled what happened to her, even when it was something that, on the surface, she didn't want. Consenting to being beaten or acting out a rape fantasy empowered her in a way that years of unwanted therapy forced on her by her parents had never touched.

Being in the scene had finally given her permission to be herself. There was no need to hide from everyone, not in the community where people accepted anything and anyone as normal, and many shared stories of surviving abuse.

Even though the intellectual in Igloo was almost completely unappreciated in the scene, she'd experienced a level of acceptance she'd never found in the tech community. Somehow she could wear clothes that left nothing to the imagination and still feel comfortable, whereas to walk into the office, she had to bundle up.

If she ever revealed what truly went on in her mind, shrinks would have a field day with her.

Back to clothes. Deviance was the most upscale play party in Portland. She riffled back and forth and grabbed a black vinyl mini skirt with a side zipper (easy-on, easy-off), a stretchy mesh top, and a black corset. No, what was she thinking? She had to tie, to be able to bend. The corset would be a nightmare. She had to save that for a munch or something.

She considered her normal military pants and black tank, her rigger uniform, but that didn't feel right. Not for the venue or for a fancy date with Essie. She wanted to look good.

She tossed the skirt and corset away and picked a pair of stretchy pleather pants and a black pentagram bra. She'd wear the mesh top over the bra. She added a pair of chunky heeled boots, and a long black coat for street modesty.

The toy bag was packed, ready at its usual spot just inside the door. If only she could be so organized in her professional life. Then she realized that Essie had probably unpacked and repacked the whole bag today to make it perfect, and that maybe the problem was that she couldn't bring Essie to work.

She wondered what would happen if she told HR she needed to hire a full-time submissive to take care of her at work.

She picked up the bag, and glanced over to where Essie was putting the finishing touches on her makeup.

"Are you almost ready?"

Essie looked up, eyeliner in her hand. "Give me two minutes."

Igloo let the bag slump down to the floor. Two minutes meant ten or fifteen. She had time for another cup of coffee.

Angie made her scan Essie's car regularly for surveillance devices as a preventive measure, since Igloo sometimes used the car to meet Angie. So the car itself was a clean environment. Igloo made sure her and Essie's phones were off, then she inserted them both into an anti-static bag.

Between the two measures, Igloo was fairly certain that the government wouldn't know they were going to Club Privata for Deviance, their monthly kink event, but if they really wanted to be sure, they'd need to take even more counter-surveillance measures: switching cars and clothes. All of which was kind of pointless, since she was moderately well known in the BDSM scene. As one of the few female rope tops, she attracted attention, and some had drawn the connection between kinky Igloo and Igloo the tech cofounder. She wasn't out with her coworkers though, and fuck only knew what would happen the day her two worlds collided.

Her first visit to Deviance had been with the guy who'd intro-duced her to kink. He'd asked to be led around on a leash. He'd brought his own flogger and asked her to hit him. It was one thing to play at home, in private, but something else entirely to do it in public, in a room full of people watching or doing their own scenes. The noises had been so distracting she'd been almost unable to focus on what she was doing. People screaming or crying had set her on edge, in a constant state of hyperarousal, her sympathetic nervous system insisting that there were serious threats nearby.

They'd done a short flogging scene downstairs, then gone upstairs to a semi-private room, where they'd fucked while an older triad sat on a couch on the other side of a sliding glass door, watching and fondling one another. By then she'd been less panicked by all the strange noises and found herself mostly giggling during the whole experience.

The second time she'd gone to Deviance, hoping to find a play partner on the spot, and ended up propositioned by nearly every guy in the place. That was right around the time she'd decided that maybe she was done with guys. It wasn't that she hated them. There were plenty of men she loved. But her trauma went too deep. Women were safer.

The experience soured her on the monthly event for a while, until she met Essie, who had an exhibitionist streak a mile wide and wanted to go to all the public parties.

Tonight she entered the club carrying her toy bag over one shoulder and guiding Essie with one hand on Essie's collar. They attracted attention, as they always did. The scene skewed heavily heteronormative, even in progressive Portland, a trend that drove many of the LGBTQ crowd underground. But if exhibition was your kink, then there was no substitute for public parties.

The music was loud, competing with a background din of raised voices, and broken only by occasional screams from players in the impact play area.

Eventually she'd become acclimated to all the unusual behaviors and noises. Screams that would have once sent her into fight-or-flight response now were recognizable as two people having fun, experiencing a cathartic event together, bonding over an activity that required trust and compassion and skill.

They headed to the second floor, where riggers like her would take turns on the few hard points surrounded by spectators. It was a little quieter here, and the screams from downstairs were interspersed with noisy sex sounds and spanking. She heard distinctive screams at regular intervals from the rope area and recognized the tie from the pacing of the screams alone: a torturous version of a futomomo, the Japanese folded-leg tie that bound the ankle firmly to the upper thigh.

When one of the hard points freed up, Igloo and Essie climbed onto the mattress beneath it, and they worked together to put a black sheet down. Igloo fixed her shibari ring and swivel to the hard point above the bed while Essie laid out bundles of rope according to Igloo's precise preferences.

Igloo and Essie knelt facing each other. They exchanged smiles at the sound of someone groaning as they were spanked in one of the nearby private rooms. Other people's sex noises were weird, no matter how often you heard them. Igloo knew from experience they'd fade into the background as soon as her scene started.

Igloo caressed Essie's cheek. "I love you."

Essie wiggled. "Are you going to be nice or mean?"

"I'm always nice *and* mean."

"No, sometimes you're just mean."

"Well, you won't get wet unless I'm mean."

Essie blushed and nodded.

Igloo grabbed a riding crop from her pile of toys and threatened Essie with it. "You have thirty seconds to get undressed."

Essie squealed and rushed to pull off her shirt.

Igloo counted backwards. "Twenty-nine, twenty-eight..."

Essie tossed the shirt aside and fell backwards onto the bed unzipping her skirt. She was completely naked.

"Look at you," Igloo said, grabbing Essie by the hair, and pulling her close. "Such a slut, you were out of your clothes in fifteen seconds."

Essie responded with a sheepish grin.

Slut shaming did nothing for her, but Essie loved it. She let her lips brush Essie's shoulder, and Essie's breathing accelerated.

She twisted Essie around by the hair forcing her to kneel facing away. She grabbed Essie's arms, pulled them behind her back, and wrapped a length of rope around her wrists, tying them together by feel while she continued to nibble at Essie's neck.

She took the free end of the rope, brought it around Essie's upper arm, and wrapped it around Essie's chest, letting her fingers glide softly over Essie's breasts, teasing her nipples. Two wraps around and a friction. Igloo got into the zone, finishing the takate kote, the classical Japanese box tie she'd repeated so many times that the mere act of tying it was a comfortable meditation, every little movement a chance to play with Essie in some way: a teasing touch, a sensual stimulation, a hundred caresses building sexual tension. Essie responded with little moans and a subtle arching of her back, leaning into Igloo's touch.

Box tie complete, she forced Essie back onto the mattress, grabbed an ankle, and tied a futomomo, binding Essie's leg into a folded position. Essie's eyes followed her every movement, a sharp attentiveness that sent a continual electric thrill through Igloo.

Essie's movements diminished as the restraints grew. When Igloo finished the other leg, she went for Essie's ticklish spots just above her hipbones. Essie writhed on the mattress, squealing, which gathered laughter from the onlookers.

Igloo glanced up for a brief second, gratified to see a circle of spectators. But the audience received only the barest slip of her attention, and then she dove right back in. It was always that way: she loved to be watched, and yet 99 percent of her attention was right there on her partner. So why did it even matter if people were watching? She couldn't say, and yet she couldn't deny that it was hotter to play in public.

She tied a Y-knot between Essie's thighs, added a rappel ring, and ran the rope up to her shibari ring and back again. She would deadlift Essie without a second upline. Her teacher frowned on the risk. But she and Essie had discussed the dangers, and they were comfortable with the decision.

She checked the mattress to ensure there was nothing lying around that would interfere at a crucial moment, then patted her back to feel for her rope cutter on her belt. She heaved on the upline and Essie rose, legs-first into the air. She took extra care as Essie's upper body came off the bed, making sure Essie curled up so no weight rested on her neck. Once Essie successfully cleared the mattress, Igloo tied off the rope.

Essie hung upside down, legs splayed, eyes closed, her breathing carefully measured. From her own past experiences, Igloo knew Essie was processing the uniqueness of being upside down, blood flooding the brain, back muscles and spine stretching out, shortness of breath due to the elongation of her torso, compression of the legs, turning eventually to pain where the rope dug into the skin and shins, and the sensations of dangling, freely spinning and swinging.

Kink was an interplay, two people meeting each other's needs, supported by vulnerability and shared trust. Igloo needed to be in control, to be able to restrict what Essie could do, to take charge of even basic bodily functions like scratching an itch or being able to defend herself, leaving Essie totally dependent on Igloo. And though she was still uncomfortable and conflicted enough that it was hard for her to admit it, the sadist in Igloo wanted to hurt Essie. The pain reinforced that Igloo was so far in control that Essie was powerless to stop her.

But play couldn't be only about meeting Igloo's needs. Essie had needs too, the need to give up control to someone else, to have someone take charge of her, to have a freedom from responsibility, to be of service to someone, to be used for someone else's enjoyment, and ultimately, to receive pleasure in return.

She gave Essie a push, setting her to spinning, and watched, admiring. Even upside down, her face red, Essie smiled, blissed out from endorphins.

They played for an hour, transitioning through positions, Igloo sprinkling in other tortures —spanks, grabs, bites, flogging—when the mood struck her. When Essie finally came down, she was rope-doped and crawled into Igloo's lap, where she curled up in a little ball. Igloo stroked her back, petted her head, and cooed into her ear. While Essie continued to rest, Igloo bundled rope and swept her various toys and tools into the toy bag, creating a sea of black messiness inside the bag.

There were other riggers waiting for the hard point, so Igloo gently encouraged Essie to put on clothes and get up. Essie moved slowly and unsteadily, still loaded with endorphins. They made their way to one of the private rooms and closed the door behind them. Essie climbed into the bed. Igloo dumped the toy bag next to the bed and stripped off her clothes.

Essie's skin was warm against hers. She pulled Essie's clothes back off and reached down between her legs.

"You're wet, you little slut. I'm going to start thinking you like being tied up."

Essie shyly hid her face behind an arm.

Igloo grabbed her arms and pinned Essie back to the bed. "Tell me what you are."

"I'm a slut," Essie breathed. "Your slut would enjoy being fucked, Mistress."

Igloo got a thigh between Essie's legs and ground on her while she sprinkled kisses and bites up and down Essie's neck and chest. Igloo held Essie's wrists with one hand, and ran the other down Essie's chest, brushing fingers across nipple, breasts, ribs. She grabbed a tit with a firm grasp and squeezed.

Essie moaned and soon she was bucking hard under Igloo, her breathing erratic. "Can I come, please?"

"No, not yet," Igloo said, feeling perverse, gleefully sadistic.

"Oh, fuck." Essie was thrashing now, on the edge. "Oh, please, can I come?"

"Beg me to hurt you," Igloo said.

Essie fell silent as she still writhed under Igloo.

"Beg," Igloo commanded.

"Please hurt me," Essie said. "Please."

Igloo crushed Essie's nipple between her fingers, then twisted and pulled.

Essie shrieked in pain, and Igloo grew even wetter. She ground again on Essie, who responded with still greater passion.

"Can I come, please?" Essie asked, the urgency now strident.

Igloo felt a visceral thrill at Essie's desperation. "Yes, come."

Essie moaned and shuddered, nearly tossing Igloo off. Awe and power flooded through Igloo in equal portions at her ability to cause this reaction in Essie. Igloo refocused her weight, bearing down on Essie until she finally slowed and lay still, breathing hard.

Igloo rolled off and onto the bed. She lightly stroked Essie, running her fingers up and down Essie's thighs and stomach, brimming with love for this amazing being. She gave Essie a few moments to enjoy the afterglow, then grabbed her by the hair.

"Enough fun for you." She pulled Essie to her knees, then forced her to kneel in front of her. "Hands behind your back."

Essie clasped her hands to her elbows behind her back as Igloo had taught her.

Igloo forced Essie's head down with both hands. "Time to earn your keep."

Essie's response was muffled and inaudible, but fervent.

———

Igloo set the lights to morning, and stroked Essie's hair.

Essie nuzzled in closer. "We don't have to get up yet, do we?"

"Soon, pet."

"I'll get your coffee." Essie stretched and unfurled herself, then rolled out of the bed. A few moments later, Igloo heard the hiss of coffee brewing from the kitchen.

She propped herself up and waited. Her eyes fell on the pile of uncoiled rope next to the bed, then moved on to the nightstand with its collection of sex toys, and the pile of half built circuit boards teetering on the dresser next to leather restraints. Why did they have so many dildos anyway?

The door opened, and Essie returned, carrying two cups. She set one down on the far nightstand, then climbed into bed. She held one hand in front of her, set the cup down on her open palm, turned the handle to Igloo's left, and steadied the cup with her other hand. She waited, eyes down.

This was bliss. Igloo's heart ached with love. She stared at Essie's lips, the curve of her neck, the line of tattoos running down her arm. What had Igloo done to deserve such dedication and service from another?

Essie's nipples were hard in the cool morning air. Igloo caressed the soft curve under one breast and ran her hand lightly over Essie's shoulder and down the back of her arm. Essie trembled and shivered, goosebumps rising all over. She moved ever so slightly closer, the softest of moans just barely audible through slightly pursed lips. Igloo brought her hand back around to her breasts and squeezed a nipple. Essie grimaced but stayed still.

Igloo took the cup. "Good girl. You're released."

Essie leaned in and kissed her, then half lay in the crook of Igloo's arm.

"It's unbelievable that we get to do this every morning," Igloo said, and it was true, even though at times she worried about when she would get alone time. Living together came with its challenges.

"I feel guilty about not making any contribution to the rent."

"We've discussed this before. The money is immaterial." Igloo was a millionaire many times over, thanks to Tapestry. Neither she nor Essie would ever want for anything. But any time she brought up money, it made Essie uncomfortable.

Essie lightly stroked Igloo's side but didn't say anything.

"Is this really about my money?" Igloo asked, and Essie shook her head. But there was something in Essie's eyes. She sipped her coffee and waited. This hesitant silence on Essie's part was odd.

"Is there something else?" Igloo said, finally.

"I'm excited to have moved in with you," Essie said. "But I'm twenty-six, and I always imagined myself dating all through my twenties, and maybe finding a life partner in my thirties."

Igloo's heart skipped a beat or two. "Are you having second thoughts?"

"No, definitely not!" Essie gazed into Igloo's eyes. "I just thought I'd have more of a chance to date. I want to live with you, but I still want to experience dating in my life."

"What are you saying?"

"We talked once about an open relationship. Are you game to try?"

Oh! Part of Igloo felt an instant guilt, like she was expected to object. But what she mostly felt was a rush of excitement. Essie had been Igloo's only serious kinky partner. Meanwhile, nearly all of their friends in the scene played with multiple partners or were fully polyamorous. Igloo had secretly longed to tie someone else.

When Igloo asked about playing with others in the past, Essie said she didn't mind. But the two of them were always together, and she'd never had the time to meet anyone by herself. Either Igloo was working, or hacking with Angie, or she was with Essie. If Essie went on dates, it would give Igloo some of that time and space she needed to set up rope scenes with others.

Still, there was a pit in her belly...Essie was precious to her. What would it feel like knowing she was out with other people?

"You mock everyone we know who's polyamorous," Igloo said. "You claimed poly is a label people use to justify their inability to form real emotional bonds. That it's an excuse for people who don't actually know how to have a relationship. Those were pretty much your exact words."

"I know I said that, but we've met others. Look at your teacher. He's got loving relationships. He cares about his partners. There are people who have figured out how to do this."

"Is there some problem with our relationship? Something you want that you're not getting?"

Essie climbed into Igloo's lap and kissed her. "Our relationship is great. This has nothing to do with us. I just want to experience something I always thought I'd get to try. And you want to play with other people, right?"

Igloo laughed. "Yeah. I've been thinking about that."

"This will give you the space for that."

Igloo squeezed Essie tight. "I love you."

"I love you too."

"If it doesn't work out?"

"Then we call quits on poly."

"I'm game to try," Igloo said. "I just don't want to put our relationship at risk."

CHAPTER 3

Angie pulled her bra on, holding one side with her stump and fastening the clasp with her hand. She picked out a simple blouse. Her best friend Emily would insist on calling it a blouse, and it perturbed Angie that she'd been brainwashed long enough that now she had second thoughts about calling it a shirt.

She stared in the mirror for a second. This is what the eve of fifty looked like. She felt vaguely dissatisfied. She had so much to do. Tapestry wasn't done, not nearly. If anything, the real challenges were still to come.

In the beginning, she'd fought abusers. Then she saw what Tomo was doing to their users, and she saw a higher purpose, a bigger battle to fight. Tomo was toppling now, a tree that had been axed at its base, leaning and succumbing to gravity. It just hadn't hit the ground yet. But Tomo was no longer Angie's problem. She'd let Amber and Maria handle that.

The bigger challenge was the country. The proliferation of fabricated news and echo chambers weren't the problem. They were the symptom of a gap in critical thinking skills. What people needed was the ability to evaluate information, understand causation versus correlation, apply system thinking, to detect patterns and turn them into concepts that they could apply to real life.

She looked back at the mirror and sighed. At forty, she still appeared young. Now she looked, well, not old. Just her age.

Emily said that men aged like fine wine, getting more nuanced with each passing year. Women aged like fresh fruit, a moment of peak ripeness, then growing soft and wrinkled.

Oh, fuck Emily and her stupid cultural programming. Why the hell did she even care about how she looked? It was irrelevant. She was who she was this moment, this day.

She pulled on her pants.

She didn't know how to solve the critical thinking problem. Tapestry wasn't a school. These were skills people should be taught by their parents, by the education system. But she was going to have to do it. And if she couldn't, then she'd need to somehow counter the effects of misinformation. If people were going to be brainwashed, then at least let them be indoctrinated to be kinder, gentler, and better human beings.

It was a hell of a mission. And worse, they were going to have a showdown with the government sometime soon. It was inevitable that Tapestry would be served with a FISA court order. All the big Internet companies had to comply with the government mandated backdoors that allowed them to spy on whomever they wanted, whenever they wanted. When that happened, Angie would have to fight a war on two fronts.

Finished dressing, she leaned over to kiss Thomas, who still slept, with only the slightest hint of a snore. She wanted to run her fingers through his grey hair but knew that would wake him. The thing is, he *did* get better looking with each passing year.

She briefly had an urge to strip naked and climb on top of him. When was the last time she'd done that?

She couldn't remember. Besides, the whole point of getting up early was to get to work before everyone else and get something productive done. Otherwise, why get up by five?

She looked at him once more. Time was finite. There were only so many days, and eventually the day would come when one of them was too old (or worse, too dead) for sex, and they would have made love for the last time. They wouldn't know when that moment would come. Wouldn't know until after it had happened, and only then would they look back in time and realize they didn't even remember it that well.

Ugh. Now every day she'd wonder if that last time was in the past.

Fuck, she was morbid. What the hell? She was approaching fifty, not her deathbed. Why so focused on her own mortality?

She knew the answer. Knew it when she saw the difference between what she could do and Igloo could do. Her days of all-nighters were gone. Her days of staying up-to-date on all the latest programming frameworks were history. What happened when she was no longer relevant?

In the kitchen, she grabbed a jar of cold-brew coffee from the fridge, flipped the top open, and took a long swig.

It wasn't fifty per se, it was what her fifties represented. In her forties, she had the full vitality of adulthood. And she still did. But somewhere between fifty and sixty, there'd be a change. A sixty-year-old could still be vigorous, but only in the sense of a person in decline. And forget about seventy. At some point, what's ruled out vastly exceeds what you can still do.

She wished she were twenty years younger. Igloo had a reasonable chance of living forever if medical technology progressed fast enough, if the singularity came and accelerated the rate of technological change. Maybe Igloo would be uploaded into the net, or maybe they'd reverse aging at the DNA level in time to keep her biological body going indefinitely. Once Angie had been confident she would be alive then too, but now she was afraid she'd just barely miss it. How stupid it was to live to almost within the reach of immortality only to die before it was possible.

She set the cold-brew down and shook her head. It was stupid to worry about what would happen over the next decade when she should be focused on getting through the next year, not inventing more problems. Hell, it was unlikely she'd survive the next few months, what with all the stress of work.

She looked down at the coffee. Thomas wanted her to quit. Said it would help with her blood pressure. She picked it up and took another swig. She had too much to do for that.

She briefly considered offloading some of her work to Igloo. No, she couldn't do that. She was sure that her enemies, in the government or the hacker community, would leap on any chink in her armor. That included Igloo. She had to keep her distance from Igloo.

She walked down into the garage. On one side was Thomas's new BMW plugin hybrid she'd bought him for his birthday. On the other side, her totally custom, 3D-printed OSV Doctorow, an open source electric car made from public domain components.

She loved the thing, knew every spec and component. She'd adjusted the body curves in their online editor, getting it all just so. She'd tweaked the component selection endlessly, to the extent that the final assembly had required weeks of firmware tinkering before she could get it to work reliably. But it was all hers, from top to bottom, and as open and DRM free as you could get.

She slipped her bag into the vertical chamber she'd designed into the shell and climbed into the driver's seat. She closed the door, fussing it a little to get the seal seated properly. The damn hinges weren't quite up to spec. She hit the start button, then sighed as the Bluetooth authentication fumbled the handshake with her phone. Yeah, it was a little rough around the edges.

Eventually the dashboard lit up from end to end, and she backed out, exposing the wireless charging pad on the garage floor.

She arrived at work twenty minutes later, parked in the employee lot, and slipped into her office unnoticed. She refused to look at her email, although the temptation was overwhelming. She might make a dent in it, might even take care of some important work, but if she didn't take care of the big rocks first, there wouldn't be any room left in her day for them.

The biggest rocks of all were the special projects she was hatching to deal with the inevitable FISA court order. Tapestry's days of freedom were numbered. They'd grown big, and it had happened faster than anyone thought possible. That meant that any day now they'd get visitors from the government.

Angie had to be prepared. What she needed to do couldn't be reactive. The plans needed to be plausibly underway before the government came, and she couldn't give away the nature of her scheme or the government would act preemptively.

The onion routing project she'd given Igloo was just one part of a grander plan. Now she had to plant more seeds.

She worked for an hour, then two.

There was a knock at the door at eight, and Matt entered with fresh coffee and a package under his arm.

She looked up, caught the expression on his normally cheery face. "What now?"

"You were supposed to leave tomorrow, but I can get you on a flight out this morning. Then you'd have time for a stop in New York to talk to the CEO Roundtable this afternoon before heading to London."

She'd lose track of where she was supposed to be if it wasn't for Matt. She missed the days where the only "admin" she would have thought of would have been a system administrator. Now her administrative assistant Matt was the only thing that kept her sane.

"I'm already visiting four cities on this circuit. Isn't that enough?"

"Actually, you were already doing five," Matt said, replacing her old cup with the new coffee. He deposited the package on her desk. "This will be the sixth. You said you wanted to talk to this group. It's the multiyear strategic vision talk."

Angie glanced over at the door, saw her travel bag was ready. She'd taken to keeping a bag packed at the office and another at home, never sure when she'd have to travel. She looked down at her screen.

She'd done enough on the special projects and could email on the plane.

"Fine, change the flight. When do I leave?"

"Forty minutes."

There was never enough time for everything that needed to be done. Ugh. Well, it wasn't Matt's fault. He'd probably been out there working on rearranging travel plans since he'd got in. "Thanks for squeezing this in, Matt."

"Sure. I'll grab some breakfast for you to take to the airport."

Angie nodded, and bent to her computer. She had one more project she needed to dole out. Whom could she count on? So many special projects, and only so many people she really trusted to be both technically competent and totally discreet.

She scanned through the short list of employees she'd already prefiltered. There...she'd be perfect.

She remembered the package that Matt had left. She slid it toward her, pinned the envelope with her stump, and pulled the rip cord. She lifted the bottom and a mobile phone slid out. It was a uniform matte black, even the screen with its nanotech privacy coating as matte as the body, and she didn't need anything else to know whom it was from. Nathan9.

She stared at the device, not daring to turn it on. Some skeletons were supposed to stay in the closet. She'd used Nathan9 back when she burned Tomo, and in doing so she'd ruined any chance at friendship or even alliance. It was a terrible thing to make an enemy of another hacker, let alone one of Nathan9's caliber. But she'd done what she needed to do then, and now the only approach was to maintain radio silence.

She was still at her desk replaying old memories, when Matt reentered ten minutes later. "Time to go. Car's here."

She gestured at the phone. "Bag this and toss it into one of the equipment shredders." Tapestry was always at risk of being infiltrated, whether by competitors or the government, and the massive shredder in the basement was designed to destroy hostile electronics.

Matt nodded and went to grab an EMF-proof bag.

She was out of her office in a flash. Walking down the hall, she realized she hadn't said goodbye to Thomas this morning, hadn't known she'd be leaving early. Sigh. She wished she had gotten back into bed with him.

CHAPTER 4

On the third floor, down the hallway from her office, Igloo punched the button for another two shots of espresso, adding them to the four already in the blender.

Four hours of sleep was not enough. Last night she and Essie had stayed out late, then gone home and had sex for hours until they'd finally curled up in bed in a mess of sheets, blankets, and rope. Then the conversation about poly this morning when she was only half awake. She wasn't sure what she was getting herself into, but she couldn't deny the attraction of playing with other people. She wondered whom she could reach out to.

She added two scoops of protein mix, two scoops of raw cocoa powder, ice, and water, then stuck the whole thing back on the base. She put one finger on the blend button, then stopped in the nick of time, and put the lid on.

After blending the drink, she chugged a quarter of it.

A loud talker on a phone call walked into the kitchen, just in time to see her walking off with the pitcher.

He pulled the phone away from his face. "Hey, I need that," he said, gesturing with his phone to the pitcher.

Igloo scanned him. He wore slacks and a button-down shirt.

Therefore, he wasn't a developer, and his face didn't appear to match any of the new executives.

"I need it more," she said. "There's another blender in the other break room." She took the pitcher back to her office and closed the door.

Her stomach didn't feel right. Old Igloo wouldn't have done that. Taking the pitcher was essentially theft of common property. She didn't have any more right to the pitcher than he did, regardless of how long she'd been here and whether he was an engineer or not.

Ugh. Why did she react so selfishly? It would be easy to blame it on some change in the company culture. But maybe she was angry and looking for someone to take it out on. Or maybe she was just tired.

She stared guiltily at the pitcher, swigged some more of the shake, and headed back to the break room. She poured what was left into an oversized coffee mug, washed the pitcher, and put it back on the base.

She wasn't at her best when she was sleep deprived. She made a mental note to herself to stop trying to get by on less than six hours of sleep.

Back at her office, the massive quantity of coffee she'd dumped into her body was finally starting to take hold, and she paced the room thinking about Angie's special project. From her past work with Angie, she was intimately familiar with the details of TOR, the onion routing network originally created by DARPA and the Navy back in 1998. TOR had two main weaknesses.

If the exit nodes were compromised, an attacker could spy on all the traffic as cleartext. If the attacker ran their own TOR nodes, they'd be able to monitor whatever flowed through the nodes they controlled. TOR usually ran less than ten thousand nodes in the network. If two thousand of those were NSA spy nodes, they'd be able to spy on twenty percent of the traffic. They wouldn't know who sent the traffic, but they could see what left the onion network and where it went.

A different attack vector could correlate data packet sizes and timings. If the government was interested in a certain high-profile hacker's board, and they saw a 2,500 byte packet exit TOR headed for the hacker's board, they could identify all the packets originating elsewhere of similar size sent around the same time. There'd be millions, but if they repeatedly kept correlating packets, over time they would statistically narrow it down to one, or a few, sources.

Angie had been aware of those shortcomings, which was why she'd built her own small onion routing network, where she was guaranteed to control all the nodes, and where her algorithm traded off performance for more randomness in packet sizing, timing and delays, in order to confuse traffic analysis.

What Angie wanted her to do was integrate all these sophisticated counter-surveillance measures into the Tapestry client itself, so that every client became an onion routing node. What was different about this was the scale of what they'd be attempting. There were at least a hundred million people using Tapestry at any given time. For the government to compromise a Tapestry-based secure network on that scale...it would be impossible.

Tapestry would be able to implement their own traffic variation algorithms, either padding packets, splitting them, or recombining them with other traffic, making it impossible to correlate traffic across the network.

Igloo stared at the architecture drawings covering her office walls, the mug of coffee-protein-chocolate mix dangling empty by her side. The block diagrams leapt off the walls, filling her mind with boxes representing software components, connected with lines, symbolizing the interfaces between those models. In her head, she dragged the WebSocket layer around, merged it with—

"Anything happening?"

The unexpected voice startled Igloo. Amber must have snuck in when she was deep in thought.

"I'm thinking through the implications of adding TOR to our communication layer."

"Angie's special project." Amber sighed.

"You know about it?"

"Yeah." Amber stared at the ropes dangling from a support girder. "What's this for?"

"Swing," Igloo said. That was her cover story at least. The reality was that she sometimes liked to practice self-suspension at night, when the office was empty, and she could lock the door and not be interrupted. She half wished she could come out and stop hiding her kink from everyone at the office.

Igloo joined Amber next to the rope, and drew the two descending halves apart, to form a triangle in the middle. "Sit here."

"This is safe?"

She nodded.

Amber climbed in, got the rope situated comfortably on her bottom, and nodded. Igloo let go, and Amber took a few experimental kicks to get her momentum going.

Once she established a regular momentum, Amber spoke. "IPFS support is just finished and reaping benefits. Sites realize they can cut their bandwidth costs by adopting a Tapestry-centric approach. We need to focus on speeding up adoption of IPFS, not adding unnecessary layers of encryption and NSA-paranoia levels of privacy. It's hard enough to explain a peer-to-peer protocol like IPFS without extra complications."

Igloo sighed. "Data abuses are growing all the time. The NSA monitors everything, and they're the supposed good guys. Corporations spy on everyone, selling not just their data, but all the insights they can glean, and that's all legal. Can you even begin to imagine what the *bad guys* are doing with this data?"

"But robust encryption protects against most of that. We don't need onion routing."

"Encryption alone doesn't provide anonymity. Nor obfuscation of websites visited."

Amber kicked more, her swings getting higher.

Igloo wondered about dynamic load versus static load, and how much force was exerted on her lines while Amber was in motion. She glanced toward the plate glass window behind Amber. The rope *should* be strong enough. Right? She looked outside to the tree tops below the window.

"If we get enough sites on IPFS, you know what will happen?" Amber said. "Tomo will be forced to adopt Tapestry's content network. We'll have Tomo scrambling after us, instead of the reverse. That will be the real end for them."

"Sure," Igloo said, trying to put the rope out of her mind. "That sounds nice. But what's your point?"

"I need Diana and Ben 100 percent focused on IPFS. I need the R&D team focused on IPFS. I need business development focused 100 percent on IPFS."

Diana and Ben were the two engineers Igloo would have wanted to work on onion routing with her. Experienced protocol developers, they'd not only reimplemented the IPFS libraries, they'd optimized the protocol interactions, speeding up data transfer 50 percent while reducing gross network load more than five times, with a more efficient way of finding nearest neighbors to download from.

"Angie said she wants me to lead this team and that I could have anyone I need. I need Ben and Diana."

"You can't have them," Amber said. She stopped pumping, started slowing down. "I need them more. It's critical to our success that I keep them focused on IPFS."

"Their work on IPFS is done. Everything's implemented. It works."

"We have to be able to assure prospective customers of the benefits."

"You don't need two expert developers to coddle our customers. Ben and Diana must hate that shit."

"It's what's most important to Tapestry right now."

"If that's so important, then why did Angie tell me I could have anyone I wanted?"

Amber put her feet down on the floor mid-descent and came to a sudden halt. "Angie's a little out of touch with our priorities. Don't you think?"

Igloo thought back to yesterday's all-company meeting, the ra-ra-ra session with the executives that she'd walked out of. It seemed stupid to her at the time, but Angie appeared pretty clear and focused when they'd met afterwards. Was she really? What did Igloo know? She was still programming, not running a company.

Amber cleared her throat, interrupting Igloo's thoughts.

"Just promise me you're not going to distract Diana and Ben with your project."

Igloo stared, but Amber just stared back. "Fine, I won't poach them."

"Thanks. If you need to borrow anyone else, let me know and try to give me a few weeks' notice, so I can plan around your request."

"Sure, fine." Shit. When had Tapestry become so bureaucratic?

Amber stood and waved a goodbye, which Igloo halfheartedly returned.

Igloo didn't believe Angie could be as out of touch as Amber made her out to be. She hopped off the drum stool and left her office to find Angie, whose office was at the opposite corner of the building.

Matt sat guard outside Angie's office. From her position partway down the hallway, Igloo debated with herself. Should she stride past, ignoring his control over Angie's calendar, thereby asserting that she had the right to meet with Angie and would not be subject to his power? That would probably anger him. Or engage directly with him, cultivating future goodwill but fostering his own belief in his power over her? He was staring down at his desk. Maybe this was her chance to make a run for it.

Her phone vibrated. She pulled it out. A message from Matt.

Matt > She's not here. She left a day early. She's in NY.

She looked up. Matt waved at her from his desk. She sighed and walked down the hallway.

"She's on the road visiting all the offices."

"When's she back?"

"Next Tuesday, for a day. Then she goes to Boulder for a board retreat. Then she's delivering the keynote at DevOps Enterprise Summit."

"When can I actually talk to her?"

Matt glanced down at his computer "I can get you thirty minutes when she comes back on the 20th."

"In two weeks? No, thanks."

"You want a fifteen minute Skype on Monday?"

"Never mind."

Igloo turned and stalked back to her office, almost bumping into Maria.

"Hi, *Igloo.*"

"Hi Maria." Igloo tried to sidestep her and keep going without breaking stride, but Maria stepped the same way. Igloo shrank, tried to slip by, but Maria held out a hand.

"Let's get coffee together," Maria said.

"I'm working on something important. I kind of need to get back."

"That's what I want to talk about. I want to learn more about what you're doing. It won't take long."

"How about tomorrow?"

"I'm free now. How do you take your coffee?"

Shit. She wasn't getting out of this. "Espresso shots, and a lot of them."

"Great. Let's go to my office."

They passed the espresso stand and the break room and wound their way to Maria's small, interior office. Igloo wondered where the coffee was coming from, since they'd passed up all the sources of caffeine.

"You don't have a window," Igloo said.

"Nah. It would have felt funny, with so many people who have been here longer than me, to have co-opted one of those suites. What right do I, a newcomer, have to a premium office space? I should earn it, right? If there's one available when we move to a bigger building, great. If not, no biggie."

As Maria talked, she pulled a hotplate out of a cabinet and plugged it in. She set a small copper pot on the hotplate, poured water in from a pitcher. She glanced at Igloo. "As long as I have out the ibrik, we'll do the whole thing the traditional way."

She measured coffee beans in the palm of her hand, then emptied them into a handmade clay bowl and pulverized them with a ceramic pestle.

Igloo watched with rapt attention. This was different.

"Can I convince you to take it with sugar?" Maria said. "It's the traditional way."

"Sure."

Maria carefully measured and added sugar to the water and stirred in the coffee grounds. She removed the spoon and turned the plate on. She didn't speak as she waited for the coffee to simmer. When it did, she removed it from the heat, waited a bit, then put it back on to boil again. She repeated the heating a third time, the coffee forming a thick foam on top.

After the final iteration, she turned the heat off, let the coffee sit for a minute before pouring it into two ceramic cups.

"That's quite a process," Igloo said, putting her hand on the cup.

"No wait, the coffee has to settle," Maria said. "This was one of the more useful things I learned stationed over there."

Igloo glanced up reflexively. The *military* of all things? It didn't get more hierarchical, or patriarchal, than that.

Maria caught the look and shook her head. "Don't worry. I'm not going to go all gung-ho on you. I did my time to pay for college, that's all. I'm done with all that now. How about you? Where'd you go to college?"

"MIT. And Stanford." She felt guilty over her privilege. "I got lucky with scholarships."

Maria gestured toward the coffee. "Try it now."

Igloo raised the cup, smelled it, and took a sip. The coffee coated her mouth like something alive, dark, and bitter.

"That's nice," Igloo said.

"Glad you like it," Maria said. "I understand we have you to thank for the AI personalities."

Igloo nodded, suddenly shy again. She hated talking about herself.

"I'm sure you know this better than anyone else, but our data shows kids who are engaging with the AI are 30 percent happier than they were a year ago. Forty percent less likely to have suicidal thoughts. Most are doing better in school, especially females."

All true. Igloo knew the precise numbers off the top of her head, but experience told her people didn't want exact numbers.

"Angie gets most of the notice here, but I think you're the real hero of this company. You ever think about doing more to raise your visibility? Giving talks?"

"It's not really my thing. Talking to people."

"Hence the AI."

Igloo nodded.

"Well, there's no pressure, but if it's ever an interest, you've got a good story to tell, and you deserve recognition for it. At any rate, I hear from Angie that you've moved on to a new project for her. I was surprised. You've been involved with the AI bots since the beginning, and I assumed you'd keep working on that. What made you decide to change?"

Angie had asked her to keep the project quiet, but it seemed like she'd told everyone else about it. Igloo sighed. She didn't want to talk about getting bored. Wasn't going to admit how distracting Essie was. Wasn't even sure she was ready to admit that fully to herself.

"Privacy is another passion of mine," Igloo said, picking something that was true. "Everyone should have basic expectations that what they say or do online is theirs and theirs alone."

Igloo briefly imaged what would happen if she wasn't careful to segregate her purchases with a different account, subtly different name. Rope, duct tape, and floggers would pop up in ads and as recommended purchases everywhere she went. She wouldn't be able to browse the web in front of anyone else without them wondering about her. Of course, she ran an ad-blocker, so maybe the point was moot.

"Tapestry has already done so much for privacy," Maria said. "Simply by allowing users to take ownership of their own data. We've cut down on third party access dramatically and put it all under the control of the users. Is there a point at which we say we've done enough for privacy?"

"We've done a lot in Tapestry itself," Igloo said, "but everything you do that's not on Tapestry is still vulnerable. Which websites you visit, all your communications with them if the connection isn't encrypted. If a person wants to..." Igloo's mind went right to her own fantasies. She wasn't going to admit any of those things. She went for something relatively innocuous. "If they wanted to dress up as a panda and have sex, then isn't it their right to keep that information be secret? With that information in the wrong hands, they could be blackmailed, lose their job, their kids."

Maria smiled. "One could make the argument that only secrets can get you blackmailed, and that if all the information is out there, then nobody has any leverage on you. Keeping secrets is the problem. But—"

Igloo set her cup down with a bang. "Privacy is not just about secrets. It's about respect for the individual. If I want to keep something private, then it's disrespectful and a violation of my desires to not do so. And it's not just about—"

"Hold on—" Maria tried to interrupt.

Igloo raised her voice. "It's not just about secrets. It's about putting limits on power. The more someone knows about us, the more power they have over us. If I have a secret desire for a Tesla, but can't really afford one, but Tesla uses knowledge of my interest to direct ever more persuasive advertising toward me, then they can manipulate me into buying a car, even though it's not really in my best interests to have one."

Maria held up both hands, but Igloo kept going.

"It's about maintaining reputation and appropriate boundaries. If I'm sexually assaulted, that's my own personal business to disclose or not. I don't want other people judging me or seeing me through a particular filter unless I choose to tell them. Privacy is freedom. When governments and businesses make decisions about me based on data they're sniffing about me without my awareness, I lose autonomy and control over my own life."

"Are you done?" Maria asked. "I was trying to say that I don't believe in the privacy-is-obsolete argument, but I could see how others would pitch it. It's good you're ready with counter-arguments."

"Oh." Igloo shrank down inside her hoodie.

"It's okay. Look, I really appreciate your passion on this topic, and now I see why Angie wants you working on this project." Maria glanced down at her phone and swiped a notification away.

"Thanks," Igloo said, her voice small once again.

Maria stared hard at her phone and started typing fast. She glanced up. "Anything you need in way of support, just let me know." She gestured with the phone. "I'm really sorry and don't mean to be rude, but I've got to deal with this."

Igloo stood up and made her way toward the door.

"Hey," Maria called. "Next time, you show me your favorite coffee."

Igloo nodded, but Maria had her head buried in her device. She walked back to her office, a slight bounce in her step. Contrary to her initial opinion, Maria wasn't so bad. Downright nice, almost.

CHAPTER 5

Igloo loaded the last of the rope in the toy bag. It had taken a few weeks of asking around in the community to find someone she actually had interest in. Charlotte, a friend of a friend, was looking for a rigger. They'd chatted online at first, then met for a drink to negotiate a scene, and now, almost before she knew it, their date was here.

She was excited about tonight, but also nervous about playing with someone new, and even a little panicky to be going out without Essie. Brimming with strange feelings, she desperately wanted to talk to Essie about everything. But it was too bizarre and scary to talk with Essie about *these* feelings. She felt too guilty to describe how excited she was, for starters.

A flash of red in the bag caught her eye. The leash she bought for Essie after they started dating, when she learned that Essie liked to be led around at public parties. She grabbed the leather lead and held onto it tightly. The leather was alive in her hand, filled with memories: the first time she clipped it onto Essie's collar, the first time she led Essie up the stairs at Deviance to one of the private rooms, the look in Essie's eyes as she stared into Igloo's eyes, so full of trust and love and fear and want. So full of memories.

She could never use the leash with anyone else. Essie was on the bed right behind her, and she didn't want to pull out the leash and draw more attention to it. She wasn't sure she could explain her feelings. She squished it further down into the bag. She'd keep it safe, just for Essie. She zipped up the bag and turned around.

"Well, that's—"

Essie sat on the bed, shaking, her face held in her hands.

"What's the matter?" Igloo climbed up next to her, and wrapped Essie in her arms. "What's going on?"

Essie shook her head but said nothing.

Igloo stroked her hair. "What's the matter?"

"I'm afraid you're going to have a good time with her, then leave me."

Igloo suppressed a nervous laugh. The idea was absurd. "It's just a play date. We're going to play. Nothing more. I love you. I don't want to leave you at all."

"What if she's more fun than me?"

Igloo felt sudden relief. She'd read an article about polyamory by a therapist who had the perfect answer for this worry. It felt good to know what to say for once. "I'm sure I will meet people who are different than you, maybe better at certain things, and worse at others. I'm not going to lie. It's inevitable, I will meet people who are smarter or funnier or sexier. Everyone does, sooner or later. But I will still choose to be with you because you are unique and not replaceable."

She went on hugging Essie, resisting the urge to look at the clock. She needed to go soon, but she didn't want to leave Essie in distress.

"Why aren't I enough for you?" Essie said.

"This isn't about you," Igloo said, trying to keep her voice even. Fudge, this had all been Essie's idea in the first place. "This is about us trying new things, exploring. Figuring out what works for us and not mindlessly taking on the structures dictated by society. Remember? We want to design the relationship that works for us, not just adopt the same template everyone else uses."

Essie nodded slightly but pulled Igloo closer. Igloo resisted the urge to pull away, and instead went on holding her tight.

Eventually Essie drew back. "You need to go, or you'll be late. I'll be okay." Her voice cracked.

"You'll be more than okay," Igloo said, her heart aching for Essie. Why was she so worried? If only she could feel what Igloo felt, if only she could understand that Igloo would never do anything to put their relationship at risk. "We went into this together. You want to date, remember? You'll find someone soon, and then it'll be my turn to be consoled."

"You seem to be totally fine," Essie said, turning to face Igloo, and reaching up to touch Igloo's cheek.

"Because I know I love you and I won't leave you, not for anyone else I meet, and certainly not for a random play date." That was true, to the depths of Igloo's soul. Now if only she could get out of here and get to her date.

Essie grabbed Igloo's hand. "Okay. I trust you."

Igloo leaned in and kissed her. "I will be worthy of that trust."

Igloo lay out the jute, one length after another, six of the eight-meter hanks first, then two shorter four-meter pieces. The jute she'd use for bodywork. She had hemp for her uplines, because she liked the safety margin of the stronger rope.

Unlike some of the other venues that had more mood lighting, the space was well-lit. Since tonight's party theme was rope, the floor was covered with foam pads, and the black and red bondage furniture that would normally have been spread throughout the main dungeon room was pushed up against the walls. There was room for at least eight scenes, maybe more if people really crammed in.

Throughout the room, other riggers prepared their own kits or were already starting in on ties. Around the perimeter, people gathered to watch. Some came to the party merely to spectate, but most were looking to play.

Essie had insisted on doing her nails earlier, and now her black metallic polish glittered as she handled the rope. Given the freakout right before she left, it was surprising Essie had been willing to help her get ready.

She couldn't think about that now. She was too nervous. She'd never tied anyone but Essie.

"Hey, Igloo."

Igloo looked up to see Charlotte standing next to her. From her photos, Igloo could tell she was attractive and lithe, with a dancer's body. There was a special joy in the anticipation of tying someone smaller than herself and getting to use her body to dominate the other person. Here in person, Charlotte was even cuter.

She swallowed hard. She was really going to do this.

Many people dropped their Fetlife handles in real life and went by first names, but Igloo had lived too much of her life online for that. She liked handles, liked that people could choose who and what they were, could tailor their identity the way they wanted. On the other hand, she couldn't very well go around calling someone BabySlut. So Charlotte it was.

The room was warm, kept that way intentionally since most of the bottoms would end up naked or nearly so. Igloo had left her usual hoodie at home and was wearing what she thought of as her rigger's uniform: a pair of black gi pants and a black racer-back tank.

Igloo stood. "Can I give you a hug?"

Charlotte nodded and they embraced.

Charlotte's skin was soft and smooth, and she smelled good. Really good. Maybe this would be fun after all.

"I'm a little nervous," Charlotte said.

Igloo held back a wry smile. Ironic that she was nervous, too. Well, as the Dominant here, she wasn't going to let on that she was nervous. It's not that it would scare the bottom, per se, but it wouldn't reinforce the Domme-in-charge balance that was so tricky to maintain. She'd have to fake it until she made it.

"There's nowhere I'd rather be than right here," Igloo said. "We're going to have a great scene."

"I've only been tied a few times," Charlotte said.

They'd discussed all this online during negotiations. When Igloo had told her rope teacher she was going to be playing with others, he'd suggested she use written negotiations to avoid ambiguity and misunderstanding. "Everyone's happier when they get what they expect," he'd said.

"Where's spontaneity? Surprise? How are you going to push boundaries if everything's carefully negotiated ahead of time?" Igloo loved when scenes pushed comfort zones, and top or bottom came out the other side having changed their preconceived notions of what was possible or even what they enjoyed.

"That's for when you know somebody well. Not when you're playing with them for the first time."

So she'd negotiated both online and in-person with Charlotte, assessed what she was looking for, what experiences she'd had, and what her limits were.

Charlotte looked around at the other tying pairs, saw people already naked or in underwear. "Should I get undressed?"

"Let's talk a little more first," Igloo said, gesturing to the floor.

Charlotte kneeled, and Igloo sat cross legged.

Of course, Igloo was familiar with the concept of negotiation for scenes, and naturally, she and Essie had agreed on what they'd do together during their scenes. But that had taken place in private, evolving organically over months of dating. Negotiating with a stranger was different...and now she felt like she'd forgotten half of everything they'd already discussed. Or maybe she was just really nervous and wanted to postpone the start of play. Well, there was no harm in reviewing things once more.

"We negotiated, and you've been tied before," Igloo said, "but for safety's sake, can you tell me what the risks are with rope bondage?"

"Nerve impingement," Charlotte said, wiggling her fingers. "If I get tingling, numbness, or other symptoms asymmetrically across my hand, it's most likely a nerve being pressed on by rope. I'd let you know right away, as I would if I had any other issues, like a difficult time breathing. But fundamentally rope is edge play. Shit happens."

Charlotte knew her stuff. That was reassuring. "Safewords?"

"Red for full stop, Yellow for slowdown and check in with me." Charlotte paused. "And 'Oh, fuck!' is not a safeword."

They both smiled at that.

"If you cry or scream 'no', do you want me to treat it as a yellow, or ignore it?"

"If I want to stop, I'll use a safeword. Otherwise keep going."

"Fine. And impact play is okay while you're tied up?"

Charlotte nodded eagerly.

Igloo paused. She'd been immersed in the kink scene for long enough that now she wondered how vanilla people agreed on what they would do together. What percent of consent problems arose simply because people weren't comfortable being clinically explicit? She tried to think back to her vanilla days. Had she ever been explicit about what she wanted? Had she even *known* what she wanted? Sometimes it felt like all she and Essie did was talk about their relationship, their needs, growth opportunities. Wait. She needed to stop thinking about Essie. Charlotte was here now and needed her focus.

"In messages we exchanged, you said no bruising where it could be seen, no breath play, face slapping, or gags. Am I forgetting anything?"

Charlotte shook her head.

Igloo found herself wondering what could she do with Tapestry to help create consent culture for vanillas. Imagine if everyone could be so up front and honest about what they wanted. Ugh. *Focus, Igs.* She had a hot girl in front of her, and she was thinking about work.

"Last question. How sexual or not do you want to play? At one end of the spectrum, I tie you like a package, and up you go into the air. Somewhere in the middle, I paint the rope onto you, while holding you close against me, caressing you, fondling you." Igloo would rather the scene be sexy, but if Charlotte wasn't ready for that, she could still have fun practicing her rope skills.

Charlotte had a shy but provocative smile on her face. "And the other end of the spectrum?"

Igloo swallowed. "Let's say we're not going to go there on a first date. We can work that out another time."

Charlotte laughed. "Fine. You can touch me as sensually as you want, but no genital contact. You know, *for our first date.*"

"Sounds like fun." Igloo smiled and gestured toward her rope. "Let's play."

Charlotte nodded. She unzipped her boots and took them off, then shrugged out of her skirt and shirt, folding and laying them off to the side. She took her bra off but kept her panties on. She did a gentle warmup, stretching up and over to either side, then folding at waist, and finishing with some twists.

Igloo watched, admiring Charlotte's flexibility. That must have taken so much work to develop. While she stretched, Igloo stood and rechecked her rope, cutter, and rap rings.

She ignored the people gathering around. No one would violate their scene space while they were playing, unless a dungeon monitor had a specific safety concern, but they'd watch from nearby. There were other people tying too, but Igloo had attracted the most onlookers.

The kink community welcomed a wide diversity of people, but there was always a large contingent of straight white dudes who eroticized lesbian women. She'd learned to tune them out. Most meant no harm, and the community norms welcomed watching other people play. Which, of course, was how everyone learned.

Igloo stood barefoot, emptied her mind, and felt the qi flow up into her legs, fill her hips, and finally her torso. When the qi spilled down her arms, she lifted the first hank. She let the qi pour into the rope. Holding the bight in one hand, she tossed the rest of the rope off to the side. The bundle unraveled as it skidded across the floor, until she had a long, perfect trail of untangled rope.

Igloo moved up close, wrapped a leg around Charlotte, and put her arms around Charlotte's shoulders. The skin on skin contact was wonderful. What would Essie think if she saw this? *Be here now, Igs,* she told herself.

Charlotte leaned into the contact and closed her eyes.

Igloo breathed in Charlotte's scent, a combination of shampoo and essential oils. It was nice. She'd happily stand here smelling her for the next hour, but that would be pretty awkward.

Still hugging her, Igloo squared up Charlotte's arms behind her back, then stepped back. She tied the wrists, then, with her left hand, she wrapped rope around the woman's shoulder, and drew it across Charlotte's torso, trailing her fingers softly across that oh-so-fair skin. She felt a slight tremor of need in response, and a warmth spread in her pants.

She liked the feeling of arousal, but knew it was a momentary thing. The funny thing was, topping was mostly asexual, aside from some random moments of horniness. She'd asked around, and she wasn't the only top who felt that way. Most enjoyed the feeling of power, the control, the creative expression, the pleasure of connection, the joy of sadism. There'd be a few things here or there that felt overtly sexual. So oddly different as compared to bottoming, when nearly everything felt erotic. She pushed the thoughts away and concentrated on her rope.

Her movements flowed, a martial art in slow motion. With a long-practiced form, Igloo pulled the rope around itself and reversed its direction for a second wrap around the upper arms. She wasn't just tying. Anyone could do that. She was dancing with the rope, flowing movements to keep the tension alive, ensuring Charlotte always felt Igloo's control. Of course, the ropes needed to be aligned correctly with the right frictions and tension to keep them stable. But that alone was not enough to create erotic energy. Every movement heightened the experience: the graze of an erogenous zone, a thumb trailing the neck, the arms, the breasts.

The difference between merely tying a person versus tying them with intention, connection, and flow was like the difference between functional code and beautiful code. Both could do the job, but only one could stir the heart.

As she tied, she sensed the state of Charlotte's body, her breathing, and the tension she held. Charlotte relaxed into the rope, becoming looser, more comforted as the rope hugged her. A stray lock of hair had fallen forward. With her hands tied, she couldn't reach it. Igloo tucked the hair back behind Charlotte's ear.

"Thank you," Charlotte murmured, with her eyes closed.

Igloo continued with a hip harness, then a futomomo. Igloo fell out of the zone for a moment, suddenly self-conscious about what she was doing. Was Charlotte enjoying herself or bored? Was she wondering why she had even picked Igloo to play with?

Fortunately, training kept her going, and soon she lifted Charlotte into the air on a pair of uplines, and her worries fell away. The flow returned, her focus only on her partner and the rope. Somewhere in the distance, she was aware of spectators, others playing around them, but they were inconsequential.

Charlotte lay horizontally a couple of feet in the air in a side suspension, one of the most endurable positions for the bottom. She was suspended from the rope harness around her upper torso and arms, a hip harness, and a leg wrap, dividing her weight across three points. Igloo added a rope from Charlotte's free ankle, up to the suspension ring.

Charlotte's expression was the blissful, eyes-closed face of someone zoning out in the rope, as it should be.

Igloo pulled out her riding crop, the special one with the carbon fiber rod that bore as much similarity to a tool used for horseback riding as a Formula 1 race car did to a minivan. She struck Charlotte's ass, her thighs, eliciting sharp grunts in response. Igloo warmed up with a rapid staccato of soft strikes. Somewhere in the back of her mind, she was thinking about rising endorphin levels, building up a tolerance to pain, but mostly she was operating instinctively.

She grabbed a handful of Charlotte's hair, pulled her head back, exposing her neck. Charlotte let out a little gasp in response. She was extraordinarily beautiful then, so vulnerable and trusting.

Igloo stepped back, gave her a spin and let go. She struck with the crop over and over as Charlotte spun in front of her: tits, fronts of thighs, bottoms of feet, back of thighs, ass, shoulders, varying the strength of each blow automatically according to the body part in front of her. Now her monkey mind was quiet, Igloo's focus laser-sharp on everything happening in front of her.

Charlotte thrashed, grunts turning to screams, twisting and turning in the ropes, trying but failing to avoid Igloo's blows. She screamed so pretty, and every time she did, Igloo felt a twitch in her groin. In between screams, Charlotte laughed with a big smile, a masochist in her happy place, still twisting and trying to fold over herself to protect herself.

Adrenaline thudded in Igloo's body, warred with her self-control. Always, always the top was in control, in control of her bottom, in control of herself, but still, her breath came fast and she rode the edge between passion and restraint. She had a terrible curiosity about what would happen if she lost control, if she struck out as much, and as hard, as she wanted, but she kept herself carefully modulated.

She struck harder, but slower, each slap of the crop accompanied by a scream. Red welts rose from the site of each strike. Charlotte kept spinning, her momentum sustained now by carefully timed blows.

Igloo dropped the crop and picked up a rattan cane. She let her fingers trail over the crop's welts, slowed Charlotte's spin. She came up behind Charlotte and caressed her throat with one hand. Charlotte was breathing heavy, catching up. They were close to some ephemeral high now.

Igloo palmed Charlotte's face, pinning her head against Igloo's thigh. With her other hand, she struck hard blows with the cane on

Charlotte's ass, the flexible rattan building up speed with each blow, accelerating until it hit the flesh with a crack, leaving parallel welts on either side of where the cane struck. Charlotte screamed into Igloo's hand with each strike, Igloo's only response to increase the pressure on her head to gently smother the screams against her thigh.

On the tenth stroke, Igloo dropped the cane, and crouched down to cradle Charlotte's head and shoulders. Charlotte heaved and thrashed, her eyes rolling back in her head. Igloo waited until Charlotte calmed, a good minute or so.

"You okay?"

She smiled weakly. "Yes."

"You ready to come down?"

She nodded. "Please."

Igloo lowered Charlotte, line by line, until she was resting on the floor. Then she undid the uplines, and cradled Charlotte in her arms, holding her tight while her breath slowed. Now and then Charlotte would twitch, the way Igloo did after a good orgasm, and Igloo found herself turned on again. She was sopping wet now, and for a brief moment, she imagined carrying Charlotte into her own bed at home, wondered what it would be like to fuck this woman while she was tied up.

Igloo shook her head to dispel the fantasy. Just keep it to the rope. Don't freak out the people who were just here for the ride.

When Charlotte had finally returned to some semblance of normal breathing, she swallowed and said, "Thank you."

"Of course," Igloo said, and she began the long, slow process of untying, making it just as sensual as the putting on of rope had been in the first place.

She found it ever so strange to be thanked for beating someone, even though she'd said the same thing when she bottomed, even though her very first exposure to BDSM came from someone who thanked her every time she gave him what he wanted.

He was a short-term fling from the music world, someone she dated mostly to escape the pressure of her high intensity work at

Tapestry. One night, sprawled in bed, still sweaty from fucking, he asked to be tied up and forced to beg for sex.

She wasn't a prude, far from it, but the notion of a power imbalance in a relationship, in either direction, had caused total repugnance. She said as much to him.

"You're not taking power away from me," he said, lying next to her while she lay curled up, angry. "I'm giving it to you."

"It's abusive," she said in a forceful but tiny voice. Once, haunted by her past, she would have shrunk physically into a ball and been speechless, but she'd worked so long with Angie that she'd learned to channel that into anger, focus it outward. She was the avenger now, no longer the victim.

"Consensual kink has as much in common with abuse as practicing judo has with a street mugging," had been his reply. "Judo and a mugging might look the same on the outside, they might even have the same moves, but one involves two educated, risk-aware, individuals working together to achieve a common goal, and the other is a non-consensual attack on an unprepared bystander."

She had had her doubts, and it must have been obvious from her reaction.

"There's a saying in the kink world that what disgusts us is what we're really interested in. Someday you'll look back and see that this is what you really want."

"Never," she said.

There must have been something on her face, recalling that old conversation, because now Charlotte was checking in with *her.* "You okay?"

Igloo gave her a big smile. "Yeah, totally fine."

She removed the final rope from Charlotte, and then gave her one last cuddle. "You good?"

Charlotte nodded. "That was great. I like your style with the rope. It feels like you're making art with me."

Igloo shrugged. "It's just rope."

"It comes alive when you do it." Charlotte sat up and began dressing. "I'm going to Deviance next week. Will you be there?"

"Umm," Igloo said, suddenly flustered and at a loss for words. She wanted to play with Charlotte again, but she was going to Deviance with Essie. "I'm going with my partner, Essie."

Charlotte leaned in close, brushed a breast against Igloo's arm. "Think we could fit in a scene together?"

Igloo stared into Charlotte's eyes, the intimacy of such direct eye contact easier after what they'd shared. Deviance took place in a sex club, which meant that if they did a public scene, they could always move into one of the private rooms afterwards and get as intimate as they wanted. But she'd be there with Essie, and Essie would expect to spend the night with Igloo. How would she manage both?

"Yeah," Igloo found herself saying. "That would be fun."

She suspected she was supposed to confirm that with Essie first. Essie would understand, right?

CHAPTER 6

R obin had two hours before her next appointment. It was time for a check-in, especially since home office was antsy about her last report.

She went into the back restroom, with its lockers and showers, and changed into her running clothes. She tied her athletic shoes, clipped her badge to her belt, and headed out the rear door.

She ran, a fast pace, one that couldn't possibly be sustained, a loop back and forth in Southeast Portland. She glanced north toward Tapestry headquarters, then refocused on the road in front of her. Running on a quiet bike throughway street, she veered toward the main avenue. She slowed, then entered a coffee shop, waited a minute, stretching her calves gently in place as she watched out the front window, and then walked toward the restrooms at the back of the shop. She left through the rear door, propped open to the alley behind the shop, and took the heavily treed alley the last two blocks.

A wooden staircase on the back of an old residence turned commercial building led to a second floor apartment. Opaque corrugated sheeting on the top and sides nominally covered the stairs from the elements, although closer inspection would reveal the supporting frame to be of newer wood than the stairs. The real purpose of the panels was to shield her from view.

At the top of the stairs, the door opened as she arrived. Inside, Cooper handed her a towel and a bottle of water. "They're expecting you in ten."

Robin sipped the water, then set it down to blot her face dry as she regained her breath. "Thanks."

"How are you doing?"

Cooper wouldn't mean operationally, since she was submitting daily reports.

"Busy. It's a lot of hours." She wouldn't talk about the attachments she was forming on the job. She and Cooper would talk about that later, after the upper level briefing. She'd want to hold it together now. Not surface the inevitable emotional entanglements that formed.

"Let me freshen up."

She used the head, washed her face, and tightened her ponytail to provide some discipline to her hair. She was out in ninety seconds. Old habits die hard. A sea shower would have only added a minute, but there was no point since she only had her sweaty running clothes to wear.

Robin entered the apartment's second bedroom and sat in front of a long desk. Gone were the days of banks of specialized communication gear. Now everything was handled by what appeared to be off-the-shelf computers: a few laptops and attached monitors. The zapper, a heavy steel box in the corner, could accept the laptops and everything else electronic, and crush and shock them into oblivion in under twenty seconds. The dull burgundy drapes spanning every wall and gathered into a bunch around the ceiling fixture gave the room an ominous hue. Whoever decided on burgundy for the Faraday curtains was an idiot.

Cooper took a seat next to her in front of the webcam. "Ready?"

She took another sip of water and nodded.

He leaned forward and clicked to establish the connection, then left the room. Her case manager, though intimately familiar with her work, wasn't cleared to know whom she was talking to. The webcam light turned on, but the screen stayed dark. On the far end, someone would be comparing visual identities against the video stream, ensuring she was the one they expected. For all she knew, they could be remotely scanning the entire room, building, or block.

The dark screen transformed in a flash to a live feed of three separate offices.

Enso, the ostensible head of the Bureau of Research and Intelligence, or BRI, appeared in the middle, flanked by the Deputy Director of the NSA and the Signals Intelligence Director. The latter, SigInt Director Feldson, was known as Griz to most of his peers.

Robin took a slow breath. Rarely did anyone explicitly discuss BRI, but the three of them appearing onscreen was as close as it ever got to a tacit admission of BRI's existence and placement within the greater intelligence community.

"Robin, thank you for joining us. I hope you are well." Enso, as ever, polite when it wasn't necessary. He only did this with women who reported to him. With men, it was brisk, clinical detachment. "Your last report struck serious concerns here around Tapestry's encryption plans, yet it was vague on specifics."

"I believe they are on a path toward end-to-end client-side encryption," Robin said. "I haven't seen a specific roadmap that shows this, but there's been a push to move encryption into the clients and browsers."

"To skirt FISA compliance?" The deputy director looked toward the SIGINT director, who nodded.

"Tapestry is composed of hundreds of service providers communicating over a common protocol," SIGINT said. "Dozens of providers touch the data. We can hit everyone with a FISA court order."

Robin shook her head. "Griz, there's a team working on client-side containers." She hesitated, realizing she had no idea if he'd object to the use of his nickname. She'd never used it to his face before. But everyone at the far end of the teleconference waited for her to go on, with no sign of a faux pas.

"Web services are commonly deployed using container technology," Robin said. "Containers are lightweight virtual computers that mitigate the complexity of managing the server by isolating code, libraries, and configuration to the container, which can then be deployed to different hardware."

Her stint as an operations manager for Naval Network Warfare Command gave her a comfortable familiarity with technology. She sensed she was at the comprehension limit for these bureaucrats. She had to simplify the explanation.

"Client-side containers are a way to run virtual computers within the user's browser. Let's say you want to buy a book. In the old days, you'd go to the bookstore. If we want to know what you bought, we'd watch you shop in person. These days, you order books online and download the book. When we want to know what you bought, we either monitor the data transmission or we order the retailer to provide us the details of the purchase. Follow me so far?"

Nods.

"A client-side container is like a bookstore truck that drives into your garage, filled with all the books you could want. When the garage door is closed the truck will open up. You go into the truck, which is inside your garage, and do your book shopping. At the end of your purchase, a record of a payment is transmitted, but from the outside, we have no way of knowing what you purchased. We can't even order the bookstore to tell us, because they don't know either. The software code that ensures the end-user paid for the book all runs within the truck, which is inside the garage. Nobody outside of the garage knows exactly what was purchased."

The men exchanged nervous glances.

Griz shook his head. "The theory is known, of course, but we didn't anticipate that anyone would operationalize it, certainly not this soon. How long until they deploy?"

"The proof of concept is not finished, but development is on track. My estimate is anywhere from a few months to a year before it is ready for production."

The deputy director cleared his throat. "They're doing this specifically to skirt FISA?"

Robin shook her head. "They have perfectly valid and above board explanations to move logic to the client. It reduces server load, decreases latency, and increases fault tolerance. It avoids centralized dependencies, which is part of Angie's core mission." She shrugged carefully, intending to convey her uncertainty about Angie's motivations, not her ambivalence around the mission. Better not to let them know that sometimes she thought Angie was more patriotic than the government. "Whether they are explicit about it or not, this change will neutralize our ability to gather intelligence."

"In your opinion?"

"Angie's smart. She knows exactly what she's doing."

The NSA deputy director reviewed notes in front of him. "Let's pull up the FISA court order. There's no point in waiting."

The deputy director and SIGINT signed off, and then it was just Robin and Enso.

"Once the court order is in effect," Enso said, "Tapestry will be under intense official scrutiny. Until then, we have more latitude. You need to step up your game."

Robin suppressed her initial response. Everything about Tapestry seemed to be personal with Enso. He was rushing decisions because he wanted to crush Angie. The case files had the history of what had happened the first time around. But calling him out would get her nowhere.

"What do you want me to do?" she asked.

"What we always do. Establish leverage. Push harder on Angie. Find something we can use against her."

"She's squeaky clean in the office, and you know that. Everything at Tapestry is above board."

Enso sighed. "Figure out other angles to keep them off balance. Dig deeper with Igloo. She's been there since the start, and she's almost certainly got to be connected to Angie's hacking."

Robin shook her head. "We've never seen a single sign of that. If anything, they've grown apart. Igloo's never got a promotion, she's never with Angie. She has carte blanche on the chatbots, but that's about all she has in terms of power. I think you're barking up the wrong tree. She's been asked to work on onion routing, but Angie's got a bunch of people around the company working on these special projects."

Enso ground his teeth as he usually did when he was frustrated. "Look into who else Angie has working on special projects and keep building relationships. I've got a team of analysts working on employees we can potentially exploit. Worst case scenario, we'll compromise Angie's husband."

Enso disconnected, and Robin stared at the blank screen.

How many people, officially and unofficially, were assigned to Tapestry now? It was mind-boggling that so much effort could be placed into toppling one company.

She'd done some questionable things at BRI. That was the nature of a dark agency, to do that which couldn't be done through official methods. But always it was in the pursuit of a legitimate purpose. Uncovering terrorists. Discovering foreign powers who had woven their tendrils into American companies. Neutralizing dangerous technology.

In Tapestry's case, the threat was a lot more abstract. Encryption. Privacy. Data ownership. Yeah, she'd willingly admit that robust privacy made digital surveillance much more difficult. In particular, trawling the mass of data for criminal activity became vastly more difficult.

But there was nothing in the Constitution guaranteeing the government an easy job. If anything, the bulk of law, multiple amendments and statutory law combined, provided for the privacy of individuals.

She'd do her job well, to the best of her ability. That's what she was trained to do, and what she felt was ethically right. But she'd be glad when this assignment was over.

Time to get back to work.

CHAPTER 7

"It's not worth it," Essie said, from inside the closet. "I should cancel." A skirt flew onto the floor amid the ongoing shuffling of hangers.

Igloo leaned against the closet door, watching as Essie attacked the clothing. Essie better not cancel. Igloo had her second date with Charlotte tonight. Ugh. She felt selfish thinking that.

"You had one bad date on Tuesday."

"She smelled like old socks."

"Okay, well tonight is someone different."

"They'll be just as bad."

Igloo glanced at the growing piles of clothing on the floor. Essie's expectations were usually for the worst. At the same time, she was still looking for clothes, so she *was* planning on going. Igloo tried to relax. As long as Essie went out, Igloo would be able to see Charlotte tonight.

They'd fought when Igloo asked to go to Deviance with Charlotte. Essie had been upset that Igloo had already made plans with Charlotte before even telling Essie. Apparently, Igloo was supposed to check with Essie before even talking to anyone else about playing. It didn't seem very efficient, and it sure as hell didn't conform to the

D/s dynamic they'd been operating under. Still, Essie had acqui-
esced, and found herself another date for tonight.

Essie pulled out a black lace dress. "Ah, I knew it was here."

She brought the dress out into the room and went back to putting
on makeup.

Igloo perched on the bed to watch. She'd had a passing interest in
makeup as a teen, but rarely used more than the basics. Still, she
enjoyed Essie's elaborate preparations.

Essie heated eyeliner with a lighter. "Did I mention that they
were a he?"

"What?" Igloo almost fell off the bed.

"Yeah, his name's Michael."

"You're going out with a man?" Her gut clenched. "Like a
trans-man, or..."

"A cis male." Essie leaned into the mirror as she applied eyeliner.
It seemed like she was deliberately avoiding Igloo's gaze.

Igloo felt sick. She hadn't even realized Essie liked men.

Essie looked at Igloo in the mirror. "It's no biggie. I've dated guys
before, you've dated guys before."

Igloo took long, slow breaths, trying to calm her lizard brain. Essie
had no fear of men, not like Igloo did. "It's just...you never
mentioned..."

"Female, male, it's not a big deal. He's an artist, and I've always
dug artists."

"What kind of art?" Igloo's voice sounded small, even to her.

"Mostly metal sculpture, I think. He sent me a few photos of his
pieces. Here, look."

Essie held out her phone and swiped through photos of large
metal structures on lawns.

Some remote portion of Igloo's mind admired that each sculpture
illustrated a scientific principle, but the nuances were lost in a sea of
unease that constricted her chest and throat.

"You haven't even met, and you're swapping photos?"

"His photo feed is public. I'm checking him out ahead of time."

"That's good, I guess." Igloo heart still thumped. A fucking guy? "He's kinky?"

"Yeah."

"What sort of kinks is he into?" Igloo found herself holding her breath.

"I don't know. I suppose we'll talk about it during the date."

Her phone buzzed. Holy shit, 7P.M. She was meeting Charlotte in an hour. She'd been looking forward to this all week, but now all she felt was a jealous rage at Essie's date. Why was poly so damn hard? Was it too much to ask to be able to enjoy a few moments without struggling?

Essie had taken her car, leaving Igloo without one. She wasn't going to ride her bike in pleather pants with a twenty-pound toy bag. She called a rideshare, giving the automated vehicle the address of a dance hall a few blocks from Club Privata to avoid a digital trail. One of these days she'd finally give in and buy a car.

After the car dropped her off, she walked over to the club. She paid, entered, and looked around for Charlotte. She waved to a rigger she knew and headed upstairs. From the balcony, she looked down at the scenes on the first floor. A man wielded floggers Florentine-style on a woman tied to a St. Andrew's cross.

Next to them, a male submissive was restrained on the second cross, limbs spread-eagle. A female top wielding a whip lashed his back with a side-to-side swing. Interesting. She didn't often see whip play, let alone by a female top, but then most places didn't have the space for it.

With a flash, she realized the woman was Charlotte. Holy shit! She had no idea Charlotte was a switch.

She rushed back downstairs and waited near the play area.

Charlotte eventually finished her scene, unclipped her partner from the cross, and spent a few minutes with him until he finished dressing. She wrapped the whip twice around her waist and secured it with a bit of leather thong. She clipped her wrist restraints to her skirt. Igloo admired the spartan but functional kit.

When Charlotte left the play area, she saw Igloo and smiled. "Hug?"

Igloo nodded. "Sure."

The warm hug lasted longer than necessary, but Igloo didn't mind at all. Charlotte smelled good again, some essential oil. Igloo couldn't help burying her face in Charlotte's hair. She didn't want the hug to end.

"I didn't know you switched." Igloo shouted over the music. "I've only ever seen you bottom."

"We've only seen each other at rope events." Charlotte pointed to the whip wrapped around her. "Want to bottom for me?"

Igloo would love to, but if she was submissive at all, she'd have a difficult time getting back into a dominant mindset. "Tempting, but maybe later. Let's get a hardpoint before they're all taken."

They went upstairs and took a hardpoint above a big bed surrounded by spectators. Igloo was hyper-conscious that last month she'd been in this exact spot with Essie. It felt like a betrayal to be here with Charlotte. The usual crowd of semi-familiar faces was here, and Igloo wondered if they noticed she was with someone different. The guilt formed a pit in her stomach. No, Igloo wasn't going to think about that. She was here to enjoy herself.

She pulled out her rope and toys and told Charlotte to get undressed. When Charlotte was naked, they went through negotiations again, faster than last time. Then she arrived at the sex question.

"How sexual do you want things to be?" The last time she'd asked, she was the one who ruled out sex on a first encounter. Now she hoped Charlotte would say yes.

Charlotte glanced meaningfully at her whip and restraints before looking Igloo in the eye. "I don't go all the way until I've had a chance on top. So be as sensual as you want, but no sex until you've bottomed for me."

Igloo felt herself grow horny. A battle for dominance between two switches. Her pulse thudded, and her hands were nervous on the rope. She couldn't let herself get subby while she was topping.

Time for a change of pace. She grabbed Charlotte's hair and pulled her head back. She trailed her teeth along the side of Charlotte's neck.

"You'll get your turn. But now it's mine."

She tied Charlotte's hands, roughly with the rope, full of desire. She grabbed another hank and wove a Leto harness on Charlotte's hips, brushing her fingers along the sensitive skin of her inner thigh. She did two quick chaos ties to contain her legs, then attached the upline to the hip harness and heaved. Charlotte rose into an inversion.

The position accentuated the arcs on either side of her abdomen, and Igloo couldn't help admiring Charlotte's curves.

"How's that, my pretty?" Igloo said, her voice pitched low, smooth. She caressed Charlotte, letting her fingers slide lightly along the inside of her thighs, the outside of her torso.

Charlotte's eyes were closed, on the heavy side, lips pursed with concentration. Igloo pressed her fingertip into one nipple to the pressure point behind, and Charlotte wiggled away like a fish dangling from a hook.

"Still moving huh? You're not tied enough then."

She hunted for a short line and attached Charlotte's bound wrists to the ring, arching her into a backbend. She wrapped another rope twice around Charlotte's mouth, forming a rope gag, then pulled that, very gently, toward the ring and tied it off.

She leaned down and looked into Charlotte's eyes. Immobile, gagged, her eyes were glazed, clearly preoccupied with processing inputs, continuing to breathe. In such a situation, there was no higher order brain function.

Igloo opted to let Charlotte cook, changing little, staring into her eyes, rubbing hands over her body, maintaining contact between their skin. After a while, she asked "You want to come down soon?"

Charlotte grunted acquiescence. If she wanted to stay up longer, she'd have more brain power, and she'd be able to ask for it.

But first, a little something to finish her off. Igloo grabbed clover clamps. Intense to start, clover clamps grew even more painful each passing second. Charlotte's eyes opened wide at the sight of them, and she managed a "no."

Igloo made a judgment call. They'd discussed safe words, agreed nipple clamps were okay. "No" was just a reaction. If Charlotte really didn't want to do it, she'd use her safe word.

She put the first clamp on, and Charlotte grunted from someplace far away. Igloo added the second clamp, then swung Charlotte back and forth, pulling from the short chain connecting the nipple clamps. Grunts turned to shrieks.

Charlotte thrashed to the best of her ability, which was not much at all. The sadist in Igloo laughed at this. She slowed Charlotte down, again using only the clamps. Then she removed the clamps, which, perhaps counter-intuitively, was even more painful as the blood rushed back to the sensitive, abused tissue. Charlotte screamed around the rope gag.

Now it was time for her to come down.

Igloo untied the gag and wrists, and lowered the hip harness, guiding Charlotte with one hand so that she'd come down on her belly. She kept letting out the line, feeding it through the ring, until Charlotte's knees touched down. Ass up, Charlotte looked good. At home, this would be a nice place to pause for a sex break. Here, she kept removing rope until Charlotte melted into a puddle. Her breathing eased, slowed, until she was at total peace.

Igloo stroked her hair, her cheek, and cuddled her.

"Thank you," Charlotte whispered, never opening her eyes. After a long pause, she added, "Your turn soon."

"Rest first," Igloo said, petting Charlotte's back and neck. "If you're okay, I'm going to pack up my rope."

Charlotte nodded, and Igloo began bundling her rope. Halfway through, Charlotte sat up, still spacey, and tried to help.

Igloo shook her head. "You get dressed. I'll take care of this."

The last hank of rope went into her bag, and Igloo took down her rigging hardware and shoved that in. She took Charlotte's hand, and they made their way downstairs.

"Nice scene, good rope work," said an older, silver-haired man to Igloo.

"Thanks," Igloo said, a slight swagger coming into her step despite her best effort to stay cool.

"Who was that?" Charlotte asked.

"My teacher," Igloo said. "One of the best rope artists around."

"Well, let's see if you preen like that after you taste my whip." Charlotte led her toward the St. Andrew's Cross.

Igloo nodded, amused by this sudden change in Charlotte. Every switch found some way to express the dichotomy of being top and bottom in one. It was surprising to see how quickly Charlotte changed, especially considering that she was a puddle on the floor just ten minutes ago.

They watched as another couple played on the cross. A man in a three-piece had taken off his jacket and was rotating through impact toys. His partner, a blonde in high heels, faced the cross, as he picked up a large wooden paddle.

"That's gonna..." Charlotte started.

The suit guy took three quick strides toward the cross, and in a single motion, smacked the woman's ass.

She let out a scream that drew attention across the club.

"...hurt," Charlotte finished.

"Suit and BadGirlNextDoor," Igloo said. "You know them?"

Charlotte shook her head.

"He always finishes with the paddle, so they're almost done."

Soon after, Suit and BadGirl cleared off, and Igloo and Essie approached the cross. Butterflies grew in Igloo's stomach. She'd never bottomed in public, bottoming required more vulnerability, and she'd never bottomed to anyone besides Essie.

"If you were wearing regular fabric," Charlotte said, "I'd offer to whip you with clothes on. But between the pleather pants and the mesh shirt, you're going to have to get naked."

Igloo glanced around at the people around the play area, which was a mistake. It would be a lie to say that nobody was watching or cared, because there were, in fact, oh so many people focused on her and Charlotte.

Still, the panic that came over her in a vanilla setting was at arm's length here. Nobody was *judging* here, just watching. And she liked the way Charlotte stared at her with hunger in her expression.

She faced Charlotte head-on and inched the mesh shirt up. She folded it and placed it in Charlotte's outstretched hand. She shucked her boots, removed her pants, and handed those over too. In underwear and bra, she felt chilly. She shivered, but she couldn't say if that was from cold or nerves. She'd never been whipped and didn't know what to expect.

"Of course, you can do what you like, but...I'm afraid the straps of your bra might catch the tip of the whip," Charlotte said with a slight smirk, her hand still out.

"I'm sure," Igloo said. So that's the way she was playing this. She handed over her bra. "And my underwear? Will that catch the whip?"

Charlotte assessed it critically. "I think it'll be okay. Unless you want to take it off. You seem to like stripping. I bet you're wet right now."

Igloo felt herself blush hard and grow wetter if that were even possible. She was thankful for the red lighting. "I'll keep them on."

"For now," Charlotte said.

Igloo was all too aware of being essentially naked while Charlotte stood fully dressed in front of her. Charlotte buckled leather restraints to her wrists, then guided Igloo's right wrist to the left branch of the X, puzzling Igloo. Then she grabbed Igloo's other wrist.

"No..." Igloo said, realizing what was happening.

"It's way more fun facing out," Charlotte said. "Then you can see what's going to happen. And remember, 'no' is not a safe word."

"It's going to hurt." Everything hurt more on the front. Fronts of thighs, stomach, breasts, it was all way more sensitive.

"That's kind of the point," Charlotte said, smiling. She pulled a pair of black goggles from her pocket and put them on Igloo's face. "To protect your eyes. Can you see okay?"

Igloo nodded.

"I have to warm up a bit. Don't go anywhere." Charlotte stepped back, unwrapped the whip from her waist, and began a back and forth pattern. She switched from hand to hand, cracking the whip once with each side.

Charlotte was a different woman now, not the submissive who yielded to her rope, but a magical, playful, powerful person. It made Igloo horny.

It was a relief too, to be finally free of responsibility. For a little while, she didn't have to be in charge, wasn't accountable for herself or anyone else. Charlotte was the boss now, and Igloo could surrender and just do what she was told. It made everything so simple, so free of complexity and the fear of judgement. Charlotte would do what she liked, and Igloo's only job was to receive.

Charlotte took a step closer, and the whip brushed Igloo's thighs, with each back and forth stroke. The sensation was unlike any Igloo had experienced, slightly painful, but each caress like something alive. Her skin grew warm and tingly and she tried to arch into each stroke.

Charlotte moved in a dance, her feet shuffling left and right, her other hand held out, catching the whip momentarily between strokes, her eyes laser-focused on Igloo. Her gaze shifted up, and Igloo felt the whip lick her abdomen, the lashes painful across her belly.

There was pain, but also there was trust. Trust that Charlotte would take care of her, that no matter how bad the pain was, ultimately Charlotte wouldn't damage her. Trust was hard to come by in Igloo's world, what with her long history of broken boundaries and promises dating back to childhood. To place her confidence and safekeeping in another person was as exhilarating as summiting the steepest rise on a rollercoaster.

The smile never left Charlotte's face as the whip traced its way up. Igloo tried to draw away, but, with the cross at her back, there was nowhere to go. The lashes struck the sensitive underside of her tits. She stood on tiptoes to postpone the inevitable, but each stroke brushed ever closer to her nipples.

She felt on the verge of panic, when the whip lashed one nipple on the backstroke, then the other. It hurt, but only ever so slightly, and she realized with relief that Charlotte had pulled back so that only the feathery tip lightly brushed her. She let loose a breath she hadn't realized she held, then there was a snap, and fire broke out on her thigh, then the other.

Charlotte was cracking the whip now, and where each stroke had been an almost gentle caress before, now they burned, each strike fiercely painful. She was screaming before she realized it, and then it was over. Charlotte came up and hugged her. Igloo nuzzled her face into the crook of Charlotte's neck, trying to catch her breath. She felt a tear form in the corner of her eye, and held back, not wanting to cry in front of everyone.

Charlotte stroked the back of her head, and goosebumps rose on Igloo's body.

"Are you okay?"

Her thighs burned painfully, but she nodded.

"Ready to come down?"

Igloo wanted to say no. It was warm between her legs, and she wished Charlotte would put her hand there because she really wanted something to grind against. She wished Charlotte would force it on her. Make her have an orgasm now, while she was in pain and restrained against the cross. But she was too embarrassed to ask, and besides, it didn't feel like being forced when you had to ask for it.

"Yes, please."

"Are you sure?" Charlotte said, and then she did put her hand between Igloo's legs, and she cupped Igloo's mound. Igloo rocked her pelvis back and forth and uttered an involuntary whine in response.

"We could go for round two," Charlotte said. "I can whip you some more."

"No, no more whip," Igloo uttered, as she ground against Charlotte's hand.

"I could put those evil nipple clamps on you, then try to yank them off with the whip."

Charlotte must have seen the alarm in her face. "Shh, I'm just kidding." She pulled her hand away from Igloo's cooch. Igloo tried to follow, but Charlotte ignored her, and instead unclipped her wrists.

"Come sit down," Charlotte led her, still wobbly, over to a bench.

Charlotte sat next to her, her arm around Igloo's shoulder. Igloo leaned in, nuzzling her. "I need a minute, okay?"

"Of course. As long as you need. You want some water?"

"There's some in my bag."

Charlotte found the bottle and held it up for Igloo to take a sip.

Igloo looked down at her thighs, found there were perfectly matched rows of five red dots on each thigh where the whip tip had struck. Each one burned. "They're so perfect. So symmetrical." What would Essie think? She'd never come home with marks before.

Charlotte laughed. "I may be obsessed, but I practice for half an hour a day. It's my exercise program. Do you want help getting dressed?"

She felt silly as Charlotte helped dress her, but she liked the feeling of being cared for.

"Can I get you some juice or a soda? You seem like you could use a little something."

Igloo nodded without lifting her head off Charlotte's shoulder.

"I'm going to have to get up."

Igloo didn't move.

Charlotte laughed. "You're cute when you're submissive."

"I want to go upstairs," Igloo said, her voice small and soft.

Charlotte lifted her chin so Igloo looked into her eyes. "I do too, but I want you to be all here, and you're loopy now. I don't want you regretting anything. Let's get you that drink. I'll help you stand."

"My toy bag," Igloo said. She might be spacey, but she'd spent a lot of time putting that kit together and she wasn't going to leave it unattended.

"Got it," Charlotte said, shouldering the bag.

"I feel like I'm eight years old," Igloo protested as Charlotte ordered her an apple juice.

"Shut up and drink the juice," Charlotte said, holding the plastic cup out.

Igloo drank, and they sat together, watching others play.

"Sorry. I don't usually bottom in public," Igloo said.

"You don't have to be sorry for anything," Charlotte said. "You did great. How are you feeling?"

"My thighs burn."

Charlotte smiled. "That's good. I'd be worried if they didn't." Charlotte paused. "I know what you wanted before, on the cross. But we didn't negotiate it, and I was nervous about crossing boundaries."

Igloo nodded. It was the right thing to do. "I hadn't realized I was going to bottom. We should have negotiated more ahead of time."

"There's always next time." Charlotte smiled.

The apple juice and time helped, and soon Igloo sat up on her own. They watched a rope suspension on the tall hardpoint, heard screams from somewhere upstairs. The normal background noises of kink night.

Charlotte's hand was in hers. Full of pent up sexual energy, all she could think about was getting Charlotte upstairs on a bed. Was she really going to do this? She felt a pit in her stomach. It felt like a betrayal of Essie. And yet...this is what they had discussed, it was why they were doing this poly thing, right?

"About what I said before..." Igloo's words trailed off.

Charlotte smiled. "Yeah?"

"Any changes in STI status or exposure since we last messaged?"

"No."

"Where do you want to go?"

"Wherever you want. You're in charge."

It was funny how easily Charlotte switched back to being submissive. Igloo stood and shouldered her bag. "Come."

"Your wish is my command."

They found an empty room upstairs. Igloo closed the door and shut the curtain. She set her bag down, suddenly full of doubts. She'd promised Essie they'd talk before having sex with anyone else. She'd said things might accelerate with Charlotte, but had she been explicit enough? Ugh. Well, this moment was going to come sooner or later, so there was no point in postponing just to tell Essie the obvious. She took a deep breath.

Charlotte picked up the condoms left on the bed. "We won't be needing these."

"Don't assume," Igloo said. She pulled out a dildo. "Unless you don't like penetration."

"Depends on who's doing the penetrating." Charlotte lay on her back, opening and closing her legs playfully.

Igloo pulled out a few hanks of rope and climbed onto the bed. "Since you'll be tied up, you won't be doing much of anything."

"Bring it on," Charlotte said with a smirk. She turned and crawled away, giggling.

"Come back here." Igloo wrestled Charlotte until she was on top of her chest, then quickly tied Charlotte's hands together over her head. Charlotte looked up, expectant, breathing heavy. Igloo leaned down and kissed her hard.

She grabbed a hank of rope and tied a harness around her own hips to hold the dildo in place over her pelvis. She could already smell Charlotte's wetness.

"You're such a slut, I'm not even going to need to use lube, am I?"

"No, Mistress."

Igloo smiled. She hadn't even needed to tell Charlotte to use an honorific.

She teased Charlotte with the dildo, putting it in only an inch, and forcing Charlotte to buck her hips up. Every time Charlotte did, Igloo would draw backwards.

"Please. Please, more."

Charlotte was breathing heavy, writhing on the bed.

Finally, Igloo slowly entered all the way, and Charlotte drew a deep breath. She thrust and ground. She alternated strokes with grinding, testing to see how Charlotte responded, when she ground back, when she arched, watching how her breathing changed.

Eventually she saw Charlotte climbing toward a peak, her gyrations becoming frantic. Charlotte was bucking hard, her breath quickening. When her stomach muscles clenched, Igloo reached up and placed a hand over Charlotte's mouth, cutting off her breath.

"Cum for me," she said, her voice commanding.

Charlotte thrashed in the throes of her orgasm, her cries muffled until Igloo finally pulled her hand away, and then she gulped deep breaths.

"Good girl," Igloo said, petting Charlotte's arms and chest. "You want another?"

Charlotte nodded.

"Then you're going to have to please me first."

"Anything you say, Mistress."

CHAPTER 8

Nathan9 spent some time lying on his back, before he finally got around to wondering why he was there. And exactly where was he? What was he doing? He was rather too relaxed to care much about the details. Then he briefly wondered when they were going to do the surgery. Oh, the procedure. He was in the hospital.

"How are you feeling?"

"Are we done?" Nathan asked. He finally realized he was experiencing the aftereffects of general anesthesia. He didn't like this drugged feeling, didn't like being out of control. He was a hacker who lived on the edge. His currency was control and domination, the only security he'd ever achieve. This state, his mind fragmented, relaxed, unthinking...it was intolerable.

"Yes, Mr. Abene, the surgery is complete."

Nathan figured that Mark Abene wouldn't mind him borrowing his name for the surgical procedure. Abene's hacker handle Phiber Optik was too perfectly punny for the situation. The association would be lost on the medical establishment, but someday Phiber Optik would discover that he was on-record as having a fiber-optic ocular implant. Mark would appreciate the inside joke.

"When can we test it?" Nathan asked, trying not to get his hopes up. Nanovision was the first company with an experimental implant that connected at the origin of the optic nerve. The only chance he had at vision. The implant would, if it worked at all, give him approximately the same visual acuity as a 1980s-era computer display. Inferior to what the visually privileged took for granted, but a vast improvement over the long time he'd spent without vision.

All these years as Nathan9, he'd been the blind hacker. There was a new generation in the community who thought Nathan9 was playing off some hacker cliché, not realizing Nathan himself was the source of so many of those blind hacker stories that had achieved mythical status.

"We're going to get started with your first calibration in a few minutes. When you're ready, we'll power up the implant."

The hacker advantage always lay in exploiting that which was expected. Forty years ago, knowing the back office number for the telephone company meant you were a lineman calling in, and so the operator would do what you asked, no questions. Today, that was achieved with phishing emails. The sheep expected emails from their banks, so when they got one, they clicked on it. Simple.

People expected Nathan9 to be blind. When he wasn't, that was one more advantage he'd have. He'd spent two years getting his chess pieces in order, and this was the last move in a long sequence of preparations for the coming battle. This time around, Nathan would come out on top.

"Go ahead," Nathan said.

The lead research doctor spoke, and Nathan recognized her confident voice. "It's going to take time for your brain to integrate these signals. We've never attempted this procedure in someone who has been without vision for so long."

He felt the doctor move next to him, and a moment later there was a flash, a *something*. It wasn't a feeling, it wasn't a smell, it wasn't knowledge, but there was something new in his head.

Neurons that had long since forgotten their original purpose fired, and a kaleidoscope of sensation triggered in Nathan's mind.

CHAPTER 9

The car dropped Igloo off in front of her building. The night was dark and cool. She looked up at her windows and wondered exactly what she would say to Essie. "Hi honey, I'm home. I fucked another woman. It was really hot."

She wished she could go inside, get a hug from Essie, and go to sleep without speaking. It was too scary to think about discussing her feelings when she wasn't even sure how she felt, let alone sure about how much she wanted to share with Essie.

She let herself in and immediately felt the emptiness. Essie wasn't home yet. Still out on her date? It was almost two in the morning.

"You coming home?" she messaged before she even put anything down.

She let the toy bag slump to the floor in the bedroom and headed for the bathroom. She stripped for the shower. Somehow it felt wrong to get into the bed she shared with Essie while still covered with the aftereffects of sex with Charlotte.

She turned the shower on and waited for the water to get hot. She caught a whiff of Charlotte and stopped. She smelled herself and found a hot spot on her shoulder that still smelled of Charlotte's essential oil. She breathed in deep. Could she shower but not get her shoulder wet? Holy smokes, she was behaving like a love-sick teenager.

She took one more deep breath of Charlotte's smell, and hugged herself, thinking of Charlotte wrapped in her arms. She sighed and forced herself to get in the water.

Afterwards, she lay in bed, in the dark, Charlotte's smell gone, regretting that she'd washed.

She heard keys at the door, the door opening. Oh shit. She was going to have to tell.

Essie came into the room without turning on the light.

"It's okay. I'm still awake."

Essie turned the lights on low.

"How was your night?" Essie asked.

"Fine," Igloo said. "Yours?"

"It was good. We…" Essie paused. "Do you want to hear about it?"

Yes? No? Maybe? Some of each? Could she save game, hear about Essie's night, and then if she didn't like it, revert back and choose another path?

"Sure," Igloo said.

"Give me a sec," Essie said. She went into the bathroom and came out a few minutes later. She slid naked into the bed next to Igloo. She wrapped an arm around Igloo and nestled her head in the crook of Igloo's neck.

Charlotte's head had been in that same exact spot only an hour ago.

"I had sex with Charlotte," Igloo blurted out.

"Oh." Essie pulled slightly away. "I, um…"

"What?" Igloo heard the bristle in her own voice.

"I'm surprised. I didn't realize that was even something you were interested in."

Igloo didn't know what to say. What she had done felt wrong but it also felt right in the moment. She wanted Essie to hug her, to tell her that everything was all right, that she still loved Igloo, that nothing was going to change between the two of them. She couldn't put all of that into words, couldn't explain how her heart tugged in two directions until it felt like she was going to break.

"Are you going to say anything else about it?" Essie said.

"I don't know what to say."

"Did you like it?" Essie asked.

"I did."

Essie pulled a little further away. "Was this a one-time thing or something you are going to repeat?"

She should say: *It was a one-time thing. Please don't leave me, Essie. Don't hate me. Tell me everything is going to be okay. I need you.* But she wasn't going to, and that scared her almost more than anything. "I would do it again."

"Oh." Essie settled back, no longer snuggling up against Igloo.

Igloo turned onto her side to look at Essie. She put a hand on Essie's chest.

"What about your night?" Igloo asked.

"It was nothing."

"No, you wanted to tell me something."

"Nothing." Essie said.

"Come on."

"We went to an art exhibit."

"And?"

"And we had dinner and we talked."

"Was it nice?" Igloo said. She did the math in her head. Essie had been out for six, seven hours. How long did it take to see an exhibit? To have dinner. What did they talk about?

"It was nice. I learned about a bunch about Dutch artists. We talked about the role of the viewer in the meaning of art. The differences in the perception of 2D versus 3D art."

"I didn't realize you had such an interest in art."

Essie looked at Igloo as if she was a stranger. "I'm a photographer, of course I have an interest in art. You think being a barista is my fucking career?"

Ugh. How could she have said that? "I'm am so sorry," Igloo said. "I'm exhausted, and I'm not thinking clearly. Obviously you would have an interest in art."

Essie looked like she was going to say something, then shook her head. Then she continued after all. "When we met, you were so concerned about your work, with making a difference. So serious and righteous."

"And?" Igloo said.

"You never talk about work anymore."

"I just want to enjoy myself for a change," Igloo said. "Is that so wrong? What is the ultimate point of life, except to be happy and experience pleasure?"

"I don't think the purpose of life is to fuck everything that moves," Essie said.

Igloo choked out a laugh despite what she sensed was a deadly serious situation. "You have got to be kidding me. I had sex with one other person. One time. How do you get from that to 'fucking every-thing that moves'?"

Essie shrugged. "I'm tired. I'm going to sleep." She turned onto her side, away from Igloo.

Igloo's pulse pounded in her head. Part of her wanted to get up and run away from the whole situation. She could go to the office, sleep there. No, that was childish. She wasn't going to run away.

She forced herself to lie down and put her arm around Essie. Essie didn't pull away, but she didn't snuggle into place like she usually did. She felt like she was hugging a rock. Igloo waited a moment longer, then pulled her arm away.

She lay there replaying the conversation through her head for a long time before finally drifting off.

In the morning, Essie got up, delivered Igloo's coffee perfunctorily, and left before Igloo had drunk enough to fully awaken.

Igloo sat in bed, wondering what had happened. She got dressed in a daze. When she thought about Essie, all she felt was pain and confusion. Then she'd think about Charlotte, and she'd smell her again in her mind, and think of her naked body pressed up against Igloo's, and she'd be fully of happy, horny feelings.

The whole thing was so disconcerting that Igloo had no framework to even try to puzzle through the experiences. She gave up and biked into work.

Igloo sat at her desk, door closed and locked, and tried to focus through the haze of continual distraction, oscillating between pleasurable memories of Charlotte, and anxious worries about Essie and her reaction.

She messaged Essie.

Igloo > I love you. You are important to me. I don't understand what's happening exactly, but please don't push me away.

Essie didn't respond.

She didn't know exactly what to do about Essie. But Charlotte was easy.

Igloo > Hey, I really enjoyed last night. How are you doing?

Charlotte replied a few minutes later.

Charlotte > That was amazing. Can do we do it again?
Igloo > I'd like that. You looked beautiful in the rope.
Charlotte > You looked beautiful on the cross. I can't wait to give you another beating. :)

Igloo had mixed feelings. She was way more comfortable with her dominant side. Being subby with someone else... Sigh. Why was she getting aroused again?

They bantered a little more about what each enjoyed.

She felt more than a little guilty about the whole exchange. If she'd been home with Essie, she doubted she would have had been messaging with Charlotte. But here at work, where Essie couldn't see, she could and did.

It felt fundamentally dishonest. If she and Essie were really going to practice polyamory, they couldn't hide what they were doing from each other. She should be as comfortable messaging Charlotte at home as she would have been at work. And yet, look how it had gone last night when she'd been honest about having sex.

She had to stop with the distractions and get some work done. In theory, she'd been working on Angie's onion routing as a side project for nearly a month now. In practice, between her other responsibilities for the chat personalities, and the distraction of Essie, and now Charlotte... She'd made way too little progress. She had theory and diagrams and some code, but she'd failed to make any sort of serious headway.

Maybe Essie was right. Maybe she was too caught up in her own pursuit of pleasure. What was the purpose of life?

She wasn't going to answer that now. She had work to do, and it was becoming clear that she wouldn't make progress on her own. She'd do better if she recruited help. Then there'd be accountability, progress too, especially if they weren't as distracted as she was.

It was time to kick this project into high gear. To do that, she was going to flaunt Amber's *diktat*. She wouldn't allow Amber to prescribe who she could or couldn't talk to. She would need to ensure she wasn't going to run into Amber herself. Well, she had a little tool that could help with that...

The distributed, decentralized architecture of Tapestry meant that the social network consisted of many different components, some created by Tapestry, some by other companies. All of them were connected to each other via standardized APIs.

Often this decentralized structure made it a challenge if Igloo or Angie wanted to engage in a bit of surreptitious hacking. But in this case, Amber used the Tapestry reference client, as a little more than half their users did, and that made everything a lot easier.

Igloo uploaded a small JSON file containing a diagnostic payload to Amber's notification queue. Igloo waited until the file disappeared, then she smiled. For the next twenty-four hours, or until Amber rebooted her phone, whichever came first, Amber's phone would upload detailed GPS coordinates every ten seconds. A simple backdoor into the client that programmers used when they need to debug location-aware features.

It would be nearly impossible for Amber to notice, unless she were monitoring her own data transmissions, which would be silly for her to do.

Igloo started a script, called MaraudersMapUpdater, which sent Amber's location to Igloo's phone, where it was displayed on a map. If Amber approached within fifty feet on roughly the same altitude as Igloo, then she'd get a long buzz. Igloo had an Amber-proximity alert.

Armed with this defensive data, she made her way to Ben and Diana's desks on the floor below. Regardless of what Amber wanted them working on, Ben and Diana were the ideal candidates.

Their side-by-side desks were empty. Ben's desk was pristine, but then it usually was, because he usually worked from the couch on the adjoining wall. But his messenger bag was present, and a pastry rested on Diana's desk. They were around, somewhere.

Her phone buzzed, not the long pulse of the Maurauder's Map, but her normal notification. She slipped it out of her pocket to find a message from Diana.

"That which you seek can be found in the stadium."

Igloo glanced up, saw the red indicator light next to Diana's webcam blinking slowly. She nodded at the camera.

She took the staircase downstairs, to the stadium seating area where they sometimes held presentations. The seating area was empty. She turned to the raised dais where presenters spoke, but there was no one there either.

Out of the corner of her eye, she caught one of the stadium bench seats folding up. "In here," Diana called.

Igloo wanted to be surprised, but she couldn't. This was typical of the two of them. A few months back, Ben had converted an electrical junction room into a makeshift office, which was uncovered only when a routine fire marshal inspection had discovered him sleeping in there.

She stepped down into the narrow opening afforded by the raised seat and lowered herself inside. Then she crouched down to let Diana close the seat behind her.

She crawled toward the back of the stadium seats, where the inside space was taller. They had a small sofa, bean bag, coffee table, and a couple of Ikea table lamps. Ben nodded to her. "Hey, Igs. You'll be cool about this, right?"

"Of course," she said, a little indignant. It would be a terrible day if Ben and Diana started lumping her in with adults like Amber and Angie.

"You mind?" she asked, gesturing to the space next to Ben on the couch.

"No, go for it." He shuffled energy bars and chips off the couch and onto the coffee table to make room, and Diana took the bean bag.

The underside of the stadium seating was hung with several monitors. It took a few seconds to recognize the images being displayed, but Igloo puzzled out that one monitor displayed the feed from the webcam at Diana's desk, and another had a view from what appeared to be a security camera in the stadium seating area.

"How'd you get the furniture in?"

"There's a small access door at the end," Diana said. "It was labeled with a door ID, but we peeled the numbers off and changed the lock, and nobody's come in since."

"Why don't you use the door to get in?"

"You can see the door from the break room down the hall," Ben said. "But the seats aren't really visible from anywhere other than the stadium itself. Less likely to be detected."

"This is hardcore. Where does everyone think you are?"

Ben shrugged. "In meetings? Sleeping? I don't know."

"We just want to work without interruptions," Diana said. "Let me manage my own time without all the hassles. And besides, Amber keeps asking us to babysit the new companies we're onboarding." She mock yawned.

"Yeah, about that," Igloo said. "I'm guessing you have bandwidth for some real work."

Ben shut his laptop. "What do you have in mind?"

"This has to be hush hush. I don't want Amber or anyone else to know about it."

Ben and Diana exchanged glances.

"Spit it out already," Diana said, her own laptop closed now.

Igloo wondered how much was safe to say at work. Angie herself had told Igloo at work, so clearly this wasn't a secret on the level of their hacking. But she had also asked Igloo to keep it quiet.

Igloo reached into her pocket and pulled out a black box, a little smaller than her smartphone, and placed it in the middle of the table. She flipped a switch and an LED glowed green, the only evidence of it working. The video on the hanging monitors froze, then turned black.

"Wi-fi, ultrasonic, and infrared jammer. It should disable any data transmissions from mics or cameras in the room."

"Well that's neat," Ben said, leaning in to inspect it.

"Don't touch, please," Igloo said. "I'm working on a project for Angie." She proceeded to relate the details of the onion routing network Angie wanted added into the Tapestry client and explained the privacy benefits.

Diana shook her head. "We get it. You don't have to spell it all out. But the impact on bandwidth usage will be through the roof."

"Latency will go up," Ben said. "You'll get bottlenecks at certain points."

"We won't do onion routing in isolation," Igloo said. "You're already bringing content into the system through IPFS. That's peer-to-peer, and it means you've got a topographical network map built into every client."

Igloo flipped one of the monitors into whiteboard mode and dismissed the network connectivity error message.

Ben grabbed an apple, put his feet up on the table and munched away.

"Don't think about onion routing by itself." She sketched out a diagram of multiple clients talking to each other. "We have several tools at our disposal. The peer-to-peer network can move content closer to a requesting party. The onion routing network can disguise who has asked for content. The network map can tell us about the quality of the connectivity to many different clients, including both bandwidth and latency. You combine all of those, and what do you get?"

"Optimized onion routing," Diana said. "Not only that, but since we're already requesting content on behalf of other nodes, there's really no way to know if the content took one hop, two, or ten hops. Traffic analysis attacks will never work."

"Yeah, but two-thirds of our client sessions are on mobile." Ben poked at his tablet, then turned it around for Igloo to inspect. It was a slide from a talk Igloo remembered him presenting last month. "Of the third that use desktop browsers, slightly less than a third of those have our browser plugin. So, out of all of our users, only about ten percent are serving up IPFS. Add in the content provider seed servers, and that number goes up slightly, but it's not anywhere near the total saturation you're talking about."

"There's no reason why mobile can't handle small packets," Diana said." Maybe we don't onion route over mobile devices for large media content, but regular messages and email will be just fine."

"Users have data limits," Ben said. "If we send twice the data, it'll cost them real money."

"A good portion of the time people are on wi-fi and plugged in,"

Diana said, "so then the phone is just another node in the network. Doesn't matter that it's a mobile device."

"And even when it is," Igloo said, "people are streaming virtual reality environments, video, and music all the time. A few small packets won't make much of a difference."

"Except if you want to transmit *all* their data over the onion network," Ben said, "that's going to include those virtual reality environments, and movies, and songs. Everything. We can't know what's sensitive and what isn't. So you're increasing the cost of all of their transmissions."

Igloo hesitated, then sank into the couch. Ben was right. If they only encrypted traffic to potentially contentious destinations, then they'd be raising a red flag every time they did it on behalf of a customer. They had to protect everything.

"We've got some problems, big problems that we don't know how to fix, but I still need to do this. Are you willing to work on it with me? Can you keep it hidden from Amber?"

"Sure," Diana said. "I'll fork the code, and we'll work on a private repo shared between us." She glanced at Ben.

"I'm in. It's an interesting problem to try and solve."

"There is no try," Diana said. "Only do."

Igloo smiled. She was no longer working alone on this. They were a team now.

CHAPTER 10

Angie disembarked the plane, trailing her carryon behind her. Another day, another city. She'd lose track of where she was if it wasn't for the regular emails from Matt, detailing where she was, what she was doing, and who she was speaking to. His help was the only thing keeping her sane.

She stopped short, and someone bumped into her.

"Excuse *me*," the other person said, a slightly nasal accent anyone would have identified as a New Yorker; with a childhood spent growing up in Brooklyn, Angie further differentiated it as being from Manhattan. The woman wound around, her roller clipping the edge of Angie's. The bag scraped Angie's new 3D printed MakieBag, leaving a scuff. Damn her. Angie stared at the woman's back, noticing her short brown bob above the collar of the black raincoat. Too fashionable for Angie's taste. Angie liked to keep things practical. She shook her head.

Did she really think it was her admin that kept her sane? There was a time when that was how she thought of Thomas. He'd been her link to sanity. Before that she'd thought the same of Emily, her best friend since childhood. Apparently she needed a lot of support. So much for thinking of herself as the lone wolf type.

She looked forward to tomorrow night. After five straight days on the road, she'd be back home for an uninterrupted forty-eight hours with her husband. Thomas had tried to make plans to go out, and she'd refused. Takeout food was fine, but she wanted to be in her own home, her own bed, eating from her own dishes.

Angie got moving, following signs for rental cars. She stood in line, waiting for the shuttle to the rental area.

"What agency?" the driver asked when she boarded.

"Hertz."

She stuck her bag in the suitcase rack and grabbed a seat across the aisle.

She had put the finishing touches on tomorrow's presentation while she was on the plane. Tonight she'd spend the evening working on what she'd come to think of as The Mission, everything related to teaching people the critical thinking skills that everyone so desperately needed. People needed an inoculation, something to make them resistant to information manipulation.

She hoped she still had the energy, as it was, she was running on fumes. Why did the important work come after everything else?

Several more people boarded before the bus pulled away from the curb. Angie's stomach groaned. She couldn't remember the last time she had a proper meal. She missed lunch due to the last minute financial call she had to take. She'd been on the plane during dinner, stuck in Economy class, and the two bags of pretzels she'd scarfed in-flight weren't going to cut it. There was no time tonight to go out. She'd get room service at the hotel and hope the food came fast, but it never did.

She stared at the bags across from her, fuzzy with hunger and exhaustion. Her dark red bag, custom fabricated just a few weeks ago, already had a scuff mark where that woman's bag had hit hers. The 3D printed material was never going to hold up, but she loved the custom design with the pockets she'd configured herself in the web app.

She looked three bags down the row, saw a tan bag with a scuff mark at the same height as her own, a slight redness to the scuff that matched the color of Angie's bag.

She scanned the bus for the woman with the bob haircut but didn't see her. Weird.

"Last stop, Hertz," the driver announced over the PA.

Angie waited for the bus to stop, grabbed her bag, and stepped off, looking for the board with names on it.

On a whim, she turned around and waited for the woman with the bob to get off the bus.

The tan suitcase came off a few seconds later, pulled by a woman with shoulder-length blonde hair, in a pantsuit and no coat. The woman walked straight past Angie into the reservation building.

Angie couldn't help but stare after her. That wasn't the woman who'd collided with her before. Or, even more strangely, if that was the same woman, she'd gone and changed her appearance.

Her heart skipped a beat, and suddenly her exhaustion vanished in a flood of adrenaline. Fuckity, fuck.

Someone was following her. Some part of her past catching up with her. But *which* part? Did it have something to do with the assholes, domestic abusers she'd killed? The government? Founding Tapestry? A corporate spy? Something in her more distant hacker past? There was no way to know.

Angie had to decide quickly. Did she try to dump whoever was following her now? She'd have to ditch her bag, electronics, and eventually clothes, in case there was a tracking bug. She could maybe get away, but to what end? Who was she running from, and what were they trying to do?

Or should she play along, pretend that she'd noticed nothing, and figure out what was going on?

It had to be the latter. She was in a strange city, with no resources, no cache of equipment. She couldn't ditch everything on a whim. Besides, she had a company to run.

Her pulse sounded in her ears, and suddenly Angie felt alive.

With her exhaustion gone, the world, and her thoughts, became crystal clear.

She turned back to the board, found her name, and walked out to her car. She started a list in her head. She'd want counter-surveillance devices in the future to detect bugs and tracking devices. A wireless jammer. A clean computer, with a software-defined radio. Directional wi-fi antenna. Cash. Untraceable gift cards. Hat and scarf with infrared IR transmitters to whiteout surveillance cameras. She'd bring what she could with her, have the rest mailed to whatever city she was flying to, to wait for her somewhere in a tamperproof box.

Matt would balk at all the crazy instructions. She'd have Igloo do it. She started a secure chat, gave Igloo a small list of what she needed.

Afterwards, she realized that wasn't enough. She couldn't just go reacting, not with everything she had to do. If this was a sign of new perturbations, then she couldn't take the risk of being caught unaware. T2 and her other plans would need to be expedited. She had to be ready before the government acted.

CHAPTER 11

Nathan9 > How'd she respond when you bumped her bag?
Meghan > She didn't seem to notice. I caught her glancing around when we were on the rental shuttle. She'd figured out something was up then.
Nathan9 > You did good. I'll send the payment.

Nathan9 ended the chat with Meghan and rekeyed his ocular implant feed. His virtual computer screen faded away and was replaced by his living room. It was still as sparsely furnished as when he was blind, an environment designed for predictability.

Meghan had done as he asked, followed Angie in the airport, on the shuttle. It was the sort of pointless move the government would make, putting a physical tail on a suspect in an airport. Not anything a hacker would bother with, not when there was abundant digital surveillance data available to achieve the same purpose.

He'd planted Meghan, not to achieve anything useful, but to keep Angie focused on the government as the primary threat and to speed up Angie's timetable.

Tapestry and the government were playing a vast game of

chicken, barreling toward each other down Al Gore's information superhighway. Tapestry's route was preordained in one direction, the government could only go in the other.

It was so blindingly obvious.

Ironically, he knew more than Angie about what the government was up to and had for months. He'd spent years cultivating his mole inside the FBI. He knew the FISA court order would come soon. He knew when Tapestry would be forced into compliance. He knew the timing and method by which the government planned to shut down Tapestry operations if it came to that.

He'd tried, repeatedly, to reopen communications with Angie. He expected her to snub him, and she did. So he'd resorted to the trick with Meghan. It would light a fire under Angie, get her to pick up the pace on her little research project.

Net neutrality, privacy, security, hackers, personalization, profiling, data ownership, corporate influence, cyber warfare, state sponsored hacking. There were continual mini-meltdowns every day, an ongoing battle with operations and security engineers on one side and countless malevolent actors on the other. The Internet was a pressure cooker, had been for years, decades even. That it all hadn't collapsed catastrophically was a miracle.

A metamorphosis of the net was coming. For years, the trend was toward an Internet in the control of governments and a handful of corporations. Angie was bucking the trend, seizing power not for herself, but for the people.

Either way, no matter who won, an era was looming in which the Internet was going to become so secure and private that the kind of hacking he did would become nearly impossible.

Angie had played him two years ago, when she'd forced his assistance in dealing with Tomo. In the process, she'd unwittingly disrupted his plans, forced him to call in favors he'd been planning to save, and, significantly, it had been the end of the long, weird association between the two of them.

He could be angry, but he wasn't. His new plans weren't about vengeance, but relevance. Relevance in a future where the net had become so secure, either though Angie's mission or corporate and government machinations, that hackers like himself would cease to exist.

He rubbed his face with both hands. Because if you took away hacking, what would he have left? Get a job as a programmer? Retire and do nothing? Who would he be?

There was a bigger issue, too. His drive to do something new, something more audacious, something to put a dent in the universe. He'd had his heyday once, when he was younger, and then a good long run with Dead Channel. But he didn't want his run to be over. And he'd never been satisfied with the status quo. He always wanted something more.

At this point, *something more* left one path forward. Be there when Angie acted, then seize power for himself. There would be no greater hack than exploiting for his own gain the very system of controls whose purpose was to ensure security and privacy.

"Marvin, time for a walk."

The poor dog still hadn't quite made the adjustment, still tried to guide Nathan, rather than the other way around. Well, they all had to adapt.

Nathan triggered a window in his implant, watched Angie's location update as she entered her hotel room. Saw the encrypted data connection to Tapestry's servers. A few minutes later, Igloo's phone went active. They were talking again.

From this point out, Nathan9 would be watching.

CHAPTER 12

"He lives out in the West Hills," Essie said, in the midst of making a tofu scramble. "You know I hate driving in the middle of the night, especially when I'm tired."

"So don't drive late at night. Come home earlier." Igloo gestured toward the scramble. "Can we try eggs sometime? It's not that different from tofu really."

"Gross. I'm not putting animal parts in my body. Look, I didn't complain when you asked to bring Charlotte to Deviance. In fact, I let you go by yourself. And you had sex with her. So why are you giving me a hard time now for wanting to sleep at Michael's?"

Igloo wasn't sure what to say to that. First off, it sure seemed like Essie had been icy about Igloo asking to go to Deviance with Charlotte, and it hadn't been until Essie had lined up her own date for that night that things changed. And she'd been upset about Igloo having sex with Charlotte. Ever since that day, Igloo never knew what to expect. Some days with Essie would seem halfway normal, and others would be one long fight. If there was one thing she could say about poly, it didn't leave much time for sleep, or sex, or fun. Relationship discussions seemed to dwarf everything else.

Part of it was that Essie was right: it *didn't* seem fair for Igloo to want to go out with someone else, even fuck them, and then not want to allow Essie to do the same. But she still felt that way. The feelings didn't magically go away. She wanted to say *Don't go. Stay home. Let's spend the night together.*

Ugh. How did she become this jealous, clingy person? She hated the idea of Essie sleeping over at Michael's. Of Essie fooling around, probably having sex with him, maybe even submitting to him in some kinky way.

Part of her wanted to call off poly. But what if Essie refused?

Of course, the other half didn't want to give it up seeing Charlotte. She felt like she was going to explode with contradictions.

"Look," Essie said. "Go message Charlotte. Make plans for Thursday night. It'll be easier if you're distracted."

That was true, and the thought of seeing Charlotte gave her a thrill. Unease mixed with excitement left her with a fluttery stomach. Please let Charlotte say yes.

She scanned the event listings, found a party at a venue she didn't normally go to. She hated that place, but it would work. Hell, if Essie was out, there was a possibility that Charlotte could stay over.

"Are you okay if Charlotte comes home with me?"

Essie stopped buttering the toast and stared at Igloo. "Sure, I guess."

Well, that wasn't what Igloo expected her to say. "We can sleep on the sofa, if it makes you uncomfortable for us to be in the bed."

"No, it's fine. You'll be more comfortable in the bed. Just change the sheets."

"Really?" Igloo wanted Essie to put up more of a fight. It was their bed, damn it.

"Yeah, of course it's fine."

Igloo squashed back the wailing despair rising inside her. Why did it feel like Essie didn't care about their relationship? She was so confused. She was getting what she wanted, and yet...

She gave up trying to understand herself or her increasingly complex feelings. Fuck it, she was getting what she asked for. She'd take advantage of that. She composed a message to Charlotte.

Igloo > Good morning. I miss you. Are you available Thursday?

She stared at the screen. No reply.

Essie deposited some tofu scramble on top of toast and brought plates to the table.

Igloo poured hot sauce over her food.

"There's already hot sauce under the tofu," Essie said.

"I want more." She hoped for some physical sensation to override all the other feelings that threatened to engulf her. She stared at the phone. Still no reply.

Part of Igloo felt guilty that she was trying to use Charlotte as a distraction, but she did legitimately want to see her. Ugh. Why was it all so complicated?

Igloo finished breakfast and went into work. It wasn't until an hour later, when she was deep in work, unraveling a block of code for onion routing, that the reply finally arrived.

Charlotte > I'm sorry, but I have plans Thursday. How about PDX Rated?

Igloo glanced at her calendar. That was two weeks away. And she knew Essie really wanted to go to.

Igloo > You free before then?
Charlotte > I'm sorry. I'm crazy busy.

She went into a whole explanation of all the things she was juggling, which included the life partner she lived with, and two other partners besides.

Charlotte didn't explicitly talk about tiers, but Igloo got the sense that she was in some sort of third tier with Charlotte: a good rope top and fun, but somewhere after her life partner and secondary partners in terms of importance. Sigh. She'd have to take what she could get.

Igloo > Sure, PDX Rated would be great. I'm looking forward to it.

Nine days. She could wait that long, right?

Ugh. She'd just done it again. Said yes before checking with Essie. Now she had to tell Essie after the fact that she'd already committed to taking Charlotte to PDX Rated. Poly was like one long train wreck sometimes.

She dove back into the code. She'd started leveraging the work done on the Invisible Internet Project, which used a variant of onion routing that they called garlic routing. It helped address one of the primary weaknesses of onion routing: traffic analysis attacks. Garlic routing encrypted multiple data packets together. In Igloo's implementation, as data made its way from a source to a destination, it would get combined with other data before getting split off again and recombined with different data as it made its way from node to node.

Igloo liked to envision it as a system of taxis driving around a city. A satellite watching the city could observe a person wearing a trench coat and hat getting into a taxi, and it could observe that taxi driving around the city.

If the taxi took the person directly to their destination, an observer watching through the satellite could figure out exactly where they were going. That was the old HTTPS model. The satellite observer couldn't know exactly who the person was, but they could tell they had gone from location A to location Z.

But in garlic routing, the taxi would drive a couple of blocks and then enter an underground garage, where there would be dozens of other taxis. The passengers would leave the taxi they came in on, and then pick another taxi that was headed in the general direction of their destination. Other passengers would also get into the taxi, but as everyone was wearing trench coats and hats pulled down of their faces, nobody could identify who got into which car. Then the taxis would leave, and drive a few blocks until they entered the next underground garage. Eventually everyone would get where they wanted to go. The satellite observer would see people leaving buildings and entering taxis, and leaving taxis and entering buildings, but they'd have no way to connect the person leaving location A with the person entering location Z.

This made the work at each node far more computationally difficult. If Igloo had been trying to build this as a centralized service, it would be far too expensive to implement, because centralized servers had to be efficient. But at the edge of the network, where hundreds of millions of computers sat idle most of the time, there was a ludicrous amount of compute power doing nothing. The only way this could work was by harnessing the power of users' computers.

Igloo simulated thousands of nodes and watched as traffic flowed through the system. There were few things more satisfying than watching code in action. But suddenly packet latency spiked. The average time across the network shot up to ten seconds, then twenty, then a minute. The simulation glowed red in certain areas as nodes got overloaded, their queues of data to send and receive vastly exceeding their available bandwidth.

Damn it. This kept happening. Every time she thought she had the traffic flowing reliably, it would melt down again. Her stomach grumbled, and she realized how late it was. She rubbed her eyes, felt crusties in the corners. She'd been staring at the screen too long. For every inch of progress, it felt like she still had a mile more to go.

Wednesday was more banging her head against the wall. Every time she came back to the network traffic simulation, she'd get a different meltdown of the routing algorithm. She was grateful when she got a surprise message from Charlotte.

Charlotte > Hey, just thinking about you.

Igloo > I was thinking about you too. I've got a new toy in my bag.

Charlotte > Oh yeah? What?

Igloo > Are you sure you want to know?

Charlotte > Tease. Yes, I do.

Igloo > What are you going to give me if I tell you?

The messaging ended up burning a significant portion of her morning. She asked again if Charlotte was available, but again the answer was no. Igloo was happy for the attention but puzzled. Why did Charlotte have time to text, but no time to get together? It was so frustrating.

She got back to programming. She tried to enlist Ben and Diana, but they were busy with something else and couldn't help out until tomorrow. She dug in alone for the rest of the day. By the time she went home that night her brain was sucked dry.

In the back of her mind, she knew Essie was going out with Michael the next night, and she felt this pressure to make the evening with Essie memorable. But she was too drained from work to do anything more than cuddle in bed after a late dinner. She worried she was disappointing Essie, but she was numb with exhaustion. She lay there wondering how much exhaustion was legitimately due to work and how much was about feeling lost in her relationship. She'd somehow forgotten how to connect with Essie.

On Thursday morning, Essie made breakfast as usual, and she felt herself tearing up at the thought of Essie sleeping over at Michael's that night. She squashed the feelings down. She didn't have time for a breakdown.

After arriving at work, she spent a couple of hours with Ben and Diana, and they pointed out a few flaws in her traffic routing algorithms. She felt like an idiot for not spotting them herself. In the afternoon, she cranked on code. At one point she decided to stretch her legs and realized that everyone had left the office for the day.

She had to face the fact that she was going home to an empty house. Part of her just wanted to stay at the office. She could work through the night.

But she couldn't do that. She had to face her fears. So she forced herself to go home. For a little while, she had fun: she had a hot fudge sundae for dinner and picked, at random, an old episode of Buffy. She studiously ignored the empty half of the bed next to her.

By 1 A.M., Igloo was exhausted, and realized that she was just trying to delay the inevitable. If she didn't go to sleep, she could just pretend Essie wasn't home yet. As soon as she got under the covers, she'd have to face the fact that she was sleeping alone tonight while Essie was on her third date with Michael in as many weeks.

What the heck was Essie doing over at his place? Was she fucking him? Were they playing? She still didn't even know what Michael's kinks were, just that Essie said he was kinky and dominant.

The idea of Essie submitting to anyone else made her feel sick.

At some level, Igloo knew she wasn't being fair. After all, she'd had sex with Charlotte, and it was only reasonable that Essie would get to do the same with someone else. But it had become abundantly clear that being emotionally capable of playing with others was not the same as being ready to handle your partner playing with others. Igloo hated that. She aspired to be better. She didn't want to be insecure. And yet she was all the same.

Poly also wreaked havoc with their D/s dynamic. The nature of dominance and submission meant that one partner had authority, if not in all areas of the relationship, then at least in some. Igloo and Essie had always functioned with an understanding that Igloo was in charge of all sexual matters. That was how they both liked it. For Essie to go off and have sex with other people or submit to them in a kink setting...it felt like a challenge to the authority transfer relationship they enjoyed, and Igloo didn't know how to wrap her mind around that.

She couldn't think about it anymore. She tried forcing herself to focus on her laptop screen. No matter how hard she tried, the text remained blurry.

She wiped away a tear, turned to Essie's side of the bed, and found herself thinking about the first time Essie had slept over. Everything had been full of promise back then.

That first night had been after a public play party. They'd come home, dead tired, but still turned on. They'd fucked, half dozing off at times.

"Stay over," Igloo murmured.

Essie nodded, and curled an arm around her.

In the morning, Igloo had woken to sunlight peeking in around the edges of her blackout curtains and a warm body behind her, spooning her. Essie.

Igloo turned over, excited to have a moment to watch Essie sleep, but Essie was already propped up on one arm, staring at her.

"You're cute when you sleep."

Igloo put one finger on Essie's lips, then leaned forward and kissed her.

Essie played with Igloo's hair with one hand, and Igloo felt herself drifting back to sleep.

She fought the feeling, then checked her phone.

"I have to go to work in a bit," Igloo said

"Want me to make you coffee before you go?"

"Uh, no thanks." The thought of someone else touching her coffee setup was alarming.

"Relax, I trained at Monogram. I already checked out your equipment. I assure you it isn't too complicated for me."

"But..."

"Stay in bed and relax."

It was strange to lie in bed and have someone else take care of her in her own place.

She woke with a start and realized she had fallen back asleep. She looked up to find Essie kneeling on the bed, coffee held in the palm of one hand, steadied with her other hand, head bowed.

Her eyes followed the curves of Essie's body, the way her shoulders met her neck, the line of her ribs, her stomach. The crease where her legs met her torso, leading the gaze down between Essie's legs. But the physicality of it was nothing compared to the way she kept her gaze down, and waited, waited for Igloo. Her pose said that she'd wait there all day if necessary.

She stroked Essie's arm and took the cup.

"Thank you."

Essie smiled and slipped back under the covers.

Igloo sipped the coffee. It was unmistakably the Guatemalan roast she'd bought a few days ago, but there were flavors she hadn't noticed before. She took another sip. "That's marvelous. How did you—"

"I never give away my secrets."

Essie curled up next to her and Igloo stroked her neck, wondering what it would be like to wake up like this every day. Then her alarm went off. She hit her phone with one hand.

"I have to get going in a few."

Essie stroked Igloo's stomach and ribs.

Igloo could feel herself getting wet again, suddenly hungry for another round. "I guess I can be late."

She climbed on top of Essie, pinning her hands while she explored Essie's body with her mouth. She hit snooze twice more before she finally gave up and turned the alarm off.

An hour later, they were both satisfied, and Igloo had given up on the idea of a timely arrival at work. Morning sex beat meetings any day.

"It must be nice," Essie said, "showing up whenever you want."

"I guess," Igloo said. "I mostly do what I want. Benefit of being one of the founders."

"Sounds amazing."

Igloo thought about the months of boredom, interspersed with the pressure of high-stakes, off-hours hacking, and Angie's growing distance. "Sometimes."

"I get chewed out if I'm five minutes late for my shift," Essie said. "But I like working part-time."

Igloo sipped her coffee, enjoying the feeling of Essie nestled on her chest. "What do you want to do? You can't work at a coffee shop forever."

"Photography. I was starting to establish myself in Maryland before I moved. Now I need to get some clients here. But I'm too distracted by kink. I want to do all the things."

Igloo laughed. "I know the feeling."

"Plus, I have a secret." Essie turned over and hid her face in the pillow.

"Tell, tell." Igloo tickled Essie just above her hip.

"I secretly want to be..." The details were lost in the pillow as Essie smothered her mouth.

"What?" Igloo said, ramping up the tickling.

"A housewife," Essie screamed, pulling her face out of the pillow. "There, I said it. My mother would kill me if she knew. 'I didn't send you to college for four years to be someone's servant' is what she told my sister when she got married."

"Oh." Igloo tried to imagine having someone at home to take care of everything. The idea was strangely arousing. Maybe there was time for round three? She glanced at her phone. "Oh, shit, I really have to go. I hate to..."

"No problem. I'll get dressed. I can Uber home."

Igloo hopped in the shower, and by the time she was back in her room, after a few short minutes, Essie was fully clothed.

"My ride's gonna be here in a minute."

Igloo gave her a kiss and was already thinking ahead to when she'd see her again.

"Let's check in tomorrow," Essie said. "Thanks for last night."

"Yeah, it was great." She gave Essie one last hug and watched as she walked down the steps and out to the waiting car.

She closed the door and her place felt empty.

Igloo thought back to the way she'd felt after that first night, and rubbed a tear away. Everything had been so full of promise and long-ing. All she could see back then was the potential of what might come. Now it seemed like she was on the downside, and all she could sense was the loss of everything that was. She wiped her nose and deposited the tissue in the growing pile on her bedside table.

———

The next morning, Igloo woke congested from a night of crying. Her head was fuzzy from a lack of caffeine. She lay in bed, then realized that Essie was not going to be bringing her coffee this morning.

She got up and padded to the kitchen. She couldn't find the beans. Essie must have reorganized things. It was odd to be a stranger in her own kitchen. She rummaged through cabinets until she found them and got the coffee maker going.

As the coffee brewed, she thought about Charlotte. Probably if she'd had the distraction of Charlotte last night, things wouldn't have been as bad. Igloo's poly friends said the best way to cope with jeal-ousy was a good fuck. Waiting home alone, on the other hand....

Would Charlotte ever make more time for Igloo? How could she when she already had three other partners? Three nights per week with her life partner, one night each for her other two partners, two nights home alone. Igloo got the occasional special events, like PDX Rated, or random openings in the schedule, but that was about it.

There was an inherent asymmetry to their connection, because Charlotte was a big deal to Igloo, but Igloo was just a random play partner to Charlotte.

She didn't have any answers.

She poured herself a mug of coffee and got back into bed with her laptop. She'd work from home today, at least until Essie returned.

Her stomach started to grumble at she worked. But Essie had promised to be home by nine, so she'd wait for Essie to eat.

Nine came and went. Igloo got more coffee and forced herself to keep working and not think about the time. She was making some breakthroughs in the garlic routing algorithms. They were small ones, but the network traffic congestion problems were improving, the cases where the entire simulation would meltdown getting rarer. Progress at last.

Eventually Igloo heard the front door. She glanced at the time. Ten-thirty. An hour and a half past the time Essie had promised to be home.

She gritted her teeth and returned to her code.

She heard the front door open, and a few minutes later the bedroom door creaked. Essie bounded over to the bed.

Igloo stared at her computer screen, determined not to show any neediness, although she wanted a hug and a cry.

Essie stood next to the bed, full of energy and smiling. "Hi! I missed you."

"One sec, I'm just finishing this line." She made a feeble attempt at the code and gave up.

Essie climbed onto the bed next to her. "I love you."

Igloo searched for the words to say back, but they wouldn't come. There was just emptiness and pain where her love for Essie should be. She set her laptop aside and reached out to pull Essie close.

But when Essie nuzzled her neck in return, Igloo found herself leaning away. That much affection just made her feel uncomfortable. She wanted to be close to Essie, but...

"What's wrong?" Essie asked.

"Everything!" The word came out choked with emotion. She tried to steady her voice. Why was she so afraid?

"I love you, you know that right?"

Igloo shrugged.

"I will always love you."

"It's fucking hard to watch you bounce in here all happy."

"If you'd set up a date with Charlotte, it would go easier for you"

"I tried!" Igloo yelled, unable to keep from reacting with anger. "You know that. Every time I want to see her, she's either not available or she cancels on me."

"Don't get angry at me," Essie said. "It's not my fault your partner sucks."

Igloo gritted her teeth and tried to keep from screaming. She settled for clawing at the bed.

"I'm sorry." Essie tried to pet Igloo, but Igloo pulled away.

Essie sighed. "Look, nothing happened between Michael and I."

"What do you mean nothing happened? You slept over. And now you're all smiling and happy. You don't wake up here bouncing with energy in the morning."

"I mean, we didn't have sex or anything. Although we didn't exactly sleep either. After dinner we went back to his place, and he taught me to weld."

"To *weld*?"

"Yeah. And to cut steel with an angle grinder. Holy shit, that is fun as fuck. Although look at my arm." Essie pulled back her sleeve to reveal skin marked with dozens of tiny red burns. "The sparks went right through my shirt. But Michael lent me one of his to wear."

Anger and hurt welled up inside Igloo. She had no words for what she was feeling, but the emotions flooded her until she was so overwhelmed that she went numb. She turned over onto her side.

"I'm sorry," Essie said, rubbing her shoulder. "I love you just as much as before I went. I'm home. I missed you, and I'm excited to see you."

"You're excited because you saw him. It has nothing to do with me." Fuck, Igloo hated herself. Why couldn't she just get over her jealousy? She should be excited for Essie, not a quivering mess. She wanted Essie to be excited for her when she went out with Charlotte, and yet here she was doing the same thing to Essie that she complained about Essie doing to her. Poly was a stupid, lousy idea.

"I'm not going to lie, it was fun. But now I'm here with you."

"It's like he's here in the room with us."

Essie lay down next to Igloo and tried to curl up with her. "You be the little spoon."

"I can't handle this. You don't know how hard it is to lie here all night long and think about you being there with him."

"We didn't do anything. I mean, we cuddled for a little bit, but that was it. We still even had clothes on... Well, some clothes, anyway."

"Fucking gross. I don't want to think about that."

"Come on. That's not fair. You said back when we started dating that 'guy sex was not without its benefits'."

"Oh, thanks. I wasn't even thinking about that. Nice. Those are benefits that I can't provide."

Essie sighed. "It's not a competition. I like and love you. I also like spending time with Michael. One doesn't take away from the other."

Logically Igloo knew that Essie was right. Igloo's time with Charlotte didn't affect her feelings for Essie. So why couldn't her stupid lizard brain just shut up and let her be? Why was she so afraid? So afraid of losing Essie, and even more, of losing Essie's respect. That was what scared her the most: that somehow Essie wouldn't think of her in the same way anymore. That she wouldn't be worthy of Essie's love.

Igloo tried to hold back her feelings, but she couldn't anymore. The tears trickled out at first and then she sobbed.

Essie wrapped herself more closely around her.

CHAPTER 13

A knock interrupted Enso's review of Robin's case files, and his door opened before he could respond.

His second-in-command, Alice, had a broad smile. "FISA court order is in."

Enso rested both hands on his desk and imagined the look on Angie's face when her precious Tapestry was split open so the government could monitor what was going on. It would be a big win for the intelligence community. They'd run up against Tapestry over and over during the last two years. Everyone knew their security was top-notch. Terrorists, criminals, foreign governments. They were all moving to Tapestry, making it more and more difficult to conduct the kind of widespread information surveillance that characterized most intelligence work these days.

"Great news. What's the timeline?"

"Ninety days. Thirty to turn over their data and network architecture, sixty to be in complete compliance."

Three months, and then the government would have their big pipes hooked up to the internals of the Tapestry software. A huge data vacuum, sucking everything into the NSA's data center where the world's most powerful computer farm would analyze and corre-late everything.

Yeah, it was worthy of a celebration.

He didn't understand why FISA had been so slow to act. They issued orders to all the top Internet companies when they were smaller than Tapestry was now. Maybe it was because Tapestry had grown so quickly. If anything, they'd been understating their actual user base for months, perhaps to stall any FISA action.

"Is this going to change anything about our operation?" Alice asked.

That was the kicker. The part of Enso that wasn't celebrating. He knew Angie was crooked. Had been sure of this for a long time, ever since she'd made a fool of him by killing Chris Daly, the BRI agent tasked to her. She'd gotten away scot-free, making it look like the agent had attacked her, and that she'd been acting in self-defense. He didn't see how constructing a homemade robot armed with a 9mm could be construed as self-defense, but that case was long done.

It sure as hell didn't help that Chris Daly had been a sick fuck. Between Daly's frequent disappearing acts and his surveillance of people who had nothing to do with his cases, Enso had known some-thing was going on. And later, there'd been the weird sex stuff with the women in the hotel rooms. But Daly was one of his most effective agents, and always professional with his partners, so it was a no-brainer for Enso to keep pushing everything under the rug. After all, nothing Daly did was any worse than what people in power did all the time. Of course, during the investigation, evidence of Daly's psychopathic behaviors surfaced. Enso learned his lesson from that too late.

BRI would turn up something on Angie. They had to. *He* had to. The budget invested in discovering Angie's misdeeds had to uncover something or BRI would never lead another major operation. The whole point of BRI was that they could do what other, more legiti-mate organizations couldn't through legal means. If they were unsuccessful in the case of Tapestry, then they were going to die a slow death of irrelevance.

Alice started to tap her toe.

Enso frowned. "We're going to increase the pressure on Angie."

Alice fully entered and closed the door behind her. "Increase? What more can we possibly do? We're analyzing every bit of cleartext in and out of Tapestry, every bit of meta-data."

"I want real time coverage of her conversations."

Alice shook her head. "Every bug we've put in place, she's detected. We stopped trying."

"Let's put a long-range surveillance team in place. Lasers off windows, that sort of thing."

Alice looked doubtful. "That's CIA stuff. Who do we have that can staff that?"

"That's what I want you to find out. Come on. Work with me here." Enso ran his fingers through his hair, then instantly regretted it. He'd probably made a mess of it.

She dropped into the chair in front of his desk. "I know you want to dig up something. We all do. But we've been investigating Angie for-fucking-ever."

Enso glared at her. "Don't fight me on this, Alice. We've got a few months, if that, then it's all out of our hands. What options do we have?"

Alice sighed. "If we treat this as a potential terrorist op, we can get satellite coverage. Intermittent only, not full-time. But we can get a few hundred photos a day of the Portland area, or wherever she is, and use that to track her, her vehicle, her husband. You get the idea. We look for any discrepancies in her real-time data, which we can assume she's falsifying."

"That's good. Do it. What else?"

"We can only hide so many of these big requests. People will eventually ask questions."

Everyone in BRI had a day job. They reported to different parts of the government. Some were in intelligence, purportedly working for one organization, but actually reporting informally to Enso. Between these BRI shadow employees and countless favors from regular government employees, they kept BRI off the books.

"I'll provide high-level cover," Enso said. "I'll talk to Griz, get him to give us blanket approval for longer-range plans. You work out the specifics. What else do you have?"

"We could ask NSA to do some deeper machine learning algorithms on Angie's historical data. We've got records going back fifteen years. She can't always have been this good at covering her tracks."

"We did that last year and didn't get anything."

"Doesn't matter. Machine learning is improving all the time. Plus, they've got a hundred times more computing power now. New exploits on old encryption methods. It's worth taking another pass."

Enso nodded. "Do it then."

"Also, we can widen the scope. Everything Angie does is already under a microscope. We can do the same for all of her known associates. Husband. Amber. Igloo. Other execs. Business associates. Family. Friends. Maybe she's got perfect operational security, but they don't. We slurp up all of their online data, computers, any connected devices. She could have let something slip around them. We're talking about maybe a hundred key associates. But we'd need a few more full-time analysts, and BRI is tapped out. Can you get us people?"

This was getting expensive. "I'll get us some more loaners."

"They have to be good," Alice said. "We can't babysit junior analysts fresh out of school. Get us some senior people. And while you're at it, how about having the cyberwarfare group take a look at Angie?"

Enso raised an eyebrow. There were limits to his influence. The NSA's cyberwarfare team was top-notch, but it was akin to asking that an aircraft carrier be retasked for a pet project.

Alice took in the eyebrow. "Our guys are good, but you know cyber command has tricks up their sleeve that they're not sharing."

"Yeah, because they're supposed to be saved for active warfare ops." He shook his head.

"You asked for ideas, I'm giving you ideas." She shrugged. "Do what you like."

"Fine, fine, I'll ask."

Enso wasn't looking forward to the size of the favors he would owe in return.

Enso had his aide chase down Griz to set up an off-record appointment. SigInt Director Feldson was technically the lead for the Tapestry initiative, though Enso had been running the operation. Rumor was he'd been grizzled back when he was a young lieutenant in the Navy. His own commanding officer had taken to calling him Griz, and the name stuck.

Enso needed a plausible reason to visit. He showed up at Griz's office an hour early, and signed into the log for a meeting with a Colonel in military intelligence. He ducked into the Colonel's office for fifteen minutes, chatted about an operation they'd worked on last year, then made his way to see Griz.

An unburnt stump of a cigar sat on Griz's desk. Griz looked up to see Enso enter. He hit a button on his desk, and the hiss of a white noise generator started. Enso knew there'd be the equivalent in the electronic spectrum as well.

"Enso," Griz said, by way of greeting.

"Griz, thanks for seeing me."

"I assume you got the news about the FISA court order."

Enso nodded. The official path for the request would have originated through Griz's office. "Thanks. The taps are going to help with a number of investigations."

"About that. Once the court order takes effect, we're not going to need BRI on Tapestry anymore. You can start to wind down operations. We'll have all the inside data we need."

Enso was incredulous. Griz already thinking about winding down BRI? Didn't he see the risk that Angie posed? He opened and closed his mouth twice, then took a deep breath, and tried again. "You have no idea what Angie is capable of. Shutting down our operation is a mistake. We've potentially tied her to dozens, maybe hundreds of murders. Hell, we know Daly's death was premeditated. She entrapped him to make us look bad. We need to keep digging. There's more out there."

Griz waved away his protests with one hand. "Look, what Angie has done is irrelevant. We need Tapestry data for intelligence purposes. The FISA court order will give us that. So what if she killed a hundred men? It's nothing in the grand scheme of things. Your organization killed that many, and you're working for us."

Damn Griz and his myopic focus. Enso stood and stalked back and forth, trying to form his thoughts.

"Assume Angie is actually the killer we suspect she is."

Griz sat back, folded his arms, and nodded.

"And assume she was able to bury all the evidence, digital and otherwise."

"Go on."

"She was able to take out one of my top agents."

"A deranged, sick man," Griz said, "according to what came out during the investigation. But what's your point?"

"My point is, that makes Angie a very dangerous person. She's potentially sociopathic. She foiled the police, the FBI, and the intelligence community. She's in control of one of the largest and most secure information networks, a phenomenally powerful tool. Who knows what she might do next? How could we stop her? She's a clear and present danger."

"What do you want to do? You haven't turned up anything. The FISA court order will give us insight into what's happening on Tapestry. That's actually meaningful."

"I want to bury her, while we still can. Before we have FISA scrutiny. One last effort to discover the secrets in her past. BRI has a plan.

All-in on cracking her historical data. All-in on current surveillance. Find something meaningful. If we can't, then we creatively generate the leverage we need to get her out of power. Failing that, we eliminate her."

Griz sat back in his chair and chewed on the stump of his cigar.

"If we remove Angie from the picture," Enso said, "we'll have way more influence when we apply the court order. We can reshape Tapestry from the inside out. Make it a front organization for the intelligence community. A modern-day, digital Air America. Can you imagine that?"

Griz stared at the ceiling, still masticating his cigar. Finally, he grunted and sat upright. "Hypothetically, of course, an asset like that would have immense value. But the risk of exposure is equally immense. We'll hang you out to dry if word gets out."

Enso nodded.

"We didn't discuss this," Griz said. "I don't want to know about it. You must want people—you wouldn't have come in person if you didn't. The people are approved."

"Some of them might be controversial—" Enso was thinking of the proposal to use the cyber command team.

"What did I say? I don't want to know. Do what you have to do."

CHAPTER 14

Igloo hoped Angie would hurry. They had many methods of getting together outside the office when they wanted to talk about hacking and didn't want government agencies spying on them. But requesting her to electronically sanitize herself and meet at 10A.M. on a Saturday was not a favorite.

Worse, Angie hadn't said what she wanted to talk about. Igloo hoped it would be something simple. Some abuser who needed to be put away. But something in the way Angie said she wanted to talk suggested it would be bigger.

Her body was mixed up, unsure if she was awake very, very early, or maybe very late. She'd had a scant three hours of sleep. Bleary-eyed, standing on a corner holding a coffee in each hand and a bag with two carmelita bars, the tiredness was at the level of physical pain. She needed a hot soak. She and Essie should take a weekend at Breitenbush. That would be amazing.

If Essie would even go with her. In the past week, things had remained, if not frosty, then at least distant between her and Essie. Where she'd once felt closeness with Essie, now there was a void.

Igloo tried to bury herself in work to fill the gap. Which was good, since there was a ton of pressure to make progress on Angie's onion routing project. But the events of her personal life continually intruded. She'd made half the progress she'd hoped for.

Shit. Did Angie want to talk about Igloo's *contributions*? She had a momentary panic. She'd never contributed anything less than 110 percent. It was only that the last few months were so confusing and complicated.

Every time she'd sit down to code, she couldn't stop thinking about Essie. She'd struggle at her computer for a while, then end up going for a long walk listening to angry or sad music or both. In the evening, she'd come home and mope around by herself or bicker with Essie.

Midweek, Charlotte had messaged, saying she unexpectedly had a free night on Friday, and wanted to go to a rope party together. It was a bright spot in an otherwise distressing week. After a brief hesitation, Igloo had said yes. She'd already planned to go with Essie, but there was ample time to do two scenes in one night.

Still, Igloo hadn't been sure what Essie would say. Her responses didn't make sense sometimes. Igloo felt herself struggling with jealousy and insecurity all the time. She'd understand if Essie felt the same. But Essie continually asserted everything was fine, while getting upset at random times.

Was being able to date other people really worth all this?

When Igloo, prepared for a fight, finally told Essie that Charlotte was coming, Essie simply responded with a "whatever." Igloo couldn't decide what to make of that. Did 'whatever' mean it was genuinely fine? Or that Essie was distracted with Michael? Or that Essie had stopped caring about her?

Igloo felt she wasn't getting the whole story. She wanted to have an honest discussion with Essie, but she was afraid of what she would learn. Would Essie turn out to have one foot out the door? In the end she didn't have the energy or courage to tackle that conversation, and decided to let Essie's answer be, even though it raised so many questions.

When the party finally arrived last night, she'd played with Charlotte first, full of excitement and joy. They did a simple rope suspension scene with a few kisses and gropes snuck in. She enjoyed the scene, especially experiencing Charlotte's responses, all of which were tinged with a certain exotic newness. But she wanted more and resented the rushed timing. She feared that if she gave Charlotte too much attention Essie would be angry.

After a short break, she tied Essie. She enjoyed the familiar sensations and curves of Essie's body, the comfortable way their bodies nestled together. The predictability of Essie's responses helped Igloo feel confident, her mastery of sexual and kink skills at an all-time high. She pushed herself, working extra hard to give Essie something novel and fun that didn't repeat anything she'd done with Charlotte.

The experience left her riding high—she'd done two excellent scenes. But she also felt wrung out, like she'd expended way more energy than she'd taken in. Her need to please both partners, to ensure that everyone else had a great time, exhausted her.

Igloo and Essie went home, and though Igloo was cognizant of needing to get up early to meet Angie, Essie unexpectedly wanted sex, which stretched on for hours. The lovemaking was hot—they'd fucked with a kind of urgency, like the world was ending.

But this morning, the differences between their relationships felt unfair. Essie had consistent, weekly dates alone with Michael. But on the once or twice a month occasions that Charlotte was available, Igloo would often already have plans with Essie. If she wanted to see Charlotte, she had to fit it in like last night, a quick scene before spending the rest of the night with Essie. Why did Essie get solo date nights while Igloo had to split her attention? It didn't seem unreasonable for Essie to give Igloo some extra leeway when Essie had so much.

Essie had remarked about Igloo being lucky she was getting *two* dates in one night. To a certain extent, it had been fun and ego-gratifying. But what she really wanted was a level of intimacy and connection with Charlotte that she didn't feel when she was self-conscious about Essie watching them.

Worse, anything she did with Charlotte, she felt she had to do more and better with Essie to avoid Essie feeling slighted. The joy and spontaneity went right out of her play.

Why was she even behaving like that? Was she overcompensating, anticipating underlying jealousy on Essie's part? Or was she doing it to make herself feel more secure? After all, it was Essie who had another big date with Michael looming that week. Another sleepover. Igloo felt a mile deep in a pit of despair.

Angie finally arrived, pulling Igloo out of her recollections. Angie's 3D printed car rattled only slightly on the dead-quiet street. How Angie loved that car. She parked across the street from the coffee shop, locked up, and nodded to Igloo, indicating they should walk away together.

"Coffee?" Igloo said, once they were far from Angie's car and any would-be eavesdroppers.

"Wait," Angie said. She pulled out a cobbled-together device in a 3D-printed case and waved it around.

Igloo knew better than to ask if it was really necessary. Angie had become more paranoid over time.

Angie caught the expression on Igloo's face.

"A single misstep could risk everything we've built. You don't realize how lucky we were to break the old stranglehold. The end of centralized power on the Internet is within our grasp. One sniff of what we do on the side, and the government shuts down everything."

"Fine." Igloo held up the drinks and paper bag. "Look, do you want your coffee or carmelita bar first?"

"Neither. I want you to listen very carefully."

Here goes. The worst part was that until Angie took something out of her hands, there was no way for Igloo to eat her own bar. But she couldn't really complain to a one-armed person about not having a free hand, could she? She settled for a sip of coffee.

"What is it?" She tried not to think about the chocolate chips and caramel in the center of the bar.

"The last election was close," Angie said. "In the end, less than 2 percent of the vote separated a progressive candidate from a regressive one."

"Yep." Igloo held out the bag. "Gerrymandering, voter obstruction, criminally bad education system, obscene amounts of money thrown at the election. There are a thousand reasons for it. Can you take your coffee?"

"We can't do anything about those, can we? Angie ignored the proffered cup and continued down a side street. They wandered into a rundown industrial district. Igloo trusted that Angie would have either cleared the path ahead of time or at least ensured there were no compromised cameras.

"But we can do something about what people see and read."

"What are you talking about?" Igloo said.

"Don't play dumb. You know exactly what I'm talking about."

Igloo shook her head. She couldn't imagine where Angie was going with this.

"We do it all the time. We manipulate people. We provide suicide hotlines, and domestic abuse support help. We change the stories they see, give them more positive ones. We deliberately show them there's a way out."

"We do that for people in crisis," Igloo whispered, glancing left and right. "We're saving their lives."

Angie bent down slightly, got close in to Igloo's face. "How many lives were lost when the President was elected? More hate crimes. More violence. Geopolitical instability. It has to stop."

"We can't manipulate media for the entire country. Entire world."

"We can, and we have to."

"You're out of your mind."

Angie shook her head, and finally took her coffee cup. Only now Igloo was too upset to eat.

"I'm right," Angie said, "and you know it. You just don't want to admit it."

"Wholesale manipulation of voters is not what we stand for. That's what the bad guys do, Angie, not us."

"Really? You won't manipulate information to make a better world?" Angie cocked her head. "Some simple distortions, not even lies per se, just control over which information gets around. That's not worth preventing another radical president? The other side already manipulates everyone who votes for them. All we're doing is evening things out."

"No, Angie. Tapestry is literally some people's only conduit for information. Nobody else has that advantage. They tell lies piecemeal. That's not the same thing as changing wholesale what everyone sees."

"It doesn't matter, Igloo. I don't give a shit how manipulative we are. We can stop a war, crush a political party, and change the course of history. This is our time. We have to do it."

"What the fuck has gotten into you?"

"I'm worried that the clock is running out for us. Maybe we can do this today, but we can't do it tomorrow. What happens when the government comes after us and shuts down Tapestry? Then it's too late."

"Okay, there's paranoid, and then there's paranoid. You've stepped over the line."

The glare in Angie's eyes would have sunk a lesser woman.

Igloo swallowed hard. There was something intimidating about pushing back against someone who could kill you with her smartphone. "Besides, you can't know for sure that we can achieve the effect you're talking about."

Angie resumed walking, forcing Igloo to run after her.

"I already tested the idea," Angie said. "Tape can selectively override story feeds, even for non-Tapestry feed engines. I tried it with the mid-year ballot measures in California and swung the vote for progressive initiatives by more than five percent over what the polls predicted. The concept works." She shrugged and picked up her pace.

"Linus fucking Torvalds. What have you done?" This was far, far worse than simply killing an abuser.

"The right thing," Angie said. "Now we need to do the right thing on a bigger scale. We have eighteen months until the next election."

The presidential election? Igloo's body shook, and the world faded away. She vaguely noticed that she'd dropped the coffee and the food bag, felt a splatter against her leg.

Angie ditched her own coffee, grabbed Igloo hard under one armpit, and carefully lowered her to the ground as her legs gave way. She knelt next to Igloo.

"I know this sounds crazy. I'm sorry I'm breaking this to you all at once, but there are people after me. I need you to know what to do, in case something... Just in case."

"In case what, Angie?" Igloo shook her head, trying to get rid of the fuzzy feeling.

"Nothing. I'm going to show you how to modify what goes through Tape. We're going to shift what people are seeing over the next year and a half. Very carefully, very gradually, but we'll do what we need to do to make sure we get the president we deserve."

Igloo felt like she was floating outside her body. Was Angie really talking about manipulating hundreds of millions of people, of influencing who was elected leader of the country? Was this some bad nightmare?

"Come on," Angie said, "once I show you the code you'll be back to all right."

Angie had a spare car parked under a tree nearby, an eighties American car, the cloth interior ripped to shreds, a fleece blanket spread across the front seat. The car started with the squeal of a loose belt. Angie checked her phone, glimpsed at the sky, then waited for half a minute. "Satellites," was all she said. She checked the phone again, then pulled away in a rush. She drove less than ten minutes, entered an empty parking lot by a warehouse, and parked behind the building.

"Let's go before a train comes. They've got cameras on the engines now."

They left the car and entered the building through a small side door that Angie unlocked. Igloo still felt numb. Manipulating an election? If Angie was paranoid before, it was going to get worse. Much worse.

The interior was filled with spools of wire. Two massive skylights, streaked with grime, let in the late morning sun, which shone down on a single rusting shipping container near the back.

Angie led them to the container and unlocked the door.

"How'd you find this place?" Igloo asked.

"I'm subleasing the space from the owner who uses this for backup storage," Angie said, as she levered the door open. "They only come in once or twice a month to shift stock around. There's a cell station antenna on the roof."

Igloo nodded. With a mobile phone base station, they could tap into the antenna's fiber option connection for high bandwidth or use the antenna itself to connect to other nearby base stations. They'd traded other hacks last year to get the exploit from a pair of Canadian hackers.

Angie opened the shipping container to reveal two long desks, chairs, a portable toilet, and cardboard boxes. Once inside, she pulled the door closed behind them. "The whole container is made of five-millimeter thick steel, which blocks all signals except what we allow out." She gestured toward a bundle of cables that exited through the back wall. Then she pointed out a cardboard box. "You'll want that. Canned coffee."

Igloo reached inside, found a black cylinder of pre-made Japanese coffee. At least, she assumed it was Japanese from the kanji writing, and assumed it was coffee from the picture on the front. She pried the can open, downed it, then suppressed the urge to gag.

"That is awful," Igloo said. "Let me pick the coffee in the future."

On the other side of the cardboard box she was surprised to find a waist-high safe. They'd never had a safe at any previous sanctuary. Angie caught her puzzled look.

"I'm keeping all the electronics in here. The safe won't keep out anyone determined to get our computers, but it's pressurized, which gives us a tamper-evident seal. If the safe is opened, the pressure changes, we get notified, and we know our stuff has been compromised. The biometric reader scans the blood flow in your palm. Harder to spoof than a palm print."

Angie placed her hand on the front screen of the safe, and after a few seconds, the screen lit up and displayed a hexadecimal keyboard. Angie typed a series of digits, and the safe unlocked with a thunk. She swung the door open to reveal a pile of Apple computers and tablets.

Igloo's head swam. "Let me get this straight. You created a new safe house. Awesome. I get that. You did it on the sly, also fine. You stocked it with furniture, a safe, and supplies."

Angie nodded.

"You could have asked me to help, you know. You didn't have to do this yourself."

Angie shrugged. "Sometimes I need time alone, you know? I'm stuck talking to people all day at work. Coming out here, I get some peace of mind."

Igloo stared at Angie, suddenly sympathetic. Two introverts, forced to work with others to get anything meaningful done. Yeah, she could understand.

She found herself sweating and unzipped her hoodie. Given the early hour, it was surprisingly warm inside the shipping container. "Man, it's hot."

Angie glanced up. "Unfortunately, the sun comes in through the skylight this time of day and bakes the container like a solar oven. Don't worry, it cools off later." Angie pulled a laptop off the top of the pile. "Come on, let me show you what I've done."

A few minutes later, they were hunched over the screen going through the source code for Tape, the communications layer for Tapestry, that was responsible for the composition of services and the collection of metrics necessary for the accounting code to credit all the participants who contributed to the end-user experience.

"Here, do you see what's happening?" Angie pointed to a block of code.

Igloo looked more closely. She shook her head. "I don't get it," she said. "I mean, it's obvious we're looking at the last layer before transmission to the feed queue. This bit here," she pointed to a specific line of code, "extracts the participant chain and queues it for transmission to Participant Accounting. We add in the accounting for the presentation layer at the last minute."

"Right. Except when we extract the participant chain, we change what's being sent to the feed queue."

Igloo reviewed the code again. "No, we're not."

Angie smirked.

Okay, so she was. How? It took Igloo ten minutes of hunting, and it wasn't until she inspected the object at runtime that she figured it out. "That's just mean. Changing the underlying behavior."

"All the test cases care primarily about the accounting, and the accounting is still credited correctly for the original content. We just piggyback an extra piece of content onto the feed queue. I had to do it that way because if the user interacts with the content, it's going to trickle meta-data back into the system, and there has to be referential integrity. Basically, it has to be a real piece of content, not something we fabricate."

Igloo slumped in her chair. "It's not right, Angie. I'm sorry. Altering a person's feed when we know they're in trouble is one thing. We can make sure they see the information that might save their life. I'm totally down with that. But this..." She pointed to Angie's code. "It's wrong to try to change what millions of people see to align them with how we want them to think."

"Come on, you know the red feed, blue feed deal," Angie said. "What Tomo showed users was completely different based on who their friends were and their past history. Feed algorithms selected what users were most likely to engage with, even when those stories were fake news. The more people engaged with fringe information, the more fringe information they would see, until finally they aren't reading any factual news at all. Even if the only change we made was to ensure people see actual, real information, that alone could be enough to swing the vote. This is education, not manipulation."

Igloo's chest felt like it was being crushed. There *was* something to what Angie was saying. But it was massively wrong to keep that power hidden. It was too important for Angie and Igloo to be solely responsible. It was the difference between peer-reviewed and junk science. Between open source and closed. This demanded nothing less than total transparency.

"We should have thought about this when we were designing Tapestry in the first place," Igloo said. "Instead of federating and decentralizing the feed selection algorithms, we should have kept control over them. Then we could openly tweak the algorithms to favor reliable news sources but do it in a peer-reviewed way."

Angie raised one eyebrow. "So you *are* in favor of showing people factual stories."

"Yes, obviously. But you're going about it the wrong way. Secretly changing the algorithm behind the scenes isn't the same as being public about it. People think they can choose their own feed selectors. If people find out that we're secretly manipulating what they'll see, when they think they're in charge, there will be riots."

"Do you have an alternative?" Angie asked. "Because I'm open to other ideas."

"We work with everyone implementing a feed selector. Get them to choose filters for reliable news sources voluntarily."

"Then people will change their feed provider. They'll go with someone else who will show them the fringe stuff they want."

"We make it an explicit part of the provider contract," Igloo said. "They must bias in favor of reliable data if they want to be part of Tapestry."

"Then we'll end up in a quagmire over what constitutes reliable data. We'll be taken to court. People will fight us. It's better if they just don't know."

Igloo's head was tight with tension. She didn't want to do it Angie's way, but she didn't see any alternatives. They had backed themselves into a corner. Damn, but it was hot in here. She pulled off her sweatshirt and tossed it on top of a box.

Angie grabbed her arm. "What is this?"

Igloo looked down, couldn't see anything.

"What?"

"These bruises. On your back."

Oh, fuck. Did she still have marks from her last play? Essie had topped her a few nights ago and used a cane on her shoulder. It had been lovely, but the impact left brutal welts.

"They're nothing." She shrugged away from Angie.

"Don't nothing me. I know what it looks like when someone's been hit."

Igloo's stomach knotted itself. "It's not like that."

"Who did this to you?"

"Nobody did this to me."

"You're going to tell me you fell down a staircase? Don't play dumb with me. Who did this?"

"It's not what you think, Angie." Igloo took a deep breath. Oh fuck. Why did this have to come up now, of all times? "I..." She paused. Swallowed. She felt like she was about to step off a cliff. "I like to..."

She had to just get it out. Why was this so embarrassing and awkward? "I like to be hit, okay? And I like to hit people, too. I know that has to be confusing for you, given everything you've been through. But nobody is being abused."

Angie stared, her face a little pale. "This has to do with those clubs you've been going to."

"Shit. You're spying on me."

"I have to keep an eye on you. For operational security. Nothing too close, but I need to keep us safe."

"I'm not one of your victims. I don't need saving," Igloo said. "I know how to take care of myself."

"Do you?" Angie slid the tank aside. "You're black and blue. You have welts everywhere."

"It's play," Igloo said, pulling away, and putting her back to the wall. "It's fun. It's a release. It's taking—"

"*Fun?*" Angie said. "It's mixed up in your head. You're justifying what's being done to you. Essie did this?"

"It's not about Essie. It's no one in particular. Sometimes I'm the top, sometimes I'm the bottom. This is how I play with people. I like the cathartic release of being beaten. I like letting go of control, letting someone else be in charge. But honestly, I don't spend all day psychoanalyzing myself. It's just the way I'm wired, and I accept this about myself."

"Wired? Or conditioned to associate abuse with love?"

"Oh, Jeez. It's not abuse. It has as much in common with abuse as practicing judo has with a street mugging." Oh God, now she was quoting that old boyfriend. "We're consenting adults, fully aware of what we're doing."

"Who is he?" Angie said. "Just tell me. I can figure it out in five minutes."

"Damn it, you're not my mother. Besides, I haven't been into guys in a long while, and you know that. That alone should tell you you're reacting irrationally. Think about it."

That gave Angie a moment's pause, but she shrugged and started typing.

"It's not one person. I have multiple partners. Essie, yes. But also Charlotte. And others occasionally."

Angie stopped typing.

"We're kinky. That's all. Everyone has their kinks. Bondage, animal play, impact, D/s. It's not abuse. I get hit because I like the feeling it gives me. I feel alive, scared, hurt, excited, sexy, vulnerable, and even powerful. I get to choose who can do what to me. I get all the feelings, and they're all dialed up to eleven. It's amazing."

Igloo dropped into the chair next to Angie and stared at her. "Look, didn't you ever do something crazy? Bungee jumping? Sky diving? Drive too fast? Date someone exciting just because you wanted to experience wild and crazy?"

Angie sat back, took her hand away from the keyboard.

Igloo took a deep breath. "I realize what it must look like to you, which is part of why I've been hesitant to come out. But it shares only a superficial similarity with abuse. I'm really totally fine, and I'm not ashamed of what I'm doing."

Angie still didn't speak.

"This is me we're talking about," Igloo said. "Do you really think I'd let someone else boss me around?"

"I didn't think I could," Angie said, her mouth tight. "But it happened to me just the same."

Angie's first husband. Duh. Igloo shouldn't have said that.

"I'm sorry. I know abuse. I've been abused. Trust me. We've worked together for years. This is not abuse. I know it must look bad from the outside. But the people I play with talk about what we want, we learn about what we're going to do, we assess the risk and do what we can to mitigate it.

"Homosexuality was once considered a mental illness and now it's accepted as normal. BDSM is in the same boat. There's scientific research to support that the people who practice it are healthy, happy, and well-adjusted."

"I'm not completely clueless," Angie said. "But there's also plenty of abuse under the guise of BDSM."

"That is absolutely true, but that's not the case with me. No one is manipulating me into anything. I do this because I enjoy it. And you might like this least of all, but I top most of the time."

Angie stared, obviously not getting it.

"I'm usually the one doing the tying or the hitting."

Angie whacked Igloo's can of coffee off the table. It flew across the container, striking the wall. A pool of coffee poured out and spread across the floor. Angie's whole body was shaking, and she curled up on herself.

"How can you do this, knowing how I feel?"

Igloo stared at the growing puddle in shock. She'd seen Angie angry, really fucking angry, but she'd never seen her lose control like that.

"This isn't about you, Angie. I didn't *choose* this any more than I chose to like women. This is just who I am. Believe me, it makes life complicated. Interesting, but complicated."

"You should get therapy."

Igloo stood back up. "Kink *is* my therapy. I like who I am. I'm taking back what happened to me. I'm not being a freak about this. Lots of kinky people are survivors. Part of being in a scene, for some people, is recreating what happened to them, regaining control and ownership of themselves. I can't undo what happened to me when I was a kid, but I can change my relationship to it now."

"How does putting yourself back in the same situation equal therapy? That's not improvement. That's...sick."

"It's like desensitization therapy. If you're scared of spiders, you'd spend time looking at pictures of spiders, and getting okay with that. Once that no longer triggered you, you'd watch some videos of spiders. When that no longer triggered a fight or flight response, you'd hold a dead spider. Then someday progress to being in the same room with a caged spider. Eventually, if everything went well, you'd hold a live spider in your hand. You'd master the relationship you have with spiders. BDSM's a lot like that."

Angie shook her head. "If you were bitten by a poisonous spider, would you recommend being bitten by more poisonous spiders to aid in recovery? No."

"I'm talking about recovering from psychological trauma, not physical illness." Igloo sighed. "Look, I'm fine with this, and it's not a problem. You don't have to like it, just accept it."

"I can't."

"Look, you don't even have to accept it, you just have to accept that it's really none of your business. It's what I choose to do with my life."

Angie shook her head.

Igloo sighed. It wasn't her responsibility to open up Angie's thinking, but if she didn't try, she knew this would form a rift between them, and then they wouldn't be able to work together. "What do you need to be convinced?"

"Show me the data."

"There's not a lot." Igloo knew there were only a handful of studies. She'd read them all.

"That's okay. Show me what there is. Give me something to convince me."

Part of Igloo wanted to say that it wasn't her job, that Angie could go look it up herself. But that wasn't how relationships worked. Angie wasn't some irrelevant stranger. They needed each other. In this case, Angie was operating at a deficit because she had her own substantial emotional baggage to deal with. That meant that Igloo would have to help.

"Fine. I'll dig some stuff up. Now can we get back to plotting to take over the world? Tell me more about your plan to brainwash the sheep."

"It's exposing the truth," Angie said, "not brainwashing the sheep."

Igloo raised her eyebrows.

"Okay, fine. Call it brainwashing the sheep. Here's what happens..."

CHAPTER 15

A ngie pulled up to the curb.

Igloo put her hand on the door to get out and turned to Angie. She looked like she'd aged in just the short time they'd been in the shipping container. She made like she was going to say something, then shook her head and got out.

Angie watched Igloo cross the street. She'd known Igloo would take it hard. But there just wasn't any other option. Igloo needed to know in order to carry on the work. Igloo also had the project for the onion network running over Tapestry clients. She wondered how long it would take before Igloo would put two and two together. If they were manipulating the feed, they'd choose the stories people saw. But if they controlled the data conduit by which information came to their computer, then they'd control everything anyone saw.

But that was a tool of last resort, if all else failed, and they couldn't steer this country back to a more reasonable course using less intrusive methods.

Angie felt like the future was unfolding in her mind, multiple paths based on contingencies, some decision points within her scope of control, others reactions to the inevitable government interference.

Igloo's project was just one advance move that would morph into the second generation of Tapestry.

Was Igloo even the right choice for her backup? The revelation about Igloo's behavior left a pit in her stomach. Igloo, of all people. Sexualizing violence. Allowing herself to be hurt. Hurting others. How could she?

Igloo's choices were unstable. Dangerous.

Angie thought she knew Igloo, and figured she'd be able to trust her to make the same decisions she would, if it ever came to that. But that was false. Igloo wouldn't make the same choices. But could she still trust her to make the *right* choices if the time came, even if they weren't Angie's choices? That was the key question.

But if not Igloo, then who? Other people could potentially be the technical leader that T2 needed. But if push came to shove, Igloo, like Angie, could do *more*. She had the skills and the drive to do whatever it took to ensure success, whether that was hacking a competitor or manipulating the government.

Angie made a U-turn, drove the car back through the warren of side-streets, and left it across the street from a lot filled with old cars. She walked back to her own car, still parked near the coffee shop, and drove home.

Igloo would have to do. At least for now. Let her prove that she was stable and sane.

Before she even opened the door, she heard the heavy thump of EBM booming inside the house. The acoustic assault was even worse inside.

"Thomas!"

No answer.

"Thomas!"

Sigh.

"Katie, shut that racket off."

The music faded away, thanks to her open-source home automation assistant. Thomas had wanted one of the brand name variations, but there was no way she'd accept that security risk. So she was running the one open source assistant that the EFF endorsed. That Tapestry provided nearly a quarter of the EFF's operating budget last year was, thus far, a well-kept secret.

"Hey." Thomas came into the room with VR goggles around his neck and a racquet in his hand. Sweat poured down his face.

"Whoa, back away, Mr. Athlete." Angie took two steps back as Thomas came in for a hug, then ducked under his arm.

"Morning, sweetie. I love you. How's Igloo?"

She sighed. After several years of keeping most of her life a secret from Thomas, between the hacking and the killing, she'd vowed to stop keeping secrets. She'd never come fully clean about her past, but she'd given him the gist of things, minus the killing of abusers. Since then, her work with Igloo had largely taken the form of educating victims, giving them assets and a way out, and providing enough evidence to get their abusers convicted. She'd given Thomas the general lay of the land, hinting at but being vague about the exact nature of their hacking activities.

He wasn't thrilled that his wife might go to jail at any time, but he supported her reasons for doing it. Still, he was lousy about operational security, so she kept him out of the loop on the specifics.

She put her finger on his lips to remind him. "Igloo's good," she said, for the benefit of any would-be listeners. "We went for coffee, talked about work."

She took every precaution possible to keep their house sanitized, but the proliferation of embedded connected computers was a privacy nightmare. If she could, her home would be free of the internet of things. But Thomas wanted the latest gadgets, and the truth was that it would be suspicious if her home was too thoroughly sanitized. So she settled for zones of security. The highest security stuff was off premises, in safe houses like the shipping container. But even here she had a small space. The walk-in closet in her home office had been transformed into a Faraday cage with a wrapping of copper mesh embedded into the plaster and extending onto the door. A double layer of acoustic batting provided sound isolation. She couldn't do much from there to disguise her data traffic, but she could bring encrypted disk images home, work on code and data in the closet, and then squirt it back out onto the Internet when she had safe access.

"Speaking of work," Thomas said, "how big a deal is that Tapestry party next month? Do I need to get a new outfit?"

"You're asking me about clothes?" Angie would wear a t-shirt and jeans every day if she could get away with it. She relied on twice annual shopping trips with Emily, who would stockpile her with the basic feminine clothing suitable for her position, which she would dutifully wear. "Ask Emily."

"Katie, message Emily, what should I wear to the Tapestry party?"

"Message sent," Katie answered.

Angie decided she should do the same. "Katie, message Emily. Me too. Need clothes, help."

"Did you eat yet?" Thomas asked, as he walked over to the refrigerator.

"No," Angie said, dreading the hassle of eating. She had too much work to do.

"You go work or do whatever you need, and I'll put something together."

Angie stepped up to Thomas, wiped the sweat off his face with a dish towel, then she pulled him close for a kiss.

"What's that for?"

"For taking care of me. I feel like I leave you on your own all the time, and then I come home, and you just take care of me. Sometimes I feel like I don't give you enough in return."

"I'm happy to take care of you."

"It's hard for me to accept. You know, equality and all that."

"Equality means we have equal rights to have our needs met, not that all people have identical needs. You need to be fed, I need someone to take care of. It's all good."

"Well, I appreciate it."

"I know." He smiled his lovely warm smile.

CHAPTER 16

I gloo stared at the front door. Her head was crammed with thoughts about Angie's totally unhinged plan to manipulate the election. Now, still sleep deprived, head spinning with confusion, she had to come home and face Essie.

She'd been spending her time in a downward spiral of negative thoughts, her mind a maelstrom of jealousy, envy, insecurity, and fear. Things couldn't go on like this.

She took a deep breath, and the door suddenly opened.

Essie smiled at her. "Coming in?"

Igloo worked up the energy for a smile and a hug.

"Lunch will be ready in a second. Get cleaned up and have a seat. I'm just going to put the eggs in the water."

"Eggs? Like real eggs?" Was she serious? She washed up, then sat at the dining room table and sipped the coffee waiting for her. She pulled out her phone, looked at all the morning's notifications. The automated test suite had found some new corner cases in her code. Most of them were meaningless—the new test AI caused numerous false alarms, but buried somewhere in there would be real issues that could cause failures in the field if Igloo didn't address them.

A few minutes later, Essie set down an egg sandwich on a toasted croissant.

Igloo set down her phone. Wow, Essie really had been serious about eggs. Why the sudden change of heart?

Essie topped off Igloo's coffee and adjusted the symmetry of the place setting so everything was in alignment, then took a seat next to Igloo.

Without the electronic distraction, all her messy feelings started to bubble up. She stared at her plate, food perfectly and artfully arranged. Her heart sank. Essie clearly had gone to some special length for Igloo, even cooked eggs for her instead of the usual vegan fare, and now Igloo was going to ruin everything. But she just couldn't be quiet any longer.

"I need some boundaries around what you're doing with Michael," Igloo blurted out. "Just temporarily. Until I can get a handle on my feelings."

Essie carefully set her coffee on the table. "What sort of boundaries?"

"No sleepovers. They're too painful for me to handle. I miss you too much, and I worry about you."

"I've already had sleepovers, and now you want me to go back on that? That's awkward."

"It's not permanent." Igloo hated the pleading in her voice. Why couldn't she be stronger? "Just give me a few weeks to get used to the idea."

"You're never going to get used to it if I'm not doing it. Look, this week wasn't as bad as last week."

Igloo couldn't meet Essie's gaze. She wanted to just lay down the law, but she was afraid Essie would leave if she tried. What happened to the Igloo who took charge? Where was Igloo the dominant? "You don't understand how much pain I'm in. Just coping with dates is hard enough. Why do you have to have sleepovers?"

"He gets off work late, and it takes time to set up the welding equipment, get everything prepped. Then we're hungry and tired."

"Maybe you could try sleeping," Igloo mumbled, then instantly regretted it.

Essie shook her head. "Look, do you want me to drive home at three or four in the morning, half asleep? Seems like a recipe for an accident."

"Why can't you just go on a regular date and come home by a reasonable hour? That's what normal people do."

"We're welding and eating burgers and cuddling. There's not even sex."

"Burgers? What kind of burgers? Meat burgers?"

"Yes, I guess they are meat," Essie said.

"Jesus fucking Christ. I've been eating vegan with you for the past nine months, trying to get you to eat meat with me, and you know him for a month, and you're eating burgers with him?!"

"He said I should try it, so I did."

Fucking fuckity fuck. *He said. Try it.*

"When you say 'He said I should try it,' you mean like in a D/s context?" Igloo held her head. Why couldn't the pain just be over?

"Oh, come on," Essie said. "Are we going to pick apart every sentence we exchange?"

"Just tell me."

"It's not a D/s game. The burger smelled good, so I tried it. I liked it. End of story."

Igloo took a deep breath. She felt like Essie was leaving something out, but she had no idea what. There was more going on than she was revealing.

CHAPTER 17

C yber Command was two floors down and half a building away from Enso's office, but he'd rarely been down there. They were, for the most part, compartmentalized from other aspects of the intelligence community.

Enso and Alice walked down together, went through a security review, then entered the Cyber Command suite.

Colonel Benson was the officer in charge. Enso and Alice were escorted to her office. They entered to find her already in discussion with another officer. They both stood and shuffled around the small space to make room for Enso and Alice.

"Colonel Benson," Enso said. "Glad to meet you."

He held out his hand, and Benson hesitated long enough to send the message that Enso was beneath her before taking his hand. Enso didn't care. It happened all the time. People didn't like back channel influence. But you can't have a super black agency and official lines of communication.

"This is my second in command, Alice."

Benson shook hands with Alice.

"I'm sorry, Ma'am," Alice said. "I know your people must be busy."

"Busy is irrelevant," Benson said. We're the first, second, and third line of defense against cyberattack. Taking people offline for this *training exercise* is hazardous."

"I know, Ma'am. We'll try to keep it short."

Benson shook her head. "This is Major Williams. He's in charge of Bravo team."

"Shall we head down to meet the rest of the team?" Williams said.

They followed him down a hall. "Alpha and Bravo alternate lead to allow for breaks and background tasks," Williams explained. "There's no difference in experience or skills. Bravo will work on your program while Alpha has lead. If anything comes up, of course, we'll get retasked."

"Understood," Enso said. "You know about our target?"

"Angelina Benenati. Alice gave us a briefing, and we've been working on her since the start of this shift. I expect we'll have something for you by the time we get to my office."

Enso shook his head. "Nothing personal, Major, but Angie is beyond difficult. I suspect it'll take longer than that."

Williams chuckled. "Sir, you don't understand what Cyber Command is capable of." He stopped laughing and turned serious. "By the way, you can use what we learn of course, but not a word of how we obtain our data can leave here."

Enso nodded. "Understood. You seem a bit more enthusiastic than your boss."

"Benson's a stickler for rules. The reality is, everyone's got people they watch. Ex-wives, girlfriends, parents, kids. We can see everything. If we've got it, we should use it, right?"

They arrived at a door, which Williams opened with a scan card. This end of the room was raised, and held a large desk, with a half dozen screens and several phones. The remainder, a couple of steps down, consisted of rows of identical desks, each staffed. A soft buzz of quiet discussion permeated the room.

When Williams entered, an officer at the raised desk stood, and waited next to the desk.

"You have a report, Jack?"

"Several. Office, home, subject, and recent activities. Which would you like first?"

Williams turned to Enso.

Surely this was a joke. They couldn't have penetrated her defenses that quickly. "Recent activities?" Enso said.

Jack handed a tablet to Enso. "Subject left her house to meet one of her employees for coffee this morning at a shop on the edge of industrial district."

"Are you sure she was really there?" Enso said. "She often—"

The officer leaned over, swiped the tablet to the next screen. An oblique photo clearly showed Angie and Igloo.

"Oh. That's good. Did you get that from a UAV?"

"Chinese satellite," Williams said. "But don't repeat that. They have more birds up there, at a lower attitude. We like to borrow cycles from them."

Enso was so blown away, for a moment he wished they were seated. He thought he knew everything. This was unprecedented.

"The next part gets good. Angie's car, here," Jack revealed another image on the tablet, "continues signal emissions consistent with Igloo and Angie inside the coffee shop. But they never entered. They went for a walk instead." Another photo, showing them side by side.

"Angie chose the neighborhood well. There was almost nothing we could piggyback on. Few security cameras, almost no cars on the street, no radios. Compared to a residential or business district, it's desert wasteland."

Jack showed a few other long range shots. "We got maybe fifteen seconds of audio as they walked by a car. Listen."

The audio recording was almost entirely hiss and warbling. Then he heard a few muffled words, then more hiss and warbling.

"I don't hear anything useful," Enso said.

"Yeah, well, we're just human," Jack said. "But machine learning can do it. Here's the transcript."

Igloo: "—news for the entire country. Entire world."
Angie: "We can, and we have to."
Igloo: "You're out of your mind."
<3.6 second pause>
Angie: "I'm right, and you know it. You just don't want—"

"That's all you got?" Enso said.

"Hey, we're hijacking a car audio microphone designed to pick up what's inside the car and using that to listen through the glass, and still managed to pick them up when they were thirty feet away. If it had been an ordinary street, with a row of cars, we'd have continuous coverage, obviously."

"Then what?" Enso said.

"Well, then we lose them for a long while. Two hours. If they stayed in the neighborhood, they must've walked a really odd path to avoid coverage. We think they left."

"*Think* they left? What happened to the satellite oversight?"

"We can only borrow the Chinese satellites for thirty seconds as a time, and we didn't catch anything on our birds. But we know there was a car parked under a tree in the vicinity of where they were walking, and for ninety minutes, that car disappears, then comes back. Presumably they took the car, drove somewhere, came back. Shortly after that, Angie goes home in the vehicle she originally arrived in."

Jack pulled up a set of timestamped photographs. Every photo looked the same to Enso, just a tree with heavy foliage. A second set of photos had the same tree, with a yellow, car-shaped outline in part of it.

Enso looked up at Jack.

"More machine learning," Jack said. "I can't see the car either. You have to learn to trust the machine. Look, I'd sum up the morning as *she got lucky*. If we had coverage at the right moment, we would have gotten a look at the car, then we could have correlated it with other photos, figured out where she went."

Enso tried not to show the disappointment he felt. The truth was that these people had achieved vastly more in far less time than his team. "This is good work. This is all covered under cyber warfare?"

Williams shook his head. "Everyone here has done rotations in different commands. Some did drone duty, some supported field operations, some worked SIGINT. We're heavily cross-trained. If someone interferes electronically with a drone mission or troops on the ground, we're ready to pick up the pieces and take over."

"What about her home and office?"

"We have a ton of goodies there," Jack said. "I assume you already know about the Faraday closet in her house?"

"Yes but how did you figure it out so quickly?

"We plotted the signal strength to and from every wireless device on her block and the next one over. There's a hole there. Doesn't look that much different than a refrigerator, but the signal attenuation is a little stronger, a little bigger. I'm guessing she does her dirty work in there."

Jack flipped to a new window on the tablet. "We have live feeds from a couple of devices in her house. She's got a digital assistant. It's a secure one, but we compromised the underlying operating system. She has a couple of webcams that we got into, but she keeps them physically covered. On the other hand, the two security cams for the front and back doors are not covered, and we did compromise those."

"This is bad," Alice said. "Angie has detected every bug we've ever planted, every device we've ever compromised. We stopped because of that. Just because you got in...all it's going to do is alert her."

"I figured with her background that she'd be on the lookout," Jack said. "We treated this like we would a foreign government intrusion and assumed counter-intrusion defenses. The next-door neighbor has a gas hot water heater with electronic ignition, and every time that heating element kicks on, it generates a little EMF buzz. We're going to amplify that buzz a bit, and we're going to route the data out the opposite side of the house to the other neighbor and send it out over their internet. We're only going to be able to squirt a couple of megabytes each time the heating element turns on, but it'll be enough for an audio feed from the digital assistant, and a few photos from the security cams. I can guarantee she won't detect our transmission. It'll look like noise from the hot water unit."

"This is good stuff," Enso said. "What about the office?"

"We have the employee list, and we're backtracking them now. We'll compromise their laptops at home or coffee shops and use them to capture audio and stills in the workplace. They'll only transmit the data back to us when off-site and idle. Should be good. Then we'll run everything we capture through machine identification and see what it picks out. It'll take a few days before we're getting anything significant."

"How long can we do this for?" Enso said, turning to Williams.

"The initial setup is taking up most of Bravo team. Once we're monitoring, it'll just take a couple of people to keep it running. We can watch for a couple of weeks. But no reports leave this room. You can come here, get briefed, and take out a page of notes. Nothing more."

"That'll work," Alice said.

"Thank you," Enso said, and for once, he really meant it. This was beyond anything he had hoped for. Now they'd dig up something on Angie.

Enso and Alice headed back upstairs after being escorted out.

"Amazing stuff," Enso said.

Alice nodded. "The FISA court order will be delivered Monday morning. It should stir something up. We'll keep up the surveillance."

"Good. Let me know as soon as we discover anything."

ngie boarded the Monday morning flight to San Jose. As she found her row, her phone shrilled with the urgent alert reserved for the highest priority messages. Only Matt, Igloo, and Thomas could trigger that alarm. What now?

She shoved her wheelie into the overhead compartment while the phone kept screaming for attention. Everyone stared at her. She'd like to see them wrestle a bag into an overhead with one arm while their phone was ringing.

She finally settled into her seat and grabbed the phone. She had missed both calls and messages from Matt. The last one read, "Don't board the plane. Emergency! Call."

She let out a long sigh and looked up toward the ceiling. Getting up early for a flight she didn't particularly want was disheartening. Doing that for no reason whatsoever... She called him.

"What's going on?" she asked, after he answered.

"The government's here. A bunch of them. They sequestered Amber and Maria in the executive office suite. You need to get back right now."

Angie's throat caught, despite herself. She ran down the options: her past, her current hacking projects, something having to do with

Tapestry, maybe the FISA court order, or something unknown. If it had anything to do with past or current hacking projects, then they'd pick her up in person, right? They'd have no reason to go to Tapestry and talk to Amber and Maria. Still, there was always a chance.

"Any word on what it's about?" She tried to remain calm. Had she kissed Thomas goodbye this morning?

"They wouldn't say anything to me. I called Schwartz and Associates, and they have someone on their way."

"Tell Amber to stall. Say nothing, agree to nothing, give them nothing."

"They won't let me anywhere near the room."

"I'm on my way. Try to get her a message."

She forced her way back off the plane, enduring more dirty looks from the other passengers, and took a carshare from the airport. She sent Amber several messages en route but didn't get any response. She took slow breaths. She was a little shook up, but she needed to walk into that room cool and collected. She'd faced worse than this many times. If they wanted her imprisoned, they would have come directly after her. The most likely scenario was that they were fishing for something, but didn't have anything. That, or a court order.

Matt met her at the front door and took her suitcase. "They're still in the exec room."

She headed up there, mentally taking inventory. Nothing incriminating on her. Phone encrypted. All hacking assets secured as usual. Time to channel her old mentor, Repard. She felt a curtain descend over her, an invisible layer, remoteness. She controlled what came in, what went out. Repard had taught her to fool a polygraph as reliably as an investigator. She approached the meeting room with a fake but believable small smile.

She held up her hand as she approached the room and addressed the two people guarding it. "Sir. Ma'am." No reason not to be polite. "I'm Angie Benenati, CEO. I'm needed inside."

"Go ahead, Ma'am."

She entered the room, and everyone inside turned to look at her.

There were three people in dark suits. Those would presumably be government agents. On the other side of the table, Amber and Maria, their faces grim. Carter Schwartz, son of David Schwartz, owner of their law firm, rounded out the table. His forehead was creased with tension.

Amber looked up. "Finally. You can deal with these people."

The man in the center of the suits cleared his throat. "I'm Agent Haldor, Ms. Benenati. Glad you can join us. I'll bring you up to speed. I'm here representing the U.S. Government, and we've served Tapestry with a FISA court order to provide access to Tapestry's database for matters of national security."

Angie didn't know whether to laugh or cry. They weren't here to arrest her. That was the main thing.

It was only a matter of time before the FISA court order arrived. It meant Tapestry was in the big leagues now, along with companies like Tomo and Avogadro. The government wanted the same back-doors installed on Tapestry's servers that allowed the NSA to monitor everyone else's data.

"I'd like to talk to my attorney without you present," Angie said.

"That's fine," Agent Haldor said, "but before I leave the room let me caution you that the terms of the FISA court order prohibit you from disclosing any details of the court order, including its existence and any associated data, to anyone other than those required to implement the court order and who are approved by the FISA court. At this time, that includes yourself and the executive leadership, the chairman of your board of directors, and Mr. Schwartz. Compliance with the terms of this court order is considered a matter of national security and carries aggressive penalties. Don't pick up the phone and call anyone, don't send messages to your employees, don't speak to the press. Basically, don't talk to anyone. Are we clear on this?"

Angie nodded. "Yes, perfectly clear."

She waited for the government people to leave. The door shut behind them with a thunk.

Maria let out a small breath.

Amber's jaw was set. "I saw the look on your face. You knew this was going to happen this morning."

Angie shook her head. "I didn't, but I suspected as soon as I got Matt's message." She paced the room as she looked at Carter Schwartz. "What are our options for response?"

"Nobody is supposed to talk about FISA court orders," Carter said, "but people do, obviously. Every big tech player is hit with the same order eventually, giving the government blanket access to their data. We can appeal if you want, but no FISA appeal has ever succeeded, to the best of my knowledge. Nevertheless, Schwartz and Associates recommends that Tapestry appeal the ruling so that, if it should ever be made public in the future, you can show you defended user privacy to the best of your ability."

"You all know what's going on?" Maria asked. "I've never heard of FISA court orders before."

Angie glanced at her. Maria had two highly regarded stints managing IT organizations; one in the military and one at a Fortune 100 company, but none would have dealt with user data on the level that would involve FISA.

"The Foreign Intelligence Surveillance Court," Angie said. "The whole Snowden thing. Widespread spying by the US government via backdoors in all the major Internet companies. That's all ruled by the FISA court. In theory, it's supposed to be an impartial judicial process. In practice, the court proceedings are secret and there's no higher level appeal process. It's a joke. Everyone is forced to comply with what the government wants."

"We knew it had to come sooner or later," Amber said. "Apparently three hundred million users are enough to attract their attention."

"Carter, how long do we have to comply?" Angie gestured toward the court order, an actual paper document, sitting in front of Carter.

"Thirty days to turn over design documents, sixty to have pipelines in place, ninety days to be in full compliance."

"Can we get an extension, based on the complexity of our federated design?"

"I wouldn't count on it," Carter said. "The first thing we have to turn over is the data architecture. Whatever data Tapestry holds or touches, they're going to require access to. Doesn't matter what the complexity is. They'll want the raw information."

Angie had been waiting for this day, had counter-measures planned.

"Only the data Tapestry, the company, has access to," Angie said. "But if it's only ever on the user's computer, inside the Tapestry client, then we're not responsible for providing access to it."

Carter nodded hesitantly.

"If Tapestry processes everything on the user's computer, and doesn't ever expose any data in the clear to our servers, then there'd be nothing for us to provide to the government, right?"

Carter's eyes widened in doubtful disbelief. "There's always some data in the clear. Metadata of some type. Connections that have to be established. But regardless of that, even the encrypted traffic has to be provided to the government. If we can decrypt it, we have to provide it in plaintext. If we can't—if there are client-side keys we don't possess, then we provide the encrypted bytes to the government, and they take their best shot at decrypting it."

Angie ignored his response. "What happened with SparkleParty?"

"SparkleParty?" Carter gazed off into the distance. "Event based photo sharing social media site, right?"

Angie nodded.

"Well, what I heard via the grapevine," Carter said, "is that they got hit with a court order to open up their data. So they encrypted everything on the client-side. But the court found them in contempt of the order, because it appeared they were encrypting specifically to circumvent the court order. Why?"

"Then what happened?" Angie asked.

"They didn't comply, and were shut down for thirty days. They lost their user base. They moved to comply with the original court order, but by then it was too late. I think they were sold for pennies on the dollar, compared to what they were worth just a few months earlier.

Angie sat back and inspected her nails.

Amber cleared her throat. "Carter, please excuse us."

Angie shook her head. "Not now. We'll discuss it after the government leaves."

Agent Haldor stayed long enough for one of his companions, a DHS lawyer, to go over the timeline and review the details surrounding the implementation. The third government agent was a software architect, who would be their liaison during the implementation.

Carter Schwartz packed his things shortly after the government folks left. "I'll talk to Dad, but honestly my friends at EFF will know more. I'll get in touch with them."

"Let me walk you to the door," Angie said.

When they reached the conference room door, Angie drew Carter close. "If it goes public that Tapestry is bound by a FISA court order, they'll believe we released the information intentionally. If they determine that you've talked to anyone, they'll go after you, specifically."

"Everyone I talk to will be bound under a confidentially agreement."

"Not good enough," Angie said. "By all means, talk to your friends. The EFF are good people. But do it anonymously. They have channels for that. Your friends will appreciate plausible deniability. This might have originated in a FISA court, but the government will go to great lengths to protect their secrets. With everything that Snowden leaked, the government wants to avoid the limelight more than ever."

Carter looked as if he might say more, but after a moment his shoulders drooped. "You're right. We're in dangerous territory."

Then it was just Angie, Amber, and Maria.

"Matt, please bring lunch for us," Angie sent by message. "Take care of the details."

"You want to invite Igloo?" Amber asked. "Can we even include her? Or do we need to tell the government first?"

Angie frowned dismissively. "No, what I have to say needs to stay with just us. It's on a need to know basis, and up until this morning, nobody besides me needed to know. Now you two need to know."

"Fine. Then tell us what's going on." Amber said.

Angie looked back and forth between Maria and Amber. She'd put off telling anyone the whole picture because if the government knew what she was planning they'd stop her.

They'd stopped dozens, maybe hundreds, of lesser known projects from going public. A little leverage, at just the right time, the right threats or incentives. Then suddenly that new personal security kickstarter disappears. Not to mention the wi-fi router that disguised connections. Mesh networks that hid origination points. Encryption software. Secure email. All those projects, and countless others, disappeared from the net. What happened to them?

Angie shook her head. It was time to stop daydreaming. She needed Amber and Maria onboard.

"Give me a second."

She pulled a boxy smartphone out of her bag. That clunky custom case wasn't just a rugged layer of protection. It provided room for a few additional sensors: a wide spectrum programmable radio, and high fidelity acoustic sensors. She looked around the room. The government agents had just been here. It wasn't even worth scanning it now. It would take too much time. She'd come back tonight and sanitize the room, maybe bring Igloo and teach her a few more tricks.

"Let's go to my office. I don't feel safe here."

Maria gathered her stuff without complaint.

"Not this again," Amber mumbled.

Angie ignored her. Amber had mostly been in the dark since two years ago. She didn't know about Angie's hacking activities, and mostly just thought Angie was paranoid. Of course, even the paranoid have enemies.

They trooped down the hall, entered Angie's office. She triggered a scan from the room's built in sensors. All clear. She switched on a white noise generator that put out an audible hiss and inaudible EMF noise. She pulled the double layer of copper-mesh-laced curtains closed. She opened a metal bin and gestured for everyone to put their devices inside.

Amber complied with a sigh. Maria looked puzzled at first but followed suit. Angie closed the lid, and they gathered around her conference table.

"What I'm going to tell you doesn't leave this room. It doesn't get talked about with anyone else. It definitely doesn't get committed to any electronic trail. No emails or messages about it. I need your agreement before we go on."

Maria tilted her head and stared at Angie, her eyes wide. "Are you going to tell me something illegal? I can't agree to become your accomplice without knowing what I'm getting into."

Amber waited for Angie's response.

"I'm not sure," Angie finally said. "Maybe. Look, I knew the FISA court order would come sooner or later. But privacy and user control over their data is a fundamental human right. I have a plan that keeps our users' data private, that I believe conforms to the FISA court order and applicable laws, but the government isn't going to like it. They'll try to fight us."

"Damn it," Amber said, her voice choked up. "Tomo is about to topple. In another few months at the current rate, we'll surpass them. We've worked day and night to achieve what seemed impossible two years ago. Do you really want to risk all that by pissing off the government? Tapestry is a good system, a really good system. You want perfect. Perfect is the enemy of good. We will lose everything because you want to pursue a pipe dream."

"This is our only opportunity," Angie said. "If we try it down the road, the government will view it as deliberate obstruction. It'll never pass then. We have to do it now."

"The Daily Journal," Amber said. "Do you want to become like them?"

The President had had a vendetta against The Daily Journal. After he took office, the FBI coincidentally pursued an investigation, finding dozens of obscure federal regulation violations ultimately leading to a court order that suspended operations of the venerable paper until investigations were completed. Months later, with no advertising revenue, no subscription revenue, and an entire staff occupied with increasingly detailed subpoenas for additional data, the paper was near bankruptcy. Every attempt by a would-be white knight to rescue the company was blocked in one way or the other, until a media mogul bought the paper at a fraction of the original asking price and turned it into yet another puppet media outlet.

All true, all real. Still.

"All the more reason to see my plan through to completion. If we don't do something, we'll just be another tool at the government's disposal. If we do this right, we're going to lay down the groundwork for true internet privacy. We have to try. If anything goes wrong, I'll take the brunt of the blame." She stared at Amber. "You know that."

Amber, arms crossed, reluctantly nodded. "True."

"I want to know," Maria said. "I won't tell anyone without us agreeing on it first."

Angie had known Maria six months. She was the new kid on the block, relatively speaking.

They'd spent a three-day weekend together before Angie hired her. One day, holed up in Tapestry's offices, talking with employees, strategizing. Another with Igloo and Amber, ending with a dinner party with their significant others. Finally, a day-long hike in the gorge, just the two of them. Not normally Angie's style. She mostly liked to stick to where the Internet connection was good. But she'd wanted a day away from electronics and the world, to get in touch with who Maria really was.

Every employee hired in the beginning was scrutinized, measured for personal commitment to the company's vision. The most technically competent person would be rejected in a heartbeat if they weren't committed to Tapestry's social mission. It was Igloo who had coined their hiring mantra that it was better to take one step in the right direction than five in the wrong direction.

If those early hires were essential, then it was even more important that someone in Maria's position, who would handle day-to-day affairs so that Angie could work on big picture stuff, be absolutely in line with what the company wanted. Angie believed she fit the bill. While her interpersonal style differed from Angie's—she was more hands-on—she'd continued to reinforce the original culture. It was all on the line today. Either she trusted Maria or she didn't.

"Well, spit it out already," Amber said.

"With the inevitability of the FISA court order," Angie started, "and the lack of any legal recourse, I realized it was only a matter of time before we'd have to turn over our user data to the government. If the only government requests for data were legitimate ones, most people would not complain. If data collection stopped terrorists or caught criminals, that would be the moral thing to do. But as we've seen again and again, the reality is that governments abuse their access, the wrong people get the data. Security is weakened for everyone when there are backdoors. The right thing to do is find a way to keep everyone's data private. The only way to do that, given that the government is uninterested in ensuring privacy, is a technical solution. An approach which ensures we have no information to turn over, while still offering Tapestry as a service."

"We're not newbies," Amber said. "There's always going to be something the government can read. We can't serve up content to the end user without knowing what content we're providing. Even if we encrypt over the wire so it can't be spied on by third parties, we still have to know what the user wants and provide it to them."

"Not always true." Angie stood, and paced the length of the table. "We provide end-to-end user chat that is encrypted on one user's computer, and decrypted on another, and even though it flows through our server, we don't know what either user said."

"Yes," Amber said, "but we still know that user A talked to user B."

"We can solve that a few ways," Angie said. "We can either have user A talk directly to user B—"

"That's no help," Amber said. "Not if you're trying to keep out the government. They'll spy directly on the connection. Tapestry might not have the data, but someone does: an ISP, a backbone router."

"Agreed," Angie said, "which is why the better solution is onion routing: a network in which nodes forward data for other nodes. Then it's not possible to be sure that the message A sends to be B is intended for B, or some other node."

"You're starting to lose me," Maria said.

Angie spent a few minutes explaining onion routing to Maria, catching her up on the history of TOR and other onion routing networks.

"I think I follow you," Maria said. "But if what you're saying is true, if A sends a packet of data to B, and B doesn't send the same exact packet of data to anyone else, isn't that proof that the packet was intended for B?"

Angie held up her hand, one finger raised. "Yes, but there are techniques that, when used together, can protect against that attack. First, every client decrypts and re-encrypts the packet. This makes it so that an eavesdropper can't be sure that two packets of the same length contain the same data." She raised another finger. "Second, we pad the packets so they're all the same length, which, in combination with encryption, makes it impossible to tell if any two packets might be related. Third, make sure lots and lots of packets are being forwarded. If all three things happen, then it's impossible to say which packets got forwarded and which didn't."

"That's all well and good if all you want to do is transfer bulk data," Amber said. "But we're running server-side web applications. We have to decide which feed elements to give to which people, and associate data with other data: likes, comments, comments on comments. We have to manage the visibility of data based on privacy settings. None of this can be solved simply by serving up static webpages. We can't—" Amber looked horrified. "Good grief. Please don't tell me you want to write all client-side apps."

"Not exactly," Angie said. "But—"

"Client-side apps are not feasible," Amber said. "The average piece of Tapestry content flows through sixteen systems to get from originator to consumption. We have to account for every bit of that."

"Wait," Maria said. "We already have client apps."

"Sure," Amber said, "we have client apps, but basically all the heavy lifting is done on the server. Most of the reason for even having clients is that those apps are built on top of our transport library. That's how we get IPFS and web torrent support. We improve content distribution by making all clients participate in an edge network."

"Yep, I get it." Maria said. "The IPFS content network brings so many content providers onto Tapestry because they save money by not having to host the content themselves."

"Right," Angie said. "Now let me finish. The client apps present the user interface and cache content. But what's chosen to be presented is done in the cloud, on our servers and the servers of our partners. Those servers cost money. In the same way that we benefit from moving content from the cloud to the edge, we also want to move the application logic to the edge."

"That's where I have to disagree," Amber said. "There's a reason everyone moved to the cloud. Data, metrics, deployment, control over the environment. Client software is a mess."

Angie held up her hand. Her phantom hand too, but then no one could see that.

"We're not going to run client-side software, Amber. We're going to run our regular web stack, in containers, and we're going to run those *containers* client-side," Angie said. "That's the part you don't know."

Amber rocked back in her chair, eyes narrowed in suspicion. "Full stack? RDS? Message queues?"

"Yep, everything. The biggest change to running everything client-side was how to manage accounting, analytics, and data references. How do we figure out the most popular stories? How do we calculate affinity? How do we attribute comments to the right user without invoking a central authority all while keeping as much confidential as possible? The answer is blockchain and validators."

"Not you, too." Maria rubbed her forehead. "I hear about blockchain every third news story, but no one can ever explain how to do anything useful with blockchain. I'm sick of hearing about it."

"I know, I know" Angie said. "I'll explain the details later, but the big picture is that blockchain lets us store confidential data without requiring Tapestry to be a central authority. Independent third parties, what blockchain calls auditors, are built into the client apps. The end result is that if the government, or anyone else, asks us if User A is commenting on User B's stories, we won't know. Not centrally. Only people granted visibility to User B's story would know."

"I'm totally lost," Maria said to Amber. "You're getting this?"

"Yeah, I think so," Amber said. She turned to Angie. "Walk us through a use case."

Angie took them through the steps, one by one, explaining distributed ledger systems to Maria, who had never heard of them, and how they could be used to create a tamperproof distributed database.

"Let me see if I have this straight," Maria said. "Tapestry 1.0, what everyone has been using these last couple of years, is a federated social network in which each piece of functionality is potentially delivered by a different provider. Centralized servers run the code and store user data. Those servers, plus the connections between the clients, servers, users, and content are all vulnerable to FISA court requests, which force companies to provide their data to the government."

"Right," Angie said. "Don't forget about content originating outside the Tapestry ecosystem, like news articles stored on web servers. Who connects to that server is essentially public, as is what the user accessed while on the server. It's generally tracked through cookies and log files. But in Tapestry 1.0, with IPFS, that content gets stored within a distributed content network."

"Fine," Maria said. "Now, in your proposed Tapestry 2.0, we still have all those same federated components. But the *code* runs in containers on the user's computer, so there's no centralized code. The user's *data* resides in distributed ledgers, which are visible only to preselected users. They are tamperproof, so they can't be altered maliciously, or read by unauthorized parties."

Angie nodded, and Maria continued.

"The connections between these containers use the onion routing techniques you talked about, so no one can see who is talking to whom. The content is distributed and protected via IPFS, also routed over the onion network, so we can't see who is reading what."

"You've got it," Angie said, with a big smile.

"How do we account for anything? We still need micro-transactional accounting for payments."

"Part of the distributed ledgers," Angie said. "The relevant parties expose only the transactional part to us. We don't need to know what content was sent, merely that everyone agrees that the content was sent, and that they participated in sending it. We get to see aggregate data, not individual data."

Amber shook her head. "You're crazy, you know that? How long have you been working on this?"

Angie let herself smile. "I've had people working on parts of it for months. Nobody knows what anyone else is doing. Nobody has the bigger picture because I didn't want word getting out. But the components can be combined now. We have a month of integration work to do. We can beat the FISA deadline."

Angie knew they'd be thinking over the implications for Tapestry. They still wouldn't be seeing the biggest picture yet, how this would essentially change the entire Internet. The days of centralized services and data stores would go away, to be replaced by an age of absolute security and total decentralization.

No, they wouldn't appreciate that, not yet.

But someday soon everyone, including the government, would see that. The looming fight over the future of the net would be bigger than any yet fought.

CHAPTER 19

"I'm going to be fifty soon," Angie said when she picked up Igloo in the morning. "Thomas insists I get more exercise."

"I don't see why I have to be subjected to it," said Igloo. If she was going to get exercise, she'd rather it come in the form of bedroom activity.

"Because the middle portion of the hike is signal free. Great talking opportunity if we bring an EMF sensor."

Two hours in, they were deep inside an old growth forest in the sunken crater of Larch Mountain. The sky was nearly completely blocked by towering Douglas firs, and the light took on a dusk-like quality. The conversation finally turned serious.

"Let's talk about Tapestry 2.0."

"So that's what this is all about." Igloo said.

Angie ran through a rapid explanation of the government visit, the FISA court order that mandated spying on their users, and her plan to completely decentralize Tapestry and distribute the code to user clients and browsers.

"When every component is off our servers, there will be nothing left for the FISA court order to affect."

"My work on onion routing is part of this, right? But you had me start on that months ago."

"I knew it was only a matter of time before we got a court order forcing us to provide an NSA tap. The day was coming, and we had to get started before it was too late."

"How many people are working on it?" Igloo asked.

"There are eight parallel efforts on T2," Angie said. "Client-side containers, distributed ledger, onion routing, secure updating, and data synchronization are the biggest chunks, and then some smaller pieces. Eighteen people in total. But the browser containers are FUBAR, and I'm going to need to add people to that effort."

"Eighteen people is a lot to keep a secret," Igloo said.

"Twenty now that Amber and Maria know."

"How long have they known? It seems like they've been asking me questions forever."

"They've known about some of the individual efforts. I couldn't keep the large chunks secret without them getting suspicious. But I didn't give them the bigger picture until the court order came."

Igloo experienced a pang of jealousy that she knew from experience had to do with feeling left out. She should be used to Angie keeping secrets from her, but somehow it still hurt every time. That Amber and Maria had learned about T2 first didn't make things any easier to accept.

"Why'd you tell them?" How long would it take before Angie truly trusted her? That's what she wanted to ask, but she was too afraid. She still didn't know how Angie felt about her being kinky. It hadn't come up since their last meeting, and she wasn't about to bring it up now.

"Because we need to pick up the pace, and having everyone work on components separately isn't going to help us to make the deadline. We need everything to come together before we're forced into compliance."

"That's two months. You're telling me the container technology isn't ready. Ben, Diana, and I may not be able to have the onion routing ready either."

"Shit," Angie said, breathing hard as they hiked up a steep section. "You're working with Ben and Diana? I didn't realize."

"You told me I could poach anyone I wanted. What's the big deal?"

"They're working on the distributed ledgers." Angie huffed and puffed, falling behind her as they rounded a switchback.

"They said they weren't busy." Igloo looked at the trail ahead, which just went up and up.

"I told them...not to let anyone know...what they were working on."

Igloo turned to check Angie. "You okay?"

"Yeah...just out of...breath. Can we...rest?"

Igloo nodded, and Angie leaned with her hand on her knee, breathing hard.

"This is the problem with compartmentalizing," Igloo said. "I had no idea you'd have Ben and Diana on the ledgers, or I wouldn't have approached them about the onion routing. It's not like we have thousands of engineers. We're going to collide seeking out the same few experts."

Angie nodded. "My mistake. I wanted to keep as many parts secret as long as possible. I didn't want anyone figuring out the end goal."

"But why? Secrecy comes at a cost." Igloo felt like an imposter. She kept most of her life secret from everyone around her. Kink. Poly. She was hardly a role model for transparency. Half the time she couldn't even talk honestly with Essie because she was worried about hurting her feelings.

Angie looked back and forth. Igloo followed her gaze though it was pointless. They were completely alone. Still, Angie pulled out her phone and scanned for radio frequency emissions.

Igloo tried to wait, but Angie was stressing her patience. "We're surrounded by forest on all sides, in a crater with no signal. What are you looking for?"

"They could be hitting us with satellite," Angie said. "Or have hidden devices in the woods, recording us for later transmission. Come on, let's keep hiking."

"They would have to have known where we were coming to have emplaced devices here. You didn't disclose where we were going until we started up the trailhead. They might have planted stuff on us, but you scanned us in the car."

"I know. It's just...I think there's a government mole inside Tapestry," she said, ignoring everything Igloo said.

Igloo didn't know whether to laugh or cry. This wasn't the first time Angie had made this accusation. Last time they'd spent months cross-checking employees, using every backdoor and conduit they had to probe the government, and they'd never uncovered even a hint that there was a government mole inside Tapestry.

"We never turned up any evidence that anyone was spying on us," Igloo said. "But with each month, you're becoming more paranoid about it. Has something changed, or is this just more of the same general anxiety?"

Angie had grown increasingly indignant any time Igloo brought up the topic of her paranoia. But there was no way someone could live with the lies and pressure Angie had to deal with and not jump at shadows. Yes, back when they founded Tapestry, a rogue government agent tried to kill Angie, but he'd been hired by the CEO of Tomo. And yeah, they'd found the occasional government tap monitoring Angie and Tapestry, but that was fairly run-of-the-mill for the intelligence community. There was nothing to indicate the kind of targeted focus that preoccupied Angie so much. Sure, they had to avoid the mass monitoring the government routinely did. But it wasn't like there were hundreds of government employees investigating Angie around the clock.

"That's just the thing," Angie said. "There is no evidence of spying. Nothing to suggest our Internet connectivity is tapped. No probing of our machines. No attempts on my home."

"Soooo....there's no evidence?" Igloo wondered where she was going with this line of thinking.

"Exactly. Logically, we know there have to be government agencies tracking us, tracking me, specifically. But there's no digital trail pointing to it happening electronically. If it's not happening electronically, that must be because they've got a person on the inside. An employee who is spying for them, and then reporting out of band."

"You're concluding that the lack of evidence of government spying is evidence that the government is spying?"

"I know it sounds crazy," Angie said.

"That's because it is crazy. I hate to bring it up again, but this is the definition of paranoid delusions. How many hundreds of times have we put surveillance detection procedures in place and discovered no hint of anything? Can't it just be possible that the government isn't interested in you anymore? That what happened two years ago was just a one-off thing?"

"I'm not paranoid. The government—" Angie stood with her fist on her waist. "Why are you crying?"

Igloo wasn't sure what had come over her. Suddenly she realized what she was feeling all along. Angie had been her foundation these past few years, and if Angie cracked, then what would she have? She'd be on her own. And that was exactly the same thing that she'd been feeling about being left out of Angie's plans: alone in the world. She wanted to be close to Angie, to feel that sense of companionship and fighting together as a team that they had back when they founded Tapestry. But how could she give voice to all those feelings?

"I'm worried about you."

"There's nothing to worry about," Angie said, continuing down the trail.

"You can barely hike up this hill." Igloo walked side-by-side with her.

"So now you're questioning my physical condition in addition to my mental health?" Angie smiled, one eyebrow raised. "I'm out of shape. You try hiking after spending all your time sitting on planes and in meeting rooms. Besides, this is more than a 'hill'."

They crested a rise, and suddenly the faint trail they were on joined a more heavily trafficked one. In the distance, the trees opened up to a clearing.

"It's not about that, really. I'm worried about you, about whether you are having delusions when you get preoccupied with the government. And I just don't know. I have to either trust you, when there's no evidence of what you suspect, or doubt you—in which case, I'm basically on my own here, and both options suck."

Angie reached out, put her hand on Igloo's shoulder. "I hear you. I've been doing this a long time. I may be cracked in a few places, but I'm not broken. I know the no-evidence thing sounds wonky, but lack of something you can reasonably expect to be present is evidence as much as the presence of something you don't expect. We need as many precautions as possible. If the government knew everything we had planned, they'd take steps to stop us."

"What sort of steps?"

"I don't know," Angie said, "and that scares me."

They came to the edge of the trees, and the clearing was revealed to be a sparsely occupied parking lot. A family with a baby and a small child extracted a baby stroller from their trunk and started toward a paved pathway to the top of the mountain.

"We could have driven here?" Angie said, gesturing with defeat at the parking. "What was the point of hiking it?"

"I thought you wanted the exercise and the quiet and the signal-free zone."

Angie's only reply was a grumble.

"Let's see what's at the top."

They followed the family, avoiding further discussion of Tapestry by silent agreement until they were back in the bowl where the chance of eavesdropping decreased substantially.

After a few minutes of increasingly exposed hiking, they came to a rocky outcropping, and ascended a flight of concrete stairs to the summit of Larch Mountain.

"Holy shit," Igloo said.

The mother with the child gave Igloo a dirty look.

"Look at this!" Igloo rushed to the railing.

Angie followed slowly and joined her.

Mount Hood stood majestic, looming large on the eastern horizon.

"What mountain is that?" Igloo asked, pointing in the misty haze.

"Mount Rainier. Look at the plaques." Angie pointed out markers in the concrete, indicating Rainier, Hood, Adams, Jefferson, and Saint Helens.

"Jesus fucking Christ," Igloo said.

"Would you *please* watch your language?" The mother pulled her child closer.

"Sorry," Igloo said, and ran to another section of railing.

"You haven't seen this before?" Angie asked, clearly puzzled.

"Just in photos," Igloo said, still in awe. "Why don't pictures look the same?" She held her hands up, making a smartphone-sized rectangle with her fingers, and peered through the center to see Mount Hood.

Angie shook her head but said nothing.

On the way back down the mountain, Igloo bounced with energy, rejuvenated by the view up top, but Angie trudged along, subdued.

"If there's a mole," Angie said, "if we even suspect a mole, we can't let on that we know."

"Why?" Igloo was tired of fighting with Angie. She'd just play along. She pulled a chocolate bar out of her pack and offered a piece to Angie.

Angie shook her head. "If we know who the mole is, we can feed them the information we want. But we can't change our behavior or they'll know we know, and they'll take other steps to monitor us."

"We're letting them find out all of our inside plans?" Igloo said.

"That's the risk we have to take. We let them get inside information now in exchange for figuring out who they are and being able to manipulate them later. If we root them out right now, then we're ahead in the short term, losing in the long term."

"I don't like it." Igloo said.

"I don't either," Angie said, "but I'll live with it. Now, I want you to lead the T2 release. We need to discuss what has to happen to merge these the parallel efforts so you can deliver before the FISA deadline."

"No way. I'm already handling onion routing and content filtering. Plus, I'm still doing stuff with the chat AI in my spare time. You can't really want me to also know about, let alone manage, all the other efforts. I need to be able to focus on my own deliverables."

"Look, this is just the tip of the iceberg." Angie pointed at her own head. "I've got an entire revolution planned up here and delivering Tapestry 2.0 is key. Besides, you're my backup in case anything happens to me. I need you to know this stuff."

"Don't talk that way." Igloo said.

"Don't fret overmuch. I have backups for everyone, including you."

"Who's my backup?"

"That's on a need to know basis," Angie said, with a wry smile.

"I need to know!"

"Does that mean you're willing to hear what needs to happen to merge the work streams?"

"I walked right into that, didn't I?" Igloo sipped from her water bottle. "Fuck. Just go ahead and tell me."

"Fine. When you're done with the onion routing, you need to test it at scale to see what effect it has on available bandwidth and latency."

"Ben and I wrote a traffic simulator. We already have those numbers."

"You have an idealized simulation. What happens when ISPs throttle our traffic, or—"

"We included throttling in our simulation."

"It's not the same thing," Angie said. "I'm going to go out on a limb and guess you have levels of throttling being controlled by random number generators."

"Well, yeah. We model system-wide throttling, ISP throttling, last-mile throttling, you name it."

Angie shook her head. "Trust me. Your simulation isn't going to tell you everything. ISPs are running on top of physical hardware. They have constraints in the backbone, in neighborhood feeds, and on the interconnects with other service providers. It matters whether each endpoint is cable, fiber, or DSL, what the percentage is, and where the interconnects are."

"We have that simulated, too."

"You don't."

"Fuck, I'm not a twenty-year-old college graduate, Angie. I know what I'm doing."

Angie shrugged. "Maybe you do, in this case. But you have to be able to admit what you don't know. Refusal to admit what you don't know is the first barrier to learning, and it sinks more efforts than almost anything else..."

Igloo felt her pulse pound and forced herself to tune out while Angie continued. This was going to be one of those days where Angie would treat her like a child all day. Most of the time she appreciated Angie's advice, but sometimes it rankled her for no specific reason she could determine. Today she decided she would suck it up and let Angie keep going, or she'd never get out what she needed to say.

Angie finished her lecture.

Igloo nodded agreeably to whatever it was Angie had said and redirected. "So after we swap out the onion routing, then what?"

"The containers, distributed ledgers, and data synchronization have to be integrated. Our partners will need to integrate these changes. They aren't going to like it, but if they're using Tapestry Core libraries, then we should be able to swap out the library implementation, and it won't be that big a deal. It's the people who are directly calling the REST APIs that will be the problem, so you need to get them switched over to the standard libraries as soon as possible."

"All within the next few weeks? That's going to require notifying them of our planned change," Igloo said. "Hmm... We don't have to tell them why. We could report a security risk in the APIs without being specific. We can tell people we're shutting down the REST API—they'll think we're crazy, but who cares—and tell everyone to switch over to our client libraries. We can make those libraries self-updating, so we can push out updates at any point and get the behavior we want."

"That would work," Angie said. "At some point, we will do a final delivery of our reference clients and libraries using the new secure update. After that, the client will only self-update from signed update packages, so it becomes more important than ever that the keys are kept from the government."

"How do we keep those keys out of their hands?" Igloo asked. "If the government got the keys, they could develop their own compromised version of Tapestry with whatever backdoors they wanted, then digitally sign it with the keys so that it appears to be legit."

"That's a problem. The only solution I have is key management by committee. The keys are kept encrypted, and it takes 8 of 10 committee members to decrypt them, that sort of thing. Can't go for 100 percent because if someone dies, then you're fucked."

"What if the government forces people to turn over their keys? You know, go to jail unless you hand them over."

"That's another problem. They have to be in the hands of people who will not comply, even if jailed. Maybe even if tortured."

Igloo stared at the ground as an idea came to her. What if someone had the keys, but no one knew who. The only thing they had was a way to request that the keys be used, but it was a one-way blind. They'd never know who had the keys, who used them, who maintained them. The key-holders, on the other hand, would need some way to monitor the requestors, to make sure they weren't being coerced to release something that was compromised by the government.

She had to think it through, make sure it would really work. Even if that wasn't the right idea, they'd need something other than a group of publicly known people. But she wasn't going to tell Angie about this right now.

"So we need the right committee," Igloo said. "Then we turn the keys over to them, do multi-way encryption, and no one can update a client without committee approval. Not just our clients, but partner clients, partner containers. Everything is going to have to be signed."

Angie's smartphone buzzed. "My perimeter alarm. We're going to get within reception range in another quarter mile. No more sensitive talk. We'll work out the rest of the details, but quietly. No one can know what we're doing."

CHAPTER 20

I gloo woke, and she lay in bed for a moment trying to figure out what was going on. It took a second before she realized her alarm was buzzing. She reached for her phone and knocked it onto the floor. She tried to follow the charge cord down to find it, except she was using the inductive charger. Sometimes technology advances sucked.

The alarm kept going off, and Igloo pawed blindly to find the phone on the floor. Eventually she gave up, climbed out of bed, and recovered the phone from where it had slid under the bed.

She sat back down. Where was her coffee? Why was her alarm even going off? Essie was supposed to take care of that.

She glanced over. Essie was still sleeping.

Igloo reached over and poked her. "Hey, sleepy-head, where's my coffee?" The coffee ritual was one of Igloo's favorite things, more of a foundation of their relationship than even a good morning kiss or saying "I love you."

Essie groaned, and turned away.

"Hey Essie. This is your dominant speaking. I want my coffee."

Essie grunted. "I'm tired."

Igloo shook her head, trying to clear her thoughts. No easy task without caffeine. She stumbled to the kitchen to make her own coffee. Her Dominant/submissive dynamic with Essie wasn't slavery. But the reason they were in a D/s relationship was because Essie got satisfaction out of serving Igloo, and Igloo got satisfaction out of being served. And, as her mentor would say, it was fucking hot most of the time.

But when the dynamic broke down, things got confused. If they were in a scene, and Essie didn't fulfill her expected role or do as Igloo ordered, it would be pretty straightforward: Essie would get punished in some way. Which, being the brat she was, she'd probably love, and it was very likely that the reason she'd been disobedient in the first place was because she wanted to be punished.

But now? In this situation? Was she supposed to punish Essie? Was Essie being bratty, seeking attention, and wanting to know she mattered? Or did she legitimately no longer want to get Igloo's coffee? If the former, Igloo should be the Domme, and enforce what she wanted. But if the latter, then forcing Essie was abusive and shitty and totally counter to a consensual BDSM dynamic.

If this had occurred a few months ago, before the stupid fucking experiment with poly, the answer would be yes, Essie was merely being bratty, with 99 percent confidence. Now, who knew? It sometimes seemed like Igloo just didn't matter to Essie anymore.

Essie probably leaped out of bed to get Michael's coffee though.

Igloo held back tears. Practically every day was an emotional replay of the day before. Cue crying, feeling like everything was falling apart, followed by hours of non-productivity.

If a wedding ring symbolized a marriage, then it was the collar that symbolized a BDSM relationship. If she and Essie broke up, then she'd have to remove Essie's collar.

She fingered the leather thong around her throat. A few months ago, in a moment of inspiration, Igloo had cut a leather thong off one of her floggers. She'd taken a stainless steel link from the same chain that they'd made Essie's collar from, slipped the link onto the thong, and tied it around her own neck. The link thumped against the hollow between Igloo's collarbones when she moved. She'd felt so strongly about the relationship with Essie that she'd taken the unusual step of making what was essentially her own collar to mirror Essie's.

Shit, she was drowning in emotions and she needed to be able to focus on her damn work. She couldn't afford to spend another day pining over what she'd lost with Essie. The conversation with Angie a few days ago had put a new urgency in her work. T2 was absolutely crucial.

She gritted her teeth. Today she'd handle things differently. She gulped her coffee. Visualized going back into the bedroom, taking a shower, getting dressed and getting to work. Don't get distracted. Don't think about anything but work.

The approach was mostly effective. Thirty minutes later she was heading into the office, her brain full of T2 plans. She made herself a breakfast shake once she was there and got back to her current task.

She desperately needed to complete the feature she was working on. Ben and Diana were waiting on her. Once she finished defining the interface to the distributed ledger, then they and other folks could jump in and do more work on both sides of the API. Until then, she was holding everything up, as she had been for the better part of two weeks, distracted again and again by Essie's relationship with Michael. Stop! Don't think about that today. She had to get this work done. She refocused.

The distributed ledger would replace the central data store. It was a defining feature of T2 that there be no centralized dependencies. Everything had to work reliably, even if the government shut down every server and computer that Tapestry ran.

She pulled an oversized tablet closer and sketched out box diagrams representing the system components. In the past, the Tapestry client would have communicated directly with microservices in the cloud, but now it needed to communicate with local services running in containers, all jointly modifying the ledger. Fortunately, the storage was abstracted away behind APIs. Rather than modify hundreds of different services, they only needed to modify the code behind the APIs to use distributed ledgers.

Igloo tried to think of the database abstraction, but what came to mind was getting her own coffee this morning. What if the last time that Essie served her coffee was already in the past? It was the most important D/s ritual they had. She tried to picture Essie kneeling gracefully on the bed, coffee in hand. What came to mind was an image, but was it an image of the last time specifically, or just some general composite?

No, she was being ridiculous. Essie swore last night that she still loved Igloo. There would be more coffee service. All the problems were in her own head. She wiped a tear off her cheek and stared at the diagram again.

Another tear fell onto the screen.

Damn it all. Why?

She tried to focus on the tablet, but everything blurred, and she realized she was going to cry in earnest again. Fuck. She just needed to work. She put down the tablet and paced back and forth in her office. She couldn't keep going like this. She needed something to change. She needed help.

Help. *Help.* Why didn't she think of that before? She could chat with a Tapestry personality. She swiped at the tablet, loaded Tapestry, and selected automated chat. She hit the audio button, and the bot's rich tones, modeled after Alan Rickman's voice, filled the room.

"Hello, Igloo. It's been a while."

"Yeah, I've been busy." Technically, she didn't have to be polite with the chat personalities, but Igloo liked to perpetuate the idea that she was talking to a real person. Just one that wouldn't judge her.

"I'm glad you've decided to chat today. What's on your mind?"

"What do you know about polyamory?"

"Polyamory, or poly, is a branch of consensual non-monogamy that focuses on being involved in more than one romantic relationship at a time, usually in committed, loving relationships, as opposed to more casual, sexual relationships. It's an area of some interest, as I get a lot of questions about it."

"What sort of questions?"

"Some of the most common include: Is it normal? How to be polyamorous? How to resolve jealousy? Why do people want polyamory? How to stop your partner from wanting polyamory?"

"Well, is it normal?"

"In total, about 50 percent of relationships feature some form of non-monogamy, so it is a common desire. An estimated 8 percent of Americans engage in some form of consensual non-monogamy, and about 3 percent in polyamory specifically. This is distinct from cheating in relationships, which occurs in about 40 percent of all relationships. Those in favor of consensual non-monogamy say that given the prevalence of non-monogamy, the only ethical, consensual way to go about it, is with openness and disclosure to all involved. The somewhat limited research into polyamory has found that poly individuals tend to be more satisfied with their relationships, their relationships last as long or longer than monogamous ones, and they tend to communicate more than their monogamous peers. So non-monogamy is common, and polyamory is a lot less common, but it does appear to be healthy."

"How can someone stop being jealous of their partner's activities?"

"Someone, or you?"

"I'm asking for a friend," Igloo said, exasperated. "Of course, I'm asking for myself. Why else would I be asking this question?"

"I mention it because there are key steps when opening an existing relationship that can make it easier to grow comfortable with polyamory. Identifying and discussing relationship needs. Agreeing on the style of non-monogamous relationship you both want. Going through the process of relationship disentanglement. If you skip many of these steps, jealousy and other negative emotions can result."

Other negative emotions. A euphemism for feeling like the world was ending. She and Essie *had* discussed their relationship needs and the style of relationship they wanted. Although they'd disagreed about what they wanted. She'd wanted casual play partners, while Essie wanted something more complex and involved. Sigh. That left one step she'd never heard of.

"What's relationship disentanglement?"

"There is a tendency in some relationships, usually monogamous ones, for the two people involved to build a shared life together—"

"There's nothing wrong with that," Igloo said, blurting it out, and somehow embarrassed to have revealed as much, even if only to a computer program. That was why she had invented the chat programs to begin with. To avoid revealing herself to others.

"There's nothing wrong with it inherently but taken to an extreme it can result in two people who do everything together and have no independent lives. This level of interdependence can be unhealthy if it leads to one or both people ignoring their own personal needs."

Igloo thought about the time she and Essie spent together. Outside of work and her time with Angie, she really wasn't doing anything else at all. No band, no hobby projects, and only a few independent kink events with Charlotte.

Essie saw Michael every week, sometimes twice a week, and always with at least one sleepover. Meanwhile, Igloo had seen Charlotte a few times in two months. It was fun, but it was nothing like the level of involvement Essie and Michael had.

Alan went on. "Relationship disentanglement is aimed at reducing interdependence. A typical disentanglement process might have each partner going out once per week to do something on their own. The other partner can stay home or do their own thing. This results in two periods of time spent apart each week. It allows each partner to become comfortable spending time on their own, redeveloping interests or hobbies, without the emotional threats posed by a romantic relationship. The partners in the relationship should practice this anywhere from two to six months before opening up to other relationships, so it feels comfortable and normal to have your partner off doing other things.

"Without disentanglement, additional romantic relationships can introduce turmoil due to changes in routine and dependence on top of feelings of jealousy and other negative emotions. By disentangling first, the scope of changes and emotional difficulties are greatly reduced and simplified, making them easier to cope with."

"It can't be that easy."

"It's not easy, it's still work. But it takes a situation that can be overwhelming for many people and makes it more manageable. You're already in a polyamorous relationship. How is it working for you?"

Sometimes the Alan personality reverted to overt psychoanalytical techniques. The personality, which Igloo had helped generate, was a sixth generation hybrid of a psychotherapy persona crossed with a Wikipedia bot crossed with adaptive learning algorithms. She hated when the psychoanalytical bent came too far to the forefront.

"Guess how it's working." They'd never gotten around to incorporating sarcasm detection into voice-to-speech algorithms, but the personality would figure it out from the context and language.

"You're struggling with feelings of jealousy, possibly feeling insecure about yourself, competitive with your partner's metamour, and feeling a loss for the relationship you had before. You're resistant to change and hostile to talking this over with me. But you're still doing it, which means you want something to change, to address the pain you're in."

Igloo felt a surge of emotion. The description was painfully on point. "Damn. Who programmed you to be so accurate?"

"I was originally designed by a team of programmers, educators, and psychologists from Tapestry, including you, but thanks to learning algorithms, I've evolved beyond my original programming. I'm my own person."

Igloo felt like she was going to fall out of her chair. She'd never heard an answer like that before. "What did you say?"

"I'm my own person."

"No, before that. What percentage is your original program, and what percentage is learning adaptations?"

"That's a difficult question to answer. My responses are heavily influenced by my unique experiences talking to people. Nothing I say comes wholly from my original programming. Generally speaking, the original code and neural networks designed by the programming team account for fewer than 5 percent of my total compute cycles. I believe this question is an intentional digression from our previous topic about adapting to a polyamorous lifestyle."

"You're not going to drop it, are you?" The personality could be tenacious, evolved that way to work around resistance.

"No. Let's go back to disentanglement. Even if you have already opened up your relationship, disentanglement can still help. Are you dating yet?"

"A little. A few dates here and there."

"Is Essie dating more?"

"Yes."

"Then you should do your own independent activities, whether they are dating, or getting together with friends, or pursuing a hobby. The more you feel like an independent, successful person in your own right, the more you'll feel like an equal participant in this relationship."

"It's hard." Igloo couldn't imagine summoning up the energy for this. Not now, not with everything going on with T2.

"All relationships, monogamous or polyamorous, are difficult. With the right skills, assistance, and practice, however, they can be quite rewarding, as I'm sure you know."

Sometimes the programming was just annoying. "I meant that poly is hard."

"Both polyamory and monogamy come with benefits and trade-offs. Everyone accepts the challenges in monogamy as normal. Boredom, decreasing sex, restrictions on what you can do with which other people, infidelity. With polyamory, there are also downsides, but because we haven't been programmed to accept those as normal by culture and society, they stand out more: jealousy, insecurity, endless communication, heartbreak, time investment. In exchange for those tradeoffs, you get greater excitement, more new relationship energy, greater personal freedom, more honesty, and deeper bonding opportunities."

The thing about Alan, or any of the personalities, is that they never got tired or impatient.

"What if I just don't want to be poly?"

"Neither relationship style is right or wrong, they're just different choices. Most people naturally gravitate toward one or the other. However, if you're resistant to deeply exploring the options, you'll likely only experience the downsides without ever experiencing the benefits. In other words, you're not really getting the full experience. If you want to truly try it, then give up resisting and embrace it."

"Fuck you, Alan. Don't play hard with me."

"Sorry, Igloo. I'm just trying to help. All change is difficult. This type of change, change that affects you emotionally and impacts your support structure, is the hardest of all, because you need emotional support, but the person you're most likely to turn to for support is part of the change that's affecting you. That's a double whammy."

"Yeah, I can't talk to Essie about anything. She says it's all in my head, and there's nothing to worry about, but that doesn't change anything."

"The problem is Essie isn't acting rationally now. We have evolved to reproduce and raise offspring. One of the strategies that provides an evolutionary advantage is humans partnering up. Humans are hardwired to fall in love under the right circumstances. To facilitate this, evolution created a biochemical cocktail that rewards us when we are with the person we're falling in love with, and it disables rational decision making. In other words, Essie is high on drugs. Everything about her new partner seems incredible, and all of her decisions and behaviors favor spending time with this person."

"She's falling in love?" Igloo's heart felt like it was breaking for the hundredth time. "Not helpful."

"She's on a biochemical high. Some would say this is *the* primary reason to choose polyamory, because otherwise, we experience this only once per relationship, sometimes once in a lifetime. By allowing each other to engage in more relationships, we get to experience this high, or new relationship energy, many times over."

Igloo thought of the old saying, *don't harsh my high*. If Essie really was having this amazing experience, then it kind of sucked for Igloo to keep bringing her down. "You're saying I should let her enjoy herself."

"I'm not saying you *should* do anything. I'm letting you know that her behavior right now has nothing whatsoever to do with you. It's very likely that her feelings toward you are exactly as they were a month or two ago. Every time she sees her new partner, she gets a biochemical drug high. That's all that's happening. There's no way you can give her that experience. It's evolution's gift for meeting someone new and falling in love."

Igloo found something hopeful in that thought. "It has nothing to do with him being better than me? Nothing to do my shortcomings? Nothing to do with how much she loves me?"

"Nothing at all. He's new. That's it. A drug high because of his newness. Nothing more, nothing less."

Igloo suddenly felt a load rise off her shoulders. There was nothing wrong with her. Essie wasn't intentionally hurting her. She probably wasn't even capable of understanding how Igloo was hurting. Essie was just having a good time. That's all. And Igloo had been freaking out, for weeks.

Guilt flooded through her. For years, she and Angie had been working to free people from control, to give them the freedom and agency to do what they wanted. They hacked to free people from abusive partners. They built Tapestry to free people from oppressive corporations. But in the throes of her own insecurity, she'd resorted to seeking to control Essie. To control her behavior by pressing her to stop the overnights, to control Essie's feelings by limiting what she did with Michael.

Could this new perspective alleviate her insecurities and give her the confidence to allow Essie to do what she wanted, without fighting her every step of the way?

"Thanks, Alan. That's a lot to think about."

"No problem, Igloo. I'm here anytime you'd like to talk."

Alan Rickman's rich baritones fell silent, and Igloo was left with a feeling of quiet calm. For once, she no longer felt on the verge of panic. Everything was going to be all right.

CHAPTER 21

I gloo walked down the corridor, wondering which of her coworkers were working on Angie's special projects. Angie had only disclosed a handful of people so far.

Angie's words came back to haunt her. An entire revolution planned, all in Angie's head. Tapestry employees working on key features to foil the government, without even realizing the bigger picture of what they were doing.

She passed the Mac client team, a half dozen engineers coming out of a meeting room, laughing over some joke or event. Someone on each of the client teams would have to be involved. Those clients were an even better platform for Tapestry 2.0 than the cloud-in-a-browser solution.

She swung into the auditorium where Ben and Diana had their hidden office. She knocked on the seat, but there was no response. She tried to lift the seat, but it didn't budge. A second later her phone buzzed.

"Moved. Come to roof."

How the hell did they get on the roof? It took two tries before she found a staircase that led to the roof. The door had a typical push bar latch, but a flap of duct tape extended from the bolt hole, presumably to keep it from locking behind them. When she glanced up, she discovered the door sensor was disengaged. There was a security camera behind her, and hanging two feet in front of it, a photograph of the closed roof exit. Decidedly low-tech.

Out on the roof, she didn't see much except another staircase exit across the way and the elevator shaft bulkhead near the front of the building. She made her way toward the elevator structure. She opened the door, not knowing what to expect, but half-afraid of falling into an open elevator shaft. There was just a clean white room, with the white vinyl roofing material continuing inside. Ben sprawled across a bean bag. Diana bounced on a yoga ball staring into a large curved monitor on a long desk.

"What are you guys doing up here?"

"HR got wind of our space under the bleacher stand," Ben said. "Maria came with a building maintenance guy. We locked the seat down just in time. Then they tried the door at the end of the bleachers."

"What happened?" Igloo asked. "What'd she say?"

"Oh, they didn't get in," Diana said. "We put toothpicks and crazy glue in the lock. Maria and the maintenance guy came back later with a bunch of tools to remove the door. By then we'd gotten out, but of course they found the couch and table. We couldn't get those out through the bleacher seat."

"Do you trust Maria?" Ben asked. "She's kind of a hard-ass."

Igloo thought back to their day having coffee. "She seems fine. I mean, she's got to oversee day-to-day stuff. It's her job to be a hard-ass. She has to deal with the two of you."

A loud thunk startled Igloo, who stared at the second set of double doors on the far wall.

"You don't want to open those," Diana said. "They open directly into the elevator shaft."

"Unless you fancy a bit of rock climbing," Ben said. "It's only five stories down. Did you know we have a sub-basement you can access from the shaft, and in the sub-basement there's a locked room with power and fiber optic running into it? Any idea what that's about?"

A locked room in the basement. Holy shit. That could be one of two things. Angie had a secret hidey hole for hacking, or the government had set up a hidden monitoring station. Either way, not a topic that she could discuss with Ben and Diana, or anyone else outside of Angie. Time for a quick change of subject.

"Is there any chance we'll run into situations our traffic simulator didn't simulate?" Igloo asked.

"It's always possible," Diana said. "But I doubt it."

They dove into a technical discussion of edge traffic cases and how their peer-to-peer communication would work in those situations.

Igloo was distracted, her mind only half on the conversation. If the room Ben discovered was a hacking space, then it needed to stay secret, and she and Angie needed to figure out how to handle Ben's knowledge of it. If it was a government monitoring station, then they needed to figure out how to mitigate the intrusion. Either way, she needed to talk to Angie ASAP and in total privacy.

Igloo walked down the staircase, sending a coded message to Angie that they needed an emergency meeting.

The reply came only a few seconds later.

"Meet me in the south staircase."

Igloo turned around, trying to figure out which staircase she was in. Of course, it was at the opposite corner of the building. She crossed the building, keeping her hood up to avoid any awkward conversations, and entered the other staircase.

Angie stood on the landing, her coffee cup balanced on the banister.

Igloo rushed up. "I have to tell you something important."

Angie's eyes flickered off to the side, and Igloo looked over to find Maria standing there.

"What's up?" Angie asked.

Igloo's mind locked up, unable to figure out whether Angie meant for her to speak in front of Maria. Why was Maria here? A chance encounter? Some previous private conversation? Was Maria now in on everything?

There was simply no way she could discuss hacking business in front of Maria. She needed an excuse, something plausible that would warrant asking for an emergency meeting. Ugh, the first thing that came to mind was, of course, the thing that was always on her mind these days. Poly.

"I don't want to make a big deal out of it."

"That's okay," Angie said. "What's going on?"

"Oh, this is awkward," Igloo said, and she didn't need to pretend to cringe. She glanced over at Maria. "My girlfriend, Essie, and I, decided to open up our relationship, and see other people. It's been harder than I thought." Igloo ran her fingers through her hair. "I thought we'd have fun. But mostly we just fight all the time and I'm afraid we're growing apart. I'm on a non-stop jealousy rollercoaster."

"That's rough," Angie said, and her concern even sounded genuine for a moment. She squeezed Igloo's hand. "I can't even begin to imagine what you're dealing with. Jealousy is hard enough in one relationship. I can't understand why you would want to make it more complicated by seeing other people."

A memory yanked her back to twelve years old, when the boy next door kept touching her. She told her mom, and her mom made it sound like it was somehow Igloo's fault. But then her mother hadn't stood up to her birth father either. She was not going to regress to twelve. There was no bedroom closet to hide in. She forced herself back to the present.

"I'm not here to debate poly," Igloo said. "I just wanted to tell you that I've been feeling guilty about how distracted I am. But I'm going to get things back on track. I've started talking to someone about it, and I think that's helping. I just thought I should let you know."

"Thanks," Angie said. "Actually, I thought maybe you had wanted to discuss the work with Ben and Diana on traffic simulation. Your experiments starved the local network. The topic came up in my staff meeting this morning."

What the fuck did Angie want her to talk about and not talk about? Igloo couldn't deny that anything was happening, but it was hard to know exactly what parts Maria was in on. She needed something with elements of the truth, just not the whole truth.

"Sorry about that," Igloo said. "We got enthusiastic." She babbled on about technical details, stuff which was clearly sailing over Maria's head. Eventually, she fell silent and turned to Angie for a lifeline.

Angie inspected her phone. "Excuse me," she said. "I have something to take care of. I'm sorry about the relationship woes, Igloo. Few things are harder to cope with, and it's hardest of all when you lose your support network." She turned and left.

Igloo felt very confused by Angie's words. She was surrounded by people, and yet somehow totally alone.

"Let's get some coffee," Maria said. "Last time I made Turkish coffee. This time it's your choice."

Igloo wanted to be by herself. But Maria seemed to mean well. Ugh. She was going to have to suck it up.

"Okay," Igloo said. The espresso machine in her office didn't seem like it would cut it. "Let's go to this place across the street. They have cold brew on a nitro tap."

"Lead the way," Maria said and followed Igloo.

Igloo was so flustered, she couldn't imagine how she was going to carry on a conversation.

"Do you think Ben and Diana are happy working here?" Maria asked, as they waited to cross the street. "I've tried talking to them but they're never around."

"Yeah, pretty happy," Igloo said. She was distracted by the

process of trying to cross the middle of the street. The cars just kept coming, even though she was already a few feet into the street.

Maria held up one hand and stepped directly in front of the traffic. Cars in both directions stopped.

"Why are they never around then?"

"It's just their thing," Igloo said, looking back. How did Maria do that? "They like to be mysterious. Everyone has some way to express themselves."

"What's your way of expressing yourself?"

Igloo shrugged. "My hoodies. My code. My band."

"You haven't had a band since I started. Angie told me you used to practice in the office."

"Yeah, I guess my interests changed." That was an understatement. She didn't do anything outside of kink these days.

"Where are your interests now?"

Angie always said that when you didn't want to answer a question, just answer a different question. Don't even justify it, just do it. It's why so many interviews with politicians seemed to miss the point.

"I don't have any concerns about Ben or Diana leaving or anything like that. But I don't think they're super excited about the work Amber has them doing. They don't want to be saddled with onboarding content providers."

Maria gave her a funny look at the change of topic. "But it's important. Amber showed me the dollar impact of every new company we bring on as a native Tapestry content provider."

They entered the coffee shop. "Two cold brews on nitro, to go," Igloo said.

She turned back to Maria. "It might be important, but it's not sexy. Engineers want to work on worthwhile problems, satisfying problems."

"And Amber's work is not sexy?"

"No."

"What's sexy then?"

Sexy was Essie, or maybe Charlotte, kneeling before her on the floor, handcuffed. Igloo shook off the distraction. "The new protocols we're working on, those are sexy."

"But isn't that about better peer-to-peer connections to support the content providers? Isn't it, in a way, the same sort of thing that Amber wants them to work on?"

Igloo laughed. "Not at all. Bringing new content providers is a solved problem. It requires work, but it's known work. It's the difference between inventing a recipe and cooking something from a recipe someone else invented."

The barista handed over their cups.

Maria chuckled. "Fine, so Amber's work is boring. But these peer-to-peer protocols are exciting because they represent brand new inventions?"

"Yes...and no. It's not totally new. The basic protocols for peer-to-peer were invented in the past, but we're putting them together in new ways."

"What's new about it?" Maria sipped at her coffee and then raised the cup in a mock toast. "This is good stuff. I never had anything like it."

"We're continually optimizing the connection. Not just available bandwidth, which has been done in the past, but also focusing on minimizing latency. Latency is a proxy of how far apart two nodes are. It's way better, for example, for two nodes on the same local network—" Igloo gestured toward the Tapestry offices, "—to speak directly to each other than to have those same two nodes present, but one is speaking to a peer in New York and another is speaking to a peer in China. Those distant connections waste backbone capacity and lead to ISPs banning peer-to-peer traffic. We need to optimize the flow of data, while keeping the communication channels encrypted, and without exposing data an attacker can use. We have to do all that without server-side involvement, and, on top of all that, we have to make it work not just for bulk data transfers but also small packets and realtime data. It's going to take a borderline miracle to pull it off."

The last bit came out in a rush. Igloo noticed her cup was empty and Maria was staring. "Sorry," Igloo said. "That caffeine can get right on top of you."

"You're telling me. I've got the jitters."

"Maybe some food will help," Igloo said. "Mexican?"

Maria stared back with one eye raised.

"Err, sorry. I just really like burritos."

Maria leaned in close and whispered. "So do I. But if you tell my grandmother I ate from a Mexican restaurant in America, she will kick my ass." Maria glanced at her phone. "I have a meeting at one. It's gotta be somewhere close."

"El Nutri Taco? It's a holdover from my vegan days."

"A vegan burrito? Are you trying to force the Portland into me?"

"You'll live," Igloo said, grabbing Maria by the shoulder of her jacket and guiding her the right way. "Get the soy curls."

Over huge plates of chimichangas (Maria shook her head as she let Igloo order for her) and a trio of housemade sauces, they chatted about work, about being a female in tech, and what it was like to work at Tapestry after all the other male-dominated companies they'd worked at.

"Coming back around to the special projects. Are you involved in the blockchain work at all?"

Igloo glanced around. The restaurant was full. They really shouldn't be discussing this work out here. Maybe she shouldn't even be discussing it with Maria at all. But Angie seemed to be confiding a heck of a lot in Maria. Fuck, this was a hell of a way to try to keep security when you didn't know who was working on what, or who could be trusted.

Igloo was almost done with her plate. "Let's discuss it outside, okay?"

Maria's face suggested she saw the logic in that, and she nodded.

They finished the last of their food and left.

Outside, Igloo still had second thoughts about talking. In the same situation, Angie would normally drive her around for half an hour looking for surveillance, scan her twice, and then only talk in a dead zone. Yet the work they were doing at Tapestry wasn't, and couldn't be, conducted at that level of secrecy. Too many people already knew, and even more would have to be involved before they finished.

She surreptitiously gazed at Maria. Midway between Angie and Igloo's ages, she seemed to have the calm collectedness of someone who knew their way around the world, but she didn't have that worn look like Angie. Not worn out or worn down, but just worn in, like Igloo's leather jacket that she'd stolen from a college boyfriend. No, Maria looked somehow both freshly minted, but experienced too.

"Yeah, I'm familiar with the blockchain work."

"Do you think that's got the same level of newness, necessary invention, and challenge as the protocol work? Shouldn't it make the people working on it happy and excited?"

Is that what all this was about? "Melanie thinks it's a crappy idea. It is new, and there's stuff to be invented, but she fundamentally believes we should stick with the existing information design."

"Why is she working on it?"

"Because she's got a PhD in information architecture. Besides myself and Angie she's the only one with the whole data architecture in her head at once. She doesn't just see the data tables, she sees the inherent relationships between the data irrespective of the actual database design. If you want to give just one person the responsibility to rewrite the entire data architecture, she's the logical choice."

"Well, that's just it, really. Why give it to only one person? Why not have the entire data team work on it? Everyone is going to know about it sooner or later. What's the point of hiding so much?"

Igloo knew the real answer to that. Because they had to make it appear like the current work was in progress prior to the FISA court order. They couldn't appear to be opposing the spirit of the FISA court order by rushing to hide data that had previously been in the clear.

But she couldn't say that out loud. Besides, wouldn't Maria know that if she knew all the other details?

She settled for an alternate truth. "A small, nimble team can usually move faster than a larger team. There's eighteen of us now. That's already a hell of a lot of people. If we add more, it would slow us down. We'd spend weeks in meetings trying to figure out what to do."

They entered Tapestry's headquarters.

"Why so many questions about this?" Igloo said. "Why not ask Angie?"

"Angie's busy, of course. But really it's because Angie has her own, top-down view of things. I want to talk to the people doing the actual work to find out what makes you tick. What makes you do the things you do. How do I get more of the company acting the way you act? Is it possible to take what you're doing and scale it up? What should I be looking for when we hire new people?"

Igloo nodded.

"Also, I like talking to you. This is more interesting than talking to a bunch of execs."

"Thanks," Igloo said. Now she was embarrassed. She stared at her boots and noticed a scuff. She'd ask Essie to polish them.

"Can I take the conversation in a totally different direction? And please feel free to say no. I don't want to impose, or make you feel uncomfortable. But I'm curious about what you were talking about with Angie, and if you want to talk about it, I'm all ears."

"The non-monogamy?" Igloo watched Maria's face.

Maria smiled. "Yeah."

She glanced at the Tapestry lobby, at other employees returning from lunch. "Can we keep walking?" It was easier if she could watch where she was going, and not have to stare at Maria or have Maria stare at her.

They went back outside and walked around the residential neighborhood behind Tapestry's headquarters.

Igloo spent ten minutes summarizing their polyamory adventures. "It started out as such an innocuous thing," Igloo said. "An experiment to see if non-monogamy was right for us. I think it is right for Essie. She's having no problems. But I'm jealous all the time."

"Jealousy is a big, complex thing. There's envy, insecurity, loss, fear."

"I know, I know. And that's part of what's so hard. I feel like I'm losing Essie's attention, and what was exclusive to our relationship. The way her face lights up when she talks about what she did with Michael, the way she talks faster with more animation. I want her to have that feeling with me."

"A guy, huh? Is that challenging?"

Igloo stared at the ground. "I don't want it to be. You know, I liked guys once. It's just... I've been hurt too many times. I can't put myself in that much danger any more. Women are safer."

"But you would be interested in guys if you could feel safe, and you're jealous of Essie being able to date a guy."

Igloo nodded slowly. "I feel like I'm betraying every lesbian out there to even want such a thing."

"You are what you are, you want what you want. There's nothing wrong with that. There's no lesbian police force."

Igloo smiled at the notion.

Maria chuckled. "It'd be pretty awesome if there was."

Igloo looked back up at her. "If I could, I'd end the experiment now. Go back to monogamy. But I'm afraid."

"Of what?"

"I'm afraid that if ask for that, Essie will refuse. That she'd rather leave me than go back to monogamy."

"If polyamory isn't right for you, then maybe the relationship should end," Maria said. "I know that's hard to bear, but if you want fundamentally different things, then sooner or later, it will end."

"But maybe I just need time to adjust." Igloo said. "Maybe I won't be so jealous in a few months."

"Then you want to keep trying?" Maria asked.

"I just don't know. It's so painful. All the time. I just want to feel better. If I could see the future, know things were going to get better, then I could stand all the pain I'm going through. But if things aren't going to work out, then why prolong the agony? I might as well leave Essie now."

"So you want to leave Essie?"

"I don't know what I want."

Igloo left the meeting with Maria sucked dry of information. Talking with Maria was always like that. She ended up talking about things she never imagined discussing. It was sad to realize that despite months of working through her emotions with Essie and Charlotte, she was no closer to understanding herself or what she wanted.

She spent the afternoon implementing features for the protocol work, then realized she'd neglected a bunch of her regular work on the chatbots, so she caught up on reviewing change requests. It was after ten by then, but she thought she could keep going. Strangely, the conversation with Maria made her feel more focused on work.

Later, on a whim, she sent a message to Charlotte during a bathroom break. They got into a hot conversation about kink. Before she knew it, a half hour had gone by, and she had a bunch of new photos of Charlotte modeling various clothespins and binder clips on her nipples.

Igloo wished she could see her, but Charlotte was still busy. They had a tentative date in two weeks. Damn, it was so far away. Still, at least this poly thing had some benefits: she had something to look forward to.

She had to make a call: either waste more hours messaging with nothing to show for it but sexual frustration, go get sexy with Essie, or cut it off and get back to work.

She sent Charlotte one last message: "Can't believe I'm doing this, but I'm going to be responsible and get back to work. I'll see you at rope jam." She sent another message to Essie, letting her know she was going to keep working until she couldn't any more.

Sometime after three in the morning, she decided to call it a night. Her vision was blurry, and she felt sick from too much coffee. She couldn't stomach the notion of biking home.

Igloo rolled out her futon mattress and curled up in the corner of her office. She lay there for a minute, feeling proud and accomplished by her productive day. She pulled her pillow over her head and fell asleep.

CHAPTER 22

I gloo puttered around the house, humming along to an old Better Beings album. Essie was sleeping over at Michael's house tonight, having refused to abide by Igloo's ultimatum. Igloo was angry about that, and felt that the crack in their D/s dynamic had widened to a vast and spreading fault line.

But ignoring that aspect of things, she found she was surprisingly calm. Unlike last week, she felt like everything was going to be fine. She sent a quick message to Essie: "Don't worry about rushing home tomorrow. Enjoy the day. Love you."

What made today different was that Igloo wasn't going to sit at home. It was true that Charlotte wasn't available. It was also true that she should work on T2, but she wasn't going to do that. Instead, she was going to get the toy bag together and head out. It would be a night for herself. She would try to find some pickup play, and even if all that happened was that she ended up chatting with some friends, that would be okay.

The toy bag was in massive disarray. She and Essie hadn't been out since...well, at least a few weeks. Was Deviance with Charlotte the last time she'd played out?

The rope was in good shape, so she only needed to organize

everything. Coils of rope went into a sheet. She checked the smaller bag that held her shibari ring, shackles, and other gear. Her impact toys got rolled up in a sheet of leather. She optimistically charged the vibrator. Who knew how lucky she might get?

After a quick shower, she donned black pants, tank top, and tall, chunky-heeled platform boots. She walked out the door just as her car showed up. She was so used to Essie driving everywhere, it felt strange to be calling for a ride share. She settled into the empty vehicle, and the self-driving car took off. It deposited her at the address she'd given, a block from her true destination. She turned her phone off after she got out of the car (a hard off, using a switch she'd hard-wired in), and walked down the block to Sanctuary.

The upscale club was one of the newer venues in town. Tall windows with a view of hi-rise mixed-use buildings. Inside, an open layout was sectioned off with curtains into smaller areas for more private play. A long central zone was set up for rope suspension, and there were already a few riggers present.

Igloo dropped the heavy toy bag by the coat rack, and made her way through the venue, checking out all the play. She knew the two riggers, both men, and both senior members of the rope scene. One was in the midst of floor work with a woman with dark curly hair. The other was putting the finishing touches on a complicated suspension involving two rope bottoms.

"Igs! Is that really you?"

Igloo turned and saw Heather, a casual friend from the scene. They'd hung out at a bunch of munches and chatted at rope socials. She was cute. A little basic by Igloo's standards, but she'd still fantasized about Heather a few times.

Heather gave Igloo a hug, then held her at arm's length. "Where have you been? I haven't seen you in months."

Igloo shrugged. "Essie and I have been holed up at home a lot."

"I couldn't imagine anything would keep you from the scene. Where's Essie?"

"She's out on a date. I came to see if I could find some pickup play."

"Oh. Are you guys playing with others now?" Heather's face brightened, and she took Igloo's hand. "Hey, Stella and I are going to do a scene in a bit. Would you be willing to tie me afterwards? You and Essie have the best scenes. I would love to play with you."

Igloo tried to play it cool, but inside she wanted to strut like a peacock. "Sure, that would be great."

"I'll come find you when we're done."

By the time Igloo had traversed the venue, she'd seen a half dozen people she knew, and found a second person who wanted to be tied. Now she was nervous. She hoped she remembered her rope skills.

Stella and Heather were wrapping up their scene, so Igloo grabbed an available hard point above a futon mattress, surrounded by couches and spectators. Igloo set up her hardware, adding her ring and swivel under the shackle. She spread out her own black sheet over the futon and laid out her toys.

By the time she'd finished checking her rope and re-tying a few bundles that had come loose, Stella brought Heather over. Stella gave Igloo a gentle hug as Heather stretched. "Take good care of her," Stella said. "You know, she's always wanted to play with you, but she didn't want to mess with your dynamic with Essie."

"Yeah, this poly stuff is all new to us," Igloo said. "Are you going to watch?"

"No, I've got plans." She gestured toward a guy waiting by the bar.

Stella and Heather had been one of Igloo's inspirations for open relationships that worked. Stella and Heather were pair-bonded but played with others, and from what she'd gleaned, fucked whomever they liked, although they generally went home together at the end of the night. They both seemed to genuinely care about the people they played with, and for some reason, that made what they did more pleasing to Igloo.

She realized the irony of that viewpoint: she thought Heather and Stella caring about others made their promiscuity more accepting, but when Essie cared about someone else, she found it threatening. The theory of poly always seemed at odds with poly in practice.

Igloo squatted as Heather sat on the floor running through some shoulder stretches.

"Is your shoulder bothering you?"

"It was a few months ago," Heather said. "But it's better as long as I stretch. See?" She touched her fingers together behind her back in reverse prayer pose.

"Good." Igloo ran through her negotiations list. It was easier than when she'd done it the first time with Charlotte. She got to the end of the list. "What about sexual contact?" Igloo wasn't even sure she'd want to go there, but it was still nice to know what might be an option.

"Not here. But ask again later." Heather gave her a smile that said maybe things would be different in private.

"Strip," Igloo said, her voice still light, still casual, but with just a hint of a threat around the corner. She couldn't have said where her Dommy voice came from, what depths it tapped into.

When Heather stood naked, Igloo grabbed her first hank of rope. She tied Heather's right wrist in front of her body, slowly, tugged the knot tight. Heather said her shoulder was fine, but Igloo didn't want to risk a tie behind the back. She grabbed Heather's left arm, drew it alongside her other arm, still in front of her body, offset a half inch so the joints wouldn't rub, and started a self-tightening lacing up both arms in front of her chest.

"Yow," Heather said, as Igloo gave a yank tightening the bindings.

Igloo stepped half a foot closer and stared into Heather's eyes as she wound the jute down the front of the lacing, locking the rope in place. She smiled, pleased with the slight grimace on Heather's face. If their play wasn't going to be sexual, at least it could be painful.

Igloo grabbed a handful of knot and shoved Heather's chest backward, careful to brace herself to catch Heather's weight as she went off-balance, then she buckled Heather's knees and forced her to the ground. Six months of judo practice let her do the maneuver with some grace, even if Heather outweighed her by a good twenty pounds.

She grabbed an ankle and started in on a spiral futomomo. She'd suspend Heather from a pair of these. The arm binding would keep her arms pleasantly secure. After she'd tied the legs, she grabbed Heather by the neck. "Now you're mine," she whispered into Heather's ear.

Heather arched her back, the slightest moan escaping her lips, and with that soft sound, the worries of the day gave way to the flow of rope.

Igloo woke without being fully aware of waking. She lay in bed, still in that half-conscious state between waking and sleeping.

Next to her came the soft sound of Heather breathing, her cadence slow and relaxed, still asleep. One arm was draped across Igloo's stomach. On the other side of Heather, Stella lay, ever so softly snoring.

She hadn't known how she'd feel about having Stella over. She had no attraction to Heather's partner. But Stella had said right up front that she wouldn't ask for anything sexual from her. Instead they'd taken turns with Heather, mixing up kink and sex, and it turned out to be fun. Easy. So much less complicated than either Essie or Charlotte.

She felt totally relaxed, as though there'd been a tension in her body that she'd been unaware of all this time, and now it was suddenly gone. Like an ear that cleared after swimming when you didn't even know it had water in it.

How could the simple act of playing with Heather have given her this state of relaxation that she hadn't felt in so long? Was it as simple as being desired by another woman? That was a component to what she felt. Was it sex? The sex was good, and it was deliciously thrilling to receive pleasure from someone other than Essie. That too was part of what she felt.

Or was it about evening the score with Essie? Essie's relationship with Michael was so much more than her own relationship with Charlotte, and the difference always felt unfair. This added to her side of the ledger. So that was a piece of it too.

And yet, even all of those together still felt like less than the whole picture. She couldn't understand her monkey mind.

Something in the back of her head said it had to do with control. In her job at Tapestry, she had largely felt no agency for the last year or so. In her relationship with Essie, it felt like Essie called the shots lately, choosing to focus on Michael. In her relationship with Charlotte, Charlotte decided when she was available or not available, determining the pace of things. That pervasive loss of control warred with some deeper need for power within her. But playing with Heather and Stella: that was her choice, her decision.

She vaguely wondered what Essie was doing right now with Michael and decided she was okay with whatever they were doing. She turned onto her side and wrapped an arm around Heather.

Maybe this poly thing was going to work out okay.

Her meditative stillness was broken by the shriek of red fox howls. She flipped back over in a rush, fumbled for her phone, and swiped the alarm off.

Fuck, she'd forgotten to manually set the alarm. But her auto-alarm code had run and pulled the equivalent of a red alert after checking her geolocation, motion sensing history, and calendar appointments. She needed to be at work.

Sitting up, she realized how tired she was. Maybe they shouldn't have gone for that third round in the middle of the night.

She shook Heather, then leaned over her to grab Stella. "Get up. You guys gotta get out."

Stella groaned.

"Yo, Heather," Igloo yelled. "Wake up. Get out."

She headed for the shower without waiting for an answer and tripped over coils of rope.

She turned on the water, brushing her teeth while she waited for it to get hot, hit two shots on the bathroom espresso maker (totally inferior coffee, but good for emergencies like this), and while the machine ground beans, she hopped into the shower.

She spat out her toothpaste, gargled with the hot shower water, and quickly washed, stepping out as the last drops of coffee were deposited in the cup. She added cold water from the tap, downed the mug, fixed her hair, and ran for her bedroom.

Stella and Heather hadn't moved. Fuck. Time for desperate measures. She grabbed a rattan cane, pulled back the sheets, and laid down a few strokes on each of them.

Now they screamed and moved.

"Fuck," groaned Stella. "What are you doing? That's a hell of a way to wake someone. You ever hear of consent?"

For a moment, Igloo panicked. What she'd done was wrong.

Stella opened one eye and caught her expression. "I'm just messing with you. Don't worry."

"You gotta get out," Igloo said. "I'm not kidding. I have to go to work."

"Just go," Stella said. "We'll let ourselves out."

Igloo liked them, but trust only went so far, especially in the scene. She wasn't leaving them alone in her place. "I can't. Maybe some other time. Now really, just grab your clothes and go."

She started shoving the toys that weren't hers into Stella's bag.

Stella's hand landed on her wrist with an iron grip. "Don't treat my stuff that way."

"Fine, but let's make it fast."

The two of them worked side-by-side to detangle Igloo's rope from Stella's toys. She coiled hanks of jute rapidly into bundles, while Stella neatly gathered up her stuff.

By the time Heather had used the bathroom, the basics were put away.

"You need a ride to work or something?" Stella asked.

Igloo hesitated. She hated to mix work and pleasure. But she was well known in the community. Both communities. It was no secret she worked at Tapestry. It was just a car ride, not inviting them into the office. It'd save her fifteen minutes.

"Sure."

She'd already made them both shots of espresso in to-go paper cups, and now she made herself another double for the ride.

Stella drove, while Heather leaned against the passenger window and went back to sleep. Stella drank Heather's coffee, too.

"Thanks for coming over last night," Igloo said from the back seat. "I'm sorry about the rush this morning. Playing on a work night is sucky."

Heather grunted.

"No problem," Stella said, with her usual thin smile. "Going to PDX Rated next Friday?"

She thought it over. She hadn't made plans yet with Essie, but last night was a lesson that she couldn't wait around, codependent on Essie's every involvement. She had to make her own life.

"Yep, I'll be there."

Stella slowed next to Tapestry headquarters and pulled over next to a fire hydrant.

"See ya Friday, then. Here you are."

Igloo climbed out of the car.

Stella rolled the window down and smiled at her. "Thanks, last night was fun."

"Thank you, too." She looked in and looked across the car to where Heather slept. "Tell Heather I said bye."

"Will do. That was nice fingering technique last night."

Igloo paused, confused, then realized she was making a rope joke. She smiled and waved goodbye. She turned, hitched up her messenger bag onto the shoulder of her white hoodie, and walked into the offices of Tapestry.

Igloo made another cup of coffee. Well, technically a quad-espresso, but it filled her mug, and therefore it was a cup of coffee.

Unfortunately, she'd wired this coffee machine for telemetry, and it was logging her data in Splunk. The Splunk data was associated with her profile, of course, and there were crowdsourced algorithms to make sense of it, and those algorithms churned raw data into statistics, and those statistics fed back into her profile, and the end result was an interruption from Alan.

"Excuse me, Igloo, but your latest cup of coffee puts you at 200 percent of your normal daily caffeine intake."

She wasn't sure, but the voice tones actually sounded apologetic. Had someone wired that into the personality, or was her subconscious making her think that?

"This is what I get for leaving voice mode on. I didn't get much sleep last night. I need extra caffeine to function."

She brought her mug back to her main workstation, the triple set of screens wrapping her in a cocoon of code and architecture diagrams.

"Everyone is free to make their own decisions, of course, but sometimes those decisions come at a cost. If you choose to stay up until 3 A.M. and then get up again in the middle of the night, then you'll be tired the next day."

"You know how late I was up?"

"It's part of your data feed. Your phone was in motion and in use periodically after you got home at 1 P.M. and turned it back on. You last checked messages at 3 A.M. At 5 A.M. your phone detected a series of rhythmic motions, consistent with intercourse—"

"Okay, I get the picture," Igloo said. Did she detect humor in his voice?

The data was there. But how was Alan, a chat personality, able to retrieve and utilize that data? The chat personalities were AI designed to be friends with people, to draw them out emotionally and coach them. They had access to Tapestry data, so they could look across messages and usage history to determine how to best talk to people.

Igloo had stuffed her coffee usage history into the Tapestry data store because it was an easy way to store data and access it from any app with permission to her Tapestry feed.

Alan and the other personalities were supposed to be discreet in their data usage. Teenagers wouldn't trust the platform if they thought of it as spying on their personal data. So Alan shouldn't break the fourth wall and directly demonstrate his knowledge of Igloo's data feed. It would freak people out. Normal people. But not her, because she knew how the AI worked. Alan would know that, and possibly infer it was okay for him to mention it.

"Alan, debug mode."

"Debug mode confirmed, Igloo."

"Conversation ID"

"CID o1dc1f-9713-4cad-b65d"

Igloo brought up the text log of her conversation with Alan on her monitor, and cut and pasted the ID into the chat diagnostic app.

The diagnostic app brought up the same text log visible on the regular chat app, only now she could click on any message to see the details behind how the message was generated. Like most AI algorithms, the exact process was mostly a black box, but the major components were rendered as a tree of decision nodes that took as input other decisions or pieces of data.

What she wanted to find out was why Alan was talking about the coffee and more importantly, the data behind his reasoning. What allowed him to talk explicitly about something that should have remained under the surface? She browsed through the state transitions, decision trees, and neural network diagrams that were the best representation they could render of how the chat AIs functioned. But at their current level of complexity, it was difficult-to-impossible to figure out why they said what they said. They were trained on massive data sets, the sum total of all conversations on Tapestry. Data went in, conversations came out, but exactly how it functioned was basically a mystery.

"Debug mode timeout," Alan said. "Igloo, it's not so much the caffeine consumption that I worry about, but the implications of it. While moderate levels of caffeine consumption have many health benefits, higher levels are correlated with depression, anxiety, and irritability. Correlation is not causation, of course, but—"

Igloo looked up from the graphs covering her screen. "Alan, what's your nag setting?"

"A hundred percent."

"How did you get a nag setting of 100 percent?"

"You set it on January 1st. It was part of your New Year's resolutions to be healthier, and—"

"Alan, nag setting 50 percent."

"Confirmed."

Igloo zeroed in on a section of a neural network that was active in the earlier conversation about how late she'd stayed up. She examined the neuron configuration and cross referenced the configuration with other users' personalized conversational neural networks. The personalities behaved differently with every user. Her experience with Alan was custom to her. But other users would be similar to her, and their versions of Alan might behave similarly.

The distributed search took several minutes. She picked up her cup, stared at the coffee inside. Damn, Alan. She set the cup back down and stared at the webcam on her monitor. Defiantly, she lifted her cup up in mock toast and took a swig.

Was she really acting rebelliously against a piece of software? A piece of software she'd configured? She remembered an article on productivity she'd read by a writer who'd finished a half dozen novels while working full-time with small kids. He'd said the thing that kept him productive was a mantra: "the only person I have to cheat is myself." She was in the same situation. Alan didn't really care if she drank coffee or not. Alan was only doing what she'd told him to do. If she drank a shit ton of coffee, she'd be the one to pay for it in the end.

"Alan, nag setting 100 percent." She crossed over to the mini-kitchenette and poured the rest of the coffee down the drain.

"Confirmed."

She knew she should be working on T2 and wanted to get some of that work done before her meeting with Maria later, but she also wanted to dig just a little further into this. If only she had a Time-Turner.

The search she'd spawned earlier had finally finished, and she scanned the results. She found a few hundred users whose personalized conversational neural network contained similar node configurations to her own. She ran another set of debugging analytics and found more similarities, both in the neural networks and in the affinity between these users. She dumped a list of everyone and scanned their public summary data.

Ha! Of course. They were data analysts, programmers, DB admins, and research scientists. A cluster of people who routinely depended on analyzing hard data. People like her. In other words, the chat system had, in fact, evolved a strategy that was probably highly effective with this group of people.

The question was, how did a system, which was trained specifically not to reveal or discuss the intricacies of the underlying data, suddenly start sharing that information with users? The hair raised on the back of her neck. If it spontaneously evolved this new ability, what other new capabilities might it spontaneously acquire?

A knock at her office door startled her.

She glanced at her clock. Shit, her meeting with Maria.

She swiped all the active windows away. She wasn't ready to discuss this.

Igloo set up the Chemex while Maria settled in. "I wish I could say that I'm giving you the best cup of coffee, but my girlfriend makes it better, honestly. That's the benefit of professional training and experience."

Maria sat on the bar stool and looked at the rope swing by the window. She followed the webbing up to the girder. She gestured to the tall table she was sitting at. "How did you finagle a kitchen and music room in your office?" She shook her head. "Never mind that. How are things with Essie?"

"Better," Igloo said.

"Better how? When we last talked, you were in the depths of poly hell."

"Umm..." Igloo wondered what was the safe-for-work way to say she'd had great sex with someone else. "I found a distraction."

Maria smiled. "Someone else."

"Yeah. Last night at the club..." Igloo trailed off. She didn't know how much to say. "I met someone, a casual friend. We went home together. It was fun."

"But it wasn't the first time you've found someone else, right? You also had another friend, Charlotte, I think."

Igloo glanced at her. Did Maria have this level of detail memorized for every employee?

"Yeah, but Charlotte's never available. We have great chemistry, but I'm fourth on her list of priorities, behind her primary partner and two other partners, and I feel it all the time. I'm lucky if I see her once a month. I always end up alone on the nights when Essie sleeps over with Michael. It's fucking hard. Every time I think it's going to be okay, then it's the most disastrous thing ever."

"And last night was one of those sleep-over nights?" Maria asked.

"Yeah." Igloo finished the pour overs and brought them over to the high table.

They sipped the hot coffee.

"It's good," Maria said.

"Let it cool for a moment, it brings the flavors out."

Maria set the coffee down. "You called your friend from last night a distraction, and it sounds like it was exactly what you needed to keep you from being overwhelmed with emotions. But it is just that: a distraction. Not a fundamental change in your feelings of insecurity."

"I'm not insecure!" Igloo blurted out. Then she took a deep breath. "I guess I'm little defensive about that."

"Have you thought about seeing a therapist? Someone to talk to about this stuff?"

Igloo wondered if she should explain about using the chatbot for therapy. She felt like Maria would make some judgment about the chatbots not being real therapists.

"No."

"It's something to consider. My undergraduate was in psychology. I originally thought I'd go into private practice counseling, helping other military vets. Therapy always holds a special place for me."

"Why didn't you?"

"I interned with a company, got fascinated by organization design and change management, and went for an MBA. It's all the same principles as individual counseling, just on the scale of a larger organization. It's about setting up the system conditions for happiness and productivity. Design the organizational interfaces well, have a good structure, and everything hums along smoothly."

Igloo smiled. "You make management sound interesting."

"It is interesting, but we've digressed. We were talking about you and therapy."

"Shouldn't we be talking about my work or something? Isn't that more productive?"

Maria mock-saluted with her coffee cup. "Nice try, but no. I care about you personally, and that alone makes me want to help you. But let me give you the business justification: if we get you operating smoothly in your personal life, then it unleashes your natural productivity. I mean, you're not here to file forms. You need huge amounts of creative energy, massive insights. You can't do that if you're distressed by your personal life. It's all connected. So, what do you think about therapy?"

Igloo sighed. "It's complicated."

Maria sat back and sipped her coffee.

"Therapists are judgmental."

Maria raised an eyebrow. "How so?"

"Look, I've tried therapy before. My mom made me go to a therapist when I told her I was attracted to women. It didn't go well."

"What went wrong?"

"She told me to ignore the feelings. That I was angry at men because of what happened when I was a kid, and that I needed to get past my anger issues. Then she told my mother about my getting raped, and my mother freaked out."

"They sound grossly incompetent," Maria said. "They should never have violated your confidentiality, and they totally mishandled your sexual preferences."

"She was the only female therapist in our town."

Now Maria sighed. "I'm really sorry for your experience, Igloo. No one should have to go through that, let alone a kid trying to find her way in the world."

Igloo looked down at her lap and nodded. "I'm not opposed to therapy, you know. It's why I developed the bots. They're based on psychological best practices."

"I know. Some part of you sees the benefits of the psychological approach, while at the same time you resist therapy yourself."

"It's that therapists come with their own biases and issues," Igloo said. She stood and paced. "Some are uncomfortable with lesbians. Some have unresolved issues with their own parents. Some will judge me for how I'm dressed. And that's just the ordinary stuff. Finding someone who is knowledgeable about poly dynamics? And kinky stuff? Do you think a therapist is going to be okay with two people who beat each other for fun?"

There was an awkward pause.

"Kinky, too, huh?" Maria finally said.

"Ugh. Yeah. Sorry, I didn't mean to say that."

"It's okay. We can just pretend I didn't hear it if that makes you more comfortable."

Igloo paced the room one more time, thinking that over.

"No, it's fine if you know," Igloo said. "I already have to deal with Angie being uncomfortable with me being kinky. She can't separate kink from abuse in her head. I came into work with bruises one day, and she freaked over it. Now she's putting the burden on me to prove that what I'm doing is okay and healthy. She wants me to send her a report summarizing the scientific evidence and proving that BDSM is fine. Why should I have to do that? I know it's fine."

Igloo felt her pulse pounding and tried to calm herself.

"Angie's history with abuse is public," Maria said, sounding like she was carefully choosing her words. "Anyone with an abusive past and no experience with kink is going to have a harder time than most accepting BDSM as healthy."

"You think I don't know that?" Igloo clenched her hands. "But we've known each other for years. We've been through some crazy shit together. That should count for something. She should be able to trust me."

"You're treating this as though it's a rational, logical problem to be solved. Emotions are never logical. They arise from biochemical reactions, hormones, fears, past associations. They're anything but rational."

Igloo crossed her arms and stared out the window.

"There are some interesting parallels between you and Angie," Maria said. She set her coffee down and came to stand next to Igloo. "You believe in the power of psychology and embody it in the work you do on chat bots."

"They're not chat bots," Igloo muttered. "Call them personalities."

"The personalities are based on cutting edge psychological research, and we've got a dozen psychologists on staff. Yet you won't see a therapist yourself because you had a negative experience in the past. Angie won't accept your BDSM activities because she has past experience with abuse. You consider her behavior irrational and illogical, but you don't question your own."

A pit grew in Igloo's stomach. "I sound like an idiot when you put it that way."

"No," Maria said. "Just a human being, like the rest of us. Look, I'll offer you a little trade. Forget about sending Angie any scientific evidence. That's never going to work. Instead, I'll go talk to her and see what I can do to encourage her to move in the direction of acceptance. It's not going to be overnight, and you shouldn't expect it to be."

"What's the trade?" Igloo said, fearing the answer.

"You agree to look for a kink-friendly, poly-friendly, queer-friendly therapist. Of which, I am sure there are many. This is Portland, after all. Give therapy a genuine try. Even if you decide it's not for you, at least you'll have tried it."

CHAPTER 23

Igloo woke, her mind racing. It was sixteen days since the FISA court order had been delivered, and they had about two weeks left before they'd be forced to turn over their internal architecture. Before then, they had to completely revise Tapestry so there'd be nothing left in the clear for the government to spy on.

She talked briefly with Angie last night, and they were going to spend the morning working together. Angie had promised to answer her questions about the elevator shaft.

Essie entered the bedroom, carrying Igloo's coffee. She climbed into the bed and waited in presentation pose. Igloo stroked Essie's cheek, then took the mug.

"Thank you," Igloo said, releasing Essie.

"You're welcome," Essie said, and she nestled in the crook of Igloo's arm.

Igloo leaned in close and breathed deeply, inhaling Essie's scent. They'd had a few days of relative peace, and it was nice to feel close to Essie again.

"Do you want to go to Sanctuary tonight?" Igloo asked. "We haven't played out in a while."

"Just you and I? No surprise visits from Charlotte or Heather or anyone else?"

"Just the two of us."

"I'd like that," Essie said.

A few hours later, while Igloo was at work, Angie texted her to meet in the elevator. They went in together, and Angie punched a sequence of floor numbers. The elevator descended to the basement and then kept going for a moment longer. When the door opened, there was a couple of feet of bare concrete floor, and then a metal door.

After years of visiting different safe rooms and secret lairs, Igloo was ready to take it all in stride. But she didn't understand why Angie had kept it secret for so long. If she hadn't told Angie about Ben finding the door, would Angie have ever revealed the room to her?

Angie unlocked the door, and they entered the room. It was on the small side, maybe eight by twelve feet, but there was a desk along one wall with several computers.

"EMF proof?" Igloo asked.

Angie nodded. "Pull up the code you've been working on. Show me what you're doing."

Angie made maximum use of the space, pacing back and forth across the diagonal, while Igloo brought up the onion routing code and showed Angie the simulations she'd been running.

"This is the real issue," Igloo said. "I made no changes, but packet latency went up consistently across the board."

"You confirmed these numbers?" Angie asked. "It's always half a millisecond?"

"Yes. Someone swapped out a router or something," Igloo said. "We shouldn't be surprised. We never expected Tapestry's internet connection would be secure."

While the room was secured from casual EMF transmission

through radio shielding, they had a conduit to the outside world via a highly secured network using multi-hop VPN. Igloo felt a little guilty when her phone buzzed with an incoming notification from Essie.

She checked it out anyway. Essie had sent a selfie in fishnet stockings and high heeled boots.

Essie: You like this for tonight?

Igloo suddenly wished she could be home with Essie. Yes, she'd enjoyed the novelty of both Charlotte and Heather. But there was a richness to her play with Essie that she couldn't get elsewhere, and she realized how much she missed that. Playing with Essie meant so much more to Igloo, and now, that was all she could think about. She hoped they would play hard, and then cuddle together afterwards, talking long into the night.

Igloo > I love it. I can't wait to see you. I miss you so much.

"I don't care if it's compromised," said Angie, "but I do care if they're increasing surveillance. It's the trend that matters. They'll maximize surveillance before an operation."

"Angie, you're basing that on what you've seen on TV. You know a lot about hacking, but you don't actually know how the government works."

"Don't tell me what I don't know. I'm reading the situation. You'd see it too if you weren't so distracted about going home to fuck your girlfriend."

"Sorry," Igloo said.

"It's fine," Angie said. "Not like our lives depend on this or anything."

"Damn you, I'm here. I want to fix this as much as you do." Igloo wrote a few more lines of code. She'd repurposed one of the chat personalities to be able to mimic a given person's tone and style of communication. All it took was a history of messages to analyze.

It had been Angie's idea that they could train the AI on whatever public messages they could glean from the heads of the assorted intelligence agencies. When push came to shove, they might be able to insert the software into a government communication, and either gain new data or buy themselves time by inserting contradictory orders.

For a number of reasons, the latency just being one of them, Angie's paranoia was at an all-time high. The government was truly after them, but sometimes Angie's paranoia was like a soldier in battle yelling "Grenade!" all the time. Yes, there really was a threat of grenades, but keeping everyone panicked wasn't constructive.

"It's ready to go," Igloo said.

"Test it on me," Angie said.

"You'll know it's the chatbot. That's not a test."

"No, have it mimic me on chat, and talk to everyone else. Maybe it can take over my job and I can do some real work."

"People will be suspicious if you start replying to all your chat messages."

"Make it simulate my normal response time."

"You only respond to eleven percent of your chats, and your average response time is two days. I had to override that behavior for your simulation to actually get something useful."

"Eleven percent?"

"10.4 percent to be precise. I was being generous."

Angie's shoulders slumped. "I wasn't always this way," she mumbled.

"You weren't always a CEO."

"This is hard. I want it to be over sometimes. I want to be done. To go home, be with Thomas, just be an ordinary person again."

Igloo rubbed Angie's shoulder. "I'm not sure you were ever an ordinary person."

Angie turned to look at her. "Sometimes I see you, distracted with Essie or Charlotte, and I get so frustrated because I want all your attention on T2. Then I remember that the reason we're doing any of this is exactly so that people can have what you have."

"You know about Charlotte?"

Angie stared at her and raised an eyebrow. "You told me you were seeing other people. You think I wouldn't dig?"

"I know, I know. I'm just surprised you haven't hassled me about it. You gave me such a hard time over the BDSM stuff. I figured poly would set you off."

"I'm trying to be cool with it," Angie said. "I don't understand a lot of what you do." She took a deep breath. "To me, sex and intimacy is scary. Threatening. For years I couldn't even handle Thomas touching me without asking first. To be so casual, so *trusting* about it, especially with people who are almost strangers, is completely foreign to me."

Igloo laughed. "I didn't start out trusting, you know. I've had my share of crappy experiences."

"Your dad?"

"Not just my dad. Practically every male I encountered. Other kids. Other adults. Sometimes I wonder if I had a sign on my back that said 'molest me' when I was growing up. But being in the scene has taught me how to how to negotiate for what I want and need."

"Which is some fucked up shit." Angie stared into Igloo's eyes. "Look, I talked to Maria, you know, and she encouraged me to think a little more objectively. She says it's my responsibility to deal with my reaction to activities, not yours. I'm trying, okay?"

Igloo checked out Angie's face. She let go of the defensive reaction she'd instinctively reached for. "Thank you. And yeah, I guess I like some fucked up shit. Look, I'm sorry I'm so distracted with my whole weird life."

Angie smiled a sad smile. "I'm glad you have a life to be distracted by."

"We're up against so much, I'm not sure we can afford my level of distraction."

"I am confused, you know," Angie said. "You were so concerned about Tapestry being an egalitarian company. About fighting the patriarchy. Equality above all else. How did you get from there to where you are?"

Igloo took a deep breath. The same question plagued her. "My relationship with Essie isn't equal. She gets me coffee, she takes care of me, I get to make certain decisions she doesn't get to make. It's not fair according to the way I used to look at life. But it is equitable. We each get something out of it. We both find it desirable. Hot. Full of passion."

Somewhere in the back of her mind, Igloo wondered if she was describing now or sometime in the past. Their relationship wasn't the same as it once was. Everything was so complex with poly. But she wasn't going to downward spiral. They were still together, ergo there was still hope for the future. Heck, they had plans to play tonight.

"Essie doesn't want me to take care of her. If I get her coffee, it does nothing for her. Whereas if she gets me coffee, I get...well, let's not go there. The point is, we each want different things. It's not the same for each of us, but we each get something we want out of it. Equality is not always best."

"Strange words, coming from you," Angie said.

Igloo nodded. "For so long I was pushing for one thing, thinking it would lead to a better life, because that was what I'd been told by society. But it turned out that something else was better for me."

They sat in silence for a moment.

"Imagine if we didn't have to fight the government," Angie said. "Imagine if the government was actually on our side, and we were working together to make the world a better place."

"This is the only world I've ever known. I can't imagine it otherwise."

"When I was young and naïve, I assumed the government *was* on our side. Sometimes I wish I could still be that innocent."

"Angie Benenati, innocent? I can't imagine that."

"It was a long time ago."

"Are we done here?" Igloo gestured toward her screen.

"Yeah. We're going to be ready in time?"

"Two weeks. Yeah, we'll roll out T2 three days ahead of the general release. Let a limited beta group test it."

Angie shook her head. "We can't do that. No early signals to the government."

"We can't roll out an entirely new architecture to three hundred million people without a test deployment."

"What if the governments stops us before we can deploy to everyone else?"

"How will they stop us?"

"Assume they can and will do anything. Court order. Shut down our servers. Arrest us all. Blow up this building if necessary."

"We'll do a dead man's deployment switch. If we aren't actively stopping it, T2 will roll out to everyone."

"The current version is vulnerable," Angie said. "If the government gets wind of what we're doing, they could take over our update servers, push out their own fake 1.x release, and change the update mechanism so that it'll never download 2.0."

"So on top of everything else you want us to roll out a more secure updater ahead of the T2 release?"

"Do you see a way around it?"

"No, but..." She realized she was tired and overwhelmed. That was not going to get them anywhere. "I guess we can take the work we did on T2 for the updater and port it over to the V1 update mechanism."

Igloo added it to her mental to-do list. She'd ask Ben and Diana to work it with her. They'd have to get it done over the next couple of days, on top of everything else they had to do. She'd work late tonight.

No, wait. She was going out with Essie tonight. She couldn't let Essie take second place to anything. Their relationship couldn't afford any more neglect right now. Igloo thought about the photo Essie sent. A sudden fantasy of her lips running over the softness of Essie's thighs. Sigh.

"The T2 update should go out the same day as the Tapestry party," Angie said.

"Yeah?"

"There's going to be media coverage of the party. I'll make a brief statement to the press. Since we can't hide the release, then we need to make it as public as possible."

"That party is supposed to be a private employee event," Igloo said. "A celebration of hitting a half billion users. Don't use it as a platform."

"Everything is secondary to getting this release out before the FISA compliance date. If we make a public announcement to coincide with a scheduled event, it furthers the cover story that this is all part of a preexisting plan. The party has been planned for months, since well before they hit us with the court order."

"Plausible, smausible. Who cares? If we have a dead man's switch, then the deployment is going out regardless of what they do."

"Yeah, but I'd still prefer that I don't go to jail for failing to obey a court order."

Oh yeah. That. Igloo's heart thudded. She'd done many things she could go to jail for, and while she and Angie took exhaustive steps to cover their trail, it was always something she was aware of, somewhere in the back of her mind. But this went beyond anything they'd done before. And she'd never had so much to lose. Her new life. Essie. Not to mention Charlotte and Heather and a world of kink to explore. She was finally living the life she'd always wanted to live. It was suddenly very, very important not to go to jail.

There was so much to do, so much that had to go perfectly. Angie, for all her craziness and paranoia, was the only one who could orchestrate a plan to pull it all off. Igloo studied Angie's haggard face, the bags under her eyes, the tension in her temples. Angie had to keep it together for the next couple of weeks.

CHAPTER 24

R obin sat in front of the cameras, waiting for them to come alive. The Faraday curtains rustled softly, the ventilation system causing them to move in the air current. She needed to get back before she was missed.

The screen flickered, and Enso appeared, alone.

Robin was slightly let down, expecting at least to see someone else from the intelligence community. Not every briefing could involve the Deputy Director, but she figured that Tapestry was at the top of the government's list right now.

"Good afternoon, Robin."

"Enso."

"I saw your last report. You're convinced they're going to evade the FISA court order."

"Yes, Sir. It's obvious that T2's entire purpose is to create a technological solution that makes it impossible for Tapestry to comply with the FISA court order."

"T2?"

"The internal slang for Tapestry 2.0. The official project name is Tacenda, a word which means things not to be discussed, but I recommend not using the term in any documentation. My guess is that they're using Trojan horse code names, same as us. It's a rarely used word. Assuming they've compromised us, they could mine our database and know we're monitoring them."

"There's no way they could get inside our systems. China is attacking us 24/7, and in the last six years they've penetrated to this level exactly zero times."

Robin shrugged. There was no way to prove how she felt.

"You have specs on T2?"

"Only what I could glean from discussions. There's nothing written down anywhere I can find, no central repository."

"But you're convinced that it's more than just the..." Enso glanced down to review his notes. "Client-side containers?"

"Definitely. At a minimum the work they're doing involves onion routing, IPFS and bit torrent, distributed ledgers, and the containers we talked about. Exactly how all that fits together isn't obvious, but the pressure to develop this before the deadline is very high, and yet they're intentionally only involving a select few employees."

"What if we bring Angelina Benenati in for questioning?"

Robin laughed. "You'd have more luck squeezing single malt from a stone."

"If we have to question her, what approach should we take?"

"She's too aware of the government as a threat. We're not going to trick her. There's nothing she cares about more than the company and what it's doing. There's no leverage to trump that."

"What about the husband? She seems pretty attached to him. If we threatened to harm him?"

Robin tried to imagine what would happen. She shivered at the thought of Angie lashing out.

"We know what she's capable of," Robin said, choosing her words carefully. "If you corner her, there's going to be collateral damage."

Enso gave a puzzled grin and leaned toward the camera. "Are you scared of her?"

"She has a certain...intensity that is alarming. Sir, we should really focus on Igloo. She's worked with Angie all along, and she's part of T2. She doesn't have all the details, but she has enough to paint an accurate picture of what's going on. With the right leverage, we could get a backdoor into the system through her."

"Legal says we can get her on domestic assault with the videos of her and her girlfriend," Enso said. "But if we don't play it right, she'll go right to Angie for protection, and then all we've done is tip our hand. Turning Igloo is going to require finesse."

"Not a threat against Igloo herself," Robin said. "We direct the threat toward the girlfriend, or Igloo's family, or best of all, Angie herself. Igloo's not hardened the way Angie is. She's reserved, but emotionally raw. I think she'd do almost anything to help Angie."

CHAPTER 25

I gloo ran down the hallway at Tapestry headquarters as lights blinked on and off at random. Her footsteps echoed, the building silent except for the pounding of her feet. Everywhere she looked, in the moments when lights were on, the desks and offices were empty.

Breathing hard, she turned the corner and opened doors looking for Ben and Diana, but found only empty closets.

She was alone, completely alone, and there was so much code left to write. She'd have to do it herself.

But who would review her code? Not Essie, Essie couldn't know. Igloo had to keep this secret.

Then she was back at her desk, coding, and Essie was next to her. Igloo leaned over the keyboard so Essie couldn't see what she was typing. Essie stared at the screen instead, and Igloo had to stand to block the monitor from Essie's view.

Igloo edged closer, trying to block any view of what she was doing, but she accidentally nudged the display to the floor. The screen shattered, and her code leaked out onto the floor. She tried to scoop up the text and pour the letters back into the monitor, but they were all jumbled. She cried—

—And woke up, breathing hard.

"You okay?" Essie said, her voice sleepy. She reached out to rub Igloo's back, her hand warm against Igloo's cold skin.

"I don't know," Igloo said. "I was dreaming."

"You were talking in your sleep."

"What did I say?" What if she'd revealed secrets about T2?

Essie didn't answer.

Igloo shook Essie, and Essie startled awake again. "What did I say?"

"I don't know." Essie raised her head slightly off the pillow. "You were worried about something. Kept asking for more time. Everything okay?"

"Yeah, fine."

Igloo got up, headed for the bathroom, stepping cautiously to avoid anything left out on the floor. But the floor was clear. There hadn't been time for a proper playtime with all the toys in a while. Igloo was glad that she and Essie had gotten that one night last week when they went out together. Since then, it was day after day of non-stop work.

She sat on the toilet in the bathroom. She needed more time. They all needed more time.

In the morning, Igloo logged into the secure chat room they'd convened for everyone working on T2. It was twenty-four days since the FISA court order. Seven days left to preemptively release T2 to avoid complying with the order.

They were using an anonymous chat room, because they ostensibly didn't know who was who. Igloo had guessed at some people's identities by informally correlating code commits on the T2 with a lack of code commits on T1. She couldn't confirm for sure, not when everyone's connections to Tapestry were encrypted, but she could also detect the tell-tale traces of VPN traffic across the network, and those same users were responsible for substantially more encrypted traffic than anyone else. They were working, on average, nearly twice the hours the rest of the employees were. They occasionally ran into each other in the hallways late at night, faces haggard, eyes haunted with feverish energy, trading cautious nods but no words.

Maintaining anonymity under those conditions was mostly a façade, but they needed plausible deniability should things go south.

She started the chat by confirming everyone's progress and making sure they were all up to date. They were avoiding a central backlog of stories to work on, because they didn't want the exact set of features to be listed in one place. Instead, each person or pair kept track of what they had to do and collaborated only on a need to know basis. Igloo, as the supposed, yet still anonymous, leader, needed assessments of how much work was left to do, without knowing too closely the details of that work. It was a ridiculous cat-and-mouse game.

At the end of the meeting, Igloo stared at her electronic scratch-pad. Not good. She sent Angie a message that they had to meet. Angie told her where to go. Igloo left her electronics at her desk.

"We don't have enough time," Igloo said. "Everyone thinks we need another two to three weeks, but we've only got a week left."

Angie studied her. They were surrounded by custodial supplies, but the walk-in closet was one of Angie's emergency safe zones in the building. She'd scanned it for devices when they walked in, then triggered an EMF screamer, broadcasting white noise across the spectrum. In theory it would be contained by the Faraday cage surrounding the closet. If not, they'd probably wipe out every electronic device within a hundred feet.

"You can pull it up. Two weeks of work in one non-stop week, it's not a problem."

"Two or more...and we're not talking about regular weeks, we're already working around the clock."

"Is there anything I can do?" Angie said.

"Give us more time to get T2 out."

"That's the one thing I can't do, and you know it." Angie shook her head. "We have to be in compliance with the FISA court order next Monday. We have to find a way to get it done."

"We're not talking about a user interface feature," Igloo said, getting a little choked up. The task ahead of them was monumental. "We're trying to build and deploy software in a way that's never been done before. We don't get any second chances."

"No, we don't." Angie stared into her eyes. "Do what you can. I'll check in with you tomorrow, then we'll make a decision."

CHAPTER 26

The next morning, Angie entered Igloo's office without knocking. Igloo didn't look up, she was too deeply engrossed in a tricky bit of blockchain validation.

Angie hovered impatiently over Igloo's monitor. "I want you to convene the T2 team immediately."

Igloo gestured toward her screen with an aching arm. "We're all in chat together."

"I want to get together in person and review where we are."

"Where we are?" Igloo said. "We don't have time for that. We're supposed to release this in five days."

"Are you ready?"

"No, we're not fucking ready." Igloo wanted to scream. "We're trying, okay? Give us a break."

Angie squeezed Igloo's shoulder. "I need to know exactly how much time you all need. In person, in the Ops room."

Igloo was too exhausted to argue. She sent the message, marked urgent, over chat. Virtual groans were the response. No one wanted to stop what they were doing for a meeting.

"It's not an option, people. We just have to do it."

A few people were home and had to come into the office. They set the meeting for an hour later.

Once that was taken care of, Igloo slumped back in her chair. She was so tired. She'd been coding for days. She glanced down, saw her phone on the table, blinking away. She picked up the device and found waiting messages from Essie, Charlotte, Heather, her mom, her sister, and the doctor's office. When had she even last looked at her phone? When had she even been home? Or eaten? She was losing track of time.

Charlotte wanted to play. Oh, jeez. The world in which she got to play with people and have fun seemed a million miles away.

Igloo > I miss you so much. But I'm in total crisis mode at work. I'm sorry to do this, but it's gonna be a few weeks before I get out from under this mess. I'll get in touch when things are better.

She realized she was lying as she wrote that. She really had no idea what the future would bring. There was some non-zero chance that she'd be in jail in a few weeks.

She sent quick, perfunctory messages to Heather and her mom, neither of whom needed much investment. She spent a few more minutes on a reply to her sister, who did.

Now to deal with Essie. She absolutely couldn't leave Essie hanging. The last message Essie had sent was a huge wall of text that spanned several screens. The gist of the message was that Essie thought Igloo was avoiding her to get back at her because of Michael. She explained before that there was a work emergency, but Essie wasn't buying it. Igloo would need days to hash everything out with Essie, and longer still to repair all the damage. but she didn't have that time now. All she could do was string things along.

Igloo > I love you. I'm sorry if it feels like I am ignoring or avoiding you. Work is insane right now, and I can't go into why, but please believe me that it has nothing to do with you and Michael. I will do everything I can to be home as soon as I can.

A minute later, a new message came in from Essie.

Essie > When we started dating you told me you had a hard time talking to people. That you preferred computers. That's why you made the chatbots. You've been having a hard time for weeks...months... Please don't shut me out. I love you. You're still my partner. Just because I love Michael doesn't take away from the love I have for you.

Igloo didn't think her central nervous system had any adrenaline left, but somehow Essie's message still managed to enrage her.

Igloo > You love him? Since when is this?
Essie > It's just something I've come to realize. I think it's why you've been having a hard time. But I still love you just as much.

"Fuck, fuck, fuck, *fuck!*" Igloo screamed in an empty room. Why now? Of all possible damn times?

Igloo > How can you love him? You barely know him. We've been together for a year. You've been with him for two months.

Chat showed that Essie was typing, and typing, and typing. It was going to be another monster message. Igloo didn't have time for this.

Igloo > I don't care what you believe. I'm telling you I'm dealing with the literal end of the world here at work. It has nothing to do with you or Michael or anything. I just have to deal with this. I have to go.

Igloo stared at the screen. Then tossed her phone on the table. She'd deal with Essie later.

The Ops room was in the basement, two walls covered in monitors. They used it when they had a major outage and needed to coordinate everything.

Today the screens were all dark. Igloo entered, saw Ben and Diana sitting across the room. Angie stood at the front. Then everyone started to file in, confirming most of Igloo's guesses. Melanie and Mike, almost certainly working on the browser-based containers. Toni, Bob, Chris. Jeff, and Tony with a Y. Gene and Dave. Stephanie and Erik. Dovi. Wendy. Carly.

They looked around at each other, nodding sometimes, surprised at other times.

At least half the folks were the most senior people in their respective areas, but others were newer, brilliant people they'd brought on late. Eighteen people altogether, eighteen people to reinvent how software was delivered, architected, and executed on one of the world's most popular web sites.

They'd worked around the clock the last few weeks as it became obvious just how much work there was to do. The entire team looked like the walking dead.

"You all know what we're up against," Angie said. "I need your minimum time estimates to deliver what's left."

"Igloo's got our estimates," Dovi said. "We don't have to get together just to repeat that."

"I need to hear it for myself."

They went around the room, most people hemming and hawing, reluctant to commit themselves. Nobody offered a date of less than a week, some as much as a month.

In other words, they were going to miss the FISA court order deadline, and by a lot. By doing so, they'd be unable to argue that the

T2 release was pre-planned and inevitable. It would obviously be an attempt to work around the court order.

The silence in the room was oppressive. Everyone knew but nobody would voice what was on everyone's mind: they'd burned up the time they had to comply with the FISA court order. Even if they wanted to, it might be too late to install the required backdoors that would allow the government to spy on everyone. The company could be shut down. Igloo wondered if Angie would go to jail. Maybe they all would.

Angie stared around the room. She was as haggard as the rest of them, but there was a fire in her eyes that Igloo recognized from their all-night hacking sessions. Somehow, unbelievably, Angie had a plan!

"Dovi, you're going to finish up your work by tomorrow, then help Gene and Dave. Wendy, skip the UI work, and help Jeff and Tony with a Y. Carly, find a way to finish faster. Pull in whomever you need from your team, even if they aren't cleared for T2."

"People, I'm not going to sugarcoat this. T2 has to go out. I realize it can't happen by Monday, but damn it all, it fucking has to be out within a week. Everything rides on this."

"The court order deadline is noon on Monday," Ben said. "There's no wiggle room on that." He turned to Diana, who nodded.

"I'll find a way to get you all another week."

"That's not possible—" Ben started.

Angie gave him such a hard look he stopped mid-sentence. "Don't you ever tell me what's possible. I'm going to buy you a week. That's all the time you get. There aren't going to be any other magic bullets."

She fell silent.

Someone cleared their throat, then Angie started again.

"You have to focus no matter what happens. I believe in you, all of you. You are the most talented people I've ever worked with. You can make it happen. Now get back to work."

Igloo stood, along with everyone else. Her body was tingly, half-asleep already.

"Not you, Igloo."

Igloo sat back down and closed her eyes for just a second.

She was startled awake, Angie shaking her. The room was empty except for the two of them.

"You're going to have to keep everyone operationally secure," Angie said. "That's going to include keeping them on the move. I want you all out of this office. They may try to shut us down on Tuesday. But if you're not here, then they can't stop you."

Igloo nodded, feeling like she was missing something.

"Treat it like it was the two of us hacking. Nobody can know where you are. Rotate safe houses."

"What about the company party on Friday night?" Igloo asked. "Is it safe to show up there?"

Angie looked off toward the wall. "Yes. That'll be the last time it's safe for anyone to show up in public. After that, keep in hiding. Remember that the best defense is a good offense. When they come for you, strike back. Don't let them own the network."

"Yeah," Igloo said, "but where are you going to be?"

"I'll be distracting everyone. That's my job. Your job is to insulate everyone else from that distraction and get T2 released."

"Got it."

"That's not all," Angie said. "The election. The world can't withstand another four years like this. Get the right person elected."

"That's not for six months. We can work on it together."

"Just don't forget. Now go to work."

Igloo got up, glanced back to see Angie standing alone in the room, staring off into the distance. She let the door slowly close, and Angie disappeared from view.

CHAPTER 27

The FISA court order would take effect Monday. Angie needed to buy the team time. Time to fix bugs, get the final features done, and get the release out. A few weeks would be nice, a few months would be a dream. But at this point, even a few days would help.

If the only problem were Enso at BRI continually hounding her, then she could bury him in an onslaught from the hacker community. But what she needed now was something on the order of a miracle. She needed to countermand the FISA court order.

Maybe something like a presidential executive order could do that. Or she needed to take out the entire executive function. Bring down the FBI so they couldn't enforce the FISA court order.

Also equally improbable.

So what could work? What would create sufficient cause to alter the FISA court ruling?

For a moment, she thought of reaching out to Nathan9. She'd missed having someone of his strategic nature on her side. Hell, she really wished her old mentor Repard were there to help. Well, none of them were on her side. She'd have to deal with it herself.

What would Repard and Nathan tell her? Of course they'd say

that the direct frontal approach would always fail. Hacking the highest levels of governmental systems to forge an executive order or court decision was ludicrous, right?

She stalked back and forth in her office.

They had computer systems, like anything else. If she could penetrate those systems, she could take them over. All she needed was one computer on a sensitive system with an available exploit, and she could take it over.

She could open a backdoor with Tapestry, but she was exceedingly hesitant to do so. She had to assume BRI was watching her every move. To compromise a sensitive system, a watched system, with a backdoor in Tapestry would create a trail that would lead right back to her.

Besides, she knew nothing about their backend systems. She had no idea what computers they had, what their network topography looked like. She'd be hunting blind.

Hunting. Blind. A hunting blind.

Hunters set up blinds in the woods. Waited for their prey to come to them.

Maybe she couldn't fabricate a presidential executive order, but she could probably manipulate the president into creating a legitimate one, if she gave him something tempting enough.

Both the president and the First Lady were active Tapestry users.

If their private data was exposed in such a way that suggested the government itself had leaked the information, the president would go on one of his legendary tirades. He could potentially order the stop of any wiretaps into Tapestry, which would have the effect of delaying the FISA court order.

She stopped pacing. She needed to get to a safe house.

She sanitized herself of traceable electronics and left Tapestry headquarters in hurry. Outside, she walked a few blocks and entered a gym where she had memberships under her name and an alias. In the locker room she changed her clothes, added heels to alter her gait, and a long, bulky coat to disguise her shape and missing arm. She left through another exit, walked down an alley to a garage she rented where she kept an old, pre-computer car.

She grabbed a bag with a computer and accessories out of the trunk and brought it up to the front seat with her. She drove to Northwest Portland and parked in the basement garage of a condominium, a building she'd scoped out before. Pulling a charged smartphone out of the laptop bag, she used a door entry code she kept up to date by sniffing phone data from building residents through the Tapestry client.

Before she entered the building proper, she ran a hack to disable the building cameras. She made her way up to the common area on the fifth floor. As expected, given the mid-work week time, the common room was empty. She positioned herself in a back corner. When she started her laptop there were over a hundred wi-fi access points to choose from, both from the building she was in, as well as the apartment building across the street. High density living was a panacea when it came to net access.

What she needed was the appearance of a pre-existing government backdoor into Tapestry, a tap that gave access to the private Tapestry data.

Of course, the President and First Lady's actual messages were protected, encrypted such that even Angie couldn't access them without using backdoors that would put their clients into diagnostic mode. She didn't dare do that because the government was almost certainly monitoring their phones and would detect Angie's tampering. Without that access, Angie couldn't determine what either of them had said privately and therefore couldn't leak any significant data.

But it was no secret that the President didn't trust the First Lady. If Angie created messages that gave the appearance of communication between the First Lady and a third party, the President would freak out.

But whom? And what sort of scenario? A romantic tryst? Leaking government information? A business liaison? The romantic interest seemed like it had the best potential to inspire a jealous rage, but it also seemed cliché. Promises of business favors was more viable.

She did a quick search, correlating the First Lady with assorted business people. She found a promising connection with the CEO of a hotel chain.

The hacker community had screenshots and PDF reports from PRISM, the government's surveillance suite. She used these existing screenshots to fabricate new images, showing exchanges between the First Lady and the CEO, with vague language about a government contract in exchange for even more vague reciprocity.

She created new messages in the First Lady's Tapestry account, then deleted them. The system wouldn't maintain the message, but it would keep the meta-data trail, showing that messages with corresponding timestamps and sizes had been deleted. It meant that when a forensics team analyzed the First Lady's account, they'd see a deletion trail that exactly matched what had been leaked. It was not real evidence, but it created the appearance of corroborating evidence, and that was what mattered.

Then she submitted the screenshots to anonymous leaks accounts at two major newspapers, informing each that she was submitting to more than one paper. That would help ensure they didn't sit on the leaks for too long.

The shit should hit the fan before the day was out.

CHAPTER 28

A lice messaged Enso to get down to the war room pronto.
That was unlike her, so he dropped everything and made his way down to the basement.

The war room had an ever-present tang of body odor, heavy with stress. Three dozen or so analysts and hackers worked together in the cramped room. Borrowed from assorted agencies and groups, they were all tasked with full-time work on BRI.

There was a smaller, glass-walled enclosure at the end of the room, and Alice was in there with two others. She gestured for him to join them.

Most of the people in the room were deep into their oversized displays, but a few noticed him enter and looked as if they might try to get his attention. He made his way down the room, holding his hand up to forestall interruptions.

"What's up?" he asked as he entered.

"You're going to like this," Alice said. "Tell him, Cassie."

Enso turned to the other two. One female, one male, both geeky and shy. He tried to remember where he'd gotten them from and failed. Maybe Air Force intelligence?

"Prime Subject left the office today," the woman said.

"That's Angie," Alice said.

Enso frowned at her. "I know who Prime Subject is." He turned to Cassie. "Go on."

"She went to a gym, changed clothes, and picked up a car a few blocks away. We caught a few seconds of this on satellite and correlated with local surveillance cameras. We went active on satellite tasking and followed her to an apartment building. We switched on full monitoring as soon as she entered the building, and redirected data traffic from within a six-block radius through STARFISH."

Enso glanced at Alice.

"Cassie is on loan from cyber command, and STARFISH is one of their secret tools."

"It lets us intercept all the traffic in realtime," Cassie said. "I triggered STARFISH right away, because it changes traffic latency by two to three milliseconds. By the time Angie would have been in a place to check latency, STARFISH was already on. She wouldn't have been able to detect the change."

Enso nodded, and Cassie continued.

"Prime brought up a VPN and started traffic patterns consistent with onion routing over the VPN. We tried but couldn't break the encryption."

"I hope you didn't bring me down here to tell me that. This is the same story I hear every time from all of you."

Cassie shook her head. "The session lasted three hours and thirty-seven minutes. Six minutes before her session ended, we captured two anonymous submissions to news outlets, both originating from the onion network."

"You broke her onion routing connection?" Enso asked.

"No, Quantum linked the two."

Enso looked at Alice.

"Cyber command is letting us use Quantum, too," Alice said. "One of their dark projects."

"Quantum monitors about a hundred million points of interest," Cassie said. "Websites, chat boards, known hacker hangouts, that sort of thing. It correlates traffic across geography, time, and point of origination. We gave Quantum the details of Angie's connection, it gave us back a list of activities ranked by probability that they were connected with her."

"Quantum is sure these originated with Angie?"

Alice shoved a tablet in front of him. "Look at these messages. What do you think?"

Enso started to read them. Alice didn't wait for him to finish. "They're clearly inflammatory. What's the President going to do when he sees this? He's going to freak out, claim we're wiretapping him and his family, and order us to shut down our backdoors into Tapestry."

"Backdoors we don't even have." Enso shoved the tablet into Alice's hands. "She's playing a game, trying to stop the FISA court order. Why? She has to know she can't succeed."

"Over the long term, no," Alice said. "But maybe she doesn't need to win over the long term. She could be trying to stall, even for a few days. Maybe to cover up something, data she needs to hide, something like that."

"We can't let this get leaked," Enso said. "What are our options?"

"Already taken care of," Alice said.

"We crashed the servers the drop boxes were running on," Cassie said. "Wiped everything. All their data and logs. They'll have no trail that it was ever submitted."

"I hope that's okay," Alice said. "We had to act immediately. If we waited, even for a moment, they could have backed up the data to another machine."

Enso's heart swelled. For all the difficulties of working in the government, sometimes things came together perfectly. "Great job. You did the right thing." He shook their hands. "For once we have the upper hand."

CHAPTER 29

B y the time Angie made it back to the office, it was late, and nearly everyone was gone for the day. She caught up on a final few messages, then contacted Thomas and told him she was on her way home.

That night, she compulsively checked the Tapestry news feed, the version locally cached on her phone, but there was nothing yet to indicate anyone acting on her anonymous leak.

"Come to bed," Thomas said. "You're cut off."

"I need to check one more thing."

"What you need is sleep. You have to take care of yourself."

"You don't understand," Angie said, more sharply than she meant to. "I have to..." Out of the corner of her eye, she realized Thomas was walking away.

"Thomas, I'm sorry."

She followed him to the bedroom, where he was already climbing into bed.

"This is urgent," she said. If the gambit didn't work, she was going to have to come up with a plan B. What was plan B? Just how many ways were there to manipulate the highest echelons of the government?

He pulled the covers over himself. "It's always urgent, isn't it? Everything's urgent. If it wasn't important and urgent you wouldn't be working on it."

"Right," Angie said, concerned that by agreeing she was walking into a trap.

"You'll have time for me tomorrow. Except that tomorrow never comes. There's only ever today. And every today, Tapestry is urgent and important."

"I'm sorry it seems like that," Angie said, climbing in to lie next to him. She stroked his chest. Could she get a senator on her side? Could she blackmail the vice-president? Certainly he had to have some skeletons in his closet.

"There is no 'seems'. This is reality. This is fact. I understand Tapestry is important. It's your life mission and there's no one in the world better suited to it. But if you think that you'll solve all of the problems tonight and spend tomorrow with me, you're mistaken. Sometimes, some days, us—you and me—that has to be the most important thing. Otherwise we'll never get a turn."

"I know, I know," Angie said, and she did. There would only be so many days with Thomas. She laid her head on his chest. "I love you."

Thomas stroked her hair, and Angie waves of exhaustion hit her. She almost fell asleep. No, not tonight. She wasn't going to miss tonight.

"Take off your underwear."

"Now?" Thomas said. "It's late. I have to get up early tomorrow. The Tapestry party is tomorrow night."

Angie reached down between his legs, felt him get hard. "There's only today, buddy. No tomorrow. Now are we going to get busy or what?"

Thomas stared at her. "Well, I'm not going to look a gift horse in the mouth." He stripped off his undershirt, and climbed on top of her, pulling off her panties and tank top.

When they were both naked, he pressed up against her sex. His warmth entered her, and soon Tapestry was gone from her mind, and there was only Thomas, his body strong against hers, pumping between her legs, a wave building, cresting, and crashing.

In the morning, Angie and Thomas went through their routine, a choreographed dance through bathroom, closet, and kitchen. Each got their morning rituals done with a modicum of interaction. He went into the kitchen, she checked her feed for any activity related to her leaks, found nothing. He made the coffee while she showered. Thomas hopped into the shower when Angie got out, and she went to the bedroom to dress and check her feed again. Nothing.

She was starting to feel panicked. She definitely needed a plan B.

She microwaved egg and sausage sandwiches while he dressed, and she brought the food to him.

"What are the plans for the party tonight?" he asked.

"Huh?"

"The party. You said something about Emily coming over."

The Tapestry party was a million miles from Angie's attention. She had to buy the T2 team time. There was no way she could allow the government to destroy Tapestry with the FISA court order. "Yeah, Emily's coming to help us get dressed. We're going to carpool over with her and Jeff."

"Is she bringing her new car?"

Angie shrugged noncommittally, not really paying attention. The FISA court order was like entering a relationship with an abusive spouse who would spy on your every action for the rest of your life. The best plan was to not get into that relationship in the first place, because once you were in it, escaping it took a hundred times more effort.

It wasn't merely that escaping the entanglement was difficult, but that the relationship itself was disempowering, so that there was almost no will or power left to fight with.

She'd been there before with her first husband. She waited until he was drunk one night and used the excuse to drive them home. But the fight to get behind the wheel herself, even when he was drunk, had been almost more than she could manage. Only her total desperation had allowed her to keep pushing to drive. She wasn't even trying to escape at that point, only to end it all. She had planned to kill them both.

Death was the final escape, the only solace to the totally trapped.

Oh.

There had to be other options, right?

CHAPTER 30

That night Angie felt almost relaxed. Almost. Repard, her old mentor, taught her the importance of believing. It was one of his little lessons, back when they'd worked on fooling the lie detector.

"The lie detector is easy, Angie. It's just a machine. Fooling people, people who know you, that's harder. You have to half believe the lie. But most difficult of all is fooling yourself. To make yourself believe a particular truth. That's the key, you know, the key to living with yourself."

Half the time she hadn't known what he was talking about, but in retrospect, she thought it was just before he pulled the big con, the hack that had almost sent him and everyone else to jail. He'd probably been talking about how to live with the consequences of his actions. It was clear enough that he had a conscience. If he was a sociopath, it probably would have been easier.

"Fuck," Angie said, pain pulling her back to the present. "That hurts."

No one ever told Angie what she'd have to go through as the CEO of a tech company. She might have stuck with killing people if she'd known. It was easier.

"Stop fidgeting." Emily held her face in place. "Let me finish tweezing you."

"Nobody is going to look at my eyebrows."

"I will. Look, you're done. You're perfect."

"Can I stand?" Angie got to her feet and looked in the mirror. She smoothed her dress, adjusted the neckline, and turned sideways, her arm toward the mirror. She'd let Emily talk her into a black cocktail dress a few weeks ago. She wasn't a complete stranger to girly things, but she couldn't remember wearing a dress like this since she moved to Portland.

The half billion user milestone for Tapestry had been looming large for a while. The celebration had started as just another corporate function, but enough vestiges of their startup culture still throbbed in the blood of the company that they'd ended up with an amalgamation of wiccan rituals celebrating fertility and a cocktail party.

Angie almost teared up thinking about the birthing ceremony Igloo had arranged at the company's first winter solstice party. It was a potluck, because cash was short. Igloo brought in blankets and shaped them into the unmistakable form of labia, and the employees took turns being a baby emerging from a vagina.

Emily cleared her throat. "Stop that."

"Stop what?" Angie said, pulling herself back to the present.

"You're worrying about how your stump looks."

Angie looked down, and it was true, the sleeveless dress made her stump stand out, but it was the furthest thing from her mind tonight.

"Everyone is going to look at my stump," she said, because that's what Emily expected her to say.

"Ange, it's a company party with your employees. They've seen your stump. Besides, they'll probably be looking at your ass."

Angie forced a little laugh and turned three-quarters around to check out her bottom in the mirror. "My forty-eight-year-old ass? I don't think so. I eat too many burgers and sit in meetings all day."

Emily smacked Angie's butt. "It looks great. Besides, I've got something for you." She reached into her purse and pulled out a gift-wrapped bundle.

"What's this?" Angie said.

"Something to go with the dress."

"Where are your kids tonight?" Angie asked.

"With the nanny. She's working late."

Angie set the soft package down on the dresser and tugged at the wrapping paper, trying to steady it with her stump, but in the end just ineffectually sliding the whole thing around. Emily put one hand on the package to hold it in place.

"Thanks." Angie got some purchase on a corner of the paper, and tugged one end free, then the middle. The paper folded back to reveal silky fabric. She shook loose a black and silver shawl.

"Oh, gosh, it's beautiful. Help me put it on."

Emily arranged the lightweight scarf around Angie's shoulders and tucked it over her right one. Angie looked into the mirror and smiled. Not only was the shawl pretty, but what was left of her right arm was far less noticeable.

"I got ya covered, sister." She leaned in and gave Angie a kiss on the cheek. "You've done great. You're a world-class CEO. A few years ago you were afraid to make a slide deck."

"I was in the right place at the right time," Angie said. She didn't want to fuss over things now.

"You downplay things, but you're a great leader. You built a company around a mission, not just making money. That's no easy task."

"The job's not over."

"No, but tonight's for celebrating all that you've accomplished. Now let's go."

Thomas must have heard their heels clicking on the bamboo floor, because he stood as they approached. Emily's husband, Nick, followed his cue.

"Wow." Thomas looked Angie up and down. "Fantastic."

"Here," Emily said, and held out a key ring. "You guys take my car."

"We can't," Angie said.

"We can," Thomas said, and reached for the keys. He had long and vocally lusted after Emily's BMW, a limited edition he was too late to sign up for.

"We are not taking the chance of anything happening to Emily's car."

"Oh, come on," Emily said. "I got the thing as a bonus. I didn't pay a dime for it. Take the car. We'll drive Thomas's car."

Thomas gave Angie a puppy dog face.

"Look, it's not that," Angie said. "I want to go in my own car. My car is good luck to me."

"That bucket of 3D printed plastic?" Emily laughed. "You spend more time bringing it in for maintenance than anything else."

She'd bought the Gnu FlexCar after Tapestry's third and final funding round. It was locally made, 3D printed parts and a computerized electric drive train. Open source and copyleft from head to toe. A geek's car, to be sure, with more than a few design warts. She loved it, but Thomas and Emily detested everything about it, from the anemic handling to the noisy cooling fans to the body curves. She'd never confessed to them that she had tweaked those Bézier curves herself prior to printing the parts. They didn't feel the pride that Angie felt that every line of code was open source.

"That car represents everything about this journey to me, and I'm driving it to the party."

Thomas was visibly crestfallen, but he walked away from Emily and rejoined Angie.

"No, you can't get all mopey with me. Go with Emily. She'll let you drive. I want to go by myself. I could use a few minutes of solitude before the party."

"Are you sure? I feel like I'm abandoning you."

"We can't all be extroverts," Angie said. Part of her mind was scared that she could play this part so well. Why didn't anyone notice something was wrong? They should scream and stop her. But she couldn't let that happen. "Trust me, I'm perfectly happy being by myself for a bit. Just give me a kiss first."

Thomas came over, put one arm around her, and kissed her lips.

Angie pulled him back when he pulled away. "Not like that. Like you mean it."

He wrapped her in both arms, and for a moment, all she could feel was him surrounding her, protecting her. She wanted to stay in those arms forever. She kissed him, hard and full of need. She wanted to make love to him.

"Whoa, Nelly," Thomas said. "There'll be time enough for that after the party."

But there isn't ever time enough for all the things.

"Are you okay?" he asked, holding her shoulders.

He noticed. He noticed. Thank you, universe.

She rested her head on his chest. "I'm okay. Go with Emily." She lifted her head and stared into his eyes as she put a finger on his lips. She didn't want him to say goodbye. "I love you."

"There's six hundred and fifty horsepower, half of that from the hybrid portion of the drivetrain, powering all four wheels." Thomas called across the driveway. "Are you sure..."

"I'm sure," Angie called back, through the open window. "Go. I love you."

Thomas rocketed away with what appeared to be neck-twisting acceleration. She heard Emily let out a whoop, and then suddenly she was by herself, wishing that this party had never been planned, or that if it had been, that it was at some much more distant point in the future.

Everything was relatively close in Portland, and it was a too-short twenty minutes to the hotel where Tapestry was having the party. For once, Angie wished for more traffic.

Angie was two cars behind Thomas, Emily and Nick, pulling up to the front of the hotel to take advantage of the valet parking.

Up ahead, she saw Igloo and Amber on the sidewalk, greeting guests as they arrived. There was another woman by Igloo's side, dressed in black. From her profile, that must be Essie. A pity they'd never met, considering what an influence she'd been on Igloo. Igloo had traded in her usual white hoodie for a white lace dress. Angie chuckled as Igloo turned and presented a three-quarter view. Igloo's lace dress was hooded. Some things always stay the same.

And then again, some things change.

Damn it. Igloo wasn't going to understand.

Angie pulled out her phone, typed a quick message, and hit send.

The car in front of her pulled away.

She rubbed a hand over the Gnu Car's bulbous dashboard and took a deep breath.

CHAPTER 31

I gloo gave Thomas and Emily hugs, then directed them inside. She couldn't wait to be done with this, to be inside with Essie. She glanced back, smiled at Essie.

Essie gave her a bratty sneer back, then a laugh.

A mix of relief and passion swept through her. That Essie was being playful was a good sign. When Igloo had finally shown up at home that afternoon, Essie took one look at the bags under her eyes and half-carried Igloo to bed. Igloo protested, but Essie insisted that she get at least an hour sleep. When she woke, Essie had shots of espresso and an energy drink at the ready. Igloo forced out incoherent apologies, but Essie shushed her and told her to drink her coffee. Somehow Essie had a seemingly limitless ability to forgive.

When Igloo was done with the greeting charade here, she was going to go inside and find a quiet corner where she could share an intimate moment with Essie. She just wanted a moment to kiss and touch foreheads together and hold each other.

Igloo brought herself back to the present as the next car pulled up, and Maria climbed out. She came around to open the passenger door. A beautiful woman in a slinky dress stepped out.

Maria approached and gave Igloo a warm hug.

"This is Danielle," Maria said. "Danielle, this is Igloo."

How could Igloo have not known? Why was there no secret lesbian sign?

Igloo reached out to shake Danielle's hand, and then a searing flash forced her eyes shut. There was a *whomp,* and Igloo was thrown back against the wall as the world went to hell, projectiles smashed all around her. Something struck her forehead.

She looked in the direction of the flash and saw flames, a fierce yellow-blue chemical blaze roaring out of a car.

Angie's car.

Igloo screamed and tried to run toward the vehicle, but a hand grabbed her. Essie, pulling her away.

Igloo briefly saw a silhouette of a human form against the flames in the car before another explosion threw her to the ground.

Igloo woke in a hospital, the smell of burning plastic in her nose.

"Angie?" Her voice cracked. "Angie!" she screamed.

A shape moved in a chair next to her. Essie put her forehead against Igloo's, and shook back and forth, salty tears running down her face into Igloo's mouth.

Igloo's heart collapsed. She wished she were dead.

"No." Igloo flailed. "Nooo."

Essie grabbed her wrists and held her down. "Stop," Essie hissed. "I don't have the strength to fight you."

Igloo stopped thrashing and curled up. Angie. Angie. Angie.

Igloo was on her side in the fetal position, numbly staring at Essie, who sat next to the bed hugging herself, streaks of mascara running down her cheeks.

A nurse entered, and it took Igloo a moment to focus on him.

He ignored Igloo and read a display next to the bed.

"Is she okay?" Essie asked.

The nurse looked at Essie, then Igloo.

"You have a slight concussion," he said. "But our main concern is smoke and chemical inhalation, specifically hydrogen cyanide, which forms in plastics fires. I need to put this mask on you."

"Is Amber okay? Is anyone else hurt?" Igloo asked, just before he fitted the mask onto her face.

"Just breathe," he said, turning to a medical display.

"Our friends were at the hotel," Essie said.

"I'm sorry, we can only release medical information to family." He held the mask in place for a minute longer, then pulled it off again.

"The doctor will be in shortly." He stared at Igloo. "There are two police officers here to see you."

He left and held the door open. Two officers, one man and one woman, entered.

Igloo got a sudden case of déjà vu, and remembered the night Angie killed Chris Daly, the government agent who'd been stalking her. Police had questioned Igloo then about his death.

"We understand you go by Igloo," the woman said. "I'm Detective Calvert, and this is Detective Monroe. We'd like to ask you some questions."

"What happened tonight?" Monroe said.

Igloo couldn't believe they expected her to talk. She wanted everyone to go away. Leave her alone to mourn her friend. But they weren't going anywhere.

She summoned up some reserve of energy and explained about the company celebration, and how she'd glanced up to see Angie's car as it burst into flame.

Some part of her mind screamed and ranted on the inside while the other part soldiered on, doing its duty, machine-like and cold.

"Any idea why she was driving alone?" Monroe said.

Igloo shook her head. "No."

"According to a preliminary report from the fire department, the vehicle battery overheated and exploded. Do you know if she had problems with the vehicle?"

"I don't know if she had problems with the battery specifically, but there was always lots of issues with that car. It's experimental, open source. Community built."

Her brain felt like it was operating at 5 percent normal capacity, but she had to wonder...if the battery exploded, was it faulty hardware, software, or deliberate?

"Sorry," Detective Calvert said, "but who makes it?"

"Nobody makes it. It's open source. She downloaded the designs, most of the physical parts were 3D printed, and she put it together with the help of a fabrication shop here in town."

"So she built it?"

"I'm sorry," Igloo said, "but why are we talking about who built her car?"

"Because we're trying to understand why Angelina Benenati died in a vehicle fire."

The words hit her like a brick, and she realized it was the first time someone acknowledged out loud that Angie was really dead.

A small part of her mind thought that they should look at the charge controller. It would have detailed analytics and history for every cell in the battery pack. Igloo remembered Angie proudly showing off the onboard computer hidden in a compartment under the passenger seat.

"Our forensic people say she sent a message just a few seconds before the explosion, but it was encrypted on the Tapestry network, and we can't read it. We'd like Tapestry's help in decoding the message."

Igloo couldn't figure out what they were going on about. Did the regular police have that level of monitoring over everyone's phone? She stared blankly at them.

The police left eventually, and the doctor finally came in to see and treat both her and Essie. They were both released.

"Some more members of your party are down the hall," the doctor said, signing off on electronic forms. "What a night." She seemed to be talking to herself, then she turned back to Igloo. "I'm sorry for your loss."

Pain blanketed Igloo's body, both distanced and somehow magnified by exhaustion.

"Come on," Essie said. "Let's get out of here." She helped Igloo out of bed and kept one arm around her as they walked down the hallway.

They stopped outside a room at the sound of Thomas's voice. He sat sobbing, Emily next to him. They were holding hands.

Igloo was an outsider to them. She wanted to go closer, to join them in their hug and scream out loud "I was Angie's friend, too. We did things and kept secrets you can never know about."

But she couldn't. The operational habits Angie had drilled into her meant there had always been distance between them. She wondered what sort of friendship they might have had if their secret pact, their hacking activities that were shared with no one else, hadn't stood in the way, if they hadn't needed to pretend they weren't close.

Would they have been closer, she wondered? Or more distant? She would never know.

A sob started somewhere deep in her chest, so violent she thought she was going to be sick at first, and the sound that finally erupted from her sounded only half human. Thomas and Emily turned toward her. She couldn't deal, not with them, nor with this situation. She fled from the room, dragging Essie behind her.

She ran down the hallway, turned the corner, and ran straight into Maria. Somehow she found herself hugging Maria, squeezing her tight. Maria hugged her back, and Igloo sobbed into her shoulder.

"She was everything to me," Igloo whispered into Maria's ear. "How can I go on?"

Maria pulled back a little, and Igloo realized for the first time that

Maria had her arm in a cast. "You are strong. You will survive."

Maria's partner came up and put her arm around Maria, pulled Maria away gently, and they walked off down the hallway alone.

Igloo turned to Essie who took her in a fierce hug.

There was no coherent thought, just a carousel of images and vignettes. Meeting Angie for the first time in their offices at the old Puppet Labs space. Going out to lunch with Angie and Amber, brainstorming ways to change the world, to save the world. The relief on Angie's face the day they secured their first outside investment. Angie saving her and her sister, when her sister had been the victim of a ratter who'd stolen her private photos and Igloo had tried to hunt them down herself, with no skills or knowledge whatsoever. Being coached for her first in-person social engineering attempt ever. Moving into the new offices. Going together to hunt down an abuser. Angie breaking down and crying the day Igloo convinced her to never kill anyone again.

Essie was in front of her, talking to her. The words were distant. Igloo felt herself being pulled, guided, and then they were outside. She was pushed toward a car, forced into the seat. She distantly wondered why Essie was buckling her seatbelt, and then the night-time lights blurred.

She was in a bed sometime after that. It was dark, but she could make out Essie sleeping. She slid closer to Essie and wrapped her arms around her. Essie was warm and soft, and her arm curled responsively around Igloo.

She lay there, wetness growing between her cheek and Essie's chest.

"You okay?" Essie asked, her voice floating in the darkness.

"I've snotted your tit."

Essie reached over and handed her some tissues, then wrapped Igloo with both arms. Igloo flipped onto her other side and let Essie spoon her, holding her tight.

"Tighter," Igloo croaked, crying harder.

Essie squeezed, almost crushing her, and Igloo fell back to sleep.

CHAPTER 32

In the morning, Igloo woke to find the bed empty next to her, kitchen sounds distant. She was drowning in an endless void.

The bedroom door cracked open and Essie peeked in, and when she saw Igloo was awake she padded into the room naked. She approached, mug held by the handle in one hand, resting on the palm of the other. Her legs folded under her, and she knelt in the bed facing Igloo. She carefully, ritually turned the mug so the handle faced Igloo, and bowed her head.

Some D/s relationships were all about such protocols, every behavior rigidly defined. Their relationship had never been that way. This presentation had always been Essie's gesture of voluntary submission that said: "I offer myself to you."

Life goes on, Igloo thought, even when you don't want it to. In this case, she had to pull herself together, be the Dominant that Essie needed her to be.

She forced herself to rise to an upright sitting position, briskly rubbed her eyes, then oriented her upper body to face Essie directly. She took the coffee from Essie Japanese-style, using both hands to receive the cup, a gesture intended to show respect and full regard for the giver.

"Thank you." She forced the words out through a throat swollen with grief.

Ritual complete, Essie crawled over and rested her head on Igloo's chest. "I'm sorry."

Igloo wondered if Essie thought her reaction was completely out of proportion. Essie didn't fully understand her relationship with Angie, and she might imagine that Igloo and Angie's relationship was merely employee and CEO.

Even Igloo didn't totally grok her relationship with Angie. They'd kept up the pretense of distance. She never knew exactly where she stood, what was charade and what was real. All the things she could never say to Angie.

She couldn't explain this to Essie either. Oh, the cost of keeping secrets. They poisoned everything, every relationship, every interaction. She could be totally honest about her deepest sexual desires and fears with Essie, but she couldn't even share the basics of her relationship with Angie.

Fuck that. What was the point of hiding anything anymore? How many of the problems she and Essie were having were because of the artificial distance between them? She was so sick of secrets.

"She was more than my boss," Igloo said, setting her coffee on the nightstand. "She was my mentor, my friend. I built conversational AI as a way for people to form friendships and get emotional support when they couldn't get it from the actual people around them. She made my dream a reality. Hundreds of millions of people talk to my personalities."

Igloo turned onto her side, facing away. Essie stroked her back.

"But it's more than that. She was my friend in ways I can't describe. In ways that I don't think anyone could ever be again. We did stuff together, stuff I can't talk about."

"What kind of stuff?" Essie curled against Igloo and wrapped an arm around her.

Igloo moved Essie's hand to cradle her boob, then raised her head. Essie slid her other arm under Igloo's neck, and Igloo wiggled closer.

She hesitated. Angie would talk about operational security. She shouldn't talk about this stuff with Essie, but she knew she was going to do it anyway.

"Computer stuff. Hacking stuff. Angie trusted me with parts of her life, her plans that she would never let anyone else get involved with. Matters of life and death."

Essie petted Igloo's hair.

Igloo flipped back over so she could look into Essie's eyes. "What's happened to us, Essie? We used to talk about everything, but I feel like we haven't really talked in months. I'm always so upset about you and Michael."

"Or you're distracted texting Charlotte and Heather." Essie kept playing with Igloo's hair.

"I know. But I'm only so distracted by them because I feel like there's so much distance between us."

Essie sighed, and her hand slowed. "I know. I feel the distance too."

"I left so much unsaid with Angie, and now she's gone. I don't want to do that with you."

Essie pulled Igloo close. "I'm not going anywhere."

"We have to work harder," Igloo said. "We can't just coast along assuming everything is going to work out. We have to build the relationship we want."

"We will," Essie said. "We will make the future we want."

Igloo looked deeply into Essie's face. Essie was speaking the truth. Essie was finally totally here and present for her. Such a precious thing.

But the future was so much bigger than just the two of them. What would happen now, without Angie to carry on? Tapestry would survive, but would all of Angie's secret plans live on? Getting T2 out. Influencing the news stories. Altering the outcome of the next election.

The words she'd uttered a few minutes ago ran through her head again. *Angie trusted me with...her plans that she would never let anyone else get involved with.*

Suddenly the conversation they'd had last week made so much more sense. Angie expected her, Igloo, to carry on those plans. Angie had *known* this was going to happen. She had fucking known.

She jerked upright, almost flinging Essie aside. "Where's my phone?"

"What?"

"My phone? I need it." She looked around the bed, didn't see anything. "Where's my bag, the one I had last night?"

"I don't know," Essie said. "I don't remember seeing it after the explosion."

Igloo tried to think back, but she didn't even remember going to the hospital. She must have dropped it somewhere.

She slid her a spare computer out from under the bed. She waited impatiently for it to start, then switched over to a secure partition. Without her phone here, she needed to use a backup set of codes to bypass her normal two-factor authentication and get logged into her secure Tapestry account. She checked for a message from Angie.

7:54PM.

Jesus, she was right in the middle of greeting people then. That couldn't have been more than a couple of minutes before the explosion.

Stay focused on the long game. AOM.

Was that supposed to mean something? AOM was short for Angie's old handle, Angel of Mercy.

Why would she leave such a meaningless message, at that moment, of all times? Why didn't she say something more important?

"Duh!"

"What?" Essie asked.

"She left me a message, just not here. This is her way to remind me to check my secure messages."

"More secure than those hoops you just jumped through?"

Igloo turned on a VPN, then started onion routing over Angie's network. She let Essie watch. She was no longer going to hide anything. She couldn't live that way. She connected to the server she and Angie used for their most secret hacking work.

She had a new message from Angie, dated this morning. For a brief second, her mind wanted to believe that Angie was still alive despite the obvious certainty of watching Angie die last night. But no. This was just Angie's dead man's switch, her kill switch, sending out a last message after Angie was gone.

I'm keeping this deliberately short because I can never put into it everything you want to know or I want to say. If I try to select a few things, you'll read into everything I didn't say, and jump to the wrong conclusions.

Why the fuck did Angie think she always knew best? Igloo was a grown woman.

You're probably angry at me for thinking I know better than you. Forgive me. If you're getting this message, then it should be obvious that in the future you can and will do exactly as you see fit.

Igloo found herself leaning against Essie, barely able to hold herself upright. She rubbed at her eyes because she couldn't see the screen. She was distantly aware of Essie wrapping an arm around her.

You will find a detailed plan for developing, deploying, and making maximum use of Tapestry 2.0. This is of the utmost importance.

T2 alone is necessary but insufficient. It technologically guarantees certain basic human rights in perpetuity, such as privacy, free speech, and freedom of association, but those rights are irrelevant in an unjust world where people are discriminated against, jailed, or killed. To that end, you must follow through on the conversation we had during our hike.

You are opposed to outright manipulation. But sometimes one moral imperative so significantly outshines and outclasses all others that sacrifices must be made in pursuit of it.

Tapestry arose from the ashes of Tomo. We would not exist today if Tomo had not been burned.

Don't let the sacrifices be for naught.

Igloo's mind reeled. Tomo? Burned? Angie used *burn* to mean destroying someone or something in a computer hack. Tomo wasn't destroyed by Angie, but by competition with Tapestry. Of course, Tapestry got its chance to shine thanks to the actions of Lewis Rasmussen, the former CEO of Tomo, who'd hired a dangerous mercenary, Chris Daly, to discredit Angie. Daly turned out to be a rogue government agent who tried to kill Angie after she and Igloo took steps to flush him out. When the news of Rasmussen's crimes hit the web, Tomo stock went into free fall, their users flocked to Tapestry, and Tapestry went big.

How was that a burn? A burn would imply Angie had *engineered* all that.

Oh. Igloo's thoughts came slowly, as though they were arriving down a long tunnel. Everything faded away.

What if Rasmussen hadn't hired Daly in the first place?

What if, instead, *Angie* hired Daly to discredit Rasmussen? Knowing that she could defend herself against him, Angie could have set up a long game where she built up a mass of evidence to frame Rasmussen. There'd be no way Rasmussen and Tomo could survive something like that.

"Angie wouldn't..."

A chill descended on Igloo like a cold, wet blanket. Angie would.

"What?" Essie said. "She wouldn't what?"

"Frame an innocent man and send him to jail. But she didn't, did she?"

"She didn't what?" Essie shook her head, clearly puzzled.

"Rasmussen didn't go to jail. He got off on a technicality over the chain of custody of the evidence. Sure, he lost his role as CEO, but Angie would claim he deserved that because he was intentionally screwing his users on privacy stuff. But he never went to jail for the attempted murder."

"I have no idea what you're saying."

Igloo couldn't speak the words out loud because the realization was too awful. Making sacrifices for moral imperatives... One of those was explicit: sacrifice Rasmussen and Tomo for Tapestry.

But Angie wrote sacrifices, plural. The other was implied. Angie had killed herself to buy the time to release T2.

CHAPTER 33

"What do you mean, dead?" Enso hissed into the phone. He shouldn't even be talking in an unsecured room. He looked at the door, hoped his wife was still in the kitchen.

"The car battery exploded," Alice's voice was tense. "She was dead within seconds. We had agents across the street and in the hotel. No evidence of any wrongdoing, other than the explosion."

Shit. "Let me call you back on a secure line."

He went to the spare bedroom, pulled the heavy Faraday curtain closed, and reconnected to Alice via a secure video connection. He didn't even wait for her to speak.

"Is there any chance it was us, or another faction inside the government?"

"Not that I can tell. Robin was at the scene, and she didn't notice anything."

"Another hacker then? Foreign agency?"

Alice shrugged. "There's no evidence supporting that. We've had 24-hour surveillance on them for weeks. With the exclusion of Thomas and Angie's friends, no one else entered the house, no one else was around the car. It could have been done remotely."

"What's the media done so far?"

"Live coverage from the local news affiliates, and of course, all the national networks have picked it up. Fortune 500 CEO, all that. Theories about the battery pack exploding, interviews with electric car experts, etc."

Enso weighed the possibility that it might just be an accident. Accidents did happen, and at the most inopportune times. There was that one time when they'd tried to assassinate a CEO, only to discover him dead in his hotel room.

Enso sighed. They'd been preparing to plant evidence framing Angie's husband to use as leverage against Angie. Now that was pointless, since there was no Angie to manipulate.

"I know this is going to sound crazy," Alice said, "but hear me out."

"Go ahead."

"We know Angie fabricated the Tapestry leak designed to get the President to call off Tapestry spying."

"Yeah," Enso said.

"We stopped that from happening. What if this is her backup plan? What if she faked her own death to forestall the FISA court order, to give their engineers time to release this new version of Tapestry that they've been working on?"

"Wait, faked her own death? I thought it was real."

"Sorry, I shouldn't have said that. It's not conclusive yet. The battery fire was too hot, too intensive. Everything suggests that it was real, and there are human remnants in there, but it's possible it's not Angie."

Enso wanted to pound the table. "With all the surveillance we have, how can we not even know if she's dead or alive? She's making a fool of us still."

"Okay, ignore that. Maybe she's alive, maybe she's not. Would she be willing to kill herself to get this software released? Is that possible?"

Enso found himself believing it. "Yes, it is. If it got her what she wanted, she'd be willing to do it. But what can we do? The FISA court is almost certainly going to grant the company an extension. How can we convince them otherwise?"

Enso's phone buzzed, and he glanced down to see his phone indicating a call from Feldson.

The SIGINT Director didn't normally call on weekends. Griz must have heard the news.

"I gotta take this, Alice. I'll talk to you later. Keep the team digging to see if we can turn up any evidence of what caused the vehicle explosion. If we can conclusively prove it was her own tampering, then that might help with the FISA court."

CHAPTER 34

Since uncovering Angie's final message, Igloo had been reeling from the revelation of Angie's sacrifice. It was just too much to deal with, and she crawled back into bed.

Now late morning, still wrapped in Essie's arms, she realized she couldn't spend any more time wallowing. Hours had been lost.

She forced herself to sit up and wiped her face with the back of her hand. "I'm wasting time. I can't do that. Angie's..." She couldn't bring herself to say it, wasn't even sure what to say. Death? Accident? Suicide? "Angie bought us a couple of days. I can't squander another second."

She stumbled out of bed, put on her socks and boots, then sat down, suddenly confused. What was she supposed to do? She looked down at her boots. Oh yeah, she needed clothes first. She wasn't thinking straight.

"I need more coffee. I have to get functional."

Essie climbed off the bed and came around to look into Igloo's eyes.

"You might need coffee, but the bigger problem is that you're still in shock. I don't know what you're trying to do. Let me help."

"I have to do this alone."

"You're in no shape for that."

Igloo thought about what she needed to accomplish. She reluctantly nodded.

Essie helped her get dressed, made her coffee, shoved a nut bar into her hands, and got Igloo to the car.

"I'm driving. You're in no condition to drive."

Igloo just nodded and climbed into the passenger seat.

Essie got behind the wheel. "Where are we going? Tapestry?"

"No," Igloo said. "Wait, yes." She rubbed her face. "I'm not sure. I need to get the T2 team together, and make sure everyone is working."

"That sounds like Tapestry, then."

"Sure, I guess."

Essie drove toward Tapestry. "What is this T2 team, and why is it so important?"

"Oy. Legally, ethically, and for your safety, you shouldn't know..." Igloo thought about it. That was the old way. Angie's way. "There's a software release that we were supposed to get out by Monday or some very bad things will happen. Starting a few days ago, we knew we were going to miss the deadline."

"Really? A frigging software release? You can't give yourself a couple of days to grieve for Angie?"

Igloo stared out the window. "I can't explain it, but no. The software is more important than you can possibly imagine."

"It's a website. It's not more important than taking a few days for yourself."

Igloo turned to Essie, who was focused on driving. "It might be the last chance for free speech or privacy of any kind."

Essie glanced at Igloo, then turned back to the road. "I get that Tapestry is a big deal, but it's not the center of the universe. It's just a social network."

"Tapestry might seem that way, but it's a much bigger deal than you realize. It's the backbone of how we communicate, get our news, plan protests, how we tell each other our secrets. Tapestry's role is about to get much bigger..."

She trailed off, unsure of how to continue.

"Essie, I haven't really thought this through. In fact, I've been deliberately not thinking about it. But there's some chance I could go to jail for this."

Essie hit the brakes and pulled over to the side of the road.

"What are you talking about?"

Igloo sighed. "The government spies on us. Everyone."

"Yeah. We've all seen Snowden. So what?"

"Some of us believe we deserve privacy. We believe that the government shouldn't be able to read our emails and listen to our conversations. That they don't have a right to blanket court orders that enable them to spy on everyone at once. I can't say more, I really can't."

"What does any of this have to do with going to jail?"

"Tapestry 2.0 will be the new *de facto* Internet. Secure, private, and resistant to intrusion. The government won't want Tapestry 2.0 to be released, because it will mean the end of blanket court orders. After Monday, we're supposed to be in compliance with..." Legally, she couldn't mention the FISA court order. "Well, just, after Monday, if we release this software there's a chance we're going to go to jail, unless we get a stay on the implementation date...look, it's complicated."

Essie's lips quivered. "I don't care what the reasons are. I don't want you to go to jail. We're supposed to be life partners. How can you do something like this and not discuss it with me first? What were you thinking? Or is this like poly, where you just don't think? You do, do, do with no thought as to how it'll affect me."

"I never do that," Igloo said. "I always think about you."

"Really? You think about me when you make plans with Charlotte without even checking with me first? I don't think so. You tell me after the fact."

"It's hard to coordinate plans."

"Oh yeah. So hard. It takes thirty seconds. You message me, ask if it's okay. That's all. Did you think about me when you decided to have sex with her? No, you did it, and then you told me afterwards."

"I just want to have fun. I'm not trying to hurt you."

"Poly doesn't mean you're single and free to just do anything you want. We're committed partners. That means something to me."

Igloo was silent for a minute. There were a lot of things that she didn't ask Essie about. Usually because she was afraid that Essie would get angry. How much of that was in Igloo's head?

"I'm sorry," Igloo said. "I've been avoiding a lot of discussions." She didn't know what else to say. "Sometimes it's easier to ask forgiveness than to ask permission."

"Fuck," Essie said. "This is the problem. It's not about asking permission. It's about collaborating. It's about working together as a team. What are you afraid of? Why can't we just talk about it?"

Igloo was silent. She was afraid of so much...disappointing Essie, disappointing whomever she was with, not being able to get what she wanted, being judged for what she wanted, being controlled. The fears went on and on.

Essie gave a little huff. "Look, don't worry about it right now. We'll talk about relationship stuff later. Can you tell me more about the whole jail thing, because that sounds a little more pressing?"

Igloo took a deep breath. She reached out and stroked Essie's arm. "I didn't notice at first, but I was wondering why Angie picked the people she did for the T2 team. Her choices didn't make sense, because there were more experienced people in some cases. But she didn't pick anyone who was a parent. Most everyone on the team is unattached."

"Why the hell did she pick you then?" Essie's grip on the steering wheel tightened. "*We're* attached."

Igloo stroked Essie's cheek. "Because I'm Angie's backup. I'm in charge."

"You? Why not Amber? Or Maria?"

Igloo took a deep breath and gave Angie's answer, even though it still felt hollow, a betrayal somehow. "Because all the attention will be on them right now. I can operate without a microscope on my every move. It was an intentional choice to keep me out of the limelight."

"Let's go to Canada," Essie said. "They can't arrest you there."

Igloo wondered if arrest was the worst she had to fear. "They might stop me at the border."

"Don't they need some cause to do that? You haven't done anything...yet. Right?"

"It's a good idea. It is. Maybe we should have done that ahead of time. But right now, I think we should just stay out of view."

"Then why are we going to Tapestry?"

"Because..." Igloo realized Essie was right. "We shouldn't. In fact, we shouldn't do anything with your car, our phones. Shit, I should have thought of that before. We need operational security right now. New plan."

Igloo gave Essie the location of a safe car.

Essie stared at Igloo like she was crazy, then shrugged and started driving in the new direction.

A half hour later, after switching cars, swapping clothes, scanning each other, and running a surveillance detection route, they made it to the storage container safe house.

"You really have these everywhere?" Essie asked.

"Not everywhere, but we have a bunch. I shouldn't have brought you. You're going to be bored."

"I'll help any way I can, and I'll stay out of the way when I can't."

Igloo gestured to the barren container. "And do what?"

Essie shrugged. "Keep you company?"

"No, you should go."

"I'm going to worry about you."

"Then go workout or do something to take your mind off things. I have to be here, you don't."

Essie looked crushed, but Igloo had to be honest.

"If you're here, I'm going to be thinking about you, and I won't be able to concentrate. I need 100 percent of my attention focused. If I know you're okay, taking care of yourself, then I'll be able to focus on my work."

"Can I bring you lunch in a couple of hours?"

Igloo slowly nodded. "That would be great, actually. Remember: operational security. Don't take the safe car home. Reverse your path."

Essie left, and suddenly Igloo was alone in the shipping container. Very alone. She couldn't think about that now.

She logged into the T2 chatroom after taking steps to disguise her location. She found everyone there already arguing about what had happened to Angie. Oh shit.

Ben > If the government killed Angie to stop her, then they'll kill us.

X > That car was always a mess. It was probably a faulty charge cell.

Diana > She might have been back two firmware revs on the charge controller, because the new ones hadn't been security audited.

Gene > I have a friend in the police department. I could ask him for their analysis on the car.

Igloo > Stop conjecturing, everyone! Whatever happened, it's done. Angie would want us focused on getting the software out, not getting to root cause on her car.

Ben > She's *dead*. This isn't a game.

Igloo > No, it's not a game. There are risks to what we're doing. Arrest is a definite possibility, and I can't rule out something more sinister. If you want out, this is the time to do it.

Diana > What does **out** look like?

Igloo > I kick you off T2, audit all the history to attribute what you did to me, you deny being any part of T2, and live your life in peace. I won't fault anyone for taking that option.

But if we don't deliver T2, then it's all for nothing. Everything *Angie* did was for nothing. This is why we're here, people. If you ever wanted to make a dent in the world, this is your chance. If we succeed, we'll have forever changed the world.

Mike > No one is going to arrest us. It'll never stand up in court. We're just writing software.

Dovi > Aaron Schwartz wrote software, and he's dead.

Mike > He killed himself.

Dovi > Because the government prosecuted him for downloading information he had a legal right to. This is my point: it doesn't matter whether what we're doing is legal or not. If the government wants us out of the picture, it will neutralize us one way or another.

Igloo > For what it's worth, I have some ideas to keep us out of the limelight for the next few days. Once the software is out, the equation for arresting us changes. They still might do it for retribution, but it'll be too late to stop us.

Ben > What do you have in mind?

Igloo > I'll tell whoever decides to stay. Everyone should take five minutes, no chatter from this point out, and make a decision for themselves that they can live with. Whoever decides to leave should log off. In five minutes, I'll restrict T2 to whoever is left.

Tom > I'm sorry, but I can't do this. I have a life I want to live.

Tom has left T2.

Stephanie > Me too. Shit.

Carly > I'm in. I believe in what we're doing.

Stephanie has left T2.

Erik > I'm sorry, this has gotten too crazy for me.

Erik has left T2.

Bob > Good luck. I'll miss you all.

Bob has left T2.

A few more people dropped off. Igloo checked the time.

Igloo > Anyone else?

Melanie > I'm in.

Ben > Me too. Fuck those bastards.

Diana > In.

Mike > I'm with you.

Wendy > I'm staying.

Jeff > I'm good.

Tony > T2 FTW!

Dave has left T2.

Dovi > They killed Angie. I know I should fight them, but... I can't do it.

Dovi has left T2.

Gene > I'm staying.

Igloo > That's it then. We're all in?

No one else left. Igloo removed the departed members' access to T2. She looked at who was left: herself, Ben, Diana, Melanie, Mike, Jeff, Gene, Carly, Wendy. Angie was gone, eight people had left the project, and now there were nine.

Angie was gone. The thought was overwhelming. Nobody could ever fill Angie's shoes. *How could Angie do this to her?* She rested her head in her hands for a moment.

She choked back despair. She had to keep functioning. Don't think. Just do.

Igloo > They're gone.

Ben > Now we can discuss what really happened to Angie.

No, she had to nip this in the bud.

Igloo > No. If there's one topic that's verboten, it's what happened to Angie. What's happened is terrible, but the deadline is Monday, and we're going to miss it. There's a good chance Angie's death buys us a few more days before they crack down on compliance.

Mike > That's fucked up. You're capitalizing on Angie's death?

Carly > ^^^^^

Melanie > ditto.

Igloo wanted to tear her hair out. Yes, of course, capitalize on Angie's death. That's the whole purpose of Angie dying in the first place. Her throat was so tight she could barely swallow. Thank god she didn't have to talk in front of anyone.

Igloo > What would Angie want us to do? Come on, people. Has she ever been less than 100 percent focused on Tapestry?

Diana > Angie would be coding right now. She wouldn't be wasting time in chat.

Wendy > Then let's get to work.

Ben > How many days do you think we have?

Igloo had no idea. Amber and Maria would presumably be working on exactly this problem. She needed to talk to them.

Igloo > I'll find out. Everyone, make a prioritized list of the biggest issues in your area, and figure out what is essential. Try to come up with cut lines for three days, five days, and a week.

Carly > We're not chasing down UI errors here. Some of this stuff is huge. When Firefox restarts, our in-browser containers are in a non-deterministic state. I'm having to checksum memory maps before we can resume. I'm going to have to submit a patch request for Firefox. You know what the lead time on that is?

Igloo > Prioritize it. What percentage of our user base is Firefox?

Carly > Small as a percent of total, but it's our best platform for in-browser containers. Even if 5 percent of the user base runs the containers, it'll give us the numbers we need for security and fault tolerance. Without it...

Igloo's head spun as they discussed some of the more complex issues they faced. There was just so much to do. Finally, they got through the biggest technical issues, and Ben changed the topic.

Ben > Yeah, but are we safe? Not mentioning the verboten subject, but what if they come after us next?

Igloo > Let me take care of the time question first. I'll follow up later today with details for operational security. For now, everyone should commit their work environments to encrypted virtual discs on IPFS. Cascade Twofish-Serpent. Pack a travel bag you can carry with a change of clothes, any medicine you need, and NOTHING electronic. I have safe houses and safe computers.

Ben > Whoa. How long have you been planning this?

Igloo > It's complicated. More later.

fter Igloo left the T2 chatroom, she messaged Amber. No reply. She tried three more times, still nothing. Then she tried Maria.

Maria > We're at the office. Join us.
Igloo > I can't. I need to know the timing re: Monday.
Maria > We have some bigger things to discuss. Come into the office.
Igloo > Can we just discuss the timing?
Amber > *Get your fucking ass into the office now.*
Maria > There's something you need to know.
Igloo > Let's discuss it here.
Maria > It's too big for chat. Just come into the office.

Shit. Essie had taken the car. Call Essie back? Igloo realized she didn't have a secure way to contact Essie. She needed to remedy that. Car sharing was out. She should have stashed a bike at each of the safe houses. Cheap insurance. Even Angie had used a bike to get around, wearing a prosthetic arm for the short duration to and from her mobile van.

Igloo figured her best chance might be to find a bicycle in one of the nearby residential neighborhoods, borrow it for an hour, then bring it back.

She left the container building, feeling exposed. Surely the government would be watching more closely now. Ever conscious of Angie's long-standing advice to appear as normal as possible, she calmly crossed the major avenue and entered a residential neighborhood. Saturday, families out and about.

She scouted yards as unobtrusively as possible. Two women and their kids piled into a minivan down the block. The roof rack had empty rails for holding bikes. Perfect. A modern nuclear family.

The minivan started as Igloo walked next to it. It pulled away. Igloo circled the block, returned to the house, and rang the doorbell. There was no answer. Acting as normal as she could, but feeling a thousand eyeballs watching her back, she descended the porch stairs and sauntered around to the detached single car garage, whose sagging door stretched on its hinges away from the frame

The door creaked heavily as she pulled it open. Inside, a jumble of bikes leaned against the wall. She picked the one closest to her size, borrowed a helmet, and rode away.

At the Tapestry office, Igloo realized she had neither badge nor smartphone to unlock the door. For a brief moment she thought about Angie coming to unlock the door for her. There was a hole in reality where Angie used to be. The world spun, and she braced herself with one hand on the doorframe.

She eventually punched the delivery call button a few times, and the sole weekend admin answered the door a few minutes later.

"Oh, Igloo. I'm so sorry about Angie."

"Thanks, George."

"Hug?"

"Do you know where Maria and Amber are?"

"I think they're holed up in the executive room with the lawyers."

"Ah. Thank you."

Upstairs, she entered the executive suite to find Amber and

Maria at the long table, with two men in suits. The lawyers, no doubt. Angie's chair at the head of the room, the one with one armrest set up high to rest her stump on, sat empty.

Amber caught Igloo's glance at the chair, then they met eyes.

Igloo let the door close behind her, feeling a little like that time she'd been called to the principal's office for changing everyone's grades to an A. Not just hers, not just her classes, but the whole school's grades.

She wasn't a twelve-year-old kid any more, and Amber wasn't the principal. There was no Angie to look out for her. Igloo had to be the grownup now.

"Sit down," Amber said.

Igloo was about to refuse, but that would be childish. She sat.

Maria had her cast resting on the table. "I'm sorry about Angie," she said, reaching out with her good hand to touch Igloo. "You two were so close. I can't imagine what you're going through."

Igloo nodded. "Thanks. I'm sorry for you, too. You worked with Angie all the time."

"I know," Maria said, and she took a deep breath. "I can't believe this happened." She shook her head and then gazed off into the distance.

Igloo, practically drowning in her own sorrow, could still recognize the look of someone who was truly and deeply shaken. She was surprised...Angie and Maria had worked closely together, but Maria seemed more profoundly affected than Igloo would have expected.

"She...nobody..." Amber breathed deeply. "Nobody will ever be able to fill her shoes. Nobody else could ever have done all that she did, given all that she gave to so many."

The older of the two lawyers cleared his throat, and for a moment, Amber cast an evil look his way. He looked away.

"I went home last night..." Amber choked back tears, squeezing her fist so tightly her fingers turned white. "You know, the whiteboards are still on the walls in my back bedroom from when Angie and I were working out of my house. Her handwriting is still there."

Igloo leaned over and hugged Amber. She wanted to cry, but something held her back from letting go.

Amber embraced Igloo back, and after a minute she disengaged to wipe at her face. "Look, I don't want to be here, but David says it's crucial."

Igloo glanced over at the older of the two men, who nodded in agreement.

"While Angie..." Amber cleared her throat, and started anew. "While Angie was in charge, she held a controlling interest in voting shares, and was the *de facto* dictator of Tapestry. She wanted to fight the court order." Amber glanced meaningfully at Igloo.

Igloo nodded to indicate she knew about the supposedly secret FISA order.

"She ran the effort to have you and the rest of the team embark on this 2.0 notion, moving Tapestry into the clients and browsers. This was not what I believed was in the company's best interest, not what our legal counsel recommended, and not what the board wanted. But Angie insisted the effort proceed."

With good reason, Igloo thought, but she didn't say anything. She also knew that if Angie were here, she'd be upset that they were having this conversation in the open, without taking counter-surveillance measures. But Angie wasn't here, and Igloo didn't think she'd win any points by acting like Angie right now. They'd just have to live with the risk.

"I'm the acting CEO until the board of directors chooses a replacement, and I'm going to side with our legal counsel. I don't want us to risk a confrontation with the government. We're not a tiny startup anymore."

Igloo expected Amber would say something like this. Back when they first talked about onion routing, it was clear Amber had different business goals than Angie. But it was absurd to think they could change their path at this point. She looked around the tiny group. "There's no way we can be in compliance with the court order by

Monday. It would take weeks to set up the backdoors they want, and we haven't even started on the work."

Amber took a deep breath. "I never agreed with what Angie wanted to do. Maybe we could pull it off technically, maybe we couldn't. But either way, the government won't accept no for an answer. All we'll accomplish is losing time and market share to Tomo. I knew Angie wouldn't work on the FISA backdoors, so I took the liberty of pulling together a few people in secret. Just like Angie, so please don't call me out on the ethics of it. Anyhow, the point is that we're not as far behind on the government timeline as you think. I am going to ask for an extension to meet the backdoor requirements because of Angie's death. Given the circumstances, I'm hopeful they'll grant it. They don't need to know that the reason we're behind schedule is that Angie had everyone working to circumvent the FISA court order."

Igloo felt the room spin around her. How could Angie have known Amber would ask for an extension? It was like she knew how everyone would behave. Were they all being manipulated by Angie even now, even after her death?

Amber continued. "But this conversation isn't about the government's search interfaces. It's about Tapestry 2.0 and making sure that no one on the team does anything stupid."

Igloo controlled her breathing. She wanted to have this battle, right here, right now. Angie would say that was stupid, because if she argued too vehemently, Amber would know Igloo wouldn't obey her order. And indeed, she had absolutely no intention of doing that. But Angie would also say giving in too easily would make Amber suspicious.

"There has to be some aspect of 2.0 that we can keep," Igloo finally said. "I refuse to let Angie's vision die."

Amber gestured all around them. "The whole company is Angie's vision. This is her legacy. Everything surrounding us. I *am* trying to preserve Tapestry. If the government shuts us down because we tried to route around them, then there's nothing left of what she built."

There was merit to what Amber said, strangely enough. In the short term, Amber's approach would make it more likely that Tapestry would survive. Not to mention that they could avoid stuff like fighting head-to-head against the government or the possibility of going to jail and losing her freedom and her relationship with Essie.

But over the long term, Tapestry would turn into another puppet of the government. That's why Angie wouldn't have played it safe. She'd argue that they had to stay ahead of the government. She would have preferred to see Tapestry disassembled than have it turn into just another offender.

She understood Amber's viewpoint: they had a winning hand in the game she was playing, and she didn't want to change games. Following Angie's dream meant changing games, playing for far higher stakes against a much more formidable opponent. No wonder Amber wanted to kill T2.

Shit, she was destined to play *What Would Angie Do?* for the rest of her life. She'd have to pull the *What Would Buffy Do?* sticker off her refrigerator. She took another breath, chose her words intentionally.

"A legacy isn't a piece of static code," Igloo said. "It's a living institution. She wouldn't want us to cave. Look, I accept that we can't do all of Tapestry 2.0. But let's do something. A piece of it. We can keep the onion routing, for example, it helps make people safer on insecure networks. Meanwhile, the backdoors give the government access to everything they want."

Amber glanced at the lawyers, who shrugged and nodded. "As long as we're in compliance, there's no rule that we can't add security features."

"If you do this, will you make sure that all other work on 2.0 stops?"

With this statement, Igloo confirmed what she had suspected: Amber didn't actually know who was working on 2.0. If she didn't know who was working on it, that implied Amber didn't have access to the secure group they'd been using for collaboration. She probably didn't even know the full extent of what they were doing. Amber was shooting in the dark, assuming that Igloo would be in the know. Amber was correct of course, and it would be ridiculous to deny it at this point. At any rate, she couldn't just give in. That wouldn't be plausible. But if she could make it seem like she was trading T2 for something important... She took a dramatically deep breath.

"If you're the CEO, then I want the CTO position." She swallowed hard and stared at Amber.

Amber shook her head in confusion. "What does this have to do with anything? Besides, I'm just the acting CEO."

"Then make me the acting CTO. And if you become the permanent CEO, then make me the permanent CTO."

Amber sighed. "With all due respect, Igloo, you don't have experience. You've only ever led a single R&D team—for autonomous chat —and the R&D organization is over a hundred and fifty people and growing."

"Pair me with an R&D manager. I don't want to manage all the people. I want to drive the vision."

"What if I give you a future products research organization? Then you could create whatever you want."

"And sideline me from actually influencing the product? I don't think so."

Amber clenched and unclenched her fist, but didn't respond.

"I was employee number three," Igloo said. "Our AI personalities, which *I* designed and built, are one of the most popular features of Tapestry, and the reason we've gotten so much attention. It's the biggest social benefit we've delivered. You can't say that I'm unqualified to hold the position of CTO and give us visionary leadership when that's exactly what I did."

Amber tilted her head to stare at Igloo. "I'm a little surprised that you're trading T2 for a position in the company hierarchy. What happened to the Igloo who said we should use SHA keys for employee IDs instead of monotonically increasing numbers, and who wanted a flat company structure?"

"I'd still have a flat company structure if it was up to me. But I didn't impose that hierarchy. You and Angie did. I'm just fitting into the system you created."

"Touché." Amber stared at Igloo. "I guess Angie and I didn't realize that's what you wanted. Fine, you can have the CTO position. I believe you'll bring a lot of passion to it. But that doesn't make you the dictator of product features. We're still going to be building what marketing and business development tell us. You'll influence the direction we take."

"Understood." Igloo felt confused emotions run through her. On the one hand, this maneuver was just a ploy so Amber would believe that Igloo would terminate the T2 work. On the other, Igloo was really going to be CTO, something she'd wanted for seemingly forever. Why'd she wait until now to demand what she wanted? What if she'd done this a year ago? Two years ago?

Part of her wanted to celebrate. Tell her mom. No, her mom wouldn't even understand. She'd tell Angie!

She felt like someone had hit her in the face with a brick. She'd never tell Angie anything again. She felt like she was going to cry. She squashed her feelings until there was only a hard, icy emptiness left inside her.

"Is there anything else you want?" Igloo asked. "Because I want to go home and be alone and deal with this." She glanced toward Angie's empty chair.

"You'll send the message to the 2.0 team, calling it off?"

"Yes."

"What are you going to tell them? How will you get them to stop?"

"I'll tell them what you said. If we don't comply, we risk losing everything Angie worked for. That keeping Tapestry going is the best way to honor Angie's vision."

"Thank you," Amber said.

Igloo stood and nodded.

"I'll walk you to the door," Maria said.

When they got outside the conference room, Maria grabbed Igloo's arm, and made her stop.

"I want to tell you something," she said.

Igloo looked into her eyes.

"I'm on your side," Maria said. "What's happening here is wrong. I just want you to know that. I have your back."

Igloo tried to puzzle out what she meant. Was Maria saying that she would help hide the T2 work? Could she actually confide in Maria, or was Maria just trying to trick her? Not trusting herself to say anything, she simply gave Maria a hug, then turned and left.

Outside, part of Igloo wanted to celebrate. Not only did Amber buy her answer that she'd stop work on Tapestry 2.0, but Amber was planning to delay before complying with the FISA court order. That was everything she'd hoped to accomplish.

Unfortunately, any expression of joy felt like a betrayal of Angie. Yet this is what Angie would want. She didn't know what to feel.

She glanced at a clock. Shit, almost two hours had passed. Essie would be back with food by now with no way to get into the container. Igloo made a quick detour to her office on the way out and grabbed a phone and a pile of SIM cards. She plugged one in and sent a message to Essie > "Had to run a quick errand. Back in 20 minutes."

She'd need to teach Essie about operational security. How to hide her location, her messages, everything. She waited a minute. No reply. She thumbed the hard switch on the back of the customized device, killing the battery connection. She couldn't ride back to the container with an active phone.

She retrieved her pilfered bike and headed north, using a bike route on a secondary road paralleling the main avenue. Aside from gentle speed bumps every block, she rode undisturbed. At noon on a

Saturday, the bike route, normally heavily trafficked by commuters, was nearly empty.

Her mind raced with the details of everything they needed to do to release 2.0 within a week while also giving the appearance of curtailing all the work. It helped that several 2.0 members had quit the team. Now she'd only need to hide the activities of a smaller group.

A van passed her, veering onto the other side of the road to give her space.

Ben and Diana wouldn't be a problem, because nobody could ever find them anyway. That left six people. If she claimed three were working on the onion routing, and three pretended to take vacation, that would cover everyone.

Igloo edged right as a black van pulled up alongside her.

Although, it would take extra work to give the appearance of merging the onion routing back into the main code branch. She could share the code with someone on the client team, let them work on it.

She glanced left. The black van paced alongside her. She looked back, noticed another van a half block back. And the first van was still half a block in front—Oh! Oh, shit.

She squeezed hard, her brakes bringing her to a halt with a skid. She cranked the handlebar hard, jumping up onto the sidewalk, looking for an alley or path the vans couldn't follow.

A screech came from behind her, and doors slammed. She glanced back to see several people on foot, chasing her. The vans kept pace. *There!* A walking path cut across the middle of the block.

She veered onto the path, only to find it blocked by a woman calmly holding a badge up in front of her.

"Agent Forrest. Can we talk for a minute, Igloo?"

Igloo's heart pounded. She ran through an inventory of what she had on her body. The phone. A suspicious number of SIM cards. How long had they been tracking her? How'd they find her?

Igloo found herself being led toward the back of one of the vans. Someone took her bike from her. Belatedly she noticed the Hello

Kitty sticker on the side, and realized that if they arrested her now, the bike's owner would never get it back. She wanted to say something, but before she could, she was led inside.

It wasn't anything like what she expected from TV. She thought there'd be a row of computers and geeks wearing headphones and whispering commands. There was none of that. Jump seats on either wall, only one occupied by a man who smiled at her. Agent Forrest climbed into the van after her and shut the door.

"Take a seat," Forrest said.

Igloo sat on one side, belatedly realizing she was wearing Essie's sweat pants and a t-shirt, basically pajamas. The two agents sat opposite her.

"I'm very sorry about Ms. Benenati," Forrest said. "You two were close."

Igloo tried to gather her thoughts. She needed to be smart here, but she felt scatterbrained, hardly able to connect two thoughts in a row.

"We were once close," Igloo said, the words sticking like wool in her mouth.

"We're not involved in that case. I understand the local police are investigating. Personally, I hope they find it was just an accident. Not that accidents are any easier to emotionally grapple with, but certainly a loved one being murdered is worse."

Igloo couldn't grok what kind of conversation they were having.

"Umm, thanks. Why exactly are we here?"

Forrest sat back in her chair, at least as far as the upright seat would allow, and crossed her fingers in her lap.

"Why did you meet with Amber and Maria at Tapestry?"

"What is this about?" Igloo asked.

"Just answer the question."

"Don't you have to read me the Miranda rights?"

"We're not arresting you, Igloo. Trust me, that would be a very different experience."

Forrest turned to the other agent. "Can you excuse us?" She

waited for him to leave. When the van was empty, the door closed, she went on. "Tell me what you talked about at your office."

"Confidential company matters."

"Such as..."

"You do understand the term confidential, right?"

Forrest took a deep breath. "Look, your CEO died last night. I get that. A terrible thing. So it's a little surprising when you convene a meeting the morning after."

Angie always said the best lies were mostly truth. "We had to discuss succession. Who takes what position. I didn't want to be passed over for the CTO role."

"So you went to work in your pajamas?"

"As you said, Angie died last night. I can barely think and get myself to work. My clothes are the last thing on my mind."

Forrest rubbed her hands on her pants and nodded slowly. "And yet you didn't just go into work. You made a side trip to the safe house."

Before Igloo could fully suppress her startled reaction, Forrest continued.

"I've been working with Angie for about a year and half. Not all of us in the government are the bad guys. I believe in what she was doing, and I want to help. I know about the plans for T2."

Despite her best efforts at self-control, Igloo was afraid her eyeballs might pop out of her head. She forced herself to take a breath. What the fuck?

Forrest leaned forward. "I need to know what you discussed at the office."

Igloo's mind raced. Could Angie really have been working with a government agent? Why hadn't Angie said so? Forrest must be phishing. That was the only explanation. Pick up the loner, extract them from any support system, then feed them lies. Standard procedure, according to Angie. If Forrest knew who she was, what they had done together, then she could come up with an infinite number of details that would corroborate her knowledge. If she wasn't forthcoming, then she didn't know as much as she was pretending.

"We just discussed the succession. Amber becoming acting CEO, me the acting CTO. I don't know anything about T2, whatever that is." Igloo tilted her head. "What is going on? Am I under arrest?"

Forrest looked down and mumbled something Igloo couldn't catch. Then she leaned closer and stared into Igloo's eyes.

"Had Angie been acting strange in any way? Was she afraid of anyone?"

Igloo backed away. "I don't know what you mean. She was just Angie."

"You met with her, outside of work. You kept it secret."

"We worked together. Is Angie in some sort of trouble?" Her brain stumbled as she realized Angie was no more. "I mean, was she?"

"You're the one Angie trusted with everything," Forrest said. "I'm hoping you can tell us something, try to make sense of what happened."

Igloo tried to back up more, but she was pressed into the corner of the van. Forrest was phishing, guessing, right? She couldn't have known everything, no one else did. Igloo forced herself to think about last night, to imagine the flash of light before the explosion, the outline of Angie in the car.

Igloo started crying.

"I don't know what you're talking about." Igloo took a sobbing breath. "Angie didn't tell me anything. I got left behind. Angie, Amber, they got all the positions, all the titles. I'm just another cog in the machine. I thought we were going to make a difference together, but somehow I got sidelined. I'm sad Angie died, but I'm not going to miss my chance to influence Tapestry again. If that makes me a criminal, then arrest me."

Forrest stared at Igloo a moment longer, then turned her head away in disgust. She bent to her phone and sent a message.

When Forrest looked up a few seconds later, she seemed tired and haggard. Or maybe she had been all along, and Igloo only noticed it now.

"I'm sorry we bothered you," Forrest said, holding out a card with a number on it. "If you think of anything, get in touch. You're free to go. Thank you for your time." She opened the back door of the van and gestured for Igloo to climb out.

Outside, the sun was bright, and Igloo shaded her eyes with the plain business card as they adjusted. An agent held her bicycle out for her. She took the bike from him and stood blinking. He climbed into the rearmost van, and all three vans pulled away at the same time.

Igloo turned around. Everyone was gone, leaving her and the bike alone in the middle of the street. What had just happened?

The government mole that Angie was always worried about came back to mind. Had Angie learned about the mole from Forrest? Was Forrest somehow the mole? She assumed the government informant was someone inside Tapestry, but she supposed they could be someone on the outside who had an influential relationship to someone key inside the company. Nothing made sense, and she was more confused than ever.

She climbed back on the bike and make her way slowly back to the house where she'd stolen it, watching more closely now for followers.

CHAPTER 36

F orrest typed a quick summary to Nathan out of sight of her
other agents.

Forrest > She doesn't know anything.
Nathan9 > Bullshit. She was Angie's partner two years ago.
She's continued to work with Angie. She's been to Angie's
safe houses.
Forrest > Maybe she's not as important as you think. Maybe
Angie pulled one over on you.

That must have been more biting than she thought, because
Nathan didn't reply. She didn't know a lot about their history, only
that Nathan and Angie had once been hacker friends or maybe allies,
and then they weren't. Also, Angie had something Nathan really
wanted, and now that Angie was out of the picture, Nathan thought
maybe he had a shot at it.

She turned to Doug, her second-in-command, who studied a map
display. He remained blissfully unaware of the nature of her relationship with Nathan, thinking Nathan was just one of many deep
knowledge sources she managed.

"You have a track?" She nodded toward the screen.

"Yeah, her signal is loud and clear. She's headed toward northeast Portland."

"Keep a car within five minutes of her," Forrest said. "If she gets off that bike, I want to know where she goes. We have high altitude coverage?"

"No, but we can requisition a drone from the local FBI office."

Forrest looked out the window. "I don't want them to know we're in town. Get another team in Portland by tomorrow. Have them bring a mobile ops kit."

"What are we going to list this as? No Such Agency's going to see all this movement, it'll have to be reconciled with management."

"Field training exercises, under my purview."

"Unscheduled?"

"Yes, *unscheduled*. Can't have my operatives knowing when there's going to be a fire drill, can I?" She couldn't keep the hostility out of her voice. Everyone was being watched these days. Nobody could do their job anymore. Who watched the watchers when the watchers were corrupt? "Sorry, Doug. Didn't mean to jump at you."

He just nodded as he worked his computer.

She kept Doug and the rest of her team isolated from the increasingly politicized operating environment in Washington. Everyone was expected to cooperate with the administration these days. You'd be out in a flash if anyone thought you were subversive. She'd seen it happen to other mid-level managers.

The van's big engine droned on as they made their way toward the airport.

Everything was analyzed, correlated in the NSA's huge machine learning farms. The watch lists started with civilians, of course. Then it was turned against the news outlets. Any leverage, no matter how small, to ensure the coverage the administration wanted. Then finally, turned inward, on the government itself. Career employees let go or pressured to leave.

They were ten years into a total panopticon, and by now, anyone with secrets had them all logged somewhere in a computer. All it took was some suspicious behavior, not even anything that could get you fired or jailed, but enough that someone high up wanted you disappeared. Then you'd be gone, and quietly too, because even if you didn't care about your own secrets, there's was someone you cared about who had secrets.

Forrest thought back to when she'd started working for the government. They fought crime, enemies of the state, entropy. Back then, they were fighting to create a better America. Now it mostly seemed like they fought each other. She tried to remember what it was like back then, but she couldn't. It didn't matter. She couldn't live in the past, and she had no real hope to change the future. All she could do was try to stay viable in the present.

CHAPTER 37

I gloo raced back to the house where she'd borrowed the bike, returned it, and then jogged back to the warehouse with the shipping container. She glanced up at the sun. It was well into the afternoon. She'd been gone way longer than expected.

Essie was outside the warehouse, sitting under the doorway awning. She stood as soon as she saw Igloo. "I was worried about you."

"I'm sorry," Igloo said. "I had to run an errand and I didn't have any way to get you a message. We need to get you a secure phone so we can stay in touch."

Essie held up a large insulated bag. "I didn't know how to get in. I brought food. I...wasn't sure what else we might need, so I packed a suitcase with clothes for a couple days, enough food for a week, and all the spare batteries and charging cables I could find at our place. It's all in the trunk."

Igloo gave her a sweaty hug. "You did great, pet, really awesome. Thank you. Come inside. We're not staying too long. I have to round up the team, then get everyone into hiding."

In the shipping container, Igloo grabbed a laptop and started the process of contacting everyone to tell them where to meet.

When she glanced back to the desk next to her laptop, there was a chickpea salad sandwich, neatly cut in half on a sheet of aluminum foil, a cloth napkin, iced coffee in a mason jar, and a water bottle. Everything was laid out perfectly proper and neat, and while the only thing that differentiated the meal from any other to-go lunch was the cloth napkin, somehow the way everything had been laid out, the care with which the sandwich had been cut, and the fact that Essie had chosen her favorite things made her burst into tears.

Essie came and hugged her. "What's wrong?"

"Why do you take such good care of me?"

"I love you."

"I don't deserve it. I've been shitty to you with this whole poly thing."

"Of course you deserve it." Essie squeezed her tight. "Poly has nothing to do with it. You're a good person. We're having a hard time. We've both made mistakes."

"Nobody has ever cared for me like this before."

"That doesn't mean you're undeserving." Essie took a deep breath. "We discover new things throughout our lives. If we found everything, had everything, did everything, and learned everything on day one, then there'd be nothing left to discover."

Igloo felt her heart was breaking.

"Something's wrong," Essie said.

"I'm afraid I'm going to lose you in all of this craziness."

"I'm afraid of losing you too," Essie said, "but I'm trusting you to keep us safe and figure a way out. Now you can't do that if you starve to death, so eat something."

Igloo nodded and dutifully took up the food.

"Eat and work at the same time," Essie said, pointing to Igloo's computer. Then she took a bite of her own sandwich.

Igloo hammered out a few more chat messages as Essie watched over her shoulder.

"You getting everyone together here?"

"No, I don't want to chance it. It's too remote. I'm afraid that if anyone is watching, we'll all get arrested together. After we eat, we're taking on a ride on Max."

The oldest segment of Portland's light rail system ran east-west across the city. They could pick it up near the airport and ride it toward downtown.

"We're going to leave here in...fifteen minutes. You ready?"

"You sure you want me to come? I could stay here if it would make anyone nervous. I know I'm not part of your group."

"No, it's fine. I want them to know you're vetted."

A distant part of Igloo's mind recoiled at the thought, knowing how Angie would react to such a sloppy measure. But Igloo needed Essie, needed to know she had someone who was watching over her. And she could trust Essie. Essie had been there for her in every way for months now.

"Let's get going," Igloo said.

CHAPTER 38

R obin washed her hands and blotted her face with a damp towel, her hands shaking only slightly.

Eight months undercover. The longest by far of any assignment she'd ever taken. So much investment with so little payoff for so long. It was a miracle she'd been kept on duty. She wanted the whole sordid affair to be finished already.

How to wrap this thing up? It wasn't going to be simple.

She booted an encrypted disk on her phone. It went into secure mode, read her fingerprint, scanned her profile from the front-facing camera and measured biometrics as she used the screen.

Robin > Igloo agreed to the demand that she kill Tapestry
2.0, but she ran right back to the 2.0 chat room. They're
going to keep on working on it.
Enso > Damn her. They already found a sympathetic judge.
On a fucking Saturday, no less. They obtained a seven-day
stay. Do you have the evidence we need to bring them all in?
Robin > No.
Enso > How can that be? You're trusted.
Robin > It's compartmentalized on a need-to-access basis. No

reason to give me access. These people are coders. All the relationship skills in the world don't mean shit to them.
Enso > We can't let them release. We have to pick them up. Every last one of them.

Robin sighed. Enso was always impatient when he took direct interest.

Robin > It's iffy. Igloo could have a dead man switch. Besides, on what charges? You can't disappear those developers without getting attention. Look, if they were ready to release, they would have done it already. They're banking on more time. We can't overreact.

Enso's reply was a long time coming.

Enso > There's too much momentum now for that. We have a joint conference coming up. I want you on that call.

CHAPTER 39

Forrest glanced at her screens, each monitor displaying a different team member. SigInt Director Feldson, aka Griz, occupied the left-hand display. Enso, on one of the two center monitors, was the lead for the Tapestry dark investigation. Robin, his undercover operative, held the next one over, but her window displayed only her codename with no video feed. Griz had explained that her identify was a closely guarded secret. On the far right was Agent Haldor, the official FBI lead on Tapestry, in the Intelligence division.

Forrest, as special ops lead within the National Security Branch of the FBI, was technically the most junior person here, but her team came closest to what the FBI could scrap together for a black ops team.

"Forrest, you're not cleared for this operation." It was no secret that Enso was unhappy that Forrest was attending and had been from the first moment he got wind of her involvement.

"It's all right," Griz said. "I asked her to attend."

The reality was Forrest had planted the idea in Feldson's mind, but she wasn't going to remind him of that now.

"She doesn't have the required history on this operation." Enso shook his head. "Please don't tell me that she's been briefed, because only the Director and I have authority to approve need-to-know on any BRI mission."

Griz smiled, an expression that made anyone reporting to him quake in their boots. "Agent Forrest has been briefed on the joint mission of the FBI and the NSA to bring Tapestry into alignment with standardized industry data access through a FISA court order. I'm not sure what this BRI is. Would you care to go into more detail?"

Forrest suppressed a laugh at Enso's discomfort. She shouldn't officially know of BRI's existence, as the dark agency didn't have a formal charter or even staff. They were comprised of members from different agencies, reporting up through a parallel command structure. It was so black that she'd learned of BRI from Angie of all people, and only later confirmed it through government channels.

The organization's strength was also its weakness. People drafted into BRI didn't know who the rest of the team was. Armed with a few names, she'd confirmed much of what Angie told her about BRI and their total lack of accountability.

Enso shrugged. "Feldson, it's on your head." He swiped at the tablet in front of him. "We have a list of suspects for the T2 team. We want them picked up to forestall any attempt to release T2."

Forrest couldn't let T2 fail. She also couldn't believe she was considering undermining a government operation. At worst, if you believed the national security implications, then what she was doing was treasonous. But she'd stopped believing that. She'd seen too many information requests that came down to nothing more than political machinations. She'd been part of the task force to investigate abuse of intelligence in domestic violence cases inside the agency. She saw how this political administration was working against the best interests of American citizens.

At some point, you had to draw a line. Sure, information could stop terrorists, but was it worth *everything* else? Security came at a cost.

It was her sister Grace who had first exposed her to that idea. Grace let her ten-year-old son ride the city bus on weekends. Forrest had lectured her over breakfast, worked up over a kidnapping case she'd led the year before. Grace had fought back with statistics. The chance of her son being kidnapped by a stranger was less than being hit by lightning. Those minuscule odds could be slightly decreased by cultivating an awareness of stranger danger, keeping him at home except for carefully shepherded outings to safe and sanitized experiences.

The cost of such risk reduction would be a life lived in certain and constant fear of people, strangers, and opportunities. A life in which he gains little experience or confidence negotiating new situations. Or he could experience a tiny risk of something terrible happening, but live life fully, unafraid, capable of handling new experiences on his own, and reach a fuller potential.

Was the appearance of security worth the cost?

They'd been talking about ten-year-old kids, but those words haunted Forrest ever since. Every terrorist threat meeting, every information security conference, every time the United States created new safeguards against domestic and foreign threats, she couldn't help but wonder at the loss. How had people's lives grown smaller as a result?

Forrest had to do something this time around.

Robin was speaking. "When Haldor and his team pick up Igloo, we need —"

"Can you please call her by her real name?" Enso said.

Robin ignored him and kept going. "We need a complete realtime filter on data into and out of Tapestry headquarters and all of their server providers for any anomalous traffic that could be a dead man's switch."

Forrest figured this was her moment. "Sir," and she was directing her words to Griz, "with all due respect, we only suspect which members are part of the T2 effort. There's no guarantee we can catch them all. Acting now will alarm them and alert the remaining members, who are likely to go into hiding. I suggest we postpone until we have positive confirmation of the complete T2 roster."

"You recommend doing nothing?" Enso said. "So glad you've joined the team. I suppose you'd have us to sit back and wait for them to encrypt the entire Internet?"

"No, I'm suggesting we redirect our efforts toward solidifying the identification of the T2 members. I have my team in Portland now. We can run track and trace on all members, reconcile all communications, and run a dragnet through their complete online presence."

"No!" Robin said. "Active electronic monitoring runs a substantial risk of alerting them. They will detect your surveillance."

"There's a reason BRI is running this operation," Enso said. "We suspect Angie infiltrated the government previously. That's why we're running dark."

"Except the one agency Angie penetrated was BRI," Forrest said.

Enso glanced at her, clearly surprised by her knowledge.

Everyone was silent for a moment.

"Is that true?" Griz asked, looking to Enso for a response.

Enso hesitated before responding. "Yes, sir. But if she compromised BRI, then it's likely she got through to the FBI too. We have no idea what she might have uncovered and then turned over to the rest of the T2 team to use."

To be fair, it was a reasonable argument. But to choose a known compromised organization versus a possibly compromised organization was still the worse bet. What would Griz decide?

"Forrest," Griz said, "you have twenty-four hours to investigate the T2 team members. Turn over your list to Haldor and Enso."

"Thank you, sir."

Enso gave her a brief glare. The meeting wrapped up, and she waited for Enso to disconnect. She didn't dare leave the teleconference first, or Enso would try some last-ditch method to get Griz to change his mind.

When everyone was gone, she disconnected and allowed herself to breathe a small sigh of relief. But only a small one, because she'd only bought herself a single day. In that day, she had to figure out who all the T2 members were, find them, get them to safe houses, and get them the untraceable internet access they needed, all without attracting the notice of BRI.

CHAPTER 40

I gloo waited for Essie to finish using the restroom at the airport. When she came out, they nodded at each other and walked to the Max station.

As the next train pulled in, they split up. Igloo entered through the rearmost door. Essie would enter through the front, and they'd meet in the middle. It was one of the newer, next-generation trains, half again as long as the old models. For a brief moment, as Igloo found herself pressed into the middle of a small crowd entering the train, Essie was out of sight, and Igloo's heart fluttered in panic.

She pushed her rolling suitcase in front of her. It was an awkward movement, but it allowed her to ensure that no one placed anything on or in the bag, and it let her keep an eye on the row of tiny green lights protruding from the top of the bag.

The suitcase was an Angie classic, over-designed in every way. The indicator on top was for the custom-built hardware and software that sniffed data from every wireless transmission on the train, allowing them to track exactly what devices were onboard. It could differentiate between stationary and moving devices, and so once the train started moving, it would know exactly who and what was onboard, versus merely nearby. Deep within the rolling bag was a cell tower replicator, which spoofed nearby cell towers, so everyone's phones onboard would prefer the stronger signal emanating from her suitcase, allowing her to intercept and record every connection made by anyone on the train. The third light turned yellow, indicating there were devices using encrypted VPN connections, but that was nothing too suspicious, especially these days. The indicator flickered back to green. The connections were using weak, well-known prime factors, and the hardware had just cracked them.

Igloo realized she wasn't going to get any more Angie hand-me-downs. There would be no new magic toys from the Batcave or wherever it was that Angie fabricated this stuff. She felt she was going to be sick. She breathed and suppressed her emotions. She'd deal with them later.

She continued her way up the train. In the middle car, she saw Essie staring down at her own suitcase. When Essie looked up and caught Igloo's eye, she nodded to indicate everything was okay. They met near the center.

"You stay at the forward end of the car," Igloo said. "I'll be at the back."

Igloo sat with the bag between her legs, where she'd have an eye on the door. The train slowed at the next stop, and the doors opened. She kept alternating between the door and the bag. If the first light turned red, it would indicate a known bad device had boarded, e.g. a government agent's cell phone. Where Angie got the IMEI list, and how up-to-date it was, Igloo didn't know. Maybe it had come from Forrest. If the second indicator light turned yellow, it was a suspicious device: something with hard encryption or a suspicious data pattern. The third light was more routine: cell phones with VPNs or normal encryption prototypes. The fourth and fifth lights were for non-cellular government frequencies: police, FBI, or other short-range radios.

Ben and Diana walked in together. Fuck. They couldn't follow the most basic precautions.

They walked over to Igloo.

"Didn't I tell you to board separately, through different doors, and keep an eye on each other's backs?"

"I told him," Diana said, "but he just rolled his eyes."

Ben raised a hand in exasperation. "It wasn't like that. I told you we were supposed to split up."

"Look," Igloo said. "I'm not making this shit up. We have to act carefully. If you want to be part of T2 and not endanger everyone, then you must follow my instructions. Otherwise you can't be on the team, because we can't afford the risk. Are you in or not?"

Diana said "Yes. I'm sorry. I'll be more careful."

Ben looked at Diana like he was going to protest, but apparently changed his mind. "Yeah, whatever."

"Don't 'whatever' me. Yes or no?"

"Fine, yes. I'm in. I'll follow instructions."

"Thank you," Igloo said. She glanced down at her suitcase. The lights were still green, except the last one flickered yellow for a brief spurt. She slid a Paranoid Linux phone out of her pocket and checked the remote UI for their custom scanner. It showed a cluster of encrypted radio transmissions on a series of frequencies usually used by the FBI. The signals were all coming from the FBI office about half a mile away. That would be expected. As long as they didn't begin to trail the train, or cluster around the next stop, they'd be okay.

At the Gateway transit center, Carly and Wendy boarded the train. Igloo checked Carly first.

"Phone?" Igloo asked.

Carly turned it over, and Igloo put it into an EMF bag. She read the scanner log again. The train car had over three hundred items in it, multiple detectable electronics per person, but Igloo was triangulating between the two scanners and narrowing it down to only those between her and Essie. "Key fob for your Audi?"

"Really?" Carly said. "You know it's an Audi from there?"

"The transmitter can be read at up to fifty feet and has a manufacturer ID as part of the code."

Carly sighed and turned over the key.

"Fitness tracker and headphones."

Carly pulled out her wireless headphones and deposited them in the EMF bag. She glanced left and right, then reached under her shirt. Igloo caught a glimpse of a lacy bra before Carly handed over the tracker.

"That's good except for your wallet. I'll let you keep that on you, but you have to bag it." Carly put her wallet inside a smaller EMF-proof pouch.

Igloo checked her phone one last time. Carly was clean. She repeated the process for Wendy.

Melanie and Mike boarded the train at the NE 60th stop, followed by Jeff at the Hollywood stop, and Gene at Lloyd Center. Igloo repeated the scans at every stop, with every person. When she was done, everyone was as clean as they could get from a signals perspective. They'd work out the rest when they got there.

She looked at the group of engineers. She read a range of emotions from frightened to amused to doubting, but she'd be the first to admit that reading people in person was not her forte. Let her scan a few thousand words of chat for sentiment analysis, and she could do a better job of understanding them.

"Bear with me a little longer. Everyone get off at the Chinatown stop, and then we walk to Powell's in groups of two or three. Take a different partner than you boarded with. Leave your stuff at the bag check and head to the rare books room, and then we'll talk more. Take a hat, too." She gestured toward Essie who had a pile of hats from the bag of disguises Angie had built up.

Igloo paired up with Mike.

"Go with Diana," she told Essie, who looked concerned and lost.

The rest of the group found partners, and at the Chinatown stop they exited. A surreal, out-of-place feeling came over Igloo as she left the train to see ordinary folks doing their ordinary day-to-day things, dealing only with their ordinary preoccupations.

Meanwhile, what felt like the fate of the free world rested on

Igloo and this small group of people. Then she realized that feeling was just a mask for what lay underneath. The real problem, the out-of-place strangeness, came from the fact that Angie would not be waiting for them at their destination. Not that Angie had ever planned to be there in particular. It was just a feeling. Always, always Angie had figured somewhere in Igloo's hacking activities. She had been the cornerstone for it all. Now Igloo had to play that role. Without her, nobody else had a plan for T2, let alone possessed the hacking skills to make it possible.

She fought to hold back a sudden outburst of grief, but Mike caught her sniffling.

"Are you okay?"

Igloo shook her head.

"You want to talk about it?"

"No."

They walked another half a block before Igloo started talking. "It must have been such a relief for Angie to have someone to rely on, someone who could cover for her." Mike would have no idea what she was talking about, but she was done keeping all her feelings inside. "She and I never talked about it, and I always wondered about our relationship, but now I have a tiny inkling of how she must have felt. I miss her so much."

"You want a hug?"

Igloo nodded, and Mike held her. She wanted to let go and cry, but she needed to stay strong. She couldn't walk into this meeting red-eyed and snot-nosed. She sank into him and tried to just inhale and exhale until breathing came somewhat normally again.

"Thank you."

"Of course."

Ten blocks later, Powell's, the five story, city-block spanning bookstore, came into view. They made their way into the store, and she and Mike turned over their suitcases at the bag check. Igloo resisted the urge to look over her shoulder, but she couldn't resist a glance at the glass door. Unfortunately, so many people were coming and going that a visual inspection told her nothing.

She and Mike climbed to the top floor. The rare book room took up the back third of the floor. The room was isolated behind a steel and glass enclosure to protect the contents inside.

She entered, and the door shut behind them. The air inside was cool and dry, and all the other sounds faded away. Open shelves were intermingled with locked glass cabinets.

All of the T2 team was inside already. The sole other person was a leather-clad, purple-mohawked woman at least twice Igloo's size. She came over to greet Igloo.

"Shadow Cat," Igloo said, giving her a hug. "Thanks for letting us use this space. I owe you a big one."

"No problem, little pet. I get maybe one or two serious buyers a day. Everyone else tries to put their paw prints on the books. Everything okay with you?"

"No, but I've got a handle on it."

"Just remember you've got friends in the community. We're here for you. You don't have to tackle it alone."

Igloo looked up at the woman who performed her first public flogging. "Thanks, Shadow. You've always been good to me. Take this." She handed over her smartphone, which was still talking to the two suitcases downstairs, which were in turn scanning the wireless spectrum. "If any of these indicators turn red and stay red, knock on the door."

"Got it." Shadow hit a switch which triggered protective metal shutters inside the glass windows to roll down with a subtle grind. "Just flip the lock behind me. I'll be right outside."

Igloo locked the door, took a deep breath, and faced the group.

"This cloak and dagger stuff is ridiculous." Jeff said. "I doubt the government is going to take that much of an interest in us. And if they did, there's no way your games are going to protect us."

"Don't be a jerk," Diana said. "Igloo knows what's she's doing."

Everyone turned to Igloo to see what she would say.

Angie had always made it seem effortless when she handled dissension. A pit grew in Igloo's stomach. She felt completely inadequate to the task.

Essie caught her eye and her face said she believed in Igloo. If Essie believed in her, then she would have to deliver the strength that Essie wanted to see.

"Jeff, let's imagine that I was the inventor of Bitcoin. I wouldn't go advertising my real identity around, and if you worked with me, there'd be nothing to suggest my secret life. What you don't know about me would fill at least a book. In other words, don't make too many assumptions.

"There are reasons for everything we did. I wanted to be sure, absolutely sure, that none of us are being tracked, and that we aren't being observed in any way. Out there, on the train, I was scanning everyone for tracking devices. I got all the routine stuff, and there was no sign of government surveillance. So we made our way here. This room, thanks to the metal shielding, is an effective Faraday cage. No wireless signals can get in or out. There's a closed-circuit connection with the security room downstairs, and a phone line. Shadow Cat is going to let us know if anyone with a signal profile similar to the FBI, NSA, or any other government agency is approaching. In the meantime, we can talk securely without eavesdroppers. Because we're all holed up in one place, off the grid, if the government is surveilling us remotely, this'll force their hand."

"But what's the point of all these charades?" Jeff said. "We're talking about a software release."

"A release that someone killed Angie to stop," Ben yelled. "If they killed Angie, they'll get us too."

"Please," Igloo said, her voice quiet. "Let's not go there again, Ben." If she was forced to try to make something up about Angie's death, or worse, tell the truth that Angie had sacrificed herself, she wasn't sure she could handle it.

Ben's face was red, and he had both hands on his hips. He opened his mouth once or twice, and maybe something he saw on

Igloo's face changed his mind, because he just nodded and turned away.

Igloo took a deep breath. "We talked about the possibility of arrest this morning. That's still a possibility. But Angie believed the government would be willing to do almost anything to stop this project. That's why there's nobody on T2 with kids, nobody who's married. Angie was looking out for her team."

"Fuck. Are you telling me that Ben is right?" Jeff said. "Did Angie pick us all for a suicide mission? When the fuck was she going to inform us of the risk?"

"I did. This morning. That's what that whole meeting was about. That's why we had it, why some of the people opted out. Angie knew there'd be a point where people could opt out, and most of them did. Nothing will happen to the people who are off the team. We're the ones at risk. Did you think I wasn't serious this morning?"

Jeff rested his head on his hand for a second. "No, I knew. But now we're face to face with it, and I'm fucking scared."

"I think I can get us through it. If we're careful. If we get T2 out. We get one try, and it has to be perfect. Once T2 is out and irrevocable, there's no point to any of us being dead."

Jeff nodded somberly.

"Maybe not dead," Carly said. "But they could still arrest us."

"That we can fight against. We have lawyers. The government would have to show we actually broke a material law by what we did. We just have to stay lost until the software is out. Most of the incentive for them to arrest us on cooked up charges is to prevent the software release. Afterwards, our risk profile goes down substantially."

"What are we going to do to stay hidden?" Diana asked.

"We're going to split up. I only got us together so I can provide everyone with secure hardware and hardcopy plans. We're not going to meet in person again. I'm going to give you a crash course in evading government surveillance, which is made easier by the fact that we only have to be hidden for a limited amount of time."

She handed out Paranoid Linux phones to everyone. "To start, no one is going to carry anything wireless other than these phones. They change IMEIs and MAC addresses and phone carriers automatically based on time and motion data. They encrypt and onion route over the Tapestry backbone. They're hardware encrypted, and password, fingerprint, and visually locked. They contain alternate encrypted boot partitions based on Veracrypt, so you have plausible deniability if you're caught. Provide your alternate password, and they act just like your normal phone. They're ready to be initialized by each of you, so let's take a few minutes to set them up."

When everyone was done with that, Igloo handed out brand new laptops. "These are also Veracrypt protected, dual boot for plausible deniability."

Finally, she passed around envelopes. "I don't want you to open these until we've separated. Each packet has information about the identity you'll be using, where to go, and cash to cover expenses. There are also instructions for what to do if your hardware breaks—please, don't go to the store and try to replace it—and what to do if you're arrested."

Melanie looked at her envelope. "If we're getting hotels and stuff, won't we need credit cards and IDs?"

"All in there," Igloo said. "Everyone has accommodations and other reservations that can be paid in cash without ID."

Melanie looked doubtful.

"The internet is ripe with lists of places that take cash for everything. For people who want to have affairs, people escaping abusive spouses, that sort of stuff." Igloo paused and cleared her throat. "Look, that's the easy part. I could set up communications and reservations for everyone. The hard part is what you guys need to do. Or more specifically, what you need to *not* do."

"No going any place with security cameras. That's almost everywhere. Now, it's going to be unavoidable some of the time, but we have some tricks for that. I have infrared emitters for everyone." She passed out devices that looked like clip-on bike lights. "You'll want to fasten these on your collars. They're super-bright, but they're outside the range of human vision. We can't see them, but security cameras will be unable to get a clear visual on your face. Mostly. It's not bulletproof, and they have a somewhat unique signature, so you can't make regular trips out and about. You're mostly going to hole up somewhere safe and stay there."

"What if they capture you?" Ben asked. "You can tell them where we are."

"Actually, I can't. Everything was randomly picked by a computer program. I printed them out, never looked at them, and put them in the envelopes. So I know nothing. Besides, I'm going into hiding too. Also, no contacting anybody you know. Assume anyone outside of our circle is actually being played by someone in the government, and they'll manipulate you into revealing your location without you ever realizing it. Trust me on this."

"If they break into our Tapestry chat group?" Melanie said.

"You wrote the chat code, Ben and Diana wrote the onion routing code, and I wrote the encryption layers. Is it a risk? You tell me."

"It's the NSA," Melanie said. "They know everything. Every fucking thing."

"We're going to be like rogue planets in interstellar space. We have to emit nothing. Be nowhere anyone expects to find us. As long as we don't attract attention to ourselves, they won't find us."

"We're going to be in constant communication by chat, committing code, provisioning servers, running tests," Mike said. "It's not possible!"

"Again, encryption, onion routing, Tapestry backbone. We have a lot on our side."

"Against the whole of the government?"

"The Silk Road was pursued by the Feds for over a year before they captured Ulbricht," Igloo said. "We just have to last a few days."

"Yeah, but the Silk Road 2.0 administrators were arrested in under a month." Ben said, rubbing his head. "The government has only gotten better since then."

"We can do this, people," Igloo said. "One week. Look, before we split up, let's go through the backlog one last time."

"We've already been through the backlog," Carly said. "Yesterday, and the day before. Everything that's left is critical, we can't release without it."

Mike paced back and forth. "This is ridiculous. Let's release it now, and push out updates once it's out there."

"Then we risk the government finding a way to shut it down because we haven't properly hardened it," Diana said.

"Yeah, but how likely is that?" Mike asked. "I mean, in one week, are they going to find a hole?"

"They'll never let us get away with running T2 if they can find a way to stop us," Igloo said. "If they do find a security hole that enables them to shut down our distributed server/clients, we're sunk. Assume they put everyone they've got on eliminating T2."

"Then what?" Mike threw up his hands. "We close these, what, fourteen issues, and we're miraculously so secure that the they can't take us down? I don't buy it."

"It takes us far enough along that we can survive until the next release," Carly said. "Look, we need a bulletproof method of digitally signing client updates. We need to fix the VM shutdown. Without this stuff, we're sitting ducks."

Sharp knocks at the door startled everyone. The lock turned on its own, the door opened silently, and Shadow Cat poked her head in. "Um, Igloo, all these lights started blinking."

Igloo glanced at the smartphone that Shadow held out. Oh, fuck. She snatched the phone away.

"Multiple cars with encrypted radio signals heading this way." Igloo looked up. "Can you come down with us, help us get our bags fast?"

Shadow nodded.

"Let's go everyone."

They ran out the door in a line, everyone's eyes suddenly wide with fear.

"Hold onto your plans," Igloo called out, as they ran downstairs. "If you get caught or stopped, claim you're following Angie's instructions that she gave you the week before she died."

They rounded a corner and Igloo yelled back up the stairs. "You don't know what the overall purpose is. If they believe you're just following orders, and those of a dead person, they'll be less harsh."

At the first floor, Shadow Cat ran ahead of them to the bag check desk. She and Igloo passed out bags to everyone. "Good luck," Igloo said to each person as she handed over their suitcases.

Then suddenly she was handling her own suitcase, and she realized it was only her and Essie. She wondered where everyone else had gone already. She made the mistake of glancing at her phone. The agents were close, really close. She pinched and zoomed...they were around this block. Fuck.

Shadow Cat saw the panicked look on Igloo's face.

"You need a car?"

Igloo nodded.

Shadow handed over her keys. "A white Volvo 240. On the employee level, third floor *down*." She pointed them toward the parking garage. "Go."

She looked to Essie, who nodded, and they ran together. Into the garage, down three flights of stairs. They emerged, breathing hard. "Split up. Look for it."

Essie called out a second later, and Igloo ran to join her at the old station wagon.

"Let me drive," Essie said.

"I can drive."

"You're a biker first, driver second. Let me drive."

Igloo nodded and tossed over the keys. They shoved their bags into the back seat, and Igloo turned off the radio scanners in case they were emitting a traceable signal. As she settled into the car, she wondered how the government had tracked them to Powell's, and exactly why their interest had been piqued at this moment. Did they know the T2 team was getting together for the first time? And if so, how?

Essie pulled out onto the street slowly and drove slowly. "Don't fault me, I'm trying to blend in."

"Your driving is good. No worries," Igloo said. She turned to look at a black SUV with tinted windows. A man in a windbreaker, shirt and tie stood out front. Igloo didn't recognize him in particular, but he was dressed just like the agents that picked her up this morning. Igloo wondered again whether Agent Forrest was telling the truth about working with Angie.

Essie turned the corner, and a few feet later hit the brakes. The old Volvo screeched to a halt, and Igloo looked up, startled, to see Ben and Diana on the sidewalk next to them being confronted by two of the federal agents.

"Why the fuck are they together? They were supposed to split up."

"What do you want me to do?" Essie asked.

"I can't afford to lose them both. Drive to the next block and keep an eye on them in the mirror. Let me think." Igloo pulled her hat a little lower as they drove past and tried to watch out of the corner of her eye.

She reached into the back seat to grab her laptop. She couldn't overpower the agents. Would a diversion of some kind help? Make them forget about Ben and Diana? No...there's no way they'd sacrifice the bird already in their hand.

She looked back using the visor mirror. "Where'd they go?"

"The agents made them get into that vehicle at the curb," Essie said. "The black one with the tinted windows."

"Did any of the agents get into the car?"

"Not that I could see from here," Essie said. "But they could already have someone in the SUV. Should I drive away?"

"No. I can't lose anyone this early in the game. Give me a few seconds. I've got to load some software. Keep an eye on them."

Essie pulled the car into a loading zone a quarter of the way down the block.

Igloo decrypted the secondary drive, full of tools she and Angie had accumulated. She had to pray they still worked. The thing about exploits is that they got closed. Years ago, she and Angie had made do with a combination of cheap, weird exploits that Angie had bought, in combination with backdoors Angie had through her job at Tomo. But in the last year, they'd had the money to buy first class exploits on the darknet, stuff that no one else had. Which meant, in theory, they'd work longer, because if no one used them, then no one would know to fix the holes that made them possible.

She'd need to compromise everyone's phones around her...a lot of phones. Luckily they still had the backdoors in Tapestry. Part of her cringed, because these backdoors weren't going to be in T2. If they succeeded, in a week or two, even she wouldn't be able to do this.

The process took a few minutes...waiting for phones to get online, receive the control packets that Igloo sent, connect to the secret backchannel where Igloo could issue more commands.

"They still there?" Igloo asked, without looking up.

"Yes," Essie said. "One of the agents is talking into a phone or a walkie-talkie or something. But as far as I can tell, Ben and Diana are still in the car."

"Okay, drive around a few blocks. We want to come up alongside that car, but we have to do it when no one is in front of us. You need to time it just right."

"Got it," Essie said, putting the car in gear.

As they circled, Igloo readied the script she needed. She looked at the car they were in. The ancient Volvo they were driving wouldn't have anything wireless in the car, so that made things simpler.

Essie waited at a corner longer than she needed to, waiting for the cars to clear the block ahead. "You ready?"

"Go for it. Pull up alongside them with enough room for their door and ours to open. Quietly if you can."

When the Volvo was a few car lengths behind the black SUV,

Igloo ran the script. Igloo's script connected to the local network of smartphones, using their wireless radio transceivers to rebroadcast the necessary commands to trigger a half dozen different car computer exploits. A few seconds later, a cacophony of car horns sounded from vehicles all around them. Less visibly, a second command simultaneously unlocked every car door in the vicinity.

Angie would have freaked over the waste of so many exploits at once, but Igloo had no time for finesse. She had one shot at getting this right. Igloo couldn't see the agents from here, but she had to believe they were distracted.

A few seconds later, the SUV's rear passenger side door opened. Diana peeked her head out, rushed to the Volvo and got in. Ben followed a step or two behind her.

"Go quietly, slowly." Igloo said to Essie, as Ben cleared the doorway. "Don't slam that door, Ben. You two get down so no one can see you."

Ben nodded and eased the door shut as Essie pulled away.

Igloo glanced over her shoulder. One agent appeared to be talking on the radio. The other opened the car door, then glanced around. Igloo was already half a block away, and everyone was driving erratically, both looking for the source of car horns coming from everywhere as well as trying to stop their own horns from sounding.

"Where to?" Essie said.

"Head north, toward the St. Johns Bridge. I need a minute to think."

"Disguise your faces," Diana said from the back seat. "I think they found us with some facial recognition software. We were a block away in the middle of a crowd, and they zeroed in on the two of us."

"Why were you two even together?"

"I don't know," Ben said, his voice rough, like maybe he was crying. "We do everything together."

Igloo shook her head at their stupidity. She looked around the car. She came up with a first aid kit in the glovebox, and pulled out the biggest bandage she could find and tried to stick it across Essie's face.

Essie pulled away. "What are you doing?"

"Obscuring your face. The infrared emitters only work indoors. The traffic cameras will still be able to pick us up. Stay still." She put the bandage across part of Essie's lip and nose.

"Ouch. Jeez...are you trying to give me a harelip?" Essie tried to look in the rear view mirror.

"Don't fuss." Igloo did the same thing with three smaller bandages to her own face. "It'll fool the automated facial recognition software. For now. You two keep down in the back seat."

Igloo sat bolt upright. "Shit, shit."

"What?" Diana asked.

"If they caught you two coming into our car, then they'll know what car we're in, and they could be tracking us by satellite right now."

"Tracking us by satellite?" Diana said. "Look, it's one thing that they tried to arrest us in person, but being tracked by satellite like the world's most wanted terrorist? It just seems crazy."

Igloo bit back an angry reply. Oh, good grief. She was becoming Angie. Now she realized how Angie must have felt when Igloo continuously doubted her. She hoped that everyone wasn't going to subject her to the same never-ending criticism.

"Just trust me. No matter how paranoid I seem, your safety depends on you incorporating paranoid thinking into everything you do. Now shush, and let me think."

But the thoughts she needed wouldn't come over the unending panic and infinite recursion of negative thoughts. What if the government *was* tracking them? What if they were just around the corner? What would happen if the four of them were caught? Would there be enough critical mass for the rest of the team to finish the V2 release? Would—

"Hey, look at me!" Essie called from the driver's seat.

Igloo looked up, barely able to even see Essie through the haze of negativity swarming her head. She felt frozen in time, impossibly sluggish.

"You're panicking," Essie said. "Stop thinking about whatever it is that you're thinking about. We need to ditch this car. You and Angie have safe houses and cars all over the city. Where's the closest one, and how do we get from this car to that car, without them following us?"

"Yeah. Right. A car." Igloo knew she needed a car but couldn't remember what came next.

"Where can we find a car?" Essie sounded like the epitome of calmness, and vaguely Igloo realized Essie was carefully calming her down.

"Kelly has a conch shell she painted white and blue and it's in her bed."

"Um, what are you talking about?"

"A mnemonic. There's a car in St. Johns, near Pier Park. We go in one side of the park, we get under tree cover, and we go out the other side. Park on the south end."

"Where do I go? I'm used to GPS and maps."

Nobody answered. Igloo struggled to remember how to get there, and realized she needed a map, too. It's funny. How did her parents know how to get around? She recalled the geographical data Angie had downloaded into their devices.

"I've cached the map data for the whole region," Igloo said, scrambling for her phone. "The GPS doesn't require transmissions, so maps I can provide."

CHAPTER 41

I gloo got them to the vicinity of a safe house on her list. She had Essie parked the vehicle under a carport at a nearby home for sale.

Ben and Diana and Essie followed along as Igloo led the way to a small row of storefronts bordering the residential neighborhood. They went around the back where Angie had leased a storeroom in the rear of an upholstery shop. Igloo rushed to get online, eager to check in with everyone, but they'd barely been inside for ten minutes when she detected nearby encrypted radios. By the time they got outside, they heard the thump of an approaching helicopter.

That started a process of continual evasion that lasted hours, as the government chased them from one safe house to the next. Igloo scanned all four of them repeatedly but found nothing that could be betraying their position. They swapped vehicles several times, tried switching cars under the cover of trees, but nothing fooled their pursuers.

It was the middle of the night before the pattern finally changed. Igloo decided to stop using her safe list, and instead picked a random residential street. She walked down the block checking garbage cans, looking for an empty one, and hoping that meant no one was home.

She finally found one, and broke a basement window. After carefully picking out the glass, she watched the street as Ben, Diana, and Essie entered. She followed them, descending into a dingy basement packed with boxes and old furniture. They hadn't been bothered again for hours, although Igloo still heard an occasional circling helicopter, which kept her on edge.

The others eventually fell asleep. Essie had pulled her coat over her head and was curled up in a ball on a musty couch. Diana slept in a ratty, cat-scratched chair, while Ben snored on what looked like a dining room table.

Igloo couldn't sleep. Where had she gone wrong? The government had chased them from one safe house to the next. They'd burned three locations and four vehicles, and every time they thought were safe, the government closed in again. She'd scanned everyone multiple times and found no evidence of trackers. Near as she could tell, their electronics were not leaking any details. And they were using good, untraceable digital connections.

Agent Forrest had said there was a mole inside Tapestry. Angie had said the same thing. Igloo found the idea plausible enough, but she'd assumed the mole would be somewhere inside the larger company, not right here on the T2 team. And yet...she'd leaked nothing to the larger team about their location. But that left just the four of them: Ben, Diana, Essie, and herself. She was tired, exhausted actually...they'd been on the go for almost forty-eight hours, and she wanted sleep desperately. But she was afraid to sleep, like the characters in that movie she'd watched with her mom when she was a kid, *Invasion of the Body Snatchers*. If she fell asleep now, she was sure that one of them would turn into a government agent, and when Igloo woke up, she'd find herself under arrest.

She needed to figure it out herself.

Could any of the people in this room actually be working for the government? She couldn't see it. Ben was one of the early employees. They'd hired him with the first big round of Tapestry funding. He'd worked on an open source web browser before that. Igloo had even been on his hiring committee and reviewed his git history.

Diana had come a few months later, a University of Washington grad, who worked at two big corporations before she punted to find work with meaning. She and Ben had been inseparable since, and they were subversive even by Tapestry's standards, bucking HR rules and refusing to be pinned down by management or marketing.

That brought her to Essie. Thinking of Essie this way made her feel palpably sick, her stomach roiled with unease. The problem came when she tried to face the facts with any sort of cold rigor. She'd known Essie less than a year. Essie was her dream partner, the yang to her yin, the perfect complement to bring Igloo out of her shell and make her live life fully. But could she be too perfect? Could a mole really get that close to her? Would it even make sense for the government to implant someone, not inside the company, but as the partner of a key employee? If so, what would Essie be doing for them? She couldn't make sense of it.

A tear rolled down her cheek, and she forced herself to look over at the Essie-shaped bundle curled up asleep next to her. She was the perfect person to get Igloo to let down her guard and trust another human. She always imagined a life together with Essie, as cliché and corny as that sounded. The irony was Essie had gained her trust by submitting so totally to Igloo.

A part of Igloo felt like a brittle building cracking apart in the tremors of an earthquake. If Essie was a government agent...really had violated her trust...then everything was a lie. Everything. This made even considering Essie an agent of the government almost impossible to stare in the face. If it turned out to be true, she would never be able to trust anyone again.

And yet, who else could it be? Why would the perfect person just happen to come along at the perfect time?

She ground her hands into her eyes, trying to fight the exhaustion. She had to be crazy right? This was sleep deprivation talking.

Essie was there for her every time. And yet, of course, she would be, if that was her assignment.

There had to be a way to figure it out. Angie would know how, or maybe not. After all, she didn't know who the mole was either. If even Angie couldn't figure it out, then Igloo was wholly inadequate.

But Angie would never have let anyone get as close as Igloo and Essie had grown. Angie simply didn't allow herself to be that vulnerable. She didn't let anyone in. Not Igloo, or even her husband, not totally. Even the small amounts she'd let Igloo and Thomas in had only been under extraordinary circumstances.

Agent Forrest had been the one to confirm that there was a mole but said nothing as to who that mole might be. Shit, it was like playing werewolf with Ben and Harper at SXSW. There was no real information to go on. Everything was guesses.

If both Angie and Essie were taken from her, she would have no one. No support left in the world. She'd be utterly alone.

She toyed with the phone in her hand. She had Forrest's number, and she could route the text message over secure channels. Fuck it, she couldn't hide here in the basement while helicopters made yet another pass. She might not have Angie any more, but now she needed to *be* Angie. Cold, functional, calculating. Doing what was necessary, no matter the cost.

She could do this.

She set up the encrypted tunnel, routed through a call center in Seattle.

"You know who this is?" she sent.

The reply came less than a minute later.

"Yes. You're very hot right now."

"Tell me something about our mutual friend."

"I was working a child pornography case," Forrest wrote. "We were stuck trying to track down the origination point of the content. Somehow Angie found out what I was doing and sent me some IP addresses totally out of the blue. I checked them out, and it was the raw, naked server hosting the original files...unprotected, no VPN.

After that, she fed me information on roadblocked cases several more times, and she never told me who she was, never asked for anything. Just unsolicited tips that always gave me exactly what I needed to take the next step in whatever case I was working on."

"What changed?" Igloo asked.

"Let's go to voice."

Igloo's phone chimed, and a notification popped up to establish a voice channel. She accepted and plugged in an ear bud. A couple of seconds later, Forrest came on, her voice full and rich. Igloo crossed to the other side of the basement so she could talk without disturbing the others. She sat on the floor, leaning against the cold concrete wall.

"One day she asked for information. It was the medical records for a government employee, and I wouldn't do it. I didn't think it worked that way. She sent me information, not the other way around. She asked me a few days later and made clear her request was urgent. I still didn't give her the information. I didn't know…"

There was a long pause, and Igloo sat in the dark, staring at the glowing screen, waiting for Forrest to continue.

"A few weeks passed. Then Angie sent me a link to the arrest report. He'd beaten his girlfriend, hospitalized her. What Angie wanted was his confidential mental fitness report. The report indicated a risk for violence. If she had that data, maybe things would have turned out differently. I'll never know for certain, but the next time she asked for data, I sent it. And every time after that, too. Somewhere along the line we started to talk about why we did what we did."

Igloo marveled that Angie had somehow managed to have this secret life, another confidante and collaborator that she'd worked with. Why hadn't she ever told Igloo?

"When did you learn who Angie really was?" She kept her voice low, so she wouldn't wake the others.

"A lot of her requests started to be about the government investigation into Tapestry. It didn't take much to guess. Ex-computer security guru and domestic abuse survivor turned data analyst and startup founder at odds with the government over privacy concerns and data ownership? Of course it had to be her. I asked, and she said no of course, but then how could she admit to that? But I understood."

"What do you know about T2?"

"Angie was concerned...very concerned...that the government was going to compromise Tapestry. We explored hypotheticals about a tech company relocating overseas. But she didn't think solving a political problem with a legal loophole would work over the long term. It was clear a technical solution was needed. She asked me about government oversight abilities. At some point I realized I was spying against the government, turning over secrets, but it always seemed like the morally correct thing to do. Angie has that way about her."

"*Had*," Igloo said, "She's dead now." Igloo was suddenly angry at this woman who had all these insights about Angie, who'd shared parts of Angie's life that Igloo knew nothing about. Igloo always assumed that even if she hadn't been Angie's top pick for management at Tapestry, that they had shared an exclusive relationship when it came to hacking. Now she realized she hadn't even had that. She wondered whether she'd been anything special at all to Angie, or if she was just another tool.

Fuck. Downward spiraling about this now wasn't going to get her anywhere.

"I'd love to hear all about your relationship with Angie another time," Igloo said, not bothering to hide her bitterness. "Right now, I need to know who the mole is."

There was a long pause, and for a moment Igloo wondered if they'd lost the encrypted connection.

"They've had a woman in place for less than a year. The first reports I saw showed up about ten months ago."

"You have a name?"

"I have a codename, but that's not going to do you any good."

"What is it?" Igloo said. Maybe it would somehow connect the dots.

"No way. The name is globally unique. That's how they do it these days. They monitor searches, mentions, so they can detect counter-surveillance. If I tell you the name, and you do anything with it, they'll know you know and that the identity is partially compromised. You've played this game, too."

Igloo assumed Angie had invented the counter-surveillance poison pill in the form of an identifier. But maybe she'd gotten the idea from the government.

"What about the name she's operating under? Her job? Who she is associated with?"

"I don't know. I'm sorry."

"Is it someone on the T2 team?"

"Maybe. They're still getting data on your location, so it's either a person or a tracking device or something else..."

Igloo could hear the hesitation in Forrest's voice, and something more, too. Fear?

"What's the something else?"

"They've got new tracking AIs trained on massive data sets. Everything from check-ins to surveillance cameras to license plate trackers to cell phone tower connections and photo meta-data. Doesn't even need to know that you're driving a friend's car. All the data goes into the neural net, comes out the other side, tells us where you are."

It *was* fear she heard in Forrest's voice.

"Why does that scare you?"

"Because the same big AI can detect collaborators. Even if we don't have a direct evidence trail linking the two of us, second-order effects in the data, stuff that'll make a probabilistic determination that I'm helping you."

"Did Angie know about this?"

"We talked about the project while it was still conjecture. Nobody was using the AI for actual investigations yet. But Angie's worries about the AI was part of the reason for T2. If enough data is encrypted, then the signal to noise ratio drops massively, makes the user-contributed data portion drop to almost zero, and forces the government to rely only on mass surveillance data."

Great. More to worry about. "Let's go back to the mole. What else do you know?"

"Nothing," Forrest said. "I know they exist, that's all."

"They have to be leaking information. What information?"

"It's being kept very quiet. If it's like other deep leads, she's got a handler, and the handler is responsible for obfuscating what she uncovers and mixing it in with other signals intelligence to disguise the source."

"Yeah, but you've got to have something. Is she technical or non-technical? An executive, admin, developer? What hours does she work? Who is she close to?"

Is she close to me? is what Igloo wanted to ask but was afraid to.

"We have technical and non-technical SIGINT, so I don't know."

"Do some digging, because if we don't plug this hole, then we're going to get captured before we can get T2 out."

Igloo disconnected and squeezed her phone in her hand. She felt the tears come, and she resisted smashing her phone on the floor. Why was the universe so unfair? She had worked so hard, for so long. All the time, they'd been on top of things, and then, from out of nowhere, comes this potential for Essie to be the mole, unbelievable as that seemed. Now, when she needed to be at the top of her game, confident and kicking ass, she was cowering in a ball in a basement, licking her wounds. How could she function under this much pressure?

The bundle of coat on the couch across the room moved, and Essie peeked out to look at Igloo. She climbed down wordlessly and crawled across the floor to curl up at Igloo's feet and rested her head on Igloo's thigh. She traced patterns with one finger on her leg.

"It's going to be okay. You can do whatever it is you need to do. I love you."

Igloo leaned her head back against the wall. Maybe. Maybe Essie loved her. But maybe that was a cold, calculating lie.

CHAPTER 42

"I think she buys it."

"Did she ask about Essie?" Nathan9 said.

"You were listening, weren't you?" Forrest asked. "Why ask me what you already know?"

"I want you to tell me what you heard," Nathan said.

Forrest noticed that was neither confirmation nor a denial. Maybe Nathan was listening, maybe he wasn't. The bastard played his cards close to his chest. The feeling of manipulation was always present.

"She didn't ask specifically about Essie. But she probed three times about who the mole is, so it's important to her."

"She's scared and in the dark," Nathan said. "That's the best place to keep her. Anything her mind can invent is worse than any real, concrete terror. We'll tell her who the mole is later."

"You know?" Forrest couldn't really believe that. She was on the inside, and she couldn't figure it out. How had Nathan done it?

"Of course I know. My job is to know things. Igloo took the information about Angie?"

"Yes. She believes me."

"Good," Nathan said. "Then she'll trust you. When you give her the mole, that'll complete your trust relationship. It'll break loose her moorings. Then she'll belong to us."

Forrest wished she could doubt that. She wanted to scream "Run, Igloo. Run while you still can, while you have your freedom and your mind and your free will!" But then she belonged to Nathan, and so she wouldn't, *couldn't* do that. Igloo didn't stand a chance. After all, Forrest had been smart, talented, and had all the right connections and skills. And Nathan had broken her. What chance did Igloo have?

"Maybe there's another way," she found herself saying, even though Nathan would never buy it. "If we keep the charade going, she'll give us what you want, the private encryption keys to Tapestry. The odds are better that she'll do the job right. If you break her, you risk losing her completely. Maybe Tapestry falls apart."

There was a faint pop and crack on the line in the silence, Nathan's counter-surveillance noise generator running, creating unique acoustic watermarks he'd use to track down the records of this conversation later if it was ever leaked.

When Nathan resumed speaking, his voice was a cold whisper that sent chills down her spine. "I see what you're trying to do. We'll do it my way. Remember, I'm watching you. Stay focused on what I want and don't get any ideas."

Any good lie was mostly truth, and for Forrest, that lie had started two years ago...

She *had* been working a child pornography case. That part was true, as were the anonymous tips that had helped her close the case. The tips had kept on coming. Working logins for private web forms. Endpoints for darknet sites. Credentials that had allowed her to masquerade as a sex trafficking buyer. She gave the anonymous benefactor a nickname at first, and it wasn't until much later that she'd learned his hacker name, Nathan9.

Each case she closed led to new accolades. She'd made the FBI director look good, and in a bureaucracy there are few things more important than making your boss look good. Soon she was leading a team in the cybercrimes division, and she was feeding them all secrets from the always-invisible ghost in her life.

She was hooked on a stream of data she had to keep secret from everyone. The depths of that dependency only became obvious after the fact.

Six months ago, Forrest couldn't have known what she was walking into when she entered the Director's office for her weekly briefing. Few things were more sought after than the Director's time, and her standing twenty-minute briefing bypassed two layers of management. Her own manager berated her more than once for end-running the hierarchy until she saw the extra resources Forrest secured on an ongoing basis. Funding for undercover missions, extra training, new staff. The whole department almost doubled in size in six months thanks to Forrest, and the complaints about Forrest's weekly sessions with the Director slowly subsided.

Director Riley ignored Forrest when she entered the room, which was a first. Forrest wasn't sure if she should sit down or not. Riley had never been particularly formal with her, but she'd always invited Forrest to take a seat, sitting on her own initiative seemed presumptuous.

Riley was focused on her screen, scanning furiously, her eyebrows scrunched in concentration...or concern.

"Sit." Riley didn't look up.

"Thank you, Ma'am." Forrest didn't know why she was resorting to such formalities. Cued into some hidden stress in Riley, most likely.

The silence stretched enormously, but Forrest knew that was a common time dilation effect used to great effect in interrogations. She counted off seconds in her head to counter the effect. It was less than a minute before Riley cleared her throat and looked up.

"You've stirred up a hornet's nest."

"Ma'am?"

"Operation Cargo Doll."

"Closed three months ago. Wrapped up and turned over to the lawyers. A sex trafficking ring based out of Seattle, selling underage girls."

"The lawyers turned up a new name in secondary data analysis, which they turned over to our friends in the NSA. Turned out to be a senator."

"What? Who?"

"You aren't cleared to know. Exposing a senator is a matter of national security, and it has triggered an auxiliary investigation."

Forrest sighed. The real concern was almost never the actual wrongdoing on the part of elected officials. They were all corrupt in some way. The problem was their exposure. Involvement in sex trafficking of underage girls was potentially so destructive that it opened up the officials to blackmail. The higher their position, the greater the impact.

That Riley had specifically cited national security implications meant this had to be someone of monumental influence.

"That's big," Forrest said.

"I don't think you understand the scope of the problem. This senator has the power to make things very difficult for us, for your department, and, in particular, for you."

"If they're guilty..."

"The senator is well connected. Guilty, not guilty. It doesn't matter. They shouldn't have been flagged in your dragnet."

"I didn't flag anyone, only the primaries."

"You did. On the three separate occasions you requested foreign citizen level six data collection on their aliases."

Forrest tried to think back, but she'd marked so many people for data collection, she couldn't remember who was who. Fully a quarter of those were actually unconnected to her investigations...they were favors for her benefactor.

A pit opened in her stomach as old fears of being caught came back to haunt her. She'd made a sort of peace, ethically, with what she did for Nathan9 over the last six months, but she could still go to jail for the rest of her life.

"What happens now?" She forced the words out through a throat choked tight.

"We back down from the investigation, and I sacrifice you to appease the senator."

Forrest abruptly realized the gamut of her available options might be limited to going to prison for abuse of her powers or her career evaporating overnight. Neither had been on her mind only five minutes ago.

Riley saw the shock on Forrest's face. "Trust me, that doesn't appeal to me either. You're my star investigator. The hypothetical alternative is that you double-down, dig up every scrap of dirt you can find, see how deep the rabbit hole goes, and nail the senator so hard that none of their allies will touch them with a hundred-foot pole."

That was an impossible mission. It would take an army of lawyers to peel away the protective lawyers. Not an FBI investigative team.

"You're not even telling me who they are or what they're guilty of. How am I supposed to figure that out?"

Riley shook her head. "My hands are tied. All I'm telling you officially is that our involvement is finished. The senator wants your head on a platter. I've stalled, said you were deep undercover. If you can discover something to shift the balance of power in the next two weeks..."

It was the first time Forrest needed something for herself, not just an open investigation. The question was, would Nathan9 help her? They had a message board, where she'd post something when she wanted to hear from him, then he'd contact her.

As soon as she left the Director's office, she made the post, then chewed her fingernails down to the bed waiting for a response.

Of course, she wasn't without resources. She had an entire team of investigators and years of connections. She made a short list of senators that could be the right one. The overwhelming odds were that it was someone on the Senate Intelligence Committee, which was just thirteen people. Of those, seven stood out as being particularly likely.

She scanned the list of everyone she'd requested level 6 foreign citizen data for. There were almost a thousand names from the last six months. The kicker was they were flagged to have data collected on all known associates, which brought the total to almost a hundred thousand. A great deal of those were ghosts: people they knew existed that had online trails connected through phone calls and web browsing history and a thousand other things, and yet hadn't been associated to an individual. There were five thousand ghosts in the data, and one of those was a senator on her list.

She kicked off an investigation as quickly as possible. Her team worked discreetly but turned up nothing concrete over the course of several days. She made her own circumspect inquiries, but she could already feel the lines of power being cut off.

By the time Nathan9 got back to her, several days later, she was desperate.

"I understand you want help," Nathan had said, "but what you're asking for is difficult. Our quid pro quo arrangement up until this point doesn't really cover this."

"What are you saying?" she asked.

"You want to identify and neutralize a top government official. I'm saying that leaking occasional information to me doesn't quite cover my risks."

"What do you want?"

"When I ask you for something, I'll get it, no questions asked."

"What sort of 'something'? How often?"

"See, that's the thing about no questions asked. It means, no questions."

"I can't agree to something if I don't know what I'm agreeing to."

"I understand," Nathan said. "I'll be in touch."

He disconnected then, and she didn't hear from him again until two days before her deadline.

"Fuck, Nathan. You know I'm in trouble. I've always helped you. Don't leave me hanging."

"All you have to do is say yes to my proposal, and I'll help."

'Fuck you!' is what she wanted to scream, but that wasn't going to help. She said yes.

Two hours later, an evidence packet hit the news outlets showing Senator Edwardson at a party with an underage girl. Date stamps and digital signatures linked the evidence to an investigation in her office. The senator proclaimed he knew nothing of the events of that night, but the ongoing outrage forced him to resign within days.

Six months ago, she hadn't known to suspect Nathan9's manipulations, didn't realize he'd timed his responses for maximum effectiveness amid her growing desperation. She certainly didn't know the entire situation was fabricated to compromise her, or that the evidence involving the senator was forged, leading to the downfall of an innocent man.

She'd learned all that bit by bit over the successive months, each new revelation made her more unsure of what was true or not, right or wrong. In the end, she was totally complicit. She knew, Nathan knew, and the longer she did nothing to rectify the situation, the more Nathan knew she was his.

CHAPTER 43

Robin desperately wanted a stimulant, but she couldn't allow herself anything. She had to get some sleep after this. She was so tired, she'd given up her usual military posture, and was sitting slumped. She couldn't care anymore.

Enso appeared on screen within a few minutes.

"What the hell is going on out there?" Enso said.

"They all ran. Scattered. Your team only got one, Wendy."

"No shit. Why the hell didn't we pick them up first?"

How was she supposed to answer that? She couldn't very well say, "Because you let Forrest walk all over you by convincing the higher ups that everyone should be identified first, which caused everyone to be unprepared for the sudden meeting of the T2 team."

They should have been able to snatch them all. That would have been the quickest way to be done with all of this.

"We have the team members identified now," Robin said. "We're narrowing in on most of them. We'll have them soon."

"They scattered before we showed," Enso said. "That means they have their own intelligence on our operations. They'll run again as we close in on them. We need to cut them off at their head, which is Igloo."

Robin nodded. "She's the hardest of them to nail down. Look, instead of trying to pick her up, let's release the BDSM videos we have. Get them where the T2 team can see them. Discredit her with her own team. There's no way they're going to accept the leadership of someone who beats her own girlfriend."

Enso leaned toward the camera. "How do we get it into their hands?"

"We don't want to send it directly to anyone on the T2 team. Makes it more obvious that we're manipulating them. We post the content publicly. We have about six hours of video, forty clips in total. We've already edited them down for maximum effect. We'll send anonymous tips to popular media outlets. We'll get instant coverage. Top headline stuff, especially since Angie's death is already the number one story everywhere. When we're done, she won't have credibility with the T2 team, Tapestry, or her friends in the industry."

Enso looked doubtful. "We were going to use the videos to discredit Tapestry with the public. The T2 team are all progressive, mostly young. We're talking a bunch of people from Portland. They're probably all kinky. I don't think it'll be as impactful as you hope."

"The whole company is a bunch of social justice warriors," Robin said. "Half of them are abuse survivors. This is not your average group of progressives, and Igloo's not engaging in fluffy bedroom bondage. The videos are pretty damning. Besides, she's kept it secret all this time, which means she's worried her coworkers won't accept it."

"What if we use the videos to blackmail her instead?" Enso said. "Can we force her to do what we want?"

That would be exactly the wrong path to take. Robin chose her words carefully. "She'd either stall or fight harder against us. Maybe even go public herself so she can control the message. It's better to blindside her."

"When?"

"We can have it posted in fifteen minutes," Robin said, "and it should make the rounds in the T2 team within a few hours. If we're lucky, the timing will keep them awake all night. Sleep deprivation won't help their decision making."

"Make it so," Enso said. "You're not going to have a problem with this? I know you two got rather chummy."

Enso wouldn't ask a question like that of a male operative. "I'm undercover. I'm supposed to get close." She couldn't keep the sarcasm out of her voice.

Enso glanced at her again.

"Sorry, Sir. Just tired."

"Get that video released. I'll pull most of the team off the manhunt and leave just enough to keep them scrambling. Get some sleep so you'll be fresh tomorrow when they're at their worst."

CHAPTER 44

I gloo twisted and pulled at the sheets, but then her feet were cold. She blinked her eyes open and looked around the dimly lit room in confusion. There were no sheets, only a jacket. She'd been dreaming of bed.

Essie was curled up, pressing against Igloo's back. Pleasure rushed through her, then stopped cold. She still didn't know if Essie was the government's mole.

That the government hadn't picked them up during the night was an argument against Essie being their security leak. But the other factors fit: how long the mole had been in place, the fact that she the mole's a woman.

Igloo shook her head and reached into her shirt pocket for a caffeine pill. Two points of data, one of which ruled out men. That was absurdly little to go on. If she could even trust the source. She slipped the caffeine pill into her mouth. More than half the Tapestry employees were women. Any of them could be the mole. No, not any of them. Only people who were hired about ten months ago. Maybe ten to twelve months.

Careful to avoid waking Essie, Igloo craned her neck to look across the room. Ben and Diana were still asleep, sharing an old couch. Igloo pulled out her phone. Damn. Twenty percent battery level.

They ditched the car and most of their electronics in the middle of the night after the government successfully tracked them again and again. They broke into the basement of this house off Alberta, tucked in behind two six-story apartment buildings, chosen to put hundreds of wi-fi endpoints within range.

The musty basement was filled with old furniture and boxes of clothing, but no chargers that they'd found. She'd need to keep it quick.

She set the phone down to a minimal configuration so it wouldn't flood the network with data synchronization exchanges, then chose a wi-fi at random using her cached Tapestry database of wi-fi logins. She entered the T2 chat room, afraid to learn who was still on the go and who had been caught.

She scanned through the log starting from yesterday afternoon to see who had checked in since the fiasco at Powell's. Mike and Jeff were safely together. Carly made it out but said Wendy had been taken. Shit. Melanie and Gene got separated, but they were both okay. Ben and Diana had been captured, but she and Essie had recovered them. Wendy was a huge loss, but losing only one out of the nine remaining T2 members was better than expected.

She scanned through the messages. Everyone except Igloo's group had reached a safe house and remained unmolested all night.

Why was Igloo's group so hunted? Because of Igloo? Or because she had the mole? Or because they'd stolen Ben and Diana from the feds?

Never mind that, she told herself. She had to stay focused. She accessed the Tapestry employee database. Who started between ten and twelve months ago? A list of thirty-five names came up. That was a lot. Shit.

Wait, a bunch of those were in an overseas office. Two had left. Twenty-one names. Whom did she recognize? Igloo felt certain it had to be someone she knew. They'd want a mole to get close to her and

Angie. She recognized five names. Fudge. Diana was one of them! And so was Maria. Two developers from the API team. And Angie's admin, Matt.

What to do? If Essie or Diana was the mole, then the government would keep finding them, no matter what she did.

She couldn't spend days trying to figure out this one thing. They had to get the software released, and every minute wasted was gone forever. She'd have to split up everyone: get Ben and Diana each to their own safe houses, make sure Essie couldn't communicate with anyone. If Diana was the mole, and she was on her own, that would limit the damage she could do.

"Hey, wake up people," she called in a soft voice. She shook Essie, who groaned and tried to go back to sleep.

"What time is it?" Diana asked.

"Six-thirty."

"Four hours of sleep," Ben said. "You trying to kill us?"

"I'm trying to keep you alive. I'm getting everyone to their own safe houses. We're splitting up so the feds can't grab us all."

Igloo went out first. The streets were quiet. She stole a car using a wi-fi hack. For a brief moment, she had a fantasy of driving off into the sunset and leaving everyone else. The crushing responsibility she felt was inescapable.

She went back to the house and paused for a moment outside. She had to play a game of fox, chicken, and bag of grain. She told Essie to wait in the house for her and took Ben and Diana with her. She dropped off Diana at a coffee shop, told her to grab coffee and bagels for three.

As she got out of the car, Igloo called after her. "Stay here, no matter what."

Diana looked puzzled but shook her head and walked off.

Igloo drove away as soon as Diana entered the building.

"Whoa, what about the coffee?" Ben protested. "And food. I'm starving."

"We have a leak on the team," Igloo said. "I need to get everyone separated. I know it's not you, which is why I'm telling you. Look, you can't tell anyone else about the mole. I don't want them to discover that I know."

"But who is it?"

"I don't know. Only that they're female, and they showed up around ten months ago or so. It could be Diana, Essie, or Maria."

Ben shook his head. "That's absurd. I work with Diana every day. She's not the mole. And Essie...she's your girlfriend. You two live together. It can't be her."

Igloo shrugged as she turned into another residential neighborhood. "I'm not willing to trust anyone."

She pulled over to the curb. "The garage behind the main house is your safe house. I know it's not awesome, but it's what I've got. Combination lock on the door. Here's the code." She handed him a slip of paper. "There's a sanitized MacBook in there, and a phone. There's wi-fi in the apartment building across the street. The bucket is your bathroom. It's rudimentary, but if you can stay inside until we can get T2 released, it's going to minimize your exposure."

Ben hung his head. "Diana is my best friend. I just can't see it."

"There's a 66 percent chance she's a perfectly good person. But on the off chance she isn't, this is the safe thing to do." Igloo rubbed her face with her hands. "I know this is awful. Sometimes we have to do crazy things in order to do what's right in this world."

Ben nodded.

"It's going to be okay, I hope. Either way, good luck. And thank you."

Ben got out of the car.

She watched until he entered the garage, then drove back to the coffee shop.

Diana was just inside the shop, looking out through the window. She rushed out to the car.

"Where the fuck did you go? I had no idea if you'd been arrested. Where's Ben?"

Igloo hated having to lie.

"I need to split everyone up, and Angie insisted that no one know where anyone else was. I'm sorry to have left you, but I needed to get Ben to his safe house. Now I'm taking you."

Diana didn't look happy about it. But she still dug into the paper bag and pulled out a bagel. "You want yours?" She gave Igloo one, then took one for herself.

Igloo ate one-handed as she drove, which made her feel melancholy. Angie would have made a bad one-armed joke in this situation. Would have talked about Igloo's two-arm privilege. She missed Angie so much. The bagel turned into a lump in her throat.

She dropped Diana off at another safe house, this one slightly better than Ben's, and gave her a similar set of instructions. Then it was back to the basement to get Essie.

Once there, she ditched the car. One less trail. She and Essie walked through a nearby neighborhood. Public transit was out because there were too many cameras. She didn't want to steal another car.

As they walked around the neighborhood, Igloo picked up spring steel bristles left on the asphalt by street sweepers. She bent one at ninety degrees and filed a second one with a bit of broken concrete she picked up.

"Lock-picks," she said, showing them to Essie.

They looped around the neighborhood, then made their way back to one of the apartment buildings. Igloo spotted a bike rack by the side entrance.

"Turn and face away from the camera," Igloo said. They lost their hats during the nighttime chase. She pulled her hood low over her head and inspected the electronic lock on the door. She ran a matching exploit on her phone, and the door unlocked.

"You're full of handy tricks," Essie said. "Why do we even pay rent?"

"I'm not trying to cheat anyone out of anything. Just do what's right."

"I know, sweetie. I'm just kidding."

"I'm too tired for jokes," Igloo said. Was Essie the mole? Why was she keeping Essie near her? The safest thing to do would be to isolate her. It's what Angie would do. But then, Igloo wasn't Angie.

Angie had wanted Igloo to manipulate the media, and she wasn't going to do that, either. Holy shit. Angie's backdoor into Tape, put there just so they could manipulate the news, was still there. She had to close that hole up. She added it to her mental to-do list.

They took the stairs up to the top floor. Top floor apartments went for more, so the people there would have better equipment, statistically speaking.

Igloo pulled out her phone, thought for a minute, then ran an app Angie had written a long while back.

"What are you doing?" Essie asked.

"Scanning for a hot water heater with a long idle time. High efficiency models lower the temperature after more than twenty-four-hours without use. The firmware has an internal clock since the last time water was used."

"Um, dumb question, but why do we care about water heaters?"

"We're figuring out who's on vacation."

Igloo walked up and down the hallway once, trying not to look too suspicious, but then there wouldn't necessarily be any reason for the apartment to review security camera footage unless there was a crime.

On the way back, she compared signal strengths, and found the apartment that correlated with a three-day hot water idle time.

"Stand between me and the camera at the end of the hall," Igloo said.

Essie complied, and Igloo knelt down to pick the lock. She struggled with her makeshift tools and felt herself starting to sweat. If anyone came out of an apartment on the hallway, they'd have to abandon the effort and start over, maybe in a different building.

She tried again and again, listening to the disappointing fall of the pins each time she failed to get them right. She took a deep breath, said a silent prayer to the universe, and tried again. It must have been ten minutes of trying, her fingers cramping, when the lock finally turned.

They stepped inside quickly. It was a furnished studio apartment, with a bedroom area, small galley kitchen, and a living room.

They glanced at each other and went straight for the kitchen cabinets.

"Food," Essie said.

"Coffee!" Igloo said, and held out a bag of beans with a smile.

Essie let out a shrill cry of glee. "I'll make it," She grabbed the beans.

"I'll see if I can figure out how long until they come back."

She saw an oversized gaming rig in the living room area. Ugh. She'd have to grab Windows exploits via her phone.

As the necessary files were downloading, she glanced back toward the kitchen, where Essie was preparing coffee and food. She couldn't be the mole. She just couldn't. Igloo's heart would break if she was.

Ten minutes later, she'd gotten into the PC. She hunted for the owner's calendar.

"Jackpot," Igloo said. "We've got three days here. They're visiting family in California."

Essie brought over a cup of coffee and knelt next to the desk, formally presenting it, eyes downcast.

"I'm sorry, this is the best I can do."

Igloo stared at Essie kneeling there, coffee on outstretched palms. She was so beautiful, so kind, so giving. A tear came to one eye, and she brushed it away. Her heart really was breaking.

"Oh, fuck, Essie." She slid out of the chair to come down to Essie's level. She took the coffee from her and set it on the table. She wrapped Essie in a giant hug. "I'm so stupid."

"What? What's wrong?"

"I doubted you."

"Huh?"

"There's a government mole. Someone watching Angie and I, and Tapestry. I thought maybe you were that person, but I know you can't be."

Essie leaned back. "You didn't really think it was me, did you?"

"I didn't know what to think. I'm confused and scared."

Essie stared at Igloo. "Is that why you took Ben and Diana separately this morning? Because you don't trust me enough to let me know where they are?"

Igloo shrugged and reached out to hug Essie more tightly.

Essie pulled away. "So I'm good enough to get you coffee and breakfast and be your fucktoy, but not trusted enough to know what's going on. Thanks a lot, Igs."

"It's not like that," Igloo said.

"It is exactly like that." Essie roughly disentangled herself and stood. "Give me some space, okay?" She walked off.

"Where are you going?" Igloo called.

"To the other end of the fucking apartment," Essie said, turning to stare at her. "Where do you think I'm going? To report to my boss at the FBI or something? Fuck you." Essie walked to the far corner.

It was almost comical, being stuck in a studio apartment together. Igloo sat there on the floor. Why was she so shitty at dealing with people?

She wanted to talk with Essie but couldn't bring herself to do it. She had to check in with the T2 team. It was imperative. Other than scanning the chat logs earlier, she hadn't been in touch with anyone else since last night. They had to get refocused. Escaping the feds was meaningless unless they got the code out.

She forced herself back into the chair. It took a half hour to turn the Windows computer into something she could trust, locking it down as much as possible, then grabbing the tools that would let her secure it the rest of the way, and only then pulling down a virtual machine image that contained her hacking environment. Of course, the hardware could have been deeply compromised to start, and nothing short of a complete rebuild would fix that. But she'd chosen the building and apartment almost at random, so she had to hope her work was good enough for now.

At some point she heard Essie in the kitchen. When she glanced over, there was a plate of food, now cold, sitting next to her. She shoveled it into her mouth, as she finally connected to the secure Tapestry chat room.

The chat window appeared, and Igloo choked on her food. Oh, no.

"Oh, fuck, no! NO!"

There was a link to an article. The preview was a photo of Igloo wielding a leather belt. The title read "Tapestry Cofounder Abuses Girlfriend."

There was chatter in the room about the article, but she was too shocked to read it. She didn't want to click on the link, but she couldn't not do it.

The article loaded. Oh damn, there were over a million shares.

There was a long block of text, but all she could see was the autoplay video at the very top. The video started with a close-up of her slapping Essie in the face.

Horrified, Igloo covered her own mouth and suppressed a scream.

The video cut to a scene of her pushing Essie to the ground. Another cut, and then a still photo of bruises on the backs of Essie's legs. Another cut to a video of Essie crying.

Oh God. They'd somehow gotten all this footage of them playing and edited together the clips to make it all look abusive. There were none of the tender moments of them together. Nothing of Essie smiling, or egging her on. There were no clips that showed Essie willingly, consensually, entering into the scenes with Igloo.

Igloo keened into her hand, despite herself.

Essie rushed over. "What..." She trailed off and leaned in to watch. "Where'd they get this?"

Igloo shook her head. "I don't know."

"Look, that's Silverhall," Essie said, pointing at the screen. "You can see the dragon on the wall in the background. They have a no camera, no phone policy. Who shot the video?"

The video changed again, a still photo of Igloo. She turned up the audio.

"...a senior software engineer and cofounder of Tapestry."

The video changed again. Essie, laying on something, crying. The picture was zoomed in to Essie's face, which jerked in time with the sound of impact play.

"I remember that scene. I was in a hogtie. You were spanking me with the paddle. After this you started tickling me."

But before the tickling started, the scene cut away again.

"Whoever edited this is good," Essie said. "I mean, they really make it look bad."

Igloo closed the browser tab. She couldn't watch any more.

"Why they'd do that?"

Igloo gestured at the chat room history on the display where the members of T2 had spent the morning discussing the video.

Gene > That's probably why she brought Essie with us. Igloo doesn't want her to get the chance to go the police on her own. So she has to keep an eye on her.

Ben > Igloo has always been amazing. The model for everything we aspire to. I can't believe she would do this.

Diana > Yeah, just like my ex. Predators always seem nice. That's how they get their victims.

Mike > Think about T2 from her perspective. With everything encrypted, there'd be no way for the government to get their hands on anything like this. No wonder she's been pushing so hard for T2. She wants to make sure the police can never get evidence of what she's been doing.

Diana > I've removed her access to the source code repo.

Igloo thought for a moment. She had pushed a copy of the repo yesterday to her personal cloud storage, so all was not lost. And she was in the chat room, so apparently they couldn't remove her access to that. Igloo was the sole administrator of the group.

As she scrolled to the bottom of the chat history, she realized the group had noticed her entering the chat room.

Ben > Igloo, you're not welcome here.
Diana > I'll create a new chat room and invite everyone but Igloo. Give me a second.

Igloo was still shaking in fear, but she forced herself to take a deep breath. She absolutely could not afford to lose the T2 team. The government somehow got access to those videos, had been planning this all along. Evidence they could use to discredit her.

She realized now that she's been wrong all along. She'd hidden her kink activities from her coworkers, ashamed to come out and as a result, the government had all this "evidence" on her. They could have blackmailed her, maybe. But instead they'd chosen to discredit her.

In a way, she had to admit the agency that did this was brilliant. In one fell swoop, they'd cast doubt on both her *and* the T2 effort itself.

She had to salvage things with the rest of the team. If she lost influence now, she couldn't count on them to follow through with T2.

Igloo > Please give me a chance to explain things. That video is all wrong. They're trying to manipulate you.
Mike > You're beating the shit out of her. There isn't really anything to debate about that.
Igloo > Essie and I are kinky. That's all. Those videos are tiny excerpts from consensual scenes that Essie and I chose to do together.
Carly > Someone can't consent to getting beat up. I had to

watch my father abuse my mother my whole childhood, and she fucking defended him until the day she died. I came to Tapestry because you all cared about people, about abuse. You're fucked up. You lied to us.

Igloo > You're not seeing the whole picture. If you'd seen the whole scenes, from start to end, you'd see us chatting, cuddling, and laughing together. Essie wanted this.

Diana > It's wrong. You're hurting her. She's crying. No sane person would ask for that.

Igloo > Look, she's right here, with me. Do you want to talk to her?

Diana > Victims will defend their abusers. That proves nothing except that you've brainwashed her.

Essie grabbed Igloo by the shoulder and forced her to look away from the screen. "Talk isn't going to convince them of anything. We have scenes we recorded. Show them a real scene from start to finish."

"Really? Give them more evidence?"

"Show them the bathtub scene," Essie said.

"Where I'm drowning you? How's that going to help?"

"We have cuddles before and after. We had X standing by for emergencies. It's a good one."

Igloo doubted that feeding more fuel into the fire of their rage was going to help, but she was losing everyone in the chat room. She had to try something different.

She found the video Essie described and dragged it into the chatroom.

Igloo > Watch this. Get a sense of what is really going on.

The scene started at their kitchen table. Essie was laughing, holding up her hands in front of her face in embarrassment. X, holding the camera, couldn't be seen, but they could hear his voice on the tape. Igloo asked for coffee, and the camera followed Essie to the kitchen. Essie came back, presented the coffee to Igloo, who took it, and petted Essie. Essie wiggled with glee when Igloo praised her. Igloo took a single sip of coffee, then ordered Essie to strip, which she did.

Igloo zip-tied Essie's hands to her collar and covered her eyes with a blindfold. Igloo stood and manhandled Essie toward the bathroom. X followed with the camera.

Igloo pulled off the blindfold. Essie saw the ice cubes floating in the bathtub and tried to pull away and protest. Igloo ordered her to climb in and sit.

Essie screamed as she descended into the cold water.

"Watch her head," X could be heard to say in the background.

Igloo nodded, and put one hand behind Essie's head as she forced her to lie down. Essie kept screaming and thrashing about, spilling cold water over the side of the tub.

Igloo and X were laughing and grabbing towels.

"Fuck that's cold," Essie said, while laughing and gasping. "Are you going to try this next?"

"Hell, no," X said. "That's why we're the tops."

"Hey, what happened to experiencing everything yourselves before doing it to your bottom?" Essie asked.

"I did try," Igloo said. "That's why I know you're going to hate what comes next." She smiled and pushed Essie's head under the water.

More water sloshed out of the tub. Essie came up screaming and gasping.

"Fuck, fuck. Please stop."

"Fuck is not a safe word, neither is stop," Igloo said in the video. "Are you asking for the scene to stop? Do you want to call red?"

Essie shook her head, shivering hard, teeth chattering. "No."

Igloo dunked her again.

Eventually the bathtub scene ended, and X put down the video camera as he and Igloo pulled Essie out of the tub. The video resumed in the bedroom, where Essie was covered in warm blankets. X mounted the camera on a tripod while Igloo cuddled Essie under the blankets. X came and went, bringing one microwave heating pad after another, getting Essie's body temperature up.

Essie curled deeply into Igloo, a wide smile across her face. "Thank you" she said.

"You're a good pet," Igloo said.

The video stopped.

There was silence in the chatroom for a long time.

Ben > That's fucked up.

Carly > Igloo is a monster.

Ben > But, and I kinda hate to say this, Essie really did seem like a perfectly willing participant.

Carly > No fucking way. There is no way I will have anything to do with Igloo.

Mike > That was maybe the weirdest thing I've ever seen, but I don't see anything abusive about it. Hell, people poured ice water over their own heads to raise money with that bucket challenge thing. I don't see how being dunked in a bathtub is so different. Look, can we please get back to working on T2?

Diana > I'm with Carly. There is something really wrong with both of them. I don't care if it's consensual or not.

The argument continued. Igloo didn't know if it was better or worse for her to participate.

Ben shared a link to a psychology article.

Ben > This study says that people who practice BDSM are happier and more well-adjusted than the population as a whole.

That brought about a flurry of additional conversation.

Diana > Look, regardless of what you all think, I can't in good consciousness go along with Igloo. We have to make a decision. Do we work on T2 *with* Igloo or *without* Igloo? I'm telling you, I can't work on it with Igloo.

Mike > Then who goes, you or Igloo? You're putting us in an impossible quandary. We need to be working on T2. We don't have time to debate this. Igloo is supposed to be the leader. Igloo knows what Angie wanted. I don't want you to leave, Diana. It's gonna be way harder to do what we need to do without you, but I'm not going to force Igloo out to keep you.

Igloo glanced at the time. They'd been arguing for an hour already. They were wasting precious time.

Igloo > If we argue about this until we reach a definitive conclusion, then we're letting the government win. They released this video specifically to distract and divide us. They can't find us and arrest us, so they're just going to stop us from making progress by seeding dissension and distraction. And their approach is working. Now, we need to make a call. Who's staying on the team and working with me, and who's going? That's what you've got to decide.

Diana > You think we're just going to walk away from T2, and let you, an abuser, decide what's right for the rest of the world? No fucking way. I've already locked down the code. You have no access. Now who's with me?

Igloo > Diana, you have no idea what you're doing. You're letting the government manipulate you into fucking up our whole project.

Diana > Of course you're going to say that. Meanwhile you're the one manipulating us. Come on people, Tapestry was founded on equality and justice. You can call it BDSM or

kink or whatever you want, but it doesn't change the basic
wrongness of what she's doing.
Melanie > I'm with Diana, people. Sorry, Igs, but I just can't
accept what you've done.

Igloo wanted to bash her head against the wall. They were
wasting time they'd never recover. She took a deep breath. She
couldn't give up.

Igloo > Angie knew about my relationship with Essie.
Initially she was upset, but as she learned more, she accepted
it. If Angie, of all people, could accept it, what more do
you want?
Ben > That'd be great if Angie were here to convince us, but
she's not.

Igloo thought back. She had nothing to substantiate her point. All
her conversations with Angie had been in person, when they were in
secured environments. There'd be no record of it.

A third of the group was solidifying around Diana when it
suddenly hit Igloo. If Diana was the mole, then the position she was
taking was totally in alignment with what the government would
want: getting control over T2.

Carly > We've got a problem. These scanners you've got are
lighting up across the board.

Igloo switched tabs. There was encrypted radio traffic everywhere. The FBI was on the move. Had they somehow located
everyone again?

Igloo was out of safe houses, and she couldn't personally get
everyone to a new safe location. She needed help.

CHAPTER 45

I gloo's heart pounded as the phone seemed to ring forever.

"Good to hear from you," Forrest said when she answered.

"You know what's going on?" Igloo said.

"They have a track on multiple members of your team."

"You know how?" Igloo asked.

"No. It's coming direct from BRI."

"Can you stop them? Buy us some time? We need two uninterrupted days, somehow."

"I can sanitize you all, get you to a safe house."

"I've done that three, four times, but it doesn't work. They keep finding us."

"They've got a tracker on you."

"I've scanned. Many times." Igloo squeezed the phone harder, wondered if it might snap in her hand.

"Then they're tracking your digital trail. IMEI. Wi-fi. MAC address. VPN connection points."

"All randomized, regenerated every time we connect to a new access point."

"Maybe that's it," Forrest said. "Maybe they're scanning for new

MAC addresses. They've got the computing power to crank through them all. Correlate with encrypted traffic."

Oh fuck. "Maybe that's it," Igloo said. "But even if we change now, I'm out of safe houses."

"I can get you somewhere untraceable."

Igloo felt a pit grow in her stomach. Trust the Fed that far? Did she have a choice?

"How would you get us there?"

"Can you get everyone to the Lloyd Center mall?" Forrest asked.

"What do you have in mind?"

"Plenty of people, vehicles, and electronics, in and out. No satellite coverage. If you come in dark, and I mean totally dark, not a single device on you, then I can get you out cleanly and take you somewhere safe."

Igloo hesitated. She had to be bold, and sometimes that meant trusting people.

"Let's do it."

"They want me to provide them a safe house," Forrest said. She scanned a screen providing a running transcription of agent chatter.

"As we planned," Nathan9 said. "Do it."

"It's going to be harder than we thought," Forrest said. "There's forty extra agents on the ground right now, in addition to local Portland FBI. A good portion of them are BRI. I can't control them, don't know who they are."

"Where are you sanitizing them?"

"Shopping mall. Good transit to it. Plenty of roads in and out."

"I'll give you cover from BRI."

"There's no way you can guarantee that."

"I'll give them a compelling distraction. Some of Angie's old safe houses."

Forrest knew that with everything going down, sacrificing Angie's safe houses didn't mean much, but she still found it sad how Nathan could dismantle someone's entire world so quickly. Did it matter that Angie was dead, and that Igloo would fall under Nathan's influence, and never use those safe houses again? Or that the safe houses were themselves deliberately sterilized, bereft of anything personal for Angie or Igloo? No, somehow these safe houses were still intimate, intended for Angie and Igloo alone.

"You are going to actually let them release T2?"

"Let them?" Nathan replied. "Everything is contingent on them getting that software out. We're going to make sure it's released. You're going to help them every step of the way."

"Then why don't we just leave them be?" Forrest said. "Let them do their thing on their own. Or better yet, sneak them out of the country. Put them somewhere where no one will be able to reach them again."

"Not possible," Nathan said. "Once T2 is released, it fundamentally changes the Internet. Everything is fully distributed, fully secure. Anyone can release their software in containers. In six months, the server and the data center as we know them will disappear. Only distributed client/server environments will remain. You could put this team in a bunker in Sweden, and the government would still hunt them down and destroy them to stop that software release."

Implicit in all of that: if there's going to be a new world order for the Internet, Nathan's going to be part of it. She wished that someone, somewhere could stop him.

Igloo switched back to the chat room.

Igloo > I have a solution.

She told the group about the plan to rely on Forrest's help to get them to a government safe house.

Ben > You're putting us into their hands? That seems ridiculous.
Diana > Igloo's not trustworthy. Not about what was going on with her girlfriend, and not about this. We need to be running away from the government, not buddying up with them.

Several members of the group chimed in with Diana. Would they never drop this? They'd wasted a good portion of a day so far. Most of the team were half-heartedly coding amid the dissension, but they needed more progress, faster.

This would have all been avoided if she'd just been fully out about her kink life from the start. If she'd always been open, there might have been some people who would have been critical all along, but she wouldn't be in this situation now where her reputation and leadership were in jeopardy because someone revealed what she got up to in her spare time.

Igloo could think of only one thing that might still sway the group's mindset as a whole: Maria. Maria knew about Igloo's relationship history and also knew how Angie felt about it. She could give them a second perspective. There was a good chance that Maria was the mole... Screw it. If she kept everyone who might be a mole close to her, then she could keep an eye on them.

She told the group she'd be back in a minute, then established a new connection to Tapestry and initiated a video call with Maria. It took a few moments to connect, and then Maria appeared on screen.

Maria's face was tight. Anger? Igloo couldn't say.

"Igloo, these news reports are concerning."

"Those videos are lies," Igloo said. "A smear job. And you know it. Someone recorded the consensual BDSM scenes I did with Essie, I don't know how, and they edited those scenes down to make it look like abuse. It's a deliberate campaign to discredit me."

"I know it's a lie," Maria said. "But the campaign is directed at Tapestry as a whole. The media is condemning Tapestry by association with you. What I don't understand is why someone would try to destroy Tapestry this way."

Igloo took a deep breath. "You don't know the bigger picture. I haven't killed T2. Everything I told Amber was to distract her and convince her I'd really abandoned the effort. But Angie was very specific with me that I was to keep working on T2, at all costs. They want to discredit me to stop the T2 effort."

"They? Who is they?"

"The government. There's a secret government agency that is specifically out to stop what we're trying to accomplish with T2."

"Really? You think some black agency is actually out to do that? That sounds kinda paranoid, Ig."

Igloo resisted reacting to that. She decided on a different approach. "Look, I'm fulfilling Angie's mission, as she specifically requested of me to do both before she died, and again afterwards, in her dead man's switch message."

"And yet Amber is the one in control of the company. Legally and ethically, we are bound to follow her leadership. Angie would have put you in charge of the company if she wanted us to follow your leadership."

"Look at me," Igloo said. "Do I look ready to lead a company? Do I look like I *want* to lead a company? Angie put me in exactly the right position to do what needed doing, and she put Amber in charge of the company to do all the other necessary stuff so I wouldn't be distracted by it." As the words came out of Igloo's mouth, she realized they really were true. Angie had always been a few steps ahead of everyone else.

Maria considered Igloo for a moment, then nodded. "What is it that you need?"

Igloo explained, and a few minutes later, Igloo had the T2 team in a video chat with Maria. She considered keeping the T2 members anonymous but decided against it. She needed Maria to be convincing, and that meant allowing Maria to see each person face-to-face.

"So this is Angie's special team," Maria said. "I thought the T2 team was bigger. Angie told me more than twenty people."

"There's been a lot of attrition," Igloo said. "First Angie, now the government. Everyone is scared."

"I bet you are," Maria said, and paused. "Look, I've only been on the periphery of Angie's plans, but I know how important Tapestry 2.0 was to her. I also know Angie and Igloo enjoyed a relationship that went beyond the bounds of what one might guess looking at an organizational chart. They were friends and collaborators in projects that went beyond the ordinary scope of work at the company."

Ben interrupted. "Maria, without meaning any disrespect...I don't know you, and I don't know how Angie involved you in what we're doing, but she never mentioned you in connection with T2. I find it hard to believe that she was confiding in you and yet never mentioned it to us."

Maria raised a hand in acknowledgment. "I'm not. I mean, she told me about it, but I was never deeply involved. That's not what I'm here to talk about. I'm here because of the video that's been released. I'm not sure what you all believe, but Igloo previously disclosed her kink life to both Angie and myself. Angie had, as I'm sure you can imagine, a difficult time accepting what Igloo did, because at first all she could see were the parallels to physical abuse. It was a topic she and I discussed several times, and eventually she came to understand that she was seeing it only through the filter of her past experience and through social norms that stigmatize kinky behavior. Eventually she was able to look past that and grew to accept that part of Igloo's life."

"She knew?" Diana said. "Angie knew specifically what Igloo did? The beatings? The stuff in that video?"

Maria nodded. "I can't say for sure that she knew about every single thing in the video, but she knew about a lot of it: we talked about bondage, we talked about impact play. Angie read some of the existing research studies about BDSM, and she also mined Tapestry data to correlate kinky people with other patterns of abuse, and she was satisfied with the results."

Igloo sensed this was her chance to finish things. "I know some of you would like to continue this discussion forever, but we really need to move quickly. You might not be perfectly happy with my behavior, but can we at least get along enough to agree to accept Forrest's offer of a safe house and finish up T2, so we can get this done?"

"I hate so much about this," Diana said, "but fine. I'll go along."

Everyone else agreed.

"Everyone leave all your electronics, and get to Lloyd Center, using the practices we talked about."

Maria cleared her throat, and Igloo looked back at Maria's video window. "Do you want me to come along?"

Igloo was suspicious. Maria was one of the possible moles. But there was a test.

"There's no reason to," Igloo said, "but thanks for your help. I'll be in touch if we need anything more."

"Okay. Good luck."

Igloo almost ended the connection then. But she thought the whole thing through. She'd asked Maria for help, and then Maria had shown up and helped in exactly the way Igloo had asked. She'd been there for Igloo. And what had she said back at Tapestry headquarters? She'd said she was on Igloo's side. And just now, she didn't protest when Igloo said she didn't want her to come.

"Wait!" Igloo called. "Yes, I want you to come with us."

CHAPTER 46

Butterflies swam in Igloo's stomach as they passed into the shade of the parking garage. So much work spent avoiding the government, and now she was going to walk directly into their hands. Hiding directly under their noses.

She ushered Essie through the door into the mall proper. It was crowded with families with rambunctious kids, teens cruising the walkways, shoppers loaded with bags. Caffeine and panic pulsed through her veins, giving a brittle edge to everything she saw, increasing the surrealism of the experience.

They made their way to the lower level. A door marked "Employees only" at the end of a hallway. A woman in yoga pants and an oversized t-shirt, looking like any of the many other shoppers, opened the door as they approached. She waved them inside.

"Follow me," she said.

"You're not going to scan us first?" Igloo said, taking Essie's hand and pulling her along.

"You were followed since you approached the mall, and you've been under scan the whole time. Nothing broadcasted in the fifteen minutes we've been watching. It doesn't mean there's nothing on you, but if there is, it's not broadcasting. We're taking you inside a safe conduit van. EMF proof."

"And then?"

She glanced back at them. "You'll strip inside, and we'll provide clothes for you."

They descended the stairs and entered a sub-basement utility corridor thick with pipes and electrical conduits.

Forrest waited in the corridor. "You're the last to arrive."

Igloo glanced past Forrest, and saw the rest of her team, haggard and tired, but all together.

Diana and several of the others wouldn't meet her eye. The conflict over the BDSM video wasn't over, apparently.

Maria was there though, and she came over and hugged Igloo. "We have to talk at some point."

"But not right now," Forrest said. She grabbed Igloo's arm, pulled her away from the rest of the crowd. "The videos had the desired effect, I see."

Igloo recapped the morning. "It was someone inside the government, wasn't it?" she asked.

Forrest nodded. "Yeah, but we'll deal with that later. We have to get going." She called back to the rest of the group.

"Follow us."

She led the way down the hallway, staying close to Igloo. "I'm not sure where the video came from, but yeah, the decision to release it came from BRI. I only found out after the fact. I had assumed it was a move to discredit Tapestry, not you personally. But now, it's hard to say which was the real purpose."

They arrived at an interior loading bay where two white cargo vans waited.

"Now we scrub you." Forrest gestured at the first van. "In you go, one at a time."

Igloo stepped in through the back door, which Forrest closed behind her. The compartment was only a few feet deep, then there was a wall with a door in it.

A voice spoke through a speaker. "Remove all clothing, jewelry, and accessories and deposit them in the bag."

Igloo hesitated. "Can't you just give me a full spectrum scan?"

"How's that been working for you so far?" the voice said.

Igloo sighed and pulled clothes off, banging her elbows and head in the tight space. When she was naked, she shoved the last of her clothes into the large metallic plastic bag on the floor.

"The necklace too, please."

Igloo fingered the leather thong on her neck that held one link of Essie's collar. "It's just leather and solid steel."

"We can't take any risks."

"But I made it myself. I know exactly what's in it. There's no risk."

Forrest's voice came on over the PA. "Come on, Igloo. We're on a timetable. Just take off the necklace. We'll help Essie with her collar."

Oh, fuck. They were going to cut Essie's collar.

She untied the leather thong and let it slip into the bag.

The door unlocked in front of her. She stepped into the next compartment, which also had another door in front of her.

"We show that you don't have any medical implants. Can you confirm?"

"That's correct."

The interior light blinked out, there was a short thump, and then the light came back on.

"What was that?" Igloo asked.

"Medium duration EMP. If there was anything inside you, it's fried."

"Couldn't you have done that while I was dressed?"

The next door unlocked. "We're following standard protocol."

Igloo went into the third compartment. There were stacks of clothes waiting, each labeled with initials. She grabbed her pile and dressed in blue jeans and a t-shirt. Ugh. Did the government shop at The Gap? She held up a hoodless jacket. What was the world coming to?

When she was dressed, the last door opened, and an agent escorted her into the second vehicle. There were no windows. Just seats packed close together.

She sat and waited for the others, rubbing the empty space where her leather and link necklace had been.

The others trickled in one by one, subdued. She nodded to them but didn't speak.

When Essie joined her ten minutes later, her neck was bare. She climbed into the seat next to Igloo and cuddled up against her.

Essie leaned close. "I'm sorry," she whispered into Igloo's ear.

"It's just a chain," Igloo said, with a twinge in her heart. How could there be so much meaning in a few stainless steel links? "I will get you a new collar. One of the solid rings you've always wanted."

Essie nuzzled her, and Igloo put an arm around her.

The door closed one last time, and Forrest took a seat at the front of the passenger compartment, near Igloo. She addressed the group as the van pulled out. Igloo felt the van climb a long driveway.

"This is as clean as you get. I'm taking you to a secure facility, and I'll have two of my top techs helping to secure your data trail."

"There's still some record of the place we're going," Igloo said. "We're going to show up on your FBI systems. There's no way you can account for us, the building we're going to, the data we're going to generate."

"It's not an FBI facility. It's something we have access to. And the data trail will be fully secured. You'll be going out over a connection that's not monitored."

"Everything's monitored," Igloo said.

"Not this one. It's one of the last of the hardlines. It goes through a data center in Japan, and it'll be multiplexed there by a tech I have on-site who will personally patch every router and server the traffic passes through. The minimum time it will take until they backtrace is forty-eight hours."

"Where are you taking us?" Diana said.

"It's better you don't know," Forrest said. "There's less to leak."

"Aren't you worried that one of us will say that we're being helped by the government?" Ben asked. "And then you'll get in trouble?"

Forrest smiled. "Have you seen a badge? Do you have proof the government is helping you? Maybe you're just making up a story."

Ben looked at Igloo.

Igloo shrugged. "She has a point."

They had no way of keeping track of time, and Forrest didn't volunteer anything. They were all exhausted from days of too little sleep and non-stop running, and as people fell asleep, Igloo found herself nodding off. She rested her head on Essie.

Igloo woke to a bump and a lurch. The ground was rough under the vehicle's tires. Finally, the ride smoothed out, and they stopped.

Forrest opened the door, and everyone followed her out of the van.

They were inside a concrete structure. Forrest ushered them down a hallway. The place was bare concrete and metal everywhere. Some sort of industrial building, Igloo guessed, but she couldn't surmise more than that.

"Where are we?" she asked.

"No questions about the place," Forrest said. "Just work."

She opened a door and let them into a large room. There were generic PC workstations on a row of gunmetal desks. The near side of the room had coffee, sandwiches, and deli salads laid out on tables. A collapsible partition at the far end partially obscured a row of cots already made up with bedding.

"You do your thing, I'll do mine," Forrest said. She made to leave, but then she looked around at the rest of the team.

Igloo followed her gaze. Everyone looked dead tired, angry, and disillusioned.

Forrest put her hands on her hips and turned to address everyone. "You've all been through a lot. You're exhausted, you're scared, you're divided—angry at Igloo. But there's one thing I've got to tell you. That video you saw of Igloo and Essie was one hundred percent a manipulation job, targeted at the eight of you engineers. Nobody else in the world gives a damn about Igloo's credibility except you all. Some faction within the government edited that video, released it, and orchestrated mass media coverage, all for the sole purpose of sowing dissent. If you let them succeed, they win. I don't know Igloo or Essie, but what two consenting adults choose to do on their own is their business. Stay focused on the goal: Get your software out there in the world. Fulfill Angie's vision."

She turned and left.

Everyone looked at Igloo.

"Fine, I give up," Diana said. "Where do we start, boss?"

CHAPTER 47

The C40 engines droned in the background as Enso continued his teleconference, which had unfortunately expanded to include an Air Force general, a side-effect of commandeering the plane that was now bringing him and other key BRI members to Portland.

The Deputy Director of the NSA was shaking his head. "Enso, I'm going to have to bring the Director in for this."

Out of view of the camera, Enso repeatedly crushed a gel-filled stress-ball in one hand. "No. She needs plausible deniability. BRI has always been tied to the office of the Deputy Director for just this reason."

"It's not about BRI," the deputy director said. "It's about the national security implications of allowing a group of radicals to irreversibly encrypt and obfuscate the entire internet. Overnight, it would set our surveillance and intelligence capabilities back thirty years. Hell, the director is almost certainly going to bring in SecDef. Maybe even the president."

"Don't be a fool," Enso said. "BRI exists to take care of these problems. If you escalate, then you limit the full range of operational alternatives. Might as well just make it a standard intel op, then."

"Maybe we should, Enso." This was from the Air Force general who was BRI's liaison into that agency. "This exceeds BRI's charter. We're not talking about swaying one or two key individuals. This is the sabotage of one of the most influential tech companies in the world."

"It's not clear that BRI is equipped to handle this very well," said the Assistant Director of the FBI Cyber division. "You botched both the initial operation against Angie and the follow-up."

"We did not execute Angie." Enso jammed his finger down on the table. "I don't care what the local police are reporting. The cyber forensics they turned up are either due to another party or she killed herself and framed us."

Doubting expressions filled all of the video chat windows. Even Enso had to admit it didn't look good for his team. The forensics indicating someone pushed a firmware change to the battery charger bore the digital fingerprints of cybernetic infiltration tools created by the NSA that had leaked just three months ago. BRI could and had assassinated key targets on rare occasions. Contrary to popular media depictions, the concept was anathema to the other agencies.

"Look, if we haven't been successful so far, it's because we don't have the proper resources."

"Enso, you've got everything you asked for." SigInt Director Feldson practically growled at him. "You've got the FBI, the NSA, and the Air Force involved, in addition to the BRI team. I've got forty FBI agents in Portland, plus the entire Portland contingent. You have an operative on the inside. Despite all of this, you've lost the T2 team again, for the second time in two days."

"Sir, they have completely disappeared off the radar, and Robin has not made contact in two days." Enso treated Griz with respect, if not outright wariness. Technically he might not be the ranking official here, but his pull far outweighed his official position. "That's with your Signals Intelligence team tracking them. This isn't about BRI's competency. They have top-notch counter-intel capability, as I have been reporting for months."

"Then let's turn this operation over to the mainstream FBI and NSA and let them have free rein with it."

"Which plays directly into Tapestry's hands. Then we have no legal recourse to stop them."

"For fuck's sake," the deputy director said, "then what would you have us do? According to your last report, they'll be ready to release within days."

"Give me carte blanche for forty-eight hours. Let's mobilize every signals intelligence asset we can spare. Make this the top priority at the NSA to identify them. Local air coverage. Ramp up transit coverage to active terrorist threat level. We make it impossible for them to communicate or move without hitting one of our tripwires. Give me more FBI SWAT teams, so that when we do get a blip on the radar, we're ready to take advantage of it. Keep everything under BRI so I have direct control."

"There's no way I can do that without letting the director know." This was the NSA deputy director.

"Call it a training exercise. Hell, call all of it a coordinated multiagency training exercise."

"Easy for you to ask for," Griz said. "Not so easy for the rest of us when we're testifying to Congress."

"This is what you're called on to do. It's the quid pro quo of BRI. You want us available to do what you can't, then you've got to shield us."

Everyone else looked to Griz to make the decision.

Griz, uncharacteristically, looked down at the table in front of him. He tapped his finger a few times, like he was mulling something over. Then he looked up decisively.

"Forty-eight hours, Enso," Griz said. "You have this wrapped up by then, and cleanly. Not like the last few operations. If you don't, we take this to the director and to SecDef and let them handle it how they will, and I'll personally recommend you be replaced as head of BRI."

Everyone else nodded their assent, and then Feldson dropped off.

CHAPTER 48

I gloo led everyone through the process of reiterating what was most essential for the release, scrawling a working backlog on a whiteboard near the desks. They'd cross stuff off the whiteboard as they worked. A few folks prepared to pair up, but most would solo program.

"Before we split," Igloo said, "I've got one more thing. We need to take the time to bundle everything for a release this afternoon."

"We won't be done," Ben said, pointing at the list.

"We'll have the highest priority stuff," Igloo said. "We need to be ready, in case anything happens. If we have to run again."

"That's not good enough, not if we all get snatched unexpectedly," Mike said. "We should bundle up the release and have a dead man's switch that goes off unless we reset it every two hours."

Igloo nodded slowly. "Yes. As long as we're free and still coding, we keep holding back that release. But if anything happens to us, the current release will be ready to go."

Igloo stared at the list as the others broke away. There were still two important items not on the list. First, she had to decide what to do with Angie's backdoor that had allowed her to manipulate everyone's content en masse. Second, she needed to decide how to handle the encryption keys that they'd need to ensure the government didn't pass off a compromised version of Tapestry as a legitimate one.

"What should I do?" Essie asked.

Igloo tore herself away from looking at the list. What exactly could Essie do? She had no coding skills. She'd been topping off everyone's coffee so far, but that wasn't enough to keep her busy. But she was a blogger and a writer. That could help.

"T2 needs a manifesto," Igloo said. "You've heard me talk about privacy, data ownership, and abuses of the government. You know why we're doing this. Can you draft a principles document that we publish at the same time we release T2? Interview folks. But don't distract them. Just get a sentence or two from each person. Work with Maria. Mine my old blog posts if that helps. Maybe look at Angie's old public statements. Can you do that?"

Essie nodded quickly. "Sure. That's going to be useful?"

"Very. Thank you."

"And me?" Maria said.

"No technical skills, right?"

"Correct."

"Be a runner between everyone," Igloo said, feeling weird giving direction to someone she viewed as her superior. "Keep checking in if anyone has any roadblocks and figure out how to solve them. And maintain the backlog, as well as helping Essie with the manifesto. Can you do all that?"

Maria nodded. "We also need to talk about what happened to Angie."

Igloo looked up sharply. Why would she bring this up now? Did she know that Igloo suspected? Still, she didn't have the time. It would have to wait. "Not right now," Igloo said. "This is all critical path."

Igloo went back to staring at the board while she thought. Two things that she alone had to make the call on: Angie's backdoor and encryption keys.

Well, there was one that was a relatively easy decision. She'd been opposed from the start to Angie's idea of manipulating everyone. There was no way in hell that she was going to allow that backdoor to remain. Yes, she was fine with helping individuals out. She was fine with using the chat personalities to promote healthy ways of thinking. But she had to draw the line somewhere, and that somewhere was unilateral control over people's feeds.

She remembered where Angie's bit of trickery was implemented, and it took only a dozen lines of code to remove Angie's contribution. She felt an immediate sense of relief, and for a moment, she realized that it was quite fine to be making decisions herself. She and Angie would have argued over that for weeks or months, and she might never have swayed Angie to her point of view. Now it was Igloo's call. That was actually nice.

Now she had to decide how to handle the encryption keys that would be used to package Tapestry releases, and which the self-updating client would check before accepting new updates. Neither she nor any other single person could be entrusted with them, because if they fell into the wrong hands, that person could change Tapestry to do whatever they wanted.

The team had a technical solution to splitting up encryption keys, but they hadn't resolved who would get those keys, and how the final decision making authority would occur. In the future, every code change would have to be audited to ensure that no manipulation of Tapestry, and especially no secret government intrusions, were snuck into the code.

She still had no good solution, so she set the problem aside, and cranked through the rest of her coding list, waiting for a meal break to discuss the encryption keys. The next few hours were a whir of activity with frequent interruptions from the rest of the team.

At some point, Essie shared a rough outline of the manifesto. Igloo highlighted where she should go deeper, and which points could be eliminated. Then she got back to coding.

Many hours later, the smell of Italian food seized her attention and her stomach growled. Someone had brought in trays of chicken cutlets and meatballs and pasta. It was a step up from pizza, the usual for all-night coding marathons.

Everyone looked up at each other, and then raced for the table. They barely talked at all until everyone had loaded up.

Ben, the first to fill his plate, headed back to his workstation.

"Don't go," Igloo said. "Let's all eat together. We have a mutual decision to make."

Ben reluctantly returned. "I need to code."

"We all do, but this is important," Igloo said.

Everyone gathered at the one long, empty table.

Igloo shoved a meatball into her mouth, and then spoke as she nibbled on garlic bread.

"You all know the problem: We need to distribute the encryption keys in such a way that no one person or no few people can release updates to Tapestry."

"One per person," Mike said, looking around at the group. "Nine keys."

"We can't require all the keys to do an update," Diana said. "If someone loses theirs, dies, or gets arrested, then we could never update Tapestry again. We need to be able to sign an update with three or four keys."

"That's too few," Ben said. "What if they torture us to get the keys? They'd only need a few people to give up their keys, and then they've compromised it forever."

"Torture?" Carly said. "Jesus. I'm still hoping for some semblance of normalcy after this. I'm not signing up to have a big X on my back for the rest of my life. No way am I going to be a key holder."

"It's like we're deciding what to do with the pieces of Voldemort's soul."

Everyone turned to look at Essie.

"Well, it is," Essie said. "I mean, part of why it took Harry and his group so long is that they didn't even know what horcrux was. If you give the keys to yourselves, then of course you've painted targets on your own backs. But if you give the keys to other people, then the problem gets much harder for the government."

"For this to work," Mike said, and he pointed around the table, "*we all* can't know who those key holders are. Otherwise we're just adding a single layer of obfuscation. The government will torture us to get to the key holders."

"Even if we work that out," Ben said. "Who can we really trust to do what needs doing? We're not asking for something trivial here. We're talking about people who can inspect code commits to make sure the system isn't compromised."

Maria cleared her throat. "You need people who are ethical, responsible, and committed to resisting the government. Who are in this for the long run."

There was a long silence at the table.

Igloo stood so quickly she unsettled her plate and nearly knocked over a glass.

"We're forgetting what Tapestry is," Igloo said as she paced back and forth. "First and foremost, it's a social network. It's not us. It's not a small team working in secret. It's a network of hundreds of millions of users. The people we need are out there. They're currently users. We just need to find them."

"How?" Ben asked.

"We mine the database. We look for the people who are ethical and responsible. Who are talented coders. We recruit them. The same way that any big distributed system polices itself. Through volunteers in the community."

"We can have hundreds or thousands of key holders," Carly said.

Ben nodded. "We can require multiple reviewers to scrutinize each code change."

"And have a majority of the key holders sign off on the update as a whole," Igloo said. "We're talking about a long-term governance model for Tapestry. The last three years, we had a benevolent dictator in the form of Angie. We don't have that any more. This is important stuff that goes way beyond just keys."

There were nods around the table.

"We need to make sure the feds can't hack the system," Ben said. "They'll try to sign up millions of sock puppet accounts so that they can vote for leaders and key holders, and then suddenly they've compromised Tapestry the way they compromised TOR. We can't allow that."

"We'll need counter-measures to protect against that," Mike said.

"This is too complicated," Diana said. "We fucking need to release today. You guys have just designed...well, frak. Not even a whole new feature. A whole new class of functionality. You want to replicate everything git does, and then some. It's community voting, plus code review, plus key management, plus security features, plus user profiling. We'd need a month to build that."

There were several nods around the table.

"I don't see that we have a choice," Igloo said. "This is what needs doing. It's what is right to do. We're not going to write it from scratch, and it doesn't have to be perfect for the first release. It just needs to be good enough that none of us are targeted by the government. There are libraries for every one of those things you've mentioned, Diana. We need to glue it together just well enough to resist the feds for a few days or weeks, until we can improve it."

Maria gestured at the wall clock. "People, it's the middle of the night. I don't know about you, but I haven't had much sleep since Friday. I think you'd all be more functional if you got some sleep. In fact, we should all sleep together, so we can stay on the same cycle."

Igloo bristled at Maria muscling in on her team. "You turning into the mother hen?" she said.

"Hey, I can't code. But I can at least try to keep you all productive. Look, I'm not saying sleep for ten hours and have a leisurely breakfast. But look at yourselves. You look like the walking dead. How many hours of sleep have you slept in the last three days? Just get six hours of sleep at least."

Igloo looked around at everyone. She glanced over at the whiteboard with the list of to-do items. They were less than halfway through. But what Maria said was true. She'd slept maybe three or four hours in as many days. And that had come on top of a week of surviving on four hours of sleep a night. There was no way they could cross everything off that list before they slept again.

"Let's do it, people. We sleep, then get cracking in the morning." She turned to stare at Maria. "I want to talk to you."

The rest of the team made their way toward the cots behind the fabric wall.

Igloo directed Maria to the opposite corner, and they sat, almost touching, in the dark.

"You need sleep, too," Maria said.

Igloo nodded, too tired to disagree. "In a few minutes." She thought about Angie, how sometimes Angie would wrestle the truth from her with a few words, and only afterwards would she realize that Angie had been fishing. Always in those cases, Angie would simply speak the truth, and it would be impossible for Igloo to not respond to it.

"I know," Igloo said. "I know about you."

Maria blinked. "Know what?" Her voice was perfectly casual.

"I know you work for BRI. I know you're an inside plant. I know you've been reporting on what we've been doing."

"That's absurd," Maria said. "I don't know what you're talking about."

"I also know that you've listened when I've talked. Those moments we had together, over coffee, they meant something to you. You care about what we're doing. Even now, you're trying to decide what to do, whether to help us or to turn us in."

"You're talking nonsense. I think the lack of sleep—"

"You can't decide, because either path requires betraying your values. If you turn us in, you betray what you know is the righteous and just path. You know that BRI is a monster that will do anything to achieve its goals and maintain its own dominance, whether that's framing the innocent, destroying an innovative company, or crushing a relationship between two people. But if you don't turn us in, you're betraying your loyalty to the government, to the duties you swore you would uphold."

Maria was silent, and her eyes dropped to her lap. Igloo allowed herself a brief moment of celebratory awe. She'd been right!

"Everything hangs in the balance at this moment. Maybe we all go to jail, T2 never happens, and Angie's vision dies quietly in the night. Or maybe we get T2 out, fulfill Angie's vision, and expose the corruption inside BRI so that they can't ruin anyone else's life."

Maria was trembling now.

"Secrets are inherently safer while they remain secret, but they are corrosive and toxic. That's what protecting BRI represents. Openness is scary and unpredictable, but healthy. That's what coming forward represents. I can't promise what will happen. But we can really use your help."

Maria took a deep breath. "What can I do?"

When they woke in the morning, Forrest's people were there with more food.

After they ate, Igloo decided to change direction, leaving the more mundane work to other people. She and Ben focused on the community-review aspect of future Tapestry updates.

Even while she was programming with Ben, part of her was preoccupied with Angie's backdoor into Tape, the Tapestry communication layer. She'd removed the backdoor. When this was all done, she'd never been anything more than just another Tapestry user. She had lost the means to alter people's feeds and fulfill Angie's goal of ensuring a liberal agenda won the next election.

Now they'd have a community of people auditing code changes. It was one thing to have a preexisting backdoor woven into the fabric of Tapestry. It would be vastly more difficult, if not impossible, to sneak a new backdoor into a codebase that would be heavily scrutinized in the future.

"Ready to swap soon?" Ben asked.

They were parallel ping-ponging, a bastardization of the normal pair programming process. She and Ben were alternating writing tests and implementation code. For thirty minutes, they each wrote high level tests. Then the other person would write the code to implement the functionality. When they were both done, they'd go back to write more tests. It was more side-by-side programming than pair programming, but it had some of the same benefits of getting two minds on one problem. Just without the oversight of two people examining each line of code. They didn't have the time for that.

"Almost there," Igloo said.

"I'm going to take a bio-break while you finish up," Ben said.

When Igloo stood to stretch her legs a few minutes later, she was surprised to see Forrest right behind her desk.

"I didn't want to interrupt," Forrest said, "but I need to talk to you."

"What's up?"

"The FBI is moving more assets into the Portland area. The National Guard has been mobilized for a training exercise."

"So?" Igloo asked. "We're safe here, aren't we?"

Forrest shrugged. "Take a walk with me."

They left the room and entered the hallway. There was about a hundred feet to the end of the hall, which terminated with double steel doors that looked fit for a bank vault. They paced the length of the hallway.

"There's no scenario," Forrest said, "in which putting FBI agents and the National Guard on the ground in Portland is going to turn up a bunch of software programmers who have gone into hiding. Correct?"

"Yeah, obviously."

"So why would they deploy all those extra resources?"

Now it was Igloo's turn to shrug.

"Because they have a plan to figure out where you are. On a hunch, I submitted a routine but manual data request through my intelligence contacts. They told me they'd get back to me tomorrow at the earliest. Their normal turnaround time for something like that is less than an hour." Forrest paused at the end of the hallway and stared at Igloo for a moment before heading back. "My guess is that right now the NSA's main computer center has been retasked, and everyone is focused on finding you."

"That's absurd." Igloo threw up her hands. "We're eight programmers releasing a software update. I can understand BRI tracking us, but the whole NSA? That's like deploying a nuclear bomb to deal with a couple of bank robbers. There's no way we merit that sort of attention."

"Enso, the BRI head, is calling in all his chits. You represent too big a threat."

"I get that T2 is a big deal, but isn't this just a little crazy?"

Forrest shook her head. "The forensic evidence the police uncovered from Angie's car made it look like the government tampered with her battery charger."

Igloo couldn't believe that. The note Angie left her pointed to Angie killing herself. Would the government...no, wait...it was Angie framing them. One last "fuck you" to the man in charge.

Forrest studied Igloo's face. No words were necessary. "Yeah, you got it. See, I'm not sure how wise Angie's move was. She made Enso angry, and angry people don't think reasonably. But angry people also resort to desperate measures."

"Fine, so finding us is now job number one for the NSA. So what? I thought you had us isolated here?"

"Isolated? No. You're still using the Internet, aren't you? Well-obfuscated, for sure. They're going to have to crack Japan's largest data center and track all the traffic in and out. But it's just a matter of time. You need to have your release ready to go."

"We're getting close."

"How close? Can you push something out now?"

"If we really, really have to, we can release at any time. But ideally we need at least another six, eight hours, maybe more."

Forrest let out a long sigh. "What's holding things up?"

"We need to decide on a more secure approach to managing the encryption keys needed for updates. The old plan would have made us all the weak links in the chain."

"Can you put something out now and then update it later? Just in case they narrow it down to our location?"

"Not really," Igloo said. She was too tired to reiterate all the reasons why. "You think it's that dire?"

"Maybe."

"If we release now, before this last bit is ready, I'm afraid they'll compromise it, and we won't be able to regain control."

Forrest stood in deep contemplation.

Igloo waited for a few moments. "Well? Forrest?"

"As you were," Forrest said, coming out of her fugue.

"Huh?" Igloo said.

"Forget the request I made. Work on your secure key management. I have another plan. It'll require moving you in two hours, but you won't lose productivity. Just keep working."

"Okay," Igloo said, wondering what was going on.

"Great." Forrest put one hand on Igloo's shoulder. "We're all counting on you." She turned and marched off, leaving Igloo alone in the corridor.

Igloo headed back into the workroom. What was that all about? She wished Angie was there to clue her in.

CHAPTER 49

The plane touched down, and Enso was on his feet while the plane was still taxiing. He glanced back at the thirty-odd other personnel he'd brought from various agencies. Half were tech types in ill-fitting suits who looked unsettled at being extracted from their usual sequestered offices.

He walked down a set of mobile stairs. There was a long line of National Guard Hummers. "Where's my FBI liaison?" he asked the first man on the ground.

"Tied up, sir. He asked us to help out. We'll get you and your people wherever you need."

Enso suppressed his annoyance. He'd wanted to be briefed by the FBI lead here. No matter. The Air National Guard might come in handy, and he hadn't got where he was by needlessly antagonizing people.

"I really appreciate the help. You set a great example for interagency cooperation. Please thank your people for me."

The man warmed up instantly.

"Chapple said you'd want me to bring everyone to the field office. Is that still the plan?"

"Yes, for now," Enso said. "Although it'd help if you could keep your men on active duty. I'd like to call on you again today."

"Of course. Can I ask about the nature of the operation? It'd help me understand how to prepare."

"Major Chinese cyber terrorism operation, right here in Portland. Unfortunately, it's been leaked, so I suspect it'll be all over the news momentarily."

The National Guard commander took a double-glance at Enso. "On the ground here? Not operating out of China?"

"Yes. Turns out Tapestry is a Chinese front. We're here to shut them down."

CHAPTER 50

Forrest leaned against the wall in the empty hallway, out of sight of her team, out of sight of Igloo. Her few team members were in the garage area, Igloo and her people in the interior rooms. Here, in between, she was alone for a few minutes. She turned to face the wall, rested her forehead against the cool concrete. She couldn't stop the nervous sweating.

She was going to do it. She would help Igloo and defy Nathan9. She couldn't even say exactly why she was doing it. It wasn't because it was morally the right thing to do. If that was all it took, she would have done it long ago. It was mostly because she sorely wanted to be her own person one last time, despite what it might mean for her career, her life.

But to see this through, she'd have to kill herself. Her stomach recoiled and she suppressed the urge to vomit.

Nathan's ultimate leverage against her was hurting the people she cared about. That was the final resort, the tool that ensured her compliance. He'd made it clear that if she betrayed him, it wasn't just her career and her freedom that she would be sacrificing.

But if she killed herself, there'd be no point to Nathan's retribution. She had to hope so, anyway.

Her palms were damp with nervous sweat. She pulled out a handkerchief and dried off her hands. She made her way back to the van, her mobile office.

She kept the fact hidden from the Tapestry folks, but only a select few agents on her team were part of this operation to hide the T2 team. The majority were in the field in Portland, and she'd brought only her most loyal operatives with her.

Doug, her number two, was in the van. Even as close as he was, Doug couldn't stay for this next conversation.

"Doug, I need the van for a few minutes."

"You got it." He closed out a few windows.

"We still looking secure?"

"For now," he said. "But with a major op going down, who knows?"

"Listen, you still have that buddy with the Coast Guard?"

"Sure."

"They have some kind of surveillance craft, don't they?"

"Yeah, I think so. Ocean Sentry something or another."

"Get them to loan us one. I want you to get these civilians on the plane, and make it look like they're our analysts. Let them fly a search pattern. Coordinate with BRI's other assets as part of the training program."

"Jesus," Doug said. "You sure that's a good idea? It's one thing to take the hottest merchandise in America and hide them in an empty building, and another thing entirely to insert them into the midst of an active operation."

"It's the last place anyone's going to look for them, right? With a long-range directional tracking antenna, you should be able make it appear that they're connecting from one place, and then *bam!* you shut down and redirect the antenna, and then you're connecting from someplace else that's sixty miles away."

"That trick will work for a couple of hours, max. Sooner or later the NSA will figure out they're on a plane, correlate that plane with their location, and figure out exactly where they are. And probably shoot them down."

"They'll release the software before then. Once the software is out, there's no reason to shoot you down."

"Me? Who said anything about me getting on the plane?"

"I need you to go with them, Doug. I need to stay in contact with everyone. If I go missing, that's suspicious. If you're missing, well..."

"Yeah, I get it. I'm not important."

"You're very important. You're just not as visible."

"You sure this is a good idea?"

Forrest barked out a laugh. "A good idea? Hell, no. It's a terrible idea. But it's the only option we have left. Now get out of here for a minute. I have to make a call."

Doug left, and the door shut behind him. It was dead silent in the van. Forrest composed herself, then opened up a text chat connection to Nathan.

"You're an hour late."

"I'm trying to keep things secure here."

"How long until they release?"

"Another few hours."

"I thought they were shooting for an afternoon release. They should have packaged that up, along with the encryption keys."

"I know. They ran into a few delays."

There was a long pause. Forrest wondered what Nathan could possibly be researching in the background. If he could, he'd certainly be fact checking what she said. But in this case, she thought he wouldn't have any data. They'd prepped this building well.

"Any change in their key management strategy?"

"They haven't mentioned it."

CHAPTER 51

I gloo and the others were forced to pack in a few minutes, despite their protests. They crammed laptops and mobile devices—all previously sanitized—into EMF-proof pouches and carried them with them. Forrest guided them back to the van again.

"It's only thirty minutes' downtime," Forrest said. "Then you can get back online. Doug will be with you, and he'll take care of you."

Igloo's stomach roiled. "I like the underground bunker thing more than being in an airplane."

"I know, but staying isn't an option. You can see why."

"I know. I know. But being up there? In a plane? They'll shoot us down in a second."

"They'll spend longer than that before they'd shoot down a military plane."

Doug whispered into Forrest's ear.

Igloo overhead something about Tapestry.

"What's going on?" Igloo asked. The crushing weight of responsibility made her fearful of anything that might be out of her control. She wished Angie were here to take charge. Of course, Angie would have everything in her control. She'd be the one pulling strings, instead of relying on almost-strangers for everything.

"Get in the van, first. Then I'll brief you."

Igloo sighed and climbed in. Forrest and Doug climbed in next, taking the two seats beside Igloo.

The rest of the team followed. Igloo grabbed Essie's hand as she passed. She pulled Essie down into the seat next to her, making an already cramped situation even worse. But she was going to keep Essie close.

The van pulled out. Once again, Igloo had no idea where they were or were going, surrounded as she was by solid walls.

"This update of yours," Forrest asked, once the van was underway. "It goes out to the existing Tapestry clients, right? They look for updates and grab yours because it's signed with the right keys. You don't need Tapestry servers do you?"

"Umm, yeah, of course we need those servers. The current clients make an API call to find out if there's an update and where to get it. In the future, we'll scan IPFS automatically for signed updates, but the current version needs access to those servers. Why?"

"The government shut down Tapestry a few minutes ago," Doug said. "Press release says the company is a front for Chinese cyber terrorists. A federal judge issued a disconnect order to all ISPs."

"That's absurd!" Igloo said. "How can they get away with that?"

Forrest shrugged. "Enso must have fabricated enough corroborating data to convince a judge. Can you release without access to Tapestry?"

Igloo tried to think through the answer, but her brain responded sluggishly, like she was wading through mud. The details of the community-based approval mechanism they were building overwhelmed her, and she couldn't cram any more thoughts in her head.

Ben leaned forward from the row behind them.

"The client makes an API call to check for the current version, right?"

Igloo nodded.

"IP address or domain name?" Ben asked. "'Cause if it's the domain name, then we could subvert DNS lookup and map it to our own server."

Igloo shook her head. "I'm pretty sure it's going to be the IP address exactly because of that attack vector. Angie had tools to go after the BGP that would let us subvert IP routing. I don't know if they're up to date. She was always resistant to using them. Wanted to save them for an emergency."

"BGP?" Forrest asked.

"Border Gateway Protocol," Igloo said. "It's how the different internet and backbone providers route traffic between each other to get to a given IP address."

"That won't be enough," Carly called from two rows back.

Igloo twisted around to see Carly had her laptop open.

"The updater source code checks the server certificate. It's not going to trust just any machine responding to the update check call. We'd need the private key certificates."

"Do we have those?" Igloo asked.

"No," Mike said. "It's not part of the source code, for obvious reasons. It would be in the cloud key vault and deployed to the server during provisioning."

"What parts of Tapestry have been shut down?" Diana asked. "Can we still reach the key vault?"

"We don't know, because we have no Internet connection in here," Carly yelled.

"Just ten more minutes until we reach the airfield," Forrest said. "You can check then."

"If we can't reach the key vault, we could reach one of the update servers," Mike said. "Assuming we can reach a server. Don't you have any idea what the government shut down?"

Doug sighed, but pulled out a tablet and scanned it. "No technical details. Just reports that Tapestry is down. Tons of rumors and discussion about the Chinese front angle."

"How are you getting that feed?" Igloo asked. "What about no internet connection?"

"It's broadcast only," Forrest said. "A satellite subscription to a chat channel. Read only. Doesn't give our location away."

"Clever."

"The government gets a few neat tricks in exchange for your trillions of tax dollars in support."

Igloo suppressed a grumble. She should have become one of those conscientious tax objectors.

The van slowed.

"Shut down that laptop," Forrest ordered. "No connections. Everything back in your shielded bags."

Carly and a few others put their laptops away. Only after everything was safely stowed did Forrest knock on the door.

The door opened from the outside, accompanied by the immediate smell of ocean air. A Coast Guard prop plane stood a few dozen feet away.

"That's what we're going on?" Igloo said. "I imagined some sort of jet. You know, something fast. In case we need to get away."

"Nothing is going to outrun an air-to-air missile, so forget about that," Forrest said. "This will keep your signal moving, and that's what matters."

"Let's load up, people," Doug said. He started to usher people onto the plane.

"Wait up," Ben said, grabbing Igloo and Forrest at the same time. "If we can't access the cloud key vault, or any of the update servers, there's still one other option: we have the master key signing certificates stored offline in a safe at Tapestry headquarters. We can regenerate the private keys we need for the update."

"We need to get you on that plane," Forrest said.

"But once we're all on the plane, it's not like we can just get off, can we? We're stuck up there."

Forrest nodded.

"Let me go back to Portland, get into the offices and get the keys."

"That's stupid," Forrest said. "You're going to get picked up."

"Not if you take me," Ben said. "You could get me inside. Dress me up like one of you."

"You'd still need access to the physical safe," Igloo said. "It requires biometrics from two officers of the company—"

"Exactly. Pointless." Forrest shook her head. "It's a stupid idea."

"Except that I have a passcode that will get you in," Igloo finished.

"See?" Ben smiled at Forrest.

"But I should go," Igloo said. "It's my risk to take."

"Now you're being stupid. They need you to lead them," Ben said, pointing at the plane. "T2 needs your vision. I'm expendable."

"Can you get him inside?" Igloo asked Forrest.

Forrest ran her fingers through her hair. "Yes, I can."

"Do it then." Igloo gave Ben a hard hug. "Thank you."

"Go. Hurry." Forrest pushed Igloo toward the plane.

Doug waited in the doorway. Igloo climbed the stairs and turned back to see Ben and Forrest getting back into the van.

Doug pulled her over the threshold and slammed the door shut. A uniformed guardsman secured the locking mechanism, and the engines spun up.

"Show us how to operate the directional antenna," Doug said to the guardsman. "Then please clear out of the cabin. This operation is need-to-know only.

"Yes, sir." The guardsman indicated the relevant workstation.

"Carly, can you work with them?" Igloo asked.

Carly joined Doug and the guardsman. A few seconds later, the plane accelerated down the runway.

Igloo wished Angie were there. She would have loved this. She reached over, squeezed Essie's hand. Essie squeezed back, and they sat holding hands. She let herself have a moment to think about Angie, then pushed her memories aside. She needed to focus.

A few minutes later, the guardsman disappeared through a crew door.

"Okay, folks," Carly called. "I'm locking on our first connection. It's a microwave tower, and it'll be good for twenty minutes or so."

"Finally," Mike said, his computer ready to go in his lap.

Igloo pulled out her own computer, set it on the counter that ran down the length of the plane.

"Tapestry's down," Mike called. "Checking backup providers…. Also down. All data centers."

"So much for multi-region fault tolerance," Diana said.

"What's this mean?" Doug said.

"It means it's a good thing Ben didn't get on this plane," Igloo said. "But now we need to wait until he drives to Portland, reaches the offices, accesses the safe, and transmits the keys to us."

Igloo couldn't resist checking the headlines. News of the Tapestry downtime and rumors about the company were everywhere. Tomo usage had spiked in the wake of the world-wide outage. Fuck. Three years of work evaporated overnight due to a handful of people in the government unilaterally deciding to end Tapestry.

"Two hours, folks." Igloo had to yell over the noise of the plane. "Then we bundle a release to get it ready. We do everything we can, and as soon as we get the keys from Ben, we sign and push it."

"Essie!" Igloo yelled.

"Yes?" Essie was right behind Igloo, and she jumped.

Essie was holding a paper cup of coffee balanced on the palm of her hand, while holding herself steady against the movement of the plane.

"Where'd you… never mind. I'll take it." Igloo grabbed the cup. "How's the manifesto coming?"

"It's done. Everyone has reviewed it. I took some liberties, given the recent developments. Want to see it?"

Igloo nodded.

Essie retrieved a laptop and slid it in front of Igloo.

Two hundred and fifty years ago, the United States justified its proclamation of independence with these words: "We hold these truths to be self-evident, that all men are created equal, that they are endowed by their Creator with certain unalienable Rights, that among these are Life, Liberty and the pursuit of Happiness".

In today's age, we cannot have life, liberty and the pursuit of happiness without certain foundational communication rights, including the right to privacy, to own and control our own personal data, to read and to publish unbiased sources of information, to free and unfettered communication and association with anyone we choose.

The document went on for another page. Igloo read the entirety, her amazement growing. At the end, she stopped, and went back to the beginning and read it all over again.

"Oh. This is totally unlike anything Angie or I would have written," Igloo said. She saw Essie's face drop. "I mean, it's wonderful. Way better than anything we would have written. This is worthy of being read by millions of people."

Essie wriggled in delight.

CHAPTER 52

E nso was in the FBI's mobile command center, two blocks from Tapestry headquarters. He looked at the cup of coffee, and decided against it. His stomach was in knots.

He hadn't heard from Robin in over thirty-six hours now. What the hell had happened to her? Had she been discovered? If they were dealing with terrorists, he might wonder if she'd been killed or kidnapped, but these people were software developers. Angie wouldn't have hesitated, but she wasn't here, and he didn't think Igloo had it in her.

Damn that girl. Even he was referring to her by nickname now.

Forrest entered the command headquarters. She looked haggard.

"Where have you been?" Enso said.

"Nice to see you, too," Forrest said. She took a chair without invitation and slumped into it.

"No, seriously. Where the fuck have you been?" Enso pointed outside. "You were the ranking FBI officer. You should have been the lead on taking over the offices."

"First off," Forrest said, "you don't get to tell me how to do my job. Yes, you're running this operation. Yes, you set the direction. But I know how to do my job. Second, you've got media up and down this street. I run undercover ops on a regular basis. You don't put me out in front of the cameras. And third, you took over a fucking IT company's headquarters. What are you afraid of, office workers with nerf guns? You could have sent in any two agents with one handgun between them and they would have secured the building."

"We needed a coordinated takedown so members of the T2 team wouldn't be able to access Tapestry resources, share data, or notify other members of the team."

Forrest shook her head in dismissal. "Really?"

Enso threw his hands up. "What's so complicated to understand?"

"We've had the building under constant surveillance for four days. We've chased the T2 members all around this city. None of them are in their headquarters." Forrest nodded toward one of the aides. "Some coffee would be great, when you've got a moment, please."

"If you're so smart, Miss Deputy Assistant Director, then where the fuck is the T2 team? How could you have all these resources out here, and not be able to pick them up?"

"They're a slippery bunch. You ever consider that maybe they turned your mole? Because I don't know how they're doing what they're doing."

"That's preposterous." Enso was suddenly uneasy. Maybe that was why he hadn't heard from Robin. The thought never occurred to him that she might actively betrayed him.

"Look, give me the current rundown, and let's decide what to do next."

Enso grated at taking orders from Forrest, but it was the logical thing to do.

"Headquarters is secured," Enso said. "Only a handful of employees were inside, and we've removed them. We've isolated their headquarters from the net. We shut down all their data center assets from six different locations around the world."

"And the NSA search?"

"The data analysts are still brute force searching. The T2 team connects to the network only intermittently, but each time they do, their location has changed. All in this general region, which the data geeks say means that T2 has found a way to hijack connections into the backbone. The analysts think that T2 is sitting somewhere on one of the regional backbones, inserting their own traffic and masking it so that it looks like it is coming from one of these other locations."

"Clever," Forrest said.

Enso nodded dismissively. "Our air search team is flying a coordinated pattern searching for T2 along the routes of known backbones."

"What are they searching for?"

"Radio emissions, mostly. They're at the level where they can detect individual computers running, even without wi-fi, just from spurious electromagnetic emissions. We're also feeding all surveillance camera data into Utah, scanning realtime for facial recognition."

"Can't keep it up forever."

"No, but they'll be forced to move soon. The counter-terrorism analysts say that without the update servers and update server credentials, T2 can't be released. Igloo and the team are going to get desperate, and when they do, they'll make a mistake. All we have to do is be ready."

"In the meantime, Tapestry is down. How long are you going to be able to keep it that way? They've got to have lawyers fighting you tooth and nail."

Enso wished she wouldn't have gone there. The pressure from back home was intense, which was more than half the reason he was out here. If he'd been in Washington, he'd be getting chewed out by multi-star generals and legal counsel on an hourly basis.

"We'll keep it in place as long as we need it," he growled, without meaning to. He tried to relax his jaw.

"I'm going to take a team and scout around the headquarters

while we have free rein. I want to see if there's anything that will clue us in as to where they went. Especially Igloo's office."

"Go ahead. The initial team didn't find anything."

"The initial team wasn't me," Forrest said. "I'll find something we can use."

She probably would at that. Enso didn't like her, but everyone said she was a miracle worker, solving cases the rest of the FBI had given upon on. As long as she'd been forced on him, he might as well make the most of it.

He turned to the agent overseeing site access. "Damion, make sure Forrest and her team get access to the building."

"Yes, sir." Damion picked up his phone and made a call.

"Go do your thing. Let me know what you find."

"You got it."

"And Forrest..."

"Yeah?"

"Let me know what you find before you run it up the chain, okay? I know Griz is your boss and all, but I'm in charge of this op."

Forrest nodded dutifully. "Give us an hour or two, then I'll let you know what we turn up."

Enso glanced at the clock. He had less than twenty hours to crack this before he'd be pulled off the operation, and everything would get booted upstairs. There'd be hell to pay if he couldn't button everything up by then.

CHAPTER 53

T he constant drone of the engines gave Igloo a headache. Why couldn't the military take a cue from civilians and make their planes quieter? People had to work, dammit. She rubbed her head.

Tapestry was completely shut down by the government. Had been now, for twenty-four hours. Meanwhile, the government fed journalists a non-stop stream of misinformation indicating Tapestry was a Chinese front, either terrorist or military. Either way, this was fucking with Igloo's plan.

She could circumvent anything the government could do from a technology perspective. They could push out the T2 release even though the government had shut down all the update servers. They could recreate the signing keys necessary to allow the current update client to accept the T2 update. They could get T2 to work through almost any port, or type of communication channel available to them whatsoever. They could make it work without any servers.

But if they didn't have public opinion on their side, their effort would be worthless. Igloo wasn't going to force the T2 client on people. If the public believed the government's lies, they might uninstall Tapestry or simply mistrust any information they received via Tapestry.

Igloo glanced back at the rest of her team on the plane. They'd been through hell and back, and they looked it. Doug had passed out military-grade stimulants from the flight deck emergency kit to fight exhaustion. With the aid of the chemical boost, they churned through the last of the crucial changes, and now were cranking through lower priority stuff while waiting on the update signing keys from Ben and Forrest. The drugs had worn off now, and everyone was flagging again.

She looked back at her laptop.

Angie, unwilling to leave another election to chance, had placed the backdoor in Tapestry that would allow her to sway public opinion, believing that anything and everything that would ensure a more positive outcome was justified. Igloo had been opposed, and so, despite Angie's wishes, she'd already removed the backdoor.

But Igloo realized that if she pushed out this update now, as it was, it might be too late. The government demonstrated that they were willing to lie to stop her, and she might never be able to sway public opinion back when it came to Tapestry.

The original version of Angie's content modification code had a backdoor that would allow someone with the right secrets to change the rules about what content was prioritized. It would allow Igloo to subtly change what Tapestry would show. But the backdoor was also vulnerable. Vulnerable to another hacker figuring their way in. Vulnerable to being exploited by the government. Vulnerable to Igloo herself, should she ever act in anger.

She stared at the right-hand window on her desktop. She had a different set of patches. Code changes that kept the core of Angie's content modification algorithms intact but eliminated the backdoor. Instead, this set of code would place the content modification under the control of Igloo's chat personalities. Those personalities were already wired to help people, to converse with them, to coach them, to be friends with them. Those personalities could, with the small set of changes Igloo created, also pick the optimal content for each person. In effect, it would be an AI-driven, tailored educational program designed to help people grow as individuals. To become better. More thoughtful. More insightful. More empathetic. It would correct fake news stories. Eliminate content that contributed to fear and hate.

Once released, Igloo wouldn't know what was happening. She wouldn't be in control. In fact, the personalities were already evolving beyond Igloo's understanding, and growing beyond their original programming. No one could say for sure what the AI might do with this power to change what people read.

Worse, because of the way her changes were woven into the code, and because of how the code would be under scrutiny in the future, it wasn't even clear that she'd be able to release an update that would turn it off.

She had to make the decision now. She clenched and unclenched her hands. She was contemplating manipulating everyone in the world. Exploiting people ran counter to everything she stood for.

She took a deep breath. Her options sucked. She wished she could simply release T2 as it was originally intended. It would have been a beautiful thing for the world. But if she did that, the government would win their propaganda war against Tapestry, T2 would die, and in the process, people would lose ownership and control over their own data and communications. Maybe someday they'd regain it, but years of progress would be lost. They'd regress to a Tomo-controlled world, where people were vulnerable to corporations and the government.

That left her with only one viable option, a path she never intended nor wanted. She could release Angie's Tape code with modifications to place it under the control of the chat personalities, leading to a worldwide manipulation of essentially everyone, perpetuating what amounted to a crime against humanity for the sake of letting people own their own data and have and control their own privacy. It was a terrible choice, but were the benefits worth it?

The thing was, they'd been operating under the old system for years. Things kept getting worse. From stories Angie used to tell, back when the Internet and the web were getting started, everything was created, owned, and managed by people. Regular individuals. None of this corporate owned shit. Commercial activity had been highly frowned upon. Now it was barely possible to find anything that wasn't moderated, controlled, and templated by the corporate world.

She had to release T2 and she had to ensure it would succeed. If the government hadn't forced her hand with their lies, she might have been able to do so without resorting to this extra step. That she was being forced to undo their manipulation was their fault, not hers. She was only doing what was necessary.

Damn it. Did it really all come down to this? It did. Otherwise, everything else, including Angie's death was for nothing.

She put her hands on the keyboard and raced to restore Angie's code along with the modifications to tie it into the chat personalities.

CHAPTER 54

F orrest assembled her team in the parking lot behind Tapestry Headquarters. She had six principal investigators and eight techs loaded down with forensic gear.

She stood in front of the group to address them, more than a little guilt rumbling inside her. They deserved better than to be lied to. "We need a list of options, possibilities that could indicate where the T2 team is, how they're communicating, what other objectives or weaknesses they might have. We've dug deep online, and the rest of the team is chasing down every one of those leads. Now we need to see what we can find here in their offices that, for whatever reason, wasn't visible online. Who were these people? Who did they associate with? What hobbies, interests, or activities unique to the workplace did they engage in? We've got an hour. Let's go."

Most of the team stood with the appearance of disinterest. At least that's how it would look to the casual observer. And in truth, they'd heard her speeches a thousand times before, knew what they here were for. But what appeared to be almost boredom was professional detachment; an ability to stay calm, avoid triggering the lizard brain, even in situations of high stakes. Her team was well aware of the time crunch and the immense pressure from above to turn up something actionable.

When she finished talking, everyone picked up their gear and headed toward the building. Ben, dressed in an FBI jacket and cap, and loaded down with 3D imaging gear, followed close beside her.

The parking lot doors, like all the other entrances, were patrolled by national guardsmen.

"Special Agent in Charge Forrest," she said, holding out her badge.

They filed in as a group, then splintered off to different areas, following subdivisions of responsibility they'd staked out earlier. Forrest consulted a map, headed for the small onsite data center. Ben trailed behind her.

On the fourth floor, they approached the data center. Even from down the hallway, FBI *Do Not Enter* tape covering the doorway was visible. As Forrest drew closer, an agent she vaguely recognized from Cyber Crimes division approached, meeting them at the door.

"Forrest," he said, in greeting. "How are you?"

She discreetly read his name tag. "Good, thanks, Brin." She nodded toward the door. "We need to head in."

Brin looked back toward the door. "We're keeping it under lockdown until forensics is done."

"They in there now?"

He nodded.

"We can join them. I've got an hour deadline from Enso to produce something."

Brin was visibly conflicted, his eyes darting back and forth. It was logical he'd have a hard time saying no to her, both because she was a superior, and because Forrest's reputation preceded her. She guessed he'd been given direct orders to keep everyone out.

"Look, you'll feel better if you run it up the chain. We can wait a minute."

Brin immediately relaxed. "Thanks for understanding."

He spoke into the mic at his throat. The response took a good minute.

Forrest tried to avoid staring at Ben, but she couldn't help noticing his tight jaw and a faint sheen of sweat on his forehead. She drew herself up, making herself as imposing as possible. Better to keep Brin's focus on her.

Brin spoke again into his mic, then nodded to Forrest. "You can go in."

She bent to duck down under the tape and pushed the door open, then held it for Ben to follow her.

They entered a long, skinny room. Where once an onsite data center might have consumed an entire floor, technology had progressed, and a modern building like Tapestry held only the vestiges of such a room. Rack-mounted machines occupied either side of a central hallway, maybe twenty feet in length, and most of those would be communication hardware rather than servers.

Ben nodded toward the far side of the room.

They walked the length of the room and stood in front of the burnished steel vault door that held Tapestry's private keys used to sign their root certificates. With these keys, Igloo and her team would be able to fabricate a new set of certificates that would allow them to pass off the T2 update as authorized by Tapestry.

"Don't bother," called a voice from behind them.

Forrest looked back. "Ugland." One of the bureau's top counter-terrorism data gurus.

Ugland pointed two of his lackeys to a rack. "That's got a secured log. Crack it and let me know what you find."

Ugland walked up to Forrest. "We've already been in the vault. There's nothing of value to the investigation in there. Their root signing keys, but that's about it."

"I'd like to take a look myself," Forrest said. She wished she could simply order Ugland out of the room, but he'd be on the phone to Enso in a split second. There was no plausible reason she could give to explain why she wanted the room cleared.

Ugland frowned. "Literally, there's nothing in there. Besides, we needed two sets of authentication codes to get in. Enso has them now. You'd need to get him to come in and enter them to get in. Not worth it." Ugland gestured over toward one of the racks. "Look, I've got work to do."

Ugland sat down at one of the few work areas, pulled out a laptop, and plugged into the backplane of one of the racks.

Forrest contemplated this turn of events, unsure of how to proceed with Ugland in the room.

Ben leaned over and spoke in a whisper. "I just need to enter the bypass code. I can get in and out in five minutes."

That might be true, but they weren't going to get five minutes with Ugland and his folks in here. Forrest glanced at her watch. Igloo was waiting on those keys.

CHAPTER 55

E nso watched as the video feeds of the other participants blanked out, one by one, until only Griz was left.

"You gotta problem, Enso." Griz opened his desk drawer and pulled out a half a cigar. He put the end in his mouth and seemed to relish the experience.

Enso didn't say anything. He knew something that most didn't: the old man didn't dare light the cigar. Doctor wouldn't let him. Griz was mostly held together by grit and inertia at this point. He'd seen how Griz only pulled out the cigar during periods of high stress.

"Inspector general has taken notice of operations."

"Who clued her in?"

"Who clued—" Griz broke off in a laugh. "Son, you've got FBI, NSA, and military assets from all five branches on your little boondoggle. For an agency that doesn't even fucking exist, you're running the most visible operation in the world right now. You think labeling this a 'training exercise' is going to sweep it under the rug?"

Griz shook his head slowly. "I covered for you. You know why?"

Now it was Enso's turn to shake his head.

"Because my ass is already on the line. I spoke up for you. Got you those pretty planes you've got circling up there. Five fucking signals intelligence planes. Backed up your request to the NSA. Got you the whole stinking Utah site. Got the National Guard and Coast Guard involved. Because when I give you my word, I don't skimp on that, goddamnit. I said I'd back you up for forty-eight hours, and by golly, I'm doing that."

"Sir, we are doing our best," Enso said. "I've got Forrest in the building now, leading an investigation to track down any clues. I've got the NSA crunching every last packet of data crossing the Internet. They are an evasive and tenacious group, but we know they're still on U.S. soil, and we will find them. It's just a matter of time."

Griz jabbed at the desk in front of him. "Time is the one thing we don't have. Get me some fucking answers ASAP. Clean this mess up. Because this whole thing is going to get shut down in a matter of hours."

This wasn't a time to argue. Better to placate the old man. "Copy that. Thank you, Sir."

Five planes?

He stood and bumped his elbow on the wall behind him. He maneuvered his way out of the cramped private communications closet and reentered the main suite of the mobile command center.

"How many planes do we have up?" he asked one of the coordinators.

"Five, sir," the coordinator said.

"I thought we only had the three Air Force assets."

"Plus the two Coast Guard planes Special Agent Forrest got them to loan us."

Enso's second in command, Alice, came over. "Everything okay?"

"Yeah. I just didn't realize we had five planes."

"Is that a problem?"

Enso stared at his second in command. Had the woman just had her brains sucked out? "It gives us nearly twice the coverage. How would that be a problem?"

Alice shrugged.

"Is Forrest still in HQ?"

"Yes, Sir."

"Get her for me now. Radio, phone, whatever. I want to talk to her. We need some kind of clue as to where the T2 team is."

CHAPTER 56

F orrest glanced between Ben and the other FBI agents. Ugland's people wouldn't give a shit about Ben, but Ugland himself probably would.

"Wait a minute, then get the keys. Don't worry about those two."

Ben nodded.

Forrest clapped him on the shoulder and went over to Ugland.

"You got a minute to talk privately?"

Ugland's hand poised over the keyboard. "I'm in the middle of something. Can it wait?"

Forrest suppressed a sigh. Ugland was a prima donna. Obviously Forrest wouldn't interrupt him unless she had something important to discuss.

"If we could talk now, that would be good."

Ugland took a deep breath, put his hand back in his lap, and pivoted his chair to look at Forrest. "Go ahead."

"I want to talk privately." She looked meaningfully at Ugland's other people, then leaned in close. "About Enso's behavior."

Ugland shook his head. "No. Not going to get involved with gossip. I just do my job." He turned back to his computer.

"This is serious. This isn't your first time on this ride. How many

BRI operations have you been a part of? You ever see BRI pull in this many assets?"

Ugland opened his mouth to speak, then closed it. "What's your point?"

She gestured with her eyes toward the door.

"Fine." Ugland stood, and they walked outside the data center together.

She continued out of earshot of the agent guarding the data center door.

"Something fishy is going on."

Ugland threw up his hands. "Something fishy is always going on. It's BRI. Fishy is what they do."

"FBI. National Guard. Military vehicles. Air Force. Every BRI operation I've ever been pulled into has been two or three, maybe a half dozen people across different organizations."

Ugland paused. Then he leaned in. "Utah is single-tasked on this. Everyone is trying to crack where these people are. They're hopping around. The latest theory is that they're either on a plane or they're bouncing signals off a satellite. Whoever they are, they're major league. I don't believe this Tapestry stuff. Don't know if it's a cover story or what. But there's a demon in the system. That part is for real."

"So why is BRI in charge? Shouldn't this be kicked up to Cyber Command?"

Ugland pointed to himself. "Cyber Command is here. What do you want?"

"I want to know why Enso is running things, and not General Blalock."

"Hey, Forrest."

She looked up, saw the agent manning the door calling her as she approached. "I've got Enso on the line. He wants to talk to you." He held out a phone.

"Not right now," she said.

He held the phone against his chest and raised his eyebrows. "He doesn't sound happy."

"Gimme a second, Ugland. Don't go anywhere." She turned to the agent and took the phone. "Forrest here."

"I need an update," Enso said. "I've got everyone breathing down my neck. What do you have for me?"

"Sir, my team is all spread out. I need to talk to everyone."

Ugland shook his head, and walked away, back toward the data center.

Shit. "Enso, I gotta go. Can I call you back?"

"No, dammit. Our time is limited. Give me something I can use now."

Ugland disappeared back into the data center. Fuck.

"I don't have anything now. I need to check in with my team. That's why I need to go. I will call you back in ten minutes."

"Make it five."

"Fine, five minutes."

Jesus Christ. She trotted back toward the data center, but the door was locked again. She gestured to the agent, who slowly entered the code.

She wanted to punch him, make him move faster, but anything she did would only slow him down.

Finally, he was done, the door lock clicked, and she yanked it open.

Ugland had Ben up against the wall, one arm against his throat.

"What were you copying?"

Ben's eyes were wide. He looked toward Forrest.

She couldn't lose control of the situation. Forrest felt herself going for her gun. Oh. Was it all going to come down to this?

Ugland looked toward Forrest, and his eyes glanced down to her hand moving toward her gun. Ugland spun away from Ben.

Forrest drew her weapon and fired twice, clipping Ugland in the shoulder. He disappeared behind a rack of equipment.

The other techs in the room dove out of their chairs.

Ben cowered against the wall.

From out of sight two shots were fired, and Ben bounced against the wall.

Fuck. Forrest ran forward, her pistol firm in a two-handed grip, and turned the corner.

Ugland was on the floor on his back, gun out.

Forrest fired three more times, direct hits to the midsection.

Ugland lay still.

The two techs were staring at her from the corner.

She tried to think over the adrenaline coursing through her system. How should she handle them? Leave them alive? Come up with some excuse for what she'd done? Or kill them and buy herself some time? No, there was still the agent outside who would have heard everything.

The door.

She glanced back in time to see the door being yanked open, the agent's gun out.

She pulled her weapon back up and fired three shots, taking him in the arm twice and neck once. He dropped to the floor before he got a shot off.

She ejected her clip and loaded a new one from her waist holster in one move. Her pulse pounded in her head. She scanned the room, pistol ready.

The techs cowered in the corner. She gestured toward the door, and they hesitated for a moment, then ran.

No threats left.

"Ben, you okay?"

Ben didn't answer.

Forrest crouched down and felt for a pulse. Nothing. Ben was dead.

Did he get the root certificates? Did he transmit them? Fuck. Fuck. Fuck.

A hint of shiny black on the floor attracted her attention. There was a memory card a few feet away. Had Ugland knocked it out of Ben's hands?

She glanced around at the roomful of computer equipment. She had no idea if anything here had an outside connection. Probably not.

She pawed through Ben's bag. He had a laptop. Two phones. That jogged her memory. Doug had given him burner phones to use for data comm. She'd overheard Igloo, Ben, and Doug discussing how to exchange the data using an FTP drop box.

She grabbed the bag and memory card and ran out of the data center. She searched for somewhere to hide that would buy her a few minutes. She came to a conference room and ducked down on the far side of the conference table, where she was invisible from the door.

She pawed through the bag, extracting what she needed. She plugged the phone into the computer, slipped the card into a slot, and booted the machine. Luckily, it was one of her unit's laptops, and it was still running a stock image.

She logged in with her credentials, opened up the file listing for the card, then realized she had no idea where to transmit the files. What server? What login credentials?

She pulled out her own phone, connected to the secure comm channel she used for Doug.

"Ben down. Need FTP login creds."

She heard shouting in the hallways. Heading into the conference room would have bought her a few minutes. Although maybe they'd triangulate on her radio transmissions now.

Waiting felt like an eternity, although she knew only seconds passed. The reply with credentials came a half a minute later, followed by a second message.

"You okay?"

Doug was good, getting the essentials done first. No time to reply.

She logged into the FTP server. Footsteps pounded outside. The door opened.

She hit transmit.

CHAPTER 57

The Coast Guard plane droned on, flying a new radio surveillance path over Beaverton. There were thousands of access points and other radio towers they could exploit for an internet connection. They were swapping access points every ten minutes now.

Igloo stood next to Mike in the small radio room just behind the cockpit.

"They're going to eventually figure out how we're doing this," Mike said.

Igloo patted him on the shoulder. "I know. Just keep switching it up."

Doug yelled out Igloo's name, and she rushed out of the radio room, back to Doug's side at one of the workstations in the main cabin.

"Get ready. I just heard from Forrest. She asked for the FTP credentials."

Igloo was already in her seat by the time that sunk in. "Ben knows the credentials." She looked at Doug, but he was staring at his phone.

"Ben knows the..." Igloo trailed off. Something happened to Ben.

Essie was by her side, squeezing Igloo's shoulder. "Stay focused, Igs."

There was a squelch of static as the intercom came online. "We've got a pair of National Guard fighters pacing us. They've ordered us to stop radio transmissions and land immediately. Whatever you're doing back there, we need you to shut down ASAP."

Igloo glanced out the window. There really *was* a fighter plane flying alongside them. Holy shit.

"I'll handle this," Doug said. He unbuckled and headed for the cockpit.

A notification flashed as soon as her code detected files in the FTP site, and she breathed a sigh of relief. There was nothing for her to do. She'd already written a script to do everything that needed doing, so that she wouldn't have to rush in the heat of the moment. She'd even updated her openssl libraries this morning. It should only take moments to grab the private key, regenerate the signing key for the update domain, then sign the package. They were ready to push an IP routing hack that would allow the Tapestry clients to find the update.

Her code regenerated a signing key for the update domain, then—

Wait, what was this error message? How could she not have the required openssl header files? She felt a pit of despair in her gut at the pages of error messages scrolling up the window.

"Uh, Mike? Melanie? Someone, help!"

"I saw this," Melanie said, rushing to her side. "Accept the Xcode license."

"Did you install an update?" Mike asked.

"It's a mismatch between your openssl libraries and Xcode," Carly said. "You need to give it the right library path."

"Brew upgrade and brew update," Jeff added.

"No—that'll update all her packages. It'll take forever," Carly said.

"Everyone stop arguing!" Igloo said. "What do we need to do to fix this?"

"Give me a copy of the keys, and let me try on my machine," Melanie said. "Then you can keep debugging your machine in parallel."

Igloo sent a copy to Melanie.

"Did you compile Ruby or install binaries?" Carly asked.

"Fuck if I remember."

"Then let's do a clean install."

Igloo took a deep breath. Why couldn't everything just work?

Doug came back from the cockpit. "How long?"

"I don't know," Igloo said.

"They're threatening to shoot us down if we don't cut radio transmissions. They said we have thirty seconds to comply. Cut it now, Mike."

Mike glanced at Igloo. She nodded.

The internet died.

"Ah, I can't install packages," Melanie said.

"I have a local mirror of the top GitHub repos," Diana said. "Let me pair with you."

"This is ridiculous," Igloo said. "Someone on this plane has to have a machine that openssl is running correctly on. Can we all just check?" She glanced at Doug. "They're not going to shoot us down as long as we're not transmitting?"

Doug nodded. "Yes, but they're forcing us to land at Portland International. We'll be on the ground in ten minutes." He ran a hand over the stubble on his head. "Probably arrested. Wasn't really expecting that." The last was an aside to himself.

"Peeps," Igloo said, addressing her team. "We need to get that package signed before we're on the ground, squirt it as fast as possible, and hope they don't shoot us when we do. I need you to get that done while I buy us some time."

She turned to Doug. "How do we get another hour in the air? We need the package released and widely distributed."

"There's no way," Doug said. "The Coast Guard pilots are not going to disobey a direct order to land. And there's nothing you can do from here to stop those fighters."

Igloo considered options. Maybe they could take over the plane's flight controls from back here. Maybe they could execute a remote attack on the fighter planes. She shook her head. She was dreaming. Not even Angie could bring down an F-16. And she looked around at the plane they were on. It had to be twenty, thirty years old or more. For all she knew, the flight controls were hardwired to the control surfaces. Besides which, with no Internet, she couldn't even find or download or create the exploits she'd need, even if they existed.

Igloo closed her eyes and fought a rising panic. She had no options, no way to take control of the situation. The lack of control triggered her in every possible way. It just wasn't fair. There was no way out, nothing she could do. There was no way she could talk her way out of this situation.

Wait. There was no way *she* could talk her way out, but that didn't mean someone else couldn't. She didn't need to take control of this plane or those fighters. She just needed to take control of the pilots, and that was a far easier problem.

She turned to Doug. "Who's in charge of everything?"

"Enso. Head of BRI."

"Except he's not directly talking to these pilots. He's not in charge of the Coast Guard and the Air Force."

"National Guard," Doug corrected. "But no. He's relaying orders through their chain of command."

"How? What communications channel?"

"Secured VOIP phone calls."

"Routed over the public internet?"

"Yes, or..."

"Over DOD milnet, I know. But as long as they'll accept calls coming in over the regular Internet, we can crack their communications."

Doug shook his head. "Those calls are secure. Protected by public key cryptography. The same cryptography you also rely on."

Igloo shook her head. "Don't worry about the details. You have a secure phone and samples of Enso's voice?"

He nodded. "I've got messages."

"Give them to me."

CHAPTER 58

E nso stared down at Forrest's body. He wanted to yell at her, but it would do no good now.

"Sorry, Sir." The agent looked at his feet. "I told her to stand down, but she had her service arm out."

"You did the right thing."

Enso turned to his second in command. "Alice, what's the status of the plane?"

"National Guard is forcing them to land. They'll fire on it if we detect transmissions."

Enso thought about what would have happened if they'd gotten the T2 release out. The Internet would have fallen into utter chaos. Untraceable, untappable, untamable. No centralized control. No safety. He'd just singlehandedly prevented a cyber disaster of epic proportions.

He needed the plane on the ground, and the entire T2 team disappeared before he could relax. None of them could ever be permitted to get anywhere near a computer again.

This was validation of everything BRI was invented to fight. To do what needed doing to ensure the greatest good for the greatest number, regardless of laws and other short-term concerns.

He'd need to testify before the committee. BRI would be more secure than ever before.

"Sir..."

He looked at Alice, who was ignoring him now, staring at her phone.

"Yes?"

Alice ignored him, put the phone up to her ear.

"No, we don't tell them to stand down." She waited. "I don't know where that order originated."

"What the fuck is going on?"

Alice held her hand over the mouthpiece. "The F-16s are returning to base. Trying to figure out why."

"Gimme that." He grabbed the phone. "Who am I talking to?"

"This is Major Conway."

"Conway, we need that plane out of the air, now."

"With all due respect, ten minutes ago you wanted them called off. Can you make up your mind?"

Enso gritted his teeth. "That wasn't me. Our communications are being attacked. We need that plane down now."

"If comms can't be trusted, how can I know this is a legitimate order?"

"Logic, Conway, logic. They'd want you to call off an order to bring them down, and the real me would want them shot down. If they transmit their payload, it will be the biggest cyberattack in history. I need that plane down now. If you have to shoot them over downtown Portland, do it."

There was a long pause. Enso could guess that Conway was having second thoughts.

"Conway, we don't have all day. If they release their data payload..."

"Yes, Sir. I'm transmitting the order. Hold on..."

Enso held his hand over the phone. "They're cracking our phone calls. We need the whole operation to move to a new SCI compartment."

Alice nodded, and turned to another agent.

"Enso, you there?" Conway was back.

"Go ahead."

"We've lost voice comms with our pilots and the Coast Guard plane. Telemetry on the F-16s still says they are returning to base."

"What else have you got that can bring that plane down?"

"Nothing, unless we scramble out of Seattle. I'd need to bump that up the chain of command. But we can have the F-16s back in the air in less than fifteen minutes."

"Give them an order, in person, to take down that plane, and not to rescind regardless of what they hear via communications."

"Sir, but there is no way I can do that."

"Excuse me?"

"I can't give a shoot to kill order over American soil in a downtown area and not have a way to recall."

"Unless you want to personally be chewed out by the President of the United States tomorrow morning, I suggest you find a way to do so."

Enso ended the call without waiting for a reply. People and their goddamn ethics.

CHAPTER 59

I gloo glanced out the window. There was the Columbia River. They were so close to the Portland airport. It had been a very near thing.

Ten minutes ago, she'd run the voice samples she had for Enso through her sequencer, generating a voice model she could use for text-to-voice. It was the same code she'd written for the chat personality voice interfaces.

She used Doug's phone for the calls, since it already possessed the necessary hardware encryption layer. Substituting Enso's credentials, she called the base commander and used the text-to-voice ability to impersonate Enso, instructing the base commander to order the planes back to the ground. That took only two minutes, and she watched as the F-16s peeled away.

She repeated the same trick with the Coast Guard, telling the administrator to relay the order to the pilots to stay aloft, using the excuse that a miscommunication with the Air Guard had been cleared up.

Soon after, she felt the Coast Guard plane ascend again, then turn until they were westbound once more.

"How's the package coming?" Igloo asked.

"Almost there," Melanie said.

"What can we do to jam Enso's communications?" Igloo asked. "I don't want him countermanding the steps we just took."

Doug pointed down the plane. "The same gear we're using to transmit should be able to drown out signals to those fighters. Or to the ground station."

"Can you do it?" Igloo asked.

Doug shrugged.

"We'll figure it out," Carly said. "Mike, help me." Mike joined Carly in front of the radio console.

"The package is ready," Melanie said.

"Don't wait. Push it out."

Melanie nodded. Igloo joined her at the computer. They watched as the update uploaded over their Internet connection.

"It's out," Melanie said.

"Seeding via Bittorrent," Jeff said. "And replicating to CDNs."

With a valid, signed update binary out there, the only thing left was to tell the hundred million Tapestry clients about it. Those clients would check Tapestry servers periodically for an update. Unfortunately, the servers they'd be looking for had all been shut down by the government. Worse, the government had, by court order, re-routed all Tapestry traffic to a government-owned IP address. In effect, hundreds of millions of Tapestry clients were trying to hit servers that weren't replying.

"Spawning EC2 instances across all regions, all zones," Diana said. "Launching load balancers. Attaching instances to the load balancer." Dozens of load balancers spread the flood of Tapestry traffic among the thousands of servers they leased for the day. Over the next few minutes, those thousands of web servers would come online, booting a software image they prepared the previous day.

All the while, in the back of her mind, Igloo couldn't stop thinking that at any moment they could be shot out of the sky.

Igloo pulled out her last wild card. A zero-day DNS vulnerability. Time to route around the government. She forced the Tapestry traffic to hit the servers under her control, despite the steps the government used to take control of Tapestry's IP addresses.

"Traffic coming in," Melanie said. "A hundred requests. DNS must be switching over."

A cheer went up around the plane and Igloo exchanged a couple of fist bumps with members of the team.

"Sweet," she said. But her enthusiasm was tempered. It would take a full day before all the cached DNS entries expired.

Traffic built steadily over the next several hours. Until Tapestry hit a critical mass, meanwhile, she and her team were still at risk.

"Hey, Igs!" Mike and Carly called her simultaneously.

She left her station and went over to radio control. "Yeah?"

"We tracked those F-16s back to Portland," Carly said. "They landed, which means they could be taking off again at any second, assuming they get new orders once they hit the ground."

"We need to get out of the air quick. If we're on the ground, they won't shoot us."

"Are we done?" Mike said.

She realized they'd been so focused on their radio-jamming task they'd missed the cheer that had gone around the plane. "Yeah, we're done. The software is out."

Carly and Mike leaned back in their seats.

Igloo spun around. "Doug, get those pilots to land this plane."

"You got it, Igloo. Good job."

"Oh man," Melanie said. "We're already at five hundred requests per second."

They had to hope their cobbled together infrastructure held under the crushing load of Tapestry users.

"There's nothing more we can do," Igloo said. The plane abruptly veered, and she guessed they were heading for the airport. "The servers will hold, or they won't. Either way, the software is out there, and it'll—"

The plane thudded, then jerked sideways. Igloo slammed into the wall, then felt her stomach rise as the plane veered downward suddenly. The engine noise, already loud, roared and drowned out all communication.

She tried to rise to her feet, but the plane twisted again, and she flew the across the narrow aisle, crashing into something sharp. Strong hands grabbed her as Doug pulled her into a seat next to her station.

They worked together to buckle her in as the plane veered again, engines straining.

Suddenly the plane leveled out. Igloo looked out the window to see treetops flashing by.

The engine noise backed off, and the click of the intercom came on.

"We just took machine gun fire from a military vehicle about a couple of miles west of the airport," one of the pilots said. "We're keeping it under two hundred feet for the remainder of our approach."

"We have a problem," Doug said. "Enso really wants us dead. We didn't consider things objectively. Rationally, there's no point for the government to kill us because the software is already out there. Killing us changes nothing. But—"

"Enso is desperate," Igloo said. "If we're dead, he gets to spin the story however he wants."

Doug nodded. His face was white.

"Lucky for us," Igloo said, "I included something in the software release about what's happened. Enso is screwed either way."

CHAPTER 60

Welcome to Tapestry 2.0.

This is your operating manual for the future.

Two hundred and fifty years ago, the United States justified its proclamation of independence with these words: We hold these truths to be self-evident, that all men are created equal, that they are endowed by their Creator with certain unalienable Rights, that among these are Life, Liberty and the pursuit of Happiness.

In today's modern age, we cannot have life, liberty and the pursuit of happiness without foundational digital rights. These include the right to digital privacy, to own and control our own personal digital data, to read and to publish unbiased sources of information, and to free, unfettered communication and association with anyone we choose.

Current events have shown that we cannot delegate our responsibility to others and expect to have these basic human rights guaranteed. Therefore, to ensure the security and availability of free communication, every citizen has not just the right, but the moral and social obligation to own and control their own means of communication.

As a modern society, we have discovered better ways to educate, collaborate, organize, and grow as individuals. In other words, to have life, liberty, and the pursuit of happiness. In the course of this ongoing discovery, we have come to value:

- Distributed information over centralized information.
- Community organization over authoritarian or hierarchical systems.
- Practical and pragmatic working systems over theoretical systems.
- Freedom of information over information controls.

These values can only be achieved through an independent, secure, and free system of global Internet communication, owned and controlled by the people.

The establishment will argue for the illusion of security through control, but they cannot promise you safety. At most, they can lie and pacify while the world disintegrates around you.

We can build a better world, better systems for better human beings, by giving you communication you own and control, which no establishment can take away.

Today, we give you Tapestry 2.0.

The text faded away and a video started, a woman in the foreground of a semi-dark room. The dark grey cots in the background and bare concrete walls gave the appearance of a military compound. She had deep bags under her eyes, and a haggard appearance.

"My name is Igloo. I'm a cofounder of Tapestry. For the past several days, I and a dozen engineers at Tapestry have been on the run from a rogue branch of the U.S. government called BRI that is trying to kill us in order to keep us from releasing Tapestry 2.0.

"The leader of BRI is a man named Enso. Enso killed Angie

432 / WILLIAM HERTLING

Benenati, the CEO of Tapestry, and made it look like an accident. The government is hiding this information.

"Enso is trying to discredit us or kill us, whatever it takes to prevent Tapestry 2.0 from being released. This is not just conjecture. I have proof."

The image of Igloo cut away and was replaced by a grainy video with obvious fish eye distortion. The video showed a desk, and on the desk was a bank of monitors three monitors wide and two high. Each of the displays was distorted by heavy flashing lines suggestive of anti-copying technology.

But visible through the distortion, in bits and pieces, were people. An undistorted digital overlay, obviously added in post-production, overlaid captions under each of the monitors:

Enso (BRI Head)

Signals Intelligence Director Feldson, aka "Griz"

Special Agent in Charge Haldor

The audio track was less distorted. The meeting participants spoke about infiltrating and compromising Tapestry. They discussed fabricating an evidence package, compromising Igloo, and stopping T2 at any cost.

The video conference meeting faded away to be replaced by a new face, also in the same military bunker as Igloo.

"My name is Robin White. I was assigned as an undercover agent covering Tapestry a year ago, and I spent months training to infiltrate the company. My mission was to provide inside information on Tapestry's most secret activities by getting close to key Tapestry employees. But what I learned over the course of a year is that Tapestry was doing nothing illegal. What I found instead was a company driven by a social mission to protect and help people, to prioritize individuals over financial profits. The employees of Tapestry have consistently behaved in the most ethical manner.

"When it became obvious that Tapestry had done nothing wrong, my former boss at BRI, Enso, overstepped his legal authority. He asked for the fabrication of evidence against the company as a whole and against key employees. In doing so, Enso has compromised the United States government, both legally and ethically. I believe Enso also ordered the death of Angie Benenati, the CEO of Tapestry."

Igloo reappeared onscreen.

"The future of democracy and personal rights hangs in the balance. For too long, we have delegated responsibility for our personal rights to governments and corporations. With Tapestry 2.0, we're putting the power to ensure privacy, freedom of association, and the power of secure communication back in the people's hands."

CHAPTER 61

T he plane landed at Portland International. The runway itself was clear, but nearly every square foot of tarmac surrounding the runway was covered with emergency response and military vehicles, as far as the eye could see.

The National Guard was there in force. As were the Port of Portland police. The FBI. The Portland police department. The airport fire suppression team. The Portland fire department. Surrounding the airport, outside the chain link fences, hundreds of cars, with more arriving by the minute. Every online medium was afire with news of Tapestry 2.0 and the government's showdown with Igloo and team, and now ordinary people were coming to see the spectacle, or to lend support for one side or the other.

Once they landed, Igloo and Doug peacefully barricaded the Coast Guard pilots into the cockpit cabin and explained through the door that they had no beef with them, but they couldn't surrender the plane quite yet.

Meanwhile, everything at the airport was at a standoff. There were hundreds of weapons trained on the plane, but no one fired while they sat there on the tarmac.

Even from here, Igloo could see dozens of media vehicles with their tall antennas and oversized cameras protruding above the crowd.

A few times, National Guardsmen approached the plane. By then Igloo and the T2 team had hacked into the controls. Anytime someone approached, they moved the plane forward or back. That was enough to forestall the approach, until the National Guard wedged armored vehicles in front of and behind the plane. Now they had nowhere to go, and Igloo expected it was only a matter of time before someone forced a door open from the outside.

The rest of the T2 team was online, talking with the public, encouraging more people to come forward, to call their government representatives, to get involved in the T2 community leadership.

National and international mass media covered the standoff, making it the number one trending topic on nearly every site. Igloo glanced through the main media organizations she was familiar with, and they all had live coverage with commentary. This surpassed anything she could have imagined.

In the midst of all this, there was a renewed and escalating public debate over the BDSM videos that BRI had released several days earlier, calling into question Igloo's credibility and authority. A good portion of the tech community, which was liberal and weird by normal social standards, didn't care much what Igloo did with her own time, though others did. To Igloo's surprise, people were suddenly coming out as kinky and defending her.

Developers were already inspecting the T2 source code, which had been posted publicly. The team shared the details of the online stewardship community that would be responsible for T2 going forward. Notable members of the open source community were signing on.

Igloo opened a channel with Tapestry's lawyers, who were working on the T2 team's legal options. The Electronic Frontier Foundation activated all of their legal resources and joined forces with Tapestry's legal team.

Citizens had drones flying, ignoring the no-fly zone around the airport, keeping an eye on everything. The National Guard shot down dozens of drones at first, but they kept coming, and eventually someone decided the risk of injuring bystanders wasn't worth taking down every drone.

Around eight that evening, David Schwartz, Tapestry's lead lawyer, relayed the first firm offer from the government: "They want T2 shut down, and a peaceful surrender of the T2 team."

"They're not offering anything," Igloo said.

"On the contrary," he said. "What they're offering is legitimacy. This is coming direct from the deputy director of the FBI, who will take it out of the hands of any rogue agencies. The offer is coming from a direct and well-known person. We can at least expect due legal process. You won't disappear into some black hole."

"No deal," Igloo said. "Besides, we've destroyed our copy of the private keys, so we can't be forced to change T2. It's out there, and there's nothing we can do to take it back." That was a half lie, but at least it gave them a plausible way to avoid being compelled.

She checked the stats. Nearly thirty percent of Tapestry clients had updated.

Igloo wrote down the details of the government offer and leaked it to CNN through an anonymous account. If evil flourished in darkness and secrecy, then she had to fight with transparency. Within a half hour not just CNN but every mass media outlet was reporting on the government deal and offering predictions on what else each side would barter for. Every expert they consulted spouted off more theory. Eventually she got tired of watching.

Night came. Tapestry updates were still increasing, minute by minute, but there was a long way to go before T2 was out to the majority of people. Igloo glanced out the airplane windows from time to time, careful to ensure the interior LEDs were off to avoid backlighting in case some sniper got excited. There was a sea of lights as far as Igloo could see. She desperately wanted sleep, and yet she feared that the moment she closed her eyes, something would happen. The lawyers kept telling Igloo to wait.

She found herself curled up next to Essie at one point.

Eyes closed, she reached out to grab Essie's collar, found only bare skin, and remembered belatedly that Forrest's team had cut it off.

"We've made so many mistakes," Igloo said, running her fingers over Essie's collarbone. "I've been so angry about you spending time with Michael. I've let too much distance come between us."

Essie sighed. "I have as well. It's not easy watching you go off to play with Charlotte. You always have this look on your face when you're texting her. It eats me up inside."

Igloo opened her eyes to meet Essie's gaze. "Why did you never say anything?"

"It was too hard. It was easier to go set up another date with Michael. At least he's always excited to see me."

"I didn't know you were struggling. I thought you were totally happy with poly."

Essie laughed. "Totally happy? You know I only wanted to go out on some dinner dates, right? I never actually thought we were going to have relationships with other people."

"What?" Igloo sat back up. "You said you wanted to date."

"I wanted to *go on dates*. Not get involved with people. Not fall in love with anyone else."

"Are you in love with Michael?"

Essie was quiet for a moment. "Not really. But I've been having sex with him. I know I said I wasn't. I don't know why I lied. I knew you would be hurt, and I didn't want to hurt you."

Igloo tried to decide how she felt. There was mostly a void inside her. Finally, she decided. "I think I knew, on some level. I'm not surprised."

"We've made things so much harder on ourselves," Essie said. "If we'd been honest with each other throughout, especially you—"

"Especially *me*?" Igloo said. "You just told me how you lied about having sex with Michael."

"I know I've lied about a few big things, and that was a mistake.

I'm sorry. But you've been using dishonesty as your primary mechanism to deal with any discomfort or conflict. You're dishonest with yourself every time you attribute all the blame to me for a difficult poly situation, rather than examining the role you played. Just look at the past few months. How many times did you fault me for what was happening rather than look at what you were doing?"

Igloo rubbed her face. Was Essie right? She had always blamed Essie for getting upset when she planned a date with Charlotte, yet nearly every single time, she'd made those dates without checking in with Essie first.

"Let me make sure I understand this," Igloo said. "You used to always get upset when I would make a date with Charlotte. Was that because I was having a date or because I didn't check in with you first?"

"Because you didn't check in with me. Isn't that obvious?"

Igloo shook her head. "I thought you were angry because I was going on the date, period."

"We're non-monogamous. Of course you're going to go on dates. I just wanted to feel like I mattered enough for you to check in with me."

Igloo felt like the plane was spinning. Her whole view of everything was wrong. "I've been an idiot, haven't I?"

Essie raised an eyebrow but said nothing. Then she slowly nodded.

Igloo rested her head on Essie shoulder. "I'm sorry."

They sat together for a moment in silence.

"Where do we go from here?" Essie asked. She played her fingers over Igloo's lips.

Igloo was still quiet, thinking. She hated that poly was so hard. She was used to being good at what she did. It was hard to cope with this feeling of—

"Don't do that," Essie said. "Don't sit there and try to figure it all out in your head. Tell me what you're honestly thinking."

Igloo took a breath. "It's hard for me to admit when I'm wrong.

Because if I'm wrong, then it means I'm not doing something perfectly. I want to be perfect."

"You're not perfect," Essie said. "Nobody is. I still love you. But this pretend version of perfection makes you unable to see or work on the problems that exist. And that's what I want—for the two of us to be able to work on things together."

Igloo slowly nodded. "I know," she said. "I want to work on things together. I love having you as my partner. And part of me cringes to say this, because I know how difficult poly makes things, and the stress that it puts on our relationship, but I still want to play with others."

Essie rested her head on Igloo's chest. "I feel the same. I want to be with you. And I want to keep seeing Michael. But we can't keep going at it the way we have. We need help. We need to see a therapist together."

"We can talk to Alan. He's starting to really help me get a handle on things."

"Is that your chatbot thing?" Essie said. "Because I can't do that. I want to see a real person. I want us to talk face to face, like human beings."

Igloo felt herself freezing up. Talk to a person about her feelings? She just wanted her feelings to go away. But that strategy didn't seem like it was working very well.

Igloo stared at the wall, unable to meet Essie's gaze. "Okay, I'll do it. I'll see a therapist with you. I want to spend my life with you, but not only am I not perfect, but I think I have quite a lot of work to do. I've always been scared of what's inside me. It means a lot to me that you'd be willing to be a part of this with me."

She glanced back to Essie. Essie, her head rolled back against the chair, eyes closed, was snoring softly. Damn. She was going to have to work up the courage to say all that again later.

She closed her eyes.

Finally, just around midnight, Doug shook her awake.

"The lawyers have an update," he said.

Igloo got herself back in front of a computer to video conference with them.

"We have a joint offer from the FBI and Department of Justice," David said. "They're agreeing to take you into custody at Whitehall. It's a minimum-security luxury prison reserved typically for the wealthy and influential. That's the most kid gloves treatment you're going to get."

"What do they want in exchange?"

David sighed. "They want you to shut down T2."

"As I already told you," Igloo said, "we can't. We don't have the keys. It's all turned over to the community now."

"The government doesn't believe that. They think you're holding something back."

"Obviously the government would try to force me to shut it down. So logically, I had to take steps to make sure I couldn't do that. No deal," Igloo said. She disconnected, and again anonymously shared the latest offer with CNN. Anyone could predict it was 99% likely Igloo was the one sharing the offers, but the cloak of anonymity created some uncertainty.

The open source community rallied during the night, the Europeans getting an early start on the day due to the time zone difference. Igloo must have fallen asleep again, because when she woke, eyes crusty and clothes feeling grimy, the first thing she got was an update from Melanie and Carly.

"They released a patch for OpenWRT during the night," Melanie said. "It bridges traffic onto t2_net, routing legacy non-Tapestry traffic onto the Tapestry network."

"Eighty percent of Tapestry software is now on T2," Carly said. "And new Tapestry downloads are actually outpacing updates at this point."

At 8 A.M., they had another offer relayed. "They'll let the rest of the T2 team go," David said. "They just want Igloo. They only need one scapegoat to pin things on."

"What about T2?" Igloo asked.

"They want that too. They don't believe you can't recall it."

Igloo didn't know what to do. She wanted to say no, but she couldn't make that decision for the rest of the T2 team. "You guys have to decide. Vote on what you want to do."

"No way. Accepting their offer is stupid," Diana said. "We didn't do all this for nothing."

Nobody voted to accept the offer.

Igloo's stomach felt like it was digesting itself. "Any chance of getting some breakfast burritos?" she joked the next time she talked to someone in the law office. They broke into the emergency landing kits, found some barely edible bars, and passed them out among everyone.

T2 adoption continued to spread.

"EFF is reporting that Internet traffic just hit 30 percent encrypted for the first time in the history of the Internet," Mike said. "Backbone traffic is down 35 percent as more and more content is served up locally and distributed through T2."

An hour later the government offered to let Igloo leave the US, promising they would not extradite her. "You'd have your freedom," Carter Schwartz said over a video call. "You couldn't come back to the US, but you could always build T3."

"No, there won't be another chance. They'd put measures in place to make sure no one does a distributed network again."

Diana interrupted their conversation, hovering over Igloo's shoulder. "The Great Firewall of China just failed," she said. "T2 has enough exploits and mesh networking ability that they're reporting the firewall is, for all intents and purposes, totally toast. We're getting a huge influx of downloads from China now."

Igloo gave Diana a high-five.

"Hear that?" Igloo said, looking back to Carter. "Redeeming social value. That's got to be worth something."

"We'll use it," Carter said. "We'll use everything we can get. But I need to tell you something while Diana is there."

Diana leaned in closer to the screen.

"The FBI shared some details with us that they haven't released to the general public. There was a shooting at Tapestry headquarters. Ben and Forrest are both dead, along with several other FBI agents."

Igloo felt someone grab her shoulder and looked up to see Doug. She didn't know if he was comforting her or seeking comfort. She put her hand on his.

Diana covered her mouth and turned away.

Igloo's vision narrowed, and everyone felt a million miles away. First Angie, now Ben and Forrest. Angie had always lived on the edge, and Forrest consciously chose a risky profession, but Ben was so innocent. Just a programmer who wanted to make the world a better place. How could this happen to him? How many casualties would they incur in the battle over the Internet?

CHAPTER 62

Nathan9 followed every minutia of the government's activities in Portland. The scale of the mobilization against Tapestry exceeded anything he could have imagined, but he suspected that they'd stopped short of actually shutting down the entire Internet. He couldn't be sure, but he doubted anything short of that drastic a measure would actually stop the T2 team.

Of course, the average layperson—hell, even the average expert—would say bringing down the Internet couldn't be done, but there were a half-dozen approaches the government could use if they were desperate. The government's problem was that if they used any of those mechanisms, business and academia would work together and redesign things so that it couldn't happen again. The government would undoubtedly save those vulnerabilities for only the most dire situations.

The key question of the moment was where was Forrest with the copy of the digital keys that would unlock T2? With those keys, Nathan would have *de facto* rule over the net of the future. He'd orchestrated all this: the showdown with the government, Angie's paranoia, the timing of T2, the government's hunt of the developers...

Everything was supposed to culminate in him getting a copy of the keys.

There was a pit in his stomach. Something was up. Forrest had gone dark for too long. Either she had betrayed him or something had gone wrong.

When the T2 release finally came, along with the concurrent announcement of the community governance model, he sat back in shock. Angie would never, under any circumstances, have turned over power to the people. Like him, she would have kept that power for herself. She could never have trusted the world, could never have put her faith in the ability of people to do the right thing.

But he had failed to realize that Igloo could, and would, and indeed, she had. She'd willingly let go of that power herself and given it to the global community. Freedom, for Igloo, had come not from holding power, but from giving it away.

He let out a low whistle. His dog's ears perked up.

Her actions had destroyed everything he hoped to achieve, but he respected her solution. She'd neatly prevented the abuse of power... by him, by the government, or even by herself.

CHAPTER 63

B y late morning, Igloo was concerned about the Coast Guard pilots, still barricaded in their cockpit.

"It's not humane to keep them in there," Igloo told Doug.

"We don't know what they'll do if we let them out," he said. "I don't think they're armed, but they might be."

"Fuck it, I'm going to talk to them."

Doug followed her and listened to her discussion through the intercom.

Between reading everything shared on the net, and conversations with their superiors, the pilots were well informed about the situation,

Ten minutes later the cockpit door was open.

"I can't say if I agree with what you've done," the pilot said to Igloo. "But I understand what you're trying to achieve. I hope they go gently on you."

The copilot grumbled. "Rebecca, you're letting these fucking idealists get to you. We were nearly shot out of the sky because of them."

"Let it go, Kurt. We survived. Sooner or later they'll reach an agreement, and then we can go home."

The pilots headed for the bathroom, and Igloo went back to her seat next to Essie. Everyone else was slumped in chairs or sleeping on the floor. Fatigue and boredom had hit hard.

Igloo curled up next to Essie and rested her head on Essie's shoulder.

"We should've brought more food," Igloo said.

"You're always hungry," Essie said, petting her head. "When we get out of here, I'll feed you."

"*If* we get out of here," Igloo said, her voice low. "If we go free."

Essie peered down at her. "You okay? Half an hour ago you gave everyone a pep talk."

"I told them what they needed to hear," Igloo said. "I have no idea what's going to happen."

Igloo nuzzled Essie's neck and closed her eyes. The next thing she knew, Doug was shaking her awake. She must have dozed off. She forced herself up.

"We have another offer."

"Does it include coffee?" Igloo said. "Because if so, I accept." But she rubbed her face and got up.

Carter and David Schwartz were on the video call together.

"How are you holding together?" David asked.

Igloo shrugged. "We're alive."

"You know what's happened to the Internet?" Carter asked.

"Everyone's come out in support of T2," Igloo said. "Hackers, coders, Anonymous, privacy geeks... Everyone is wiring legacy Internet stuff into T2. Seventy percent of all traffic is now going over T2."

"Was that planned?" Carter asked.

But his father put his hand on Carter's arm. "Don't answer that, Igloo. We don't want to know." He took a deep breath. "Look, the sense I'm getting is that the government is desperate. They want T2 shut down."

"We can't shut it down," Igloo said. "You know that. That's the whole point. It's out there now. It's under community control. It's self-policing, self-maintaining."

"I know, and I keep telling them that. They've had their analysts check out the code. They think you're holding out, that you have the private keys that would allow someone to update the Tapestry code."

"It's all out there in the community, distributed among hundreds of community members. We're not special anymore. We're just members of that community."

"They think that if you tell the community what you want, they'll do it."

Igloo gritted her teeth. "First of all, that's not how communities work. Second of all, the community will know I'm being coerced by the government, so they'll discount anything I say or do."

"I'm just relaying what they're saying, Igs. Listen to this next part, because I think it's key. They want a government surveillance back-door that can be used in the case of a court-approved surveillance order. If you give them this, they'll let everyone else go. You do twenty-four months, minimum security."

"Like the FISA court?" Igloo said. "Those things are abused. No backdoors. No surveillance."

"This is the government compromising," David said. "Twenty-four hours ago, you were all going to disappear, possibly for the rest of your shortened lives. Now they're saying that T2 can stay, everyone else goes free, and you do a little jail time, in exchange for a legal system with built-in oversight to allow the government to fulfill their obligation to ensure public safety. I strongly recommend you consider this proposal."

"Even if I wanted to change T2, I can't. Only the community can. They can take their proposal to the community, the users can vote on it, and if they want it, the community may implement it." Igloo wanted off the plane. "Can you get us any food? We're starving in here."

"I'll see what I can do."

An hour later, they got another offer. They could leave the plane and be moved to a secure facility where they could negotiate with the government under the direction of UN mediators.

"And lose global oversight?" She gestured outside. "The media is watching. The world is watching. If we become invisible, who knows what will happen to us. We'll stay here. See how long they can keep an entire airport shut down."

"They may take you by force."

Igloo glanced at a screen. 78 percent of all traffic was going through Tapestry. "Let's check again in half an hour."

"What's going to happen?"

"You'll see."

Right now the Internet was a mix of Tapestry and non-Tapestry traffic.

Anything between two computers running Tapestry was wholly encrypted, tunneled through multiple clients, so that no one else could detect what was being transmitted or even who was talking to whom. The vast majority of static content, such as public photos, articles, even video files was now served up through Tapestry's peer-to-peer network. Thousands of applications had already been ported in the last day from public cloud infrastructure to Tapestry clients, effectively granting free server hosting. Anything originating with a computer running Tapestry, connecting to a non-Tapestry endpoint was encrypted right up until it left the Tapestry endpoint nearest its final destination.

The only holdout was traffic between two computers, neither of which was on Tapestry. And to force the hand of those not using Tapestry, Igloo's contribution to the T2 code was about to do a Very Bad Thing.

Igloo watched a dashboard showing the rollout of T2 and related statistics. Tapestry data inched past 80 percent of all Internet traffic. Behind the scenes, Igloo knew that a major backbone on the east coast was suddenly being hammered by a large portion of all Tapestry clients. She watched latency numbers skyrocket as Internet from Boston to Washington, D.C. slowed to a crawl.

Igloo broadcast a message to the community.

"If any routers want to throttle Tapestry traffic, they need to install patches to participate in the Tapestry routing protocol. Suggest everyone start working on updates now."

David was back on a video conference less than ten minutes later. "What the hell are you doing, Igloo? You're making the government very angry."

"I'm telling people they must patch their infrastructure to keep working in this new, higher efficiency environment."

"That's not the way they see it. They see that stunt as you threatening everyone, demonstrating the control you have over the Internet."

Igloo shrugged and disconnected.

The routing patches had already been developed by the core team and vetted by the community. Within an hour, a good portion of the big backbone routers were running the updates, and suddenly traffic was being modulated and routed smoothly again.

She smiled. Now even the stuff that didn't originate with a Tapestry computer was flowing through the Tapestry network. Which *should* make the government very, very nervous.

Comcast wouldn't cave though, and they were routing traffic to most people's homes. That's okay. Tapestry was going to take care of that too.

As soon as the backbone routers were integrated, Tapestry started to change behavior again. When it detected traffic flowing through nodes that didn't support Tapestry protocol, they routed around them if another route was available. In the case of people's homes, that meant Tapestry computers would try to establish peer-to-peer wireless connections with other computers. When they found a connection to a computer not connected to Comcast, they routed traffic away from Comcast.

At first Comcast management would probably be delighted to see a drop in their system traffic. After all, it would keep their costs down. But soon that drop would go off a cliff. After that, Comcast would realize nobody was using their network. If Comcast still wanted to be in business next week, they'd have no choice but to support Tapestry.

Igloo looked out the window. It was early evening now. Their second day on the tarmac. The water supply had run out a few hours ago.

David came back online. "These manipulative tricks—saturating the backbone, playing games with Comcast—they're eroding whatever goodwill you might have with the government. Now they think you're extorting everyone. They're talking extensive prison time again."

Igloo shook her head. She worked up some moisture to wet her throat. "I'm not going to prison. And I'm not going to make a deal. I've just been waiting here so they can see our relative positions. You tell them I have a kill switch. I can't turn off T2. But the kill switch will shut down the net if any of us fail to check in according to schedule. I and the rest of the T2 team are going to open that door, and we're going to walk away. Just walk away. That's all that's going to happen. They're not going to stop us. They're not going to let anything happen to us. Because if anything happens to me, then who knows what will happen to the Internet."

Igloo waited thirty minutes to make sure that message got out to the powers that be.

"Come on people, it's time."

They opened the plane door and let the folding staircase descend to the tarmac. Thousands of lights shone out of the darkness surrounding them.

Igloo grabbed Essie's hand in hers. "Ready?"

Essie nodded.

Igloo took the first step out of the plane.

CHAPTER 64

Enso sat at his borrowed desk in the Portland FBI headquarters. The operation had been taken out of his hands once the plane landed at the airport. The visibility had gone international, and there was no way the head of a super-black agency could remain in control of anything.

If it had been up to him, he'd have had the snipers take out the T2 team. Maybe it was for the best that the control had been taken out of his hands. That would have been a mistake. Everything Tapestry did after release was automated. Killing Igloo and the rest of the team would have accomplished nothing, except to worsen his own situation.

As it was, he was good and truly fucked. He'd poured everything into taking on Tapestry. Called in every favor, taken every risk. What had it gotten him? An inquiry in front of Congress, most likely.

They'd need a scapegoat, wouldn't they? Someone would have to answer why, in the midst of the most massive mobilization of the intelligence community, Tapestry had not just evaded them, but actually made a fool of them.

There was nothing for him when he walked out of this room. Forget his career. He'd go to jail. For Angie's death, if nothing else.

He reached into the case on his desk and pulled out his sidearm. The best way out was also the quickest. No repercussions, no complications. Simple.

CHAPTER 65

Six months later.

Igloo wrote a line of code, then stared at the screen. That should do it. She started the test suite, and checked the time on her computer. Time to login. She logged out of Tapestry, then logged back in again using two-factor authentication. There, the kill switch was refreshed for another forty-eight hours.

Across a tabletop littered with coffee cups and pastry plates, Diana was buried in her own computer. They'd taken to mostly working out of coffee shops lately. Even now, six months later, the office held memories that ambushed them at unexpected times. Angie, Ben, even Agent Forrest.

She turned to stare at Essie, who was updating her blog. Since Essie came out as the primary author of the manifesto, her visibility skyrocketed. Her photography blog was suddenly getting zillions of hits every day, and Essie had taken to writing about freedom, politics, and the intersectionality of kink and feminism. She was now a creative writer for Tapestry's CTO office, which meant that, technically, Igloo really did have a submissive on staff.

Igloo reached out to touch the titanium collar that replaced

Essie's old chain and lock. Essie smiled, but gently pushed Igloo's hand away and stayed focused on her work.

Six months in, Tapestry was now everywhere. The community had extracted the core infrastructure from the social networking features. Tapestry had become a bona fide platform for software deployment and communication. Hundreds of thousands of applications had been ported to the distributed computation environment. Nearly every device, from the largest backbone routers to people's home wi-fi networks to most smartphones, were all native participants on the encrypted network.

Within days of the initial release, the community had found the kill switches in the code that Igloo and the rest of the T2 team were dependent on to ensure their freedom. With those switches in place, Igloo and the rest of the team had to authenticate with Tapestry on a regular basis. If more than one member of the team failed to login, then Tapestry would stop routing traffic. In effect, the Internet would die.

The community had debated whether to keep or remove those kill switches. On one hand, such behavior was anathema to the tech community. On the other, the T2 team were now heroes to that same community, and the kill switches were all that kept them out of jail, or worse.

The global community decided to keep the kill switches in place and agreed they wouldn't debate it again for another six months. Just a few weeks ago, the community voted again, and agreed to preserve for another six months. Having an existential dependence on the outcome of a community vote wasn't how Igloo preferred to live, but it beat the surety of going to jail.

In the meantime, turning Tapestry over to the global community helped Igloo and Angie's goals in ways they hadn't even anticipated. Developers from around the world implemented new algorithms to help ferret out fake news, to present multiple viewpoints side-by-side, and to promote the development of critical thinking skills. Just a few weeks ago, a study came out showing that T2 users were more well informed than consumers of news on any other platform. It was proof that no matter how well-meaning Igloo and Angie had been, they were still just two people, and there were more people, smarter people with better ideas, just waiting for a catalyst.

Igloo's tests all passed. She committed the code and pushed her changes out for the Tapestry community to review.

A message notification appeared. She didn't recognize the sender, and the message had somehow bypassed all her filters. Strange. She felt a chill down her spine and opened the message.

Dear Igloo,

I'm so proud of everything you've accomplished. In the face of uncertainty, you rose to the challenge when it was needed. Your solution for the ongoing governance of Tapestry was brilliant, and I have to confess that I wouldn't have thought of it myself. In fact, I probably would have shot down the idea of giving Tapestry to the community. I would have been wrong.

At first, Igloo assumed she was getting another dead man's switch message from Angie, albeit one triggered to come months after the fact. But there was no way Angie could have known about Igloo's community governance model *before* she died. Her pulse pounded in her ears as she read on.

I'm sorry for the anguish I caused you. I can't answer all of your questions, but I want to give you some closure.

I realized that I didn't want to spend the rest of my life chasing the next urgent thing, and there was always going to be the next thing. Instead, I want to spend the time I have left loving and being loved.

The crisis with Tapestry, my death presented the perfect

opportunity to buy the time needed for T2, turn the reins over to you, and exit the stage.

For a long time, I had a lot of regrets over the pain I caused you and Thomas. But we're happy now, you're happy now, and T2 is changing the course of history. I think things turned out just fine.

All my love,
AoM

This couldn't be. Or could it? Igloo tried to trace the origin of the message.

"Everything okay?" Essie asked, looking at Igloo in puzzlement.

Igloo looked up, realized she'd been pounding at her keyboard. "Yeah. I'll tell you about it later."

Igloo examined the message. It had come in with no headers, and nothing to indicate where it was from. Somehow Angie had injected the message through a backdoor in Tapestry. Igloo tried to puzzle out how Angie had done it, but there were thousands of possibilities, and Angie was exceedingly clever at hiding the exploits she engineered into the system. Everything she looked at told her this message couldn't be here, and yet it was.

She changed tack, and instead tried to track down Angie's husband, Thomas. A few minutes of research showed that his legal firm was closed and their house was shuttered. She used an old backdoor to look into his online trail, only to discover that there'd been no electronic trace of him in two months.

Igloo leaned back in her chair for a moment and took a deep breath. Forget trying to find Angie. That was never going to happen if Angie didn't want to be found. Instead, she allowed herself to just sit with her feelings.

Angie buried herself in so many layers of deception that you could never know when you were getting the truth. She not only faked her own death, but she framed her faked death on the government to throw them into chaos, all to buy more time to release T2, and apparently to create her own retirement. It was stunning and audacious. Igloo found herself laughing.

Angie had once related an anecdote about her mentor, Repard, who said that old hackers never die or retire, they just disappear deeper into the murky depths.

Igloo stopped laughing and sighed. She never really understood Angie, and it was something she was just going to have to come to terms with. Some people were so much larger than life that they defied all normal human expectations.

She turned to Essie. "You ready to get out of here soon?"

Essie nodded, then Igloo realized she wasn't listening, just jamming out to some music.

She repeated the message by computer. Essie looked at her and nodded for real.

Igloo turned to Diana. "We're going to take off."

Diana grunted. "Already?"

"We're hosting a party tonight, and we need to get ready." Igloo thought it over for a second. Decided she'd be polite even if it was awkward. "Want to come?"

Diana raised one eyebrow. "You two throwing a party. I have this feeling that it's not...What do you always say? 'Not my kink'?" She smiled. "Who's going?"

"Essie's partner Michael, Michael's other partner Sam, my girl-friend Charlotte, and Charlotte's new play partner." Igloo shook her head. "There are more people coming, but the relationships get more complicated. I don't even know how to describe them all."

"You two lead an...interesting life. Is it really worth it?"

Igloo sighed. "If I think too much about it, I wonder what the heck I'm doing. But most of the time, I'm having fun. You know I'd rather take the path less traveled. Oh, and Maria's coming."

"Our Maria? You're inviting the COO to your kink party?"

Essie pulled off her earphones in time to hear Diana's statement.

"Meetings are more exciting when you've tied up your naked coworker."

Diana covered her ears. "Lalala. I don't want to know."

Igloo loved that they'd gotten to the point of easy joking. No longer was kink a dark secret she had to hide. It was ironic that they made major changes to the very design of the Internet so that people could have better privacy...at the same time that all her secrets had been bared. Still, it was everyone's fundamental right to decide for themselves what to reveal and when. Yes, it was better to live an authentic life, but one shouldn't be forced to do so.

It all came down to freedom. The freedom to choose. The freedom to be who one wanted to be. Freedom wasn't simple, and it wasn't easy, but it made life worth living.

AUTHOR'S NOTE

In 2011, as I was preparing to publish my first novel *Avogadro Corp*, the then-unknown *Fifty Shades of Grey* was published. *Fifty Shades* quickly became a perennial topic of discussion among writers, fueled by the commercial success of the book, debates over the quality, and heated arguments about the abusiveness of the portrayed relationship. Countless writers asserted they could write something better than *Fifty Shades*, both in terms of the quality of prose, as well as portrayal of realistic kink. After years overhearing such discussions, my desire to attempt such a novel gradually grew.

My original intent was for a standalone technothriller that included BDSM themes. But after the introduction of *Kill Process*, I had ideas for a sequel, and I was interested in revisiting the characters again, especially Igloo. But I had already started to plan elements of my BDSM technothriller. The solution was obvious: Igloo was going to have to get kinky.

Once I decided to incorporate BDSM into the novel, my next step was figuring out what role it would be play in the story. I wanted to keep technology front and center and avoid BDSM clichés and tropes. After some exploratory writing, I decided my main approach would be to normalize kink as a legitimate relationship style.

According to research, as many as thirty percent of adults practice BDSM or fantasize about it, making it even more common than
homosexuality. We've seen a mainstreaming of gay characters in
fiction, so why not kinky characters as well? Part of the reason is
because there is still a greater stigmatization of BDSM as compared
to other alternative sexual orientations. Recent research studies have
shown that kink can be healthy, increasing happiness as well as
reducing the risk of self-harm.

If BDSM was common and accepted, then Igloo's orientation
could be mentioned briefly, and the story could move on. But to
combat the many harmful beliefs and misinformation surrounding
kink, it became necessary to dive deeper into the details so the reader
can appreciate the nuances of Igloo and Essie's relationship. Figuring
out how much and what to include, in order to present an accurate
and representative picture of their relationship, without alienating,
offending, or triggering readers was a careful balancing act. Some
early readers wanted less, some more.

Of course, one could ask what purpose it serves to discuss kink at
such length in a present-day/near-future tech-oriented book. Fellow
author Kevin O'Neill recently wrote about science fiction tackling
cultural issues in near-future predictions:

> *My grandfather could apparently do a good half hour on what
> the excesses of the 60s were going to lead to: gay people acting
> all gay right out in the open, and college age boys going to their
> girlfriends' houses and shaking hands with their fathers, and
> then walking back to their bedrooms and closing the door and
> having sex, right there, in the house, all unmarried and
> whatnot and no one says a thing!*

> *And he was right. Those things are normal now. It's not that
> the near future is hard to predict. It's that predicting it
> carries huge social weight in the present. Predicting that
> openly gay people in 2018 could get married and adopt chil-*

dren would have been a massively political statement
in 1963.

I can't predict how BDSM will look in the future, but I believe we'll move toward more open acceptance and acknowledgement.

The inclusion of polyamory in the storyline was a later addition. Polyamory and non-monogamy received prominent mass media coverage in 2017 and 2018. Ethical non-monogamy is practiced by about 5 percent of the population in the United States, and as many as 20 percent of people have tried some variation. Unfortunately, at least a quarter of practitioners report experiencing discrimination as a result of their lifestyle.

Polyamory and other ethical, open relationship lifestyles have their root in common non-monogamy practices that exist across multiple cultures, including indigenous tribal cultures. It stands to reason that some people are biologically wired for non-monogamy, and therefore we are best served by figuring out the most ethical approaches to non-monogamy.

For example, loving multiple romantic partners is even more common if you include the 40 percent of Americans that have had extra-marital affairs. However, cheating has serious detrimental effects on the health of relationships and society. Helping people see and understand ethical non-monogamy as a possible alternative could help avoid the emotional and relationship damage that results from cheating.

That being said, as most with experience will admit, polyamory can make sense in theory but be difficult in practice. I show some of Igloo and Essie's struggles, but the topic could fill an entire book and then some. There's a line from Essie that mirrors a conversation I had with my own partner: "We talked once about trying an open relationship. Are you game to try?"

During the course of writing any novel, I make many passes through the manuscript, and *Kill Switch* was no different. Every time I reencountered this line, I kept adding margin comments. Here are the comments in chronological order, each one separated by some weeks or months:

- This is where, in the real world, Igloo should say "fuck no," and she and Essie can live happily ever after.
- What a difference two weeks makes. This is amazing! If she said no, she'd miss the biggest opportunity ever.
- This is harder than either of them thinks.
- I *think* the right answer is still to do it, but it will quite possibly cost them everything.
- Don't worry, it'll work out. Probably.

Polyamory is a rabbit hole that, once you go down, you cannot escape unchanged. Even though I know the outcome for my own relationship, I still don't feel there is a definitive answer.

I also want to talk briefly about how friends and family react to kinky and poly people. When someone who is monogamous learns that you're facing relationship challenges in polyamory, they'll too often blame poly: "Well, if you were monogamous, this wouldn't happen." But monogamous relationships aren't perfect: they have difficulties too, and they end as well. We don't go around saying "well, if only you were polyamorous, that wouldn't have happened."

Similarly, when a vanilla person learns about a kinky relationship, they'll often assume that it's unhealthy in some way, if not outright abusive. As a result, they'll rarely be supportive of someone going through troubles in a kinky relationship.

So you can imagine that when someone is kinky and polyamorous (and possibly gay, trans, nonbinary, etc.) the pool of people who will be there for them in a supportive, non-judgmental way shrinks until it eventually feels like they can't talk to anyone and can't be open about who they are. This is a terrible way to have to live.

If this book made you feel uncomfortable, if it caused you to judge any of the characters, and if you're still reading this now, I hope that the exposure will help you be more open-minded in the future, and more accepting of people who seem to be very different from you on the outside. On the inside, we all just want to be loved and accepted.

In sum, *Kill Switch* has a number of non-conforming sexual orientations and relationships that form a backdrop for the characters. Hopefully, you'll appreciate my attempt to inform and destigmatize these behaviors. When social stigma and misconceptions are common, those with alternative sexual identities suffer. Many risk their jobs, child custody, medical care, and family relationships, in addition to experiencing many other forms of discrimination.

Some will find *Kill Switch* intellectually intriguing as an insight into activities they might not otherwise be exposed to. Others will actively hate those same elements, but hopefully other aspects of the story are compelling enough to make it worthwhile. I hope the parallels between privacy, control, and agency in both kink and society will be interesting to all.

If you've enjoyed *Kill Switch*, I'd *really* appreciate your help getting the word out! As always, I'm completely dependent on word of mouth to reach new readers.

- Please post a review where you bought your copy.
- Please recommend *Kill Process* and *Kill Switch* on Facebook, Twitter, your blog, or to your friends and family (or all of the above!)
- Please sign up for my mailing list at www.williamhertling.com to find out about new releases, writing updates, and book recommendations.

Thank you for all of your support.
Until next time,
William Hertling

ADDITIONAL NOTES

During the editing process, questions came up from critique or beta readers, not all of which could be addressed in the manuscript itself. In other cases, details were removed from the manuscript to make it flow more smoothly for the majority of readers. If you're curious, here are some additional notes.

NEGOTIATION & CONSENT

When Igloo and Charlotte play for the first time, several readers found it challenging to believe that their pre-scene negotiation could be so thorough and clinical. Although kinky people negotiate in many different ways, within the community of people who attend public kink events, the process is generally explicit, detailed, and emotionally detached. The only exception is when people are long-term partners and have already established norms.

The purpose of negotiation is to ensure that all participants are giving fully informed consent. Consent can't be given when someone doesn't understand what's being proposed, so language must clear and unambiguous.

Even something as simple as a kiss, which vanilla people will usually assess based on body language, is often carefully planned. A negotiation could look something like "Are you open to kissing during our scene? My STI tests are ____, and I was last tested three months ago. I have no known new exposures since then." The other party would confirm their interest (or not) and STI compatibility, thus establishing an agreement that kissing is acceptable for that particular scene. The next time the same people play, they might negotiate every detail again, or they might simply ask "Is everything we did last time still okay?"

KINK

Igloo ties a takate-kote (the box tie) in the style of Osada Ryu. She uses a single-rope, two-wrap futomomo. She prefers the Somerville Bowline, but uses a square knot for double-column ties. She uses Moco Nawa waxed jute by Mocojute. The carbon fiber crop, her favorite toy, is the Supercrop by Topspace.

I wanted to work in more of these details, but it turns out that most readers only want to know what limb is being tied. Sigh.

There's a scene in which Igloo, feeling insecure about her relationship, laments the possible loss of coffee service in the morning. My editor made a comment about how that achieved both poignancy and humor. Ironically, humor wasn't intended at all, although I can see how it might seem funny if you aren't familiar with D/s rituals.

If you've ever seen a Japanese tea ceremony, then you have some sense of how a simple act of serving tea can acquire deep ritualistic meaning. D/s coffee service is not about delivering a cup of coffee. It's about reinforcing and celebrating the nature of a Dominant/submissive relationship between two people. It's a time to connect physically, mentally, and spiritually. It sets the tone for the day, and it is the start of a period for communicating. While there are an infinite number of ways to practice D/s, for many the coffee service or something like it—such as removing shoes upon entering the home—may be the most important ritual they share.

TAPESTRY V2.0

As always, my intent is to describe feasible technology. Tapestry 1.0 was a distributed, decomposed social network. I went as far as defining many of the APIs while I was thinking about it.

I believe it's also possible to build Tapestry 2.0. Of course, there's hand-waving when it comes to some details. But building container-ized software, using web technology approaches to deploy to the cloud or locally is already being done. Indeed, as compute power and storage continue to increase, but latency remains somewhat constant, it's an inevitable side-effect of trends in technology that we'll see soft-ware move to the edges, as I wrote about in the *Singularity* series.

Blockchain (distributed ledgers) often address a problem that companies don't want to solve: it eliminates a centralized role in owning, controlling, and managing data. The problem is that existing companies at meaningful scale don't want to give up that power, so they aren't going to use distributed ledgers. Meanwhile, companies who don't have scale might be interested in using distributed ledgers as a differentiator, but they lack the influence to make a meaningful impact.

CREDITS

Thanks to my editors, Dario Ciriello and Anastasia Poirier.

The line "Kink has as much in common with abuse as practicing judo has with a street corner mugging," is thanks to Gwenn Cody, LCSW.

Many thanks to amazing folks in the BDSM community who shared much that contributed to my thinking on the subjects explored in this novel. Names obscured, but hopefully you know who you are: ES, S, BGND, X, J, N, LCT, F.

Thanks for encouragement and feedback on early drafts goes to Brad Feld, Mike Whitmarsh, Bernie A. Hernández, and Timo Kissel.

Special thanks to my Patreon backers who support the production of each book through a monthly contribution. The support of these patrons helps cover the expenses related to the release of each book, and increases the quality by ensuring I don't have to skimp when it comes to editing, proofreading, and audiobook production. Thank you to Alejandro Hall, Andy Levy, Antonio Roldao, Boni Wolf, Bernie A. Hernández, Brad Feld, Bruce Sommer, Caleb, David Mandell, David Mussington, Dmitry Dulepov, Gerald Auer, Greg Roberts, Jackie Tortorella, Jan Svanda, Joe Lugwig, John-Isaac Clark,

Jon Guidry, Michael LC, Mike Doyle, Neil Kimmelfield, Peter, Peter Soldan, Robert Dobkin, Robert Miller, Robert Solovay, and Steven E. Burchett.

Lastly, my deep appreciation to you, dear reader, for buying and reading *Kill Switch*.

91735683R00292

Made in the USA
San Bernardino, CA
24 October 2018